THE
NEIGHBORHOOD

A TWIN ESTATES NOVEL

STYLO FANTÔME

STYLO FANTÔME
Published by BattleAxe Productions
Copyright © 2017
Stylo Fantôme

ISBN-13: 978-1542356435
ISBN-10: 1542356431

Critique Partner:
Ratula Roy

Cover Design
Najla Qamber Designs
najlaqamberdesigns.com
Copyright © 2017

Formatting: Champagne Formats

DEDICATION

To laughter and big adventures and late
nights and still not giving a fuck.

THE NEIGHBORHOOD

A TWIN ESTATES NOVEL

1

Your First Date with an Eros Match! Rate On Our Scale of 1 to 10 To Unlock Other Potential Matches.

K ATYA TOCCI STARED ACROSS THE TABLE, NOT EVEN BOTHERING TO HIDE the fact she wasn't paying attention to her date at all. If she bothered with the Eros dating site's rating system, she would've scored this gentleman in the negatives.

Maybe that was a bit harsh – he was clean, and attractive, and hey, at least he was struggling to make it through the evening. Katya had given up two glasses of wine ago, so really, *she* should be given the negative rating.

I'll polish off this third glass and call it a night.

Mr. Henry *"no relation, though boy, do I wish! HAHA"* Ford really couldn't be found at fault for the awful encounter, she knew. Henry had shown up expecting a sex kitten who'd be down for a good time. What he'd gotten, though, was a bitter woman wearing too much makeup.

She never set out to the be that way, though. Each time she found a match, she promised herself it would be the return of "new-Katya".

The sex kitten who'd been brazen enough to waltz into a sex club and have her wicked way with the owner. The saucy minx who'd brought a real estate tycoon to his knees. She would dress sexy, and she would flirt, and she would use these guys up like tissue paper. Just like a pair of boys had used her.

Unfortunately, new-Katya had gone into hibernation. Or died. In her place was a girl who looked the part – bold lipstick and heavy eyeliner, short dresses and plunging necklines – but could barely even break a smile. No, this new chick was most definitely a downer, and sex was the last thing on her mind.

God, I don't ever want to have sex again. Sex got me into this mess.

Katya shook her head and tried to focus. Thinking about sex was never good. Once she started thinking about it, she inevitably thought of Liam Edenhoff, and of course, Wulfric Stone, and she wasn't allowed to think about either of them. They were permanently on time-out from her brain. From her *life*.

They were in such deep shit, in fact, that she'd cut them out entirely. Hadn't spoken a word to either of them in two weeks. Two weeks of dealing with hurt and anger and no closure … it felt more like several lifetimes. Lifetimes and sooooo many pints of ice cream.

Then on top of dropping them, just to prove to herself that she could be a modern, liberated, independent, sexually progressive woman without them, she'd reactivated her dating profile – the fake one her roommate had made for her.

One matching sexy profile pic later and Katya was making matches left and right. She managed to send flirty messages, and she put on sexy outfits, but every date she showed up for, she just couldn't muster the energy to seal the deal.

All of the men were attractive. Some were even well spoken. But they all seemed … *boring*, to her. Lackluster. Like she was talking to dolls. There was no *spark*, and as much as she hated to admit it, Katya needed that to be attracted to someone. Gone were the days of being with a guy just because he belonged to the right country clubs and had graduated from the right schools. She'd been spoiled – she needed someone who made her blood boil and her skin tingle. Unfortunately, it didn't seem like any of the men in San Francisco had that capability.

Well, technically that's not true – there were two who were very good at it.

Before she could chastise herself for letting that reminder sneak through, her date interrupted her thoughts.

"So, uh, wanna come back to my place for some coffee?" Henry Ford asked, complete with cheesy grin. Katya snorted. Was this guy for real? She'd barely looked at him twice – did he really think he had a chance?

"No thanks. Big day tomorrow," she said, then she swallowed the last of her wine and went to stand up.

"Oh yeah? Doing what? Anything I could help with?" he asked, standing as well while looking at her chest the whole time. She grabbed her purse off the back of her chair.

"Not even a little. Thanks for dinner. Sorry I wasted your time," she said, struggling to pull her jacket on.

"What? No, you didn't waste my time. Besides, the night's still young, we can stop somewhere for a night cap," he suggested.

"The night is over. I'm sorry, really."

Politeness wasn't part of her nature anymore – Wulfric Stone had wrestled that trait it to the ground, then Liam Edenhoff had shot it. She didn't particularly care that she was offending the poor guy. She ignored Henry Ford as she hurried out of the restaurant, cinching the belt of her jacket tight before heading out into the chilly night.

Summer was officially over and fall was making itself known in the port city. She shivered as she hurried down the sidewalk. Her date still had to pay the bill, so he couldn't really chase after her, but still. She wanted some distance between them before she called for a ride.

This isn't working.

3

It wasn't the first time Katya'd had that thought. She'd hoped to find some peace of mind in her little adventure. Become even more of a badass bitch. But really, she was just annoyed with herself and bored most of the time.

She would give it one more chance. *Eros! A Site for Lovers* was a San Francisco based company, specifically made for people living in and around the metropolitan area. As a promotional tool, they were having an event – cocktails and speed dating. She'd signed up on a whim, though at the time, she'd assumed she'd be swimming in dudes before the event even happened.

Now she was looking at it as a finish line. If she couldn't grow the balls to have some sort of sexual adventure by the end of the party, she would take it as a sign that she really and truly wasn't cut out to be a dating-app-vixen.

One more. One more song-and-dance, then I'll hang up my slutty profile for real and say goodbye to new-Katya.

2

BREATHE. BREATHE. DON'T THINK. BREATHE. BREATHE. DID I SIGN THAT *paperwork the office sent over? Breathe. Breathe. Have to check that escrow deal. Breathe. Breathe. God, what is she doing right now? How did this get so fucked up. I knew I should have fucking listened to myself and kept walking – DON'T THINK. Breathe. Breathe.*

While Wulfric Stone's natural habitat was an Olympic sized swimming pool, it wasn't the only form of exercise he got – he had a stressful job, he had lots of different ways of burning off the tension. Running came a close second to swimming for clearing his head. It created a different sort of burn in his muscles, created a whole new plethora of aches and pains.

Sometimes, when he was particularly angry about something, he preferred it over swimming. With the swimming, after doing a couple miles worth of laps he could just float away. Literally. Lay on his back and be weightless for a while.

Not with running, though. How cruel – a sport that takes a person miles away from their starting point, and then when they push themselves too hard, they still have to turn around and do the same distance back. Feel like collapsing? No weightless pond to float in.

No, the best case scenario meant hopefully finding a cool patch of grass to fall onto and praying his muscles didn't cramp up, all while gravity put pressure on every limb.

Yes, running was a very punishing sport, and Wulfric Stone was a very bad man who definitely deserved some punishing.

Breathe. Breathe.

His calves were burning and sweat was *pouring* down his body. He was pretty sure his lungs were getting ready to stage a coup and walk out on him. Still, he kept pushing, pounding his feet down harder against the ground.

How can I breathe when everything is so wrong?

Wulf let out a frustrated shout and ripped his earphones off. This wasn't working. He slowed to a stop. He knew it was a bad idea, he should jog for a while, reducing his pace slowly, but fuck it. Running away from his problems clearly wasn't helping. Maybe a massive charlie horse would successfully distract him.

Or maybe it would give him a heart attack, that would be *perfect*.

He veered off the pathway, heading straight into the woods. A breeze hit his sweat slicked skin, causing him to shiver. He grabbed the hem of his t-shirt and brought it to his forehead, mopping up the sweat. When he lowered the material, he glanced around and realized he'd wandered so far that he couldn't see where the trail was anymore.

Good. Maybe I'll be lost in here forever. That would solve everything. Jesus, how did everything get so fucked up?

It was a rhetorical question, Wulf knew the answer. *He* had fucked it all up. Broken his own rules, gone against his own advice, and look what had happened. He was a mess, wandering around in the woods, cursing at trees.

And what was worse – he could've avoided it all. He'd known just how bad the ending between them could be, he'd seen it all unraveling from early on, and he'd tried to avoid it by doing what he did best. Being an asshole. After all, if he told her about their little scam, she'd leave him. If he didn't tell her and she found out, she'd leave him. If Liam told her, she'd leave him. It was very clear to Wulf that the only possible outcome was Katya leaving him.

So, like a true gentleman, Wulf had left her first.

Why did she come back? If she'd just stayed away, everything would be fine. Fucking fine.

Except it wouldn't be fine. He'd be a shell of man – or at least, a worse version than the one he'd already been – and she'd be convincing herself Liam was the perfect guy for her. Wulf couldn't stand that thought. Couldn't bear the idea of Liam touching her and kissing her and seeing her naked and making her sigh and gasp.

"*AH!*"

His fist slammed into the tree before he even knew his arm was moving. He hadn't pulled the punch at all, striking the trunk as hard as he could, but Wulf barely felt anything. He was numb.

So he hit it again. And again. And didn't stop till blood was running down his fist, and even then, he still didn't feel a thing. It was only the red staining his white t-shirt that gave him pause.

Of course I didn't feel anything. I'm Wulfric Stone, and stones don't have feelings.

Crimson liquid ran down the back of his hand, stark against his pale skin. Like turning the channel on a television from black-and-white to technicolor. It shocked him a little, seeing his own blood like that. He finally looked up and took in his surroundings.

Jesus, I'm brooding in the woods and hitting trees. When did I turn into this person?

For the first time since Katya had walked away from him, he stood outside of himself and looked in on the situation.

He'd sent her text messages. He'd sent flowers. He'd gone to her apartment once, only to be turned away by her rabid roommate. Nothing worked, Katya had completely frozen him out.

And I just let her.

That wasn't like him. Since when did Wulfric Stone ever accept no for an answer? Since when did he pout and sulk and whine? When did throwing temper tantrums in the middle of the woods become the norm?

He turned in a circle, searching for the way back to the trail. He was breathing fast, his mind racing at a million miles an hour. Since she'd walked away, he hadn't been acting like himself.

So *of course* nothing was working. She'd started to fall in love with him, she'd claimed. The man he'd been before she'd left. Brash and rude and ballsy and demanding. The kind of man who kicked down doors, and ignored anything he didn't like, and *always* got what he wanted.

As he started jogging through the underbrush, he laughed at himself. He couldn't believe he hadn't realized it sooner. This whole time, he'd been asking himself what she needed from him to make things right. What she would want him to do. He hadn't been asking the right questions, not at all.

What would Wulfric Stone do?

3

L IAM EDENHOFF STARED AT HIS COMPUTER SCREEN.

Holy shit. Goddammit. Holy shit.

Katya Tocci stared back at him. Only she didn't look like the Katya he knew. Not the sweet, semi-innocent, cake baking, lovable goddess.

The girl on the computer was pouting her red lips at him while her bedroom eyes screamed "*fuck me*". To say she looked transformed was an understatement. He'd never seen her in clothing like that, so sexy. It was strange. He'd seen her naked and in all sorts interesting positions, but somehow the tight shorts and crop top were almost more provocative.

She was a head turner when she was wearing pajamas and hanging out at home. Sexified and wearing slutty make up? Liam's mouth had gone dry, which made him nervous. If her picture was having this effect on him, what were all the other thousands of men on the Eros dating site thinking?

*How many matches has she made? How many dudes has she anger-banged? No, she wouldn't do that. Shit, would she? **Shit**.*

In the short time they'd been friends, Liam and Katya had gotten pretty close. He felt like he'd known her pretty well, could guess how she'd react to certain things. So to say he was shocked with how easily she'd cut him out of her life would be an understatement.

Yes, he'd done an awful thing. He'd lied and manipulated and just generally been a bastard. But still. Friends forgave each other, that's what they did. He considered Katya to be a very good friend. A best friend, even. It was killing him, not being able to see her and talk to her. How could she just let him go?

Of course, maybe it wasn't so simple. Clearly, the profile was in retaliation to what he and Wulfric Stone had done to her. Hell hath no fury like a woman scorned, and apparently a woman who was manipulated into sleeping with two men at once could get furious enough to sleep with a lot of other men to get revenge.

Liam groaned and rubbed his hands over his face. What to do? He glanced at his phone. He hadn't spoken to Wulf since the day Katya had walked in on them talking about her. Since she'd discovered that they knew each other and had only been pretending they didn't.

Liam could admit it, Wulf was more decisive. Wulf was more likely to take action. He would want to know about Katya's profile, and he would want to do something about it. Would have ideas on *what* to do about it.

But Liam was competitive by nature. Both he and Wulf had started sleeping with Katya around the same time. It had turned into somewhat of a game, who could get her to do what. Then it had evolved into who could win her, and though it killed Liam to say it, Wulf had definitely been winning.

So if he called Wulf, and the other man came up with some great plan to make her see the light, it might only serve to make her see that Wulf was the one for her. And Liam refused to believe that. Katya was light and love and happiness. She deserved someone who would cherish those parts of her. Someone who would devote his life to making her smile. And he just knew Wulfric Stone wasn't that person.

*No. No, I can do this on my own. I'm smart, I can figure out a way. I can do **something**. I don't need him, and neither does she.*

Liam pushed up his sleeves and leaned forward again. Began typing on the keyboard. He may not have been as smart or as rich or as impressive as Wulf, but he had a couple tricks up his sleeve. He may have lost the first battle, but he wouldn't lose the war.

It's not over yet, angel cake.

4

"ARE YOU SURE YOU WANT TO DO THIS?"
Katya turned around at the sound of her roommate's voice.

Tori Bellows stood in the hallway, picking at her nail polish. It was six o'clock, but she was already in fishnets, tight shorts, and a cropped vest. Dressed for work at Liam's club. She had the body to pull it off, and the attitude to make sure people kept their hands to themselves.

"Of course, I already paid for my ticket," Katya replied, turning back to the mirror and smoothing her hands over her outfit.

"You know what I mean. You're not proving anything, you know. Neither of them even call anymore. They have no clue you've gone on dates with half the men in San Francisco," Tori was blunt. Katya winced, but wasn't mad. They were complete opposites and had been friends for years. Tori's rough edges worked well with Katya's soft tones. They balanced each other.

"It's not about them," she responded, her voice calm. "This is about *me*. Proving something to myself."

"What? That you can be just as big a skank as the rest of the girls out there?"

"Maybe. Or maybe that I can go out and find a man without it being some elaborate hoax. That I can be sexy and appealing without some great charade. That I can … that I can control who I see, and what I do with them," she finished.

Tori grumbled, but it was hard to argue with someone trying to find their independence. After a minute, though, she found a way.

"See," she sighed. "I would agree with you, normally. I'm all for you being in charge and whatever. You literally could sleep with half of San Francisco, and I wouldn't judge you. Hell, I'd throw you a party. IF that's what you really wanted for yourself. But I don't think that's what you want. I don't think you even want to do this speed-dating thing, and that I won't throw a party for. That I will totally judge you for."

Katya paused for a long moment, staring at her friend. The other girl was still looking at her hands, picking the black polish apart.

"It's sort of for me," Katya whispered, then cleared her throat. "And yeah, sort of because of them. They … they stole something from me. I'm just trying to get it back."

"Oh, honey," Tori hurried into the room. "You won't find it out there, with some random dude. You've still got it. You just need to give yourself a chance to get over those guys. Heal a little bit. Realize it was *never* about them. *You* went on that first date. *You* made that first move. Nothing that happened after can ever take that away from you."

Katya took a deep breath and stepped sideways. She could feel the impending hug, and if they hugged, she'd start crying, and she wouldn't ever stop. She laughed and patted at her hair, making sure it was all in place.

"I know, I know. Just let me wallow for a little while longer. The male attention is good for my ego."

"Kat-"

"Seriously. I'd already planned on deactivating that stupid

account after tonight. I committed to being at this event, I don't want them to be short a girl just because I make shitty choices. I'm gonna go and have fun and score some free drinks. Then tomorrow it's back to life as normal," she assured her friend.

"Well, hopefully not *too* normal. New-Katya was fun. You don't need to serial date everyone on a dating app to find a man. Going clubbing with your bestie works pretty good, too," Tori laughed.

"Sounds like a solid plan."

She almost got out the door unscathed, but Tori surprised her by following her into the hallway and jumping on her. They crashed into a wall and Katya couldn't help but laugh. Probably her first real laugh in weeks.

I don't deserve such a good friend.

She actually felt good as she took a taxi across town. Tori had made sense – Katya wasn't really proving anything to anyone. She was just forcing herself to be something she wasn't. She didn't have to go back to being old-Katya, but she didn't have to always be new-Katya, either.

And the best part, she finally felt like neither of those personalities needed Liam or Wulf. Sure, she missed them and hated that she missed them and kind of wished dysentery on both of them. But she wouldn't let them control her anymore, not even in absentia.

When she got to the event, Katya was actually impressed. It was held on a rooftop terrace. It was cold out, but there were lots of outdoor heaters and cute little gas fireplaces. Singles mingled all over the place, enjoying cocktails at the open bar. She realized she was one of the last to arrive, almost half an hour late, and she'd barely grabbed a Cosmo before someone started tapping on a microphone. She turned towards the stage and watched as a blonde woman cleared her throat.

"Welcome, Lovers!" she shouted, and a lot of people cheered.

Introductions were made and the website was explained – despite the fact that everyone there already had a profile. Then speed dating was explained, which Katya actually did find interesting. She'd never done it before, so she listened closely.

There were an even number of men and women, which she'd already known. The entire back half of the terrace was covered in two-top tables, and the women would all go take a seat at each one. Then the men would all go sit down. After five minutes, a bell would ring, and the men would shift to the table on their right. If either of them enjoyed the other person, they would go on the app and get into the event's page, then click a "yes" button on the attendee's profile. At the end of the night, anyone who matched yeses would get an e-mail with their match details and contact info.

Katya was already pretty sure she wouldn't make any matches, but she did like meeting new people, and the five minute rule kind of made it exciting. So she chose a table in the last row and waited for the first man to take his seat.

It was an interesting process. With some of the men, five minutes felt like an eternity. They laughed at her career choice or stared at her breasts or talked about their exes. With others, though, five minutes wasn't nearly long enough. She met a guy who was three days out of the army, just trying to get back into the habit of talking to "normal" people again. Another was a father of two, who admitted to usually keeping that fact a secret till the second or third date, but he shared some photos with her when she said she liked kids. Still, no spark. Lots of potential new friends, but she wasn't naive enough to think any of these men were looking for friends. She would take the night with a grain of salt and just enjoy herself.

About half way through the event, the bell rang and she said goodbye to Al the accountant. She was tucking his business card into her purse when the next man took his seat. Without looking up, she held out her hand to shake his.

"Hi, sorry, this zipper is stuck. I'm -"

"Katya!?"

She sat upright, immediately on guard. Then she let out a sigh of relief when she recognized the guy.

"Hey! What are you doing here?" she laughed.

"Hey, I could ask you the same question," he teased, shaking her hand even though they'd met a long time ago.

Gaten Shepherd lived next door to her, in Liam's building. They'd bumped into each other when he'd first moved in – he'd been fighting to get his couch through the lobby door. Katya and Tori had shoved while he'd pulled, then they'd stuck around and helped him unload the rest of his truck.

They'd hovered somewhere between acquaintances and friends ever since. She'd watered his plants when he'd gone on vacation, he'd fixed some wobbly shelves in her living room. They would chat outside when she had to wait for the bus, and one time in a down pour he'd given her a ride, even though her work place was out of his way.

She hadn't seen him in a couple weeks, though. She'd been too busy with her multiple-men problem, and she knew he had a busy schedule, too. He was a well sought after carpenter and handy-man, and on top of that, his model girlfriend required a lot of his time.

Hmmm, must be an ex-girlfriend now.

"I thought you were dating that one dude," he commented. Katya froze for a second, then shook it off.

"No, that *dude* and I aren't dating," she chuckled. "What about you and Mimi?"

"Oh, that ended a week or so ago. She got a contract in Italy and got pissed that I wouldn't drop everything and leave. I was just … I was done, you know? I think I was done a long time ago," he explained.

"Oh. Well … I guess that's good, then?" Katya offered, and he laughed again.

"Yeah. So, this is crazy, huh? Bumping into each other here, when we live like two hundred feet apart. I could've just asked you out at the dumpster," he said, and she burst out laughing.

"Hey, I haven't clicked yes, yet. Don't get ahead of yourself," she warned him. He held up his hands.

"My mistake. Is this the part where I should prattle off all my accomplishments? My credit score?" he checked.

"Credit score?"

"The lady at table four asked me."

"She did not!"

"She really did."

It was nice talking to Gate. They'd always had a comfortability with each other, right off the bat. He told her about a classic 1940's house he was helping to restore. Normally hearing someone describe cabinets would be boring, but he was so in love with his work, it came out in his voice. She was fascinated and actually a little sad when she heard the bell ringing.

"But I never got to hear your credit score," she joked as he climbed to his feet.

"Well, click yes, and maybe you'll find out," he suggested.

"I'm sorry, but I think I'm done dating neighbors for a while," she told him. He pressed a hand to his heart.

"Oh, c'mon, I'm nothing like that guy! I don't own one surfer t-shirt, and I have a full time job," Gate pointed out.

"Excellent qualities, though he has a full time job, too," she corrected him. Some sort of scuffle was happening next to them, a group of guys shuffling around. She realized Gate was holding up the line somewhat.

"He does? He always seems to be hanging around. Look, match or no, call me sometime. I'll take you to see the house," Gate said, scribbling his number down on the back of a card. Katya stood and took it.

"That would be nice. This was fun, Gate. Thanks."

He surprised her then by squeezing between the tables and giving her a hug. She sighed and leaned into him. He must have come straight from work, he smelled like saw dust. She smiled and pulled back a little. Another man had finally taken his seat across from her, and she hadn't even acknowledged him yet. She had to sit back down.

"It was. See you at the dumpster," Gate joked as he headed to the next table.

She was still laughing as she took her seat.

"I'm sorry, we actually know each other, and I hadn't seen him in …"

Katya's voice trailed off as she looked at her new suitor.

"I would just like to say," Liam Edenhoff started quickly. "That I'm not always 'hanging around' the building, and there is nothing wrong with 'surfer' t-shirts."

She didn't even think about it, she just stood up. Her thighs hit the edge of the table, threatening to overturn it. Liam slapped one hand down, keeping it upright, and grabbed her drink with his other hand. The candle bit the dust, though, and rolled across the floor.

"You can't be here," she said, falling back into her seat, then trying to stand up again. He let go of her drink and grabbed her wrist.

"Please. Please, Katya, five minutes. You gave ten other strangers five minutes. Just give me the same," he begged. She glanced around and realized some people were staring at them. She groaned, then yanked her arm free of his grip.

"What are you even doing here!? How did you get to this table?" she demanded. She would've noticed if he'd been sitting right next to her that whole time.

"I was at table fifteen, but I saw how you were talking to that guy, then I recognized him. So I skipped up here and paid the next dude to take my place," he explained.

"Typical."

"Hey, desperate measures."

"You're down to four minutes. Why are you here? Are you stalking me?" she suddenly gasped as the idea popped into her head.

"*Yes*," he groaned. "Stalking you, praying to you, dying for you to just look at me again."

"Uh …" she'd never heard Liam be so poetic before – she didn't know how to handle it.

"I saw your new profile. You won't return my calls, you won't see me – I had to do something. I saw that you were coming to this event. I know the bar that's catering, they got me inside," he told her.

"So let me get this straight. You stalked me online, you snuck into a private event, and then you bribed someone for this seat," she laid it all out.

"Yeah. Yeah, I did."

That was it. No defense. No apologies.

"You can't do this!" she hissed. "You can't just … you're like a child! You do whatever you want and expect no repercussions, and then when there are, you lie and cheat and steal and do whatever it takes to get out of paying the consequences."

"I know, but you know what? If the punishment for everything I've done is losing you, then damn right I'm gonna do all that crazy shit to win you back. I'm willing to do whatever it takes to get you to forgive me," he assured her.

"Oh really? How about *just be a decent human being*," she growled.

They were really attracting an audience at that point, which Katya didn't want. She'd already made a fool of herself once for this man. Not again. She stood up, taking care not to bump the table this time, and she walked away. Of course he got up and followed her, but she refused to acknowledge him. She threw open the door to the stairs and started stomping her way down them.

"You can't just cut me off," he called out behind her.

"Yes I can!" she yelled back.

He started to say something else, but she couldn't hear him. The bottom floor of the building was a crowded bar and the noise drowned him out. Katya bee-lined for an emergency exit and pushed her way out into an alley. She was almost jogging when she heard him burst out the door behind her.

"Katya," he chuckled as he came up along side her. "Are you

seriously trying to run away from me? In those heels?"

"Yes," she said through clenched teeth.

"You're about as athletic as a lame duck. C'mon, you're gonna trip and break your neck, then I'll have to carry you, and last time I did that, I think I threw out my back -"

Arguing and fighting were fine, it just reminded her of how angry she was at him. But him being funny? Nice? It reminded her of how much she loved being around him. About what a wonderful friendship they'd had. And that hurt. Hurting was so much worse than anger.

"*I fucking hate you!*" she screamed, whirling on him and beating him with her purse.

"Whoa! Calm down!" he yelled, trying to get a hold of her arms.

"No!" she yelled back, managing to avoid capture. "You don't get to do what you did to me and act like everything is fine. You don't get to violate me and manipulate me and use me, and then just crack jokes and be funny and awesome and make me hate myself and *you can't just do this to me!*"

"Stop," he said in a low voice. He finally got a hold of her wrists but she kept pulling.

"No. You stop. Stop following me, and stop calling me, and stop showing up at my apartment. I swear to god, I'm gonna move," she growled, trying to yank away. He laughed. Actually laughed at her.

"How? You just renewed a year lease last month."

She gasped.

"You'd let me out of that lease."

"No, I wouldn't. Not till you forgive me."

"This is blackmail."

"Hardly."

"Wulf manages your buildings, I'll make him let me out of that lease."

"Are you serious? Get out of a contract with Wulfric Stone? Have you met him?"

This time, she laughed. Actually laughed. Tears pricked the corners of her eyes.

"Yeah. Yeah, he's kind of a bastard," she agreed.

"He really is."

She finally straightened up and pulled away from him a little, though he still clung to her wrists.

"He is. I mean, what else do you call someone who lies to you? Manipulates you? Humiliates you? Uses you? Shares all your most intimate, secret moments with another person?" she asked, staring Liam very directly in the eyes. He swallowed thickly, but didn't look away.

"Bastard may not be harsh enough. Would loser work?"

"Asshole?"

"Dickhead?" he threw out another insulting name for himself.

"How about … worst person ever?" Katya suggested, her voice barely above a whisper. He smiled, but it didn't reach his eyes.

"No. Close, but I'm not quite there yet," he whispered back. She took a deep, shuddering breath.

"I have to go."

"No."

"I don't have anything to say to you, Liam. I want to go home, I'm tired."

"Katya, I'm not going away. I'll be here tomorrow, and the day after, and the day after that," he warned her.

"What can I do to make you understand that I don't want you in my life?"

"Nothing."

"We're talking in circles. Good night," she sighed, unsuccessfully trying to pull free.

"Then let's have some straight talk – would you treat Tori this way?" he suddenly asked.

"What do you mean?"

"Tori's your best friend."

"Yeah."

"And I was, too."

"*Do not* compare yourself to her. I've known her for years, and she's never treated me the way you did," Katya warned him.

"You can't deny that what you and I had was special," he kept going. "She may have been in your life longer, but you and I were almost as close."

Katya wasn't going to lie to him or herself – he was telling the truth. But still.

"I don't care. It's comparing apples and lying sacks of shit."

"Still. If Tori did something awful to you – lied to you, kept secrets from you, hurt your feelings, would you just drop her like a bad habit? Cut her out of your life without giving her a chance to make up for it?" he asked.

"She would never -"

"Jesus, Katya, use your imagination. What if you found out she slept with your ex-boyfriend? And she lied to you about it, for months? Or she stole money from you? That would be it?" he was insistent with his questioning.

"Yes!" she bit out. "Now let me go."

"I don't believe that. Really think about it. Could you just stop talking to her? Forever? After everything you guys have shared?"

She didn't want to think about it. Not at all, because he was right. She couldn't. Sure, if Tori had ever done any of those things he'd suggested, Katya would've been upset. Furious. Maybe would even threaten to stop speaking to the other girl. But when all was said and done, she couldn't imagine her life without her best friend in it. She would try her hardest to work through the problem with Tori, and would hope they'd come out the other side as better friends.

"It's not the same," she whispered. He squeezed her wrists and pulled her closer, forcing her into his personal space.

"How is it not the same?" he asked.

"Because," a tear finally escaped and slid down her face. "Even if she did all those things … it's not the same. You guys .. *you broke my heart*."

"Oh, angel cake," he breathed, closing the small gap between them and wrapping his arms around her.

It was wrong. To want to be comforted by the person that hurt her. To find such relief in the arms that had brought her so much pain. But facts were facts, and as she cried into the front of Liam's shirt, some of the weight she'd been carrying around for two weeks came off her shoulders.

"It's not the same," she breathed. "She could never hurt me the way you two hurt me. It's not the same, Liam."

"I know, I know. But still. I was an awful person. The things we did to you … I don't deserve your forgiveness, but I'll never stop until I earn it," he told her.

"What if that never happens?" Katya was honest. She wasn't sure she had it in her to forgive him.

"I don't believe that," he replied. "I may be an asshole, and Wulf is quite possibly the devil incarnate, but you, Katya. You're a good person. You would never let something as amazing as what we had slip away, just out of spite. You would fight for it, at least until you were sure it wasn't worth fighting for anymore."

His words. They struck way too close to home. They reminded her of words she had spoken – only she'd been saying them to a different man. It sent a chill down her spine. Had Wulf told Liam about that night? Her gut instinct was no, Wulf wouldn't do that. But of course, her gut didn't know diddly squat when it came to these men. She stepped out of Liam's embrace.

"Maybe I'm already sure," she sniffled, wiping at her face.

"You're not, and I'm prepared to spend a lot of time convincing you of that," he told her.

"I can't …" she let her voice trail off. She didn't know what to do. Was she really prepared to spend the rest of her life hating Liam? And how did Wulf play into it all?

"I'm not asking for a lot. Just … maybe answer the door when I knock, once in a while. Maybe have a cup of coffee with me," he suggested. She took a deep breath.

"I don't know, Liam. We'll see. You'll just have to knock, and we'll see," she replied.

"That's all I wanted."

"And what about Wulf?"

"What about him?"

"Are you here as his ambassador? Do you speak for the two of you? Because I don't want him at my door," she said in a stern voice.

"I haven't spoken to Wulf in two weeks, I hope he doesn't show up at your door," Liam assured her.

"And I am *not* going to sleep with you again, *ever*," she assured him.

"Hadn't even crossed my mind."

"*Liar.*"

"You know, I think you missed me a little bit," he teased her. She glared at him.

"And don't be cute. I haven't made any promises, and Tori still owns those steel-toed boots."

The last time Liam had pleaded outside her door, Tori had opened it and kicked him in the balls – "just to shut him up", she'd insisted.

"Tell her if she does that again, I'm firing her."

"Fire her and *I'll* kick you in the balls."

"Okay, maybe you didn't miss me, but I missed you. I missed you so much, angel cake," he sighed, smiling down at her. She frowned and looked away.

"Good. Remember that feeling every time you think about what you did to me, or every time you think about telling a lie," she suggested. His smile fell away.

"I knew this was gonna be hard. I can handle it," he assured her.

"Don't be so sure. I have to go," she said, stepping around him.

"Can I walk you home?"

"*No.*"

"Alright, baby steps. Baby steps."

She walked in silence for a moment, but then realized she could hear him walking behind her. She stopped and whirled around on him.

"Can't walk me home, and can't follow me home!" she snapped.

"But I live in the same place," he pointed out.

"I don't give a shit! Go to work, or go get tacos, or grab a taxi! Stand here for all I care, but *stop* following me," she said.

"This is ridiculous, I have to -"

"So help me god, if you don't turn around right now, I will move out tomorrow and I will see you in court over that broken lease," she threatened.

Liam took a deep breath. He was a jovial person by nature, but she knew he didn't handle being told "no" very well. He was usually able to talk his way around anything. But not this situation.

He finally nodded, and without saying another word, he turned on his heel and marched off in the opposite direction. Katya glared after him for a while, then turned as well and stomped towards a BART stop.

5

THOUGH SHE WAS ON "SABBATICAL" FROM HER JOB, KATYA WAS STILL GOING to make some of the wedding cakes that had been commissioned. Specifically, she wanted to make her friend Lauren's cake. It was a massive undertaking, actually three cakes, all of them elaborate, and it had to be perfect for the big day. Katya didn't trust the task to anyone else.

Lauren had witnessed the epic cake fight between Katya and Wulf. They'd met up several times since then, to go over more of the design elements for the fancy dessert, and Lauren had asked about Wulf. Asked if Katya would be bringing a date to the wedding.

Katya said yes, she would. Tori would be her plus-one. Lauren laughed and had said she'd hoped for another repeat food fight.

The wedding was on Saturday, and Katya only had two days to finish making all the flowers and sugar pearls and edible lace. The interns at the bakery were making the cake layers and covering them in fondant, but everything else was up to Katya.

Which was why she was rushing out the door Thursday morning. She'd accidentally slept in – she always tried to get to the bakery around six in the morning, so she could get the bulk of her work done before the shop opened at ten. It was already eight, though, which meant she only had a couple hours before customers started coming and going, which inevitably meant she'd receive a barrage of questions from the clerks and interns.

She stood at the elevator for what felt like forever, but it remained seemingly stuck on the seventh floor, the top of the building. Someone must have been holding the door open. She cursed and hurried into the stairwell. She lived on the fifth floor, and by the time she got to the bottom, she was huffing and puffing, wondering if she would make her bus stop on time.

She was looking at her watch when she burst into the lobby area of her building, so she wasn't paying attention. She rammed into what felt like a hollow wall and stumbled backwards. She was so stunned, it took her a second to take in what had happened.

That is the biggest sofa I've ever seen.

She'd slammed right into the back of it. Moving men stood at either end, holding the large piece of furniture up off the ground and barely sparing her a glance. They were clearly straining with the effort it took to hold up the couch, and Katya realized they were waiting for the elevator.

How do they think they're going to get it in there!?

"Sorry," she said, tapping one of the big men on the shoulder. "But I think someone blocked the door. I was waiting for it for a while on the fifth floor, but it never came down."

"Oh yeah, that's Barry," the guy replied.

"Barry?"

"He's unloading the buffet table. It's a bitch to move, with that entire marble top. We told him to wait. He's probably having trouble getting it unwedged," the guy explained, as if Katya not only knew Barry, but knew all about the marble topped buffet table.

"Unwedged?" she asked.

"Yeah. It didn't really fit, we had to swing it in at an angle, tilt it up on its end. I tell ya, I didn't think the elevator was gonna move, that sonnuva bitch was so heavy."

Katya glanced up as the elevator made a dinging sound. Barry must have gotten the table out, because the doors in front of her slid open. The couch started moving, but when it became even more obvious that the behemoth wouldn't fit, the guys started going about uncoupling the sectional pieces.

She was confused. A lovely elderly Korean couple lived in the penthouse on the top floor. They owned a jewelry store down by the water front where Mr. Han was a gemologist. They'd somewhat adopted Katya and Tori as their grandchildren, since their real ones lived in New York. Katya had spent a fair amount of time at their place, helping Mrs. Han bake, eating dinner with them, or taking down their trash when she went to take her own.

So she knew that their apartment was decorated in mostly dark woods, with high end vintage sofas and arm chairs. Lots of mid-century pieces. Not large sectionals like the one in front of her.

Were they completely redecorating? The huge sofa that was now being dismantled was definitely super modern. Over-stuffed and done in a linen colored upholstery that was so soft, she wondered if it was a kind of chenille. She reached out and ran her hand across the top cushions. They felt comfortable and luxuriant. *Expensive.*

She shivered and glanced at the front of the building. There was a regular push door on the right, and then a super large revolving door in the center, with only one divider. Through them, she could see the end of a large moving van and more furniture. A huge chair that matched the couch. A large credenza and a sideboard, both in matching gray wood. Thick wood, at that – heavy pieces. She assumed Barry's marble topped buffet was made out of a similar material. Expensive. She looked back down at the couch.

"The Hans ordered all this?" she asked, watching as an end piece of the couch was disconnected finally and dragged into the waiting elevator.

"Who?"

"The Hans, the people whose apartment you're moving all this into," she told the moving guy.

"Look, lady, I don't know no Hans, I just know the guy who booked this gig offered us two hundred extra bucks each if we get it all unloaded in an hour, so unless you're gonna help, I'd appreciate it if you'd move your fine ass outta the way," he grunted, then the doors slid shut.

Katya didn't care about his sexist undertones. Her mouth fell open and she was sure her jaw was brushing the ground. Out the corner of her eye, she saw the other moving man start to head for the exit. Presumably to get more furniture. Two hundred bucks was two hundred bucks, after all.

"... *the guy who booked this gig* ..."

What kind of guy bought high end furniture and then offered a ridiculous bonus to his moving men?

"Hey," she called out, moving to step around the couch. "What guy is your friend talking -"

Again, she wasn't paying attention. Bad habit she had. She walked into someone, shoulder checking him hard enough to send her off balance. She bumped up against the corner piece before catching her balance.

"I'm assuming he was referring to me."

Katya couldn't lift her eyes. If she did, it would be real. And it couldn't be real. Dealing with Liam was hard enough, but at least he was soft. Like a blanket, he wrapped around her and enveloped her. It was easy to forget he could hurt her.

With Wulfric Stone, though, it was impossible to forget. He was carved out of ice and had razor sharp edges. He'd cut her to pieces once already. If she slipped again, he'd slice her right in half.

"What are you doing here?" she whispered, still staring out the front door. Moving man number two was struggling with the large chair outside. She watched him for a second, then felt a finger under her chin. Forcing her to turn and face forward. A pair of blue eyes froze her in place.

"You don't seem happy to see me," Wulf informed her.

"Probably because I'm not. Why are you delivering all this stuff to the Hans?" she asked.

"I'm not delivering it to them."

"Then why are you sending it up to their apartment?"

"It's not their apartment anymore."

"What? Yes it is, they've lived there forever, I was just …"

Katya's voice fell away as a light bulb went off over her head.

"They haven't lived there since last night, since about seven o'clock," Wulf told her.

Seven o'clock. Right about when she'd been getting off a train to go to the Eros speed dating party.

"So what, you evicted them!?" she was aghast. He rolled his eyes.

"Please. You always favor the dramatic. They're currently settling in to a new home in a four story Victorian, three blocks from their store."

"How did you manage that?"

"Easy, I own the building and I offered it at half the rent they were paying here. They all but begged me to let them move in," he explained. Katya held up her hands.

"So let me get this straight. You own a four story Victorian down near the water, that you offered to the Hans at half the price of their old place, just so you could move in, presumably to make my life hell?" she double checked.

"Something like that."

"Doesn't anyone know what the definition of stalking is!?" she shouted, her voice echoing in the small lobby.

Wulf went to respond, then paused when his cell phone started ringing. He held up a finger and checked the screen. Katya was about to grab it and throw it into the revolving door, but then he shocked her by locking the device and sliding it into his pocket.

"You did this to yourself," he told her. "I've left you messages.

Many times. I even sent you flowers."

"Your *secretary* sent me flowers."

"Ayumi is more than a secretary, and I assure you, she double checked with me to sign off on the final decision."

"You're amazing."

"Thank you."

"It wasn't meant as a compliment."

"I'm choosing to take it as one, anyway."

"What about your amazing ivory tower penthouse apartment? You're just gonna leave it empty so you can slum it down here with us plebeians?"

"No. As it so happens, I've already found the perfect tenant to sublet it," he said. She barked out a laugh.

"Please. You wouldn't even let me into your precious sanctuary, you expect me to believe you just let some stranger live there?" she asked.

"While it had been some time since I'd last spoken to her, my sister is hardly a stranger," he replied.

"Vieve? You got Vieve to move in!?" she was shocked. It was hard to picture his soft spoken younger sister taking part in one of his dastardly schemes.

"She's been there for the last week. When I finally got the Hans out of their place, I gave her the keys to mine."

"You can't," Katya stood away from the back of the sofa. "You can't do this. First Liam showing up last night, now – *oh my god*. Did you two plan this!? He distracts me at speed dating so you can move the Hans out without me knowing!?"

"Oh sweet jesus, don't tell me you did something as desperate as speed dating."

The night before, Katya'd had some long conversations with herself. About growing up and being mature and analyzing her emotions and actions. Not being so rash or hot headed. But it all flew out the window and she started swinging her heavy tote bag, bashing it against Wulf's side.

"No! Speed dating was just for fun! Going to the swingers' orgy afterwards was the act of desperation!" she yelled at him. Unlike Liam, he didn't make a move to stop her. He took the blows as if nothing strange was happening at all.

"I always knew you were holding back," he sighed. "But to answer your question, no. I knew you weren't in the building. I had no clue where Eden was, he and I haven't spoken in a while."

"He doesn't know you're just … moving people around and moving in?" Katya asked.

"Why should he? He's not involved in the rental process at all," Wulf said.

"He's gonna be pissed if he finds out you moved in!"

"I don't care."

"But he's the owner – he has some say in who does or doesn't live here. I'll get him to make you leave," Katya threatened. Wulf laughed.

"Go ahead and try. I have an iron clad contract with him that entitles me to any and all business decisions for these buildings, short of remodeling or selling, as well as a lease for that apartment. I'm not going anywhere, Tocci."

"Then *I'll* move out."

"And I'll sue you for breach of contract," he warned her.

"You wouldn't dare."

"Test me. I have an entire legal department that would love to have something to do."

Katya felt like she was drowning. She just wanted to get on with her life. After two weeks of feeling sorry for herself, she had felt like she'd begun to make some headway. Had begun to heal. Then boom, she'd gotten knocked down by Liam, then bowled over by Wulf.

"Why can't you just leave me alone?" she whispered, desperately trying not to cry. He sighed and stepped up close to her. It wasn't like with Liam, though. She wasn't comforted by Wulf's presence. She wasn't sure she ever had been. Being close to Wulf was like being full of static electricity and standing too close to something metal. She could feel the charge, was bracing herself for the shock.

"Because. We made promises to each other. I intend to keep them," he whispered back. She glared up at him.

"You never made any promises," she hissed.

"Not out loud," he agreed. "But they were made. You felt them."

She lurched away from him. The last time they had spoken – really spoken, not just her screaming at him in the rain – it had been intense. Almost life changing. She had felt herself really falling in love with him. Then a day later, she'd found out it had all been a lie. So yes, there had been promises made. Made with lips and tongues and hearts and souls. Which made the fact that he'd broken them all that much worse.

"I am not okay with this, Wulf. I can't be won back by intimidation and stalking. I can't be won back, *period*," she warned him. He smirked and stepped up close again.

"See, there's one problem with that statement," he said.

"What problem?"

"I don't have to 'win you back.'"

"Excuse me?"

"Because I don't think I ever lost you."

Katya didn't say anything. She just turned around and walked out the door, not even giving him a backward glance.

———————◇———————

Katya was able to keep her mind clear for almost two solid hours. She poured every ounce of her concentration into her work, finishing the last of the edible flowers and pinning almost half of them in place on the actual cakes. She was hanging the remaining flowers in an air tight cabinet when the events of the past eighteen hours finally caught up with her. She hurried into the break room, then screamed into her heavy jacket.

She wasn't sure she could ever forgive Liam Edenhoff for his part in what they'd done to her, but she was positive she wouldn't ever forgive Wulfric Stone. He didn't know what compassion was, or empathy, or sincerity. He didn't have normal human emotions. He didn't deserve forgiveness, nor did he probably care if he ever got it.

I'm just a challenge to him. That's what it is. The one that got away.

With that thought, Katya finally stopped screaming. Wulf wasn't used to losing, and he'd been so close to winning her. To have that victory ripped away, it must have really stung.

Over the past two weeks, she'd had a lot of time to think about her predicament and the men that had caused it. To go over all the signs she'd missed, all the ways they'd tried to one-up each other. Liam, giving her a pool on the roof. Wulf, driving her home to her family.

Even when she'd thought Liam hadn't known who she'd been seeing, she'd been able to sense a feeling of dislike from him. And his disdain for his "business partner" had been clear and palpable. Liam had spent most of his life feeling second best to his twin brother – it was obvious Wulf inspired similar feelings. That had fed into Liam's drive to win her over.

But a desire to prove himself to an absentee father was what Wulfric's foundation was built on. He *did not* come in second, and especially not to a man like Liam Edenhoff. Wulf was rich and smart and intelligent and, if truth were told, a total snob. A slacker who'd come into an inheritance? Wulf had probably taken delight in helping Liam, and had most definitely rubbed his encounters with Katya in the other man's face.

She paused as she started putting on her jacket. If that were all true – which she thought it was – then it would also kill him if she started speaking to Liam again, but kept refusing to speak to him.

She shook her head and finished gathering her stuff. She wasn't like that, Liam was right. She didn't do things out of spite or anger. Not even new-Katya – she may have been a sex kitten, but she wasn't a raging bitch.

Why couldn't she be? Being Miss Good Girl hasn't gotten me very far ...

No. No, she didn't want to go down this road. She didn't want to become *that* girl, who wound up in a viral video, keying her ex-boy-friend's car and running down his new girlfriend, or whatever. Things had been dark, right after the "break up" had happened. She'd halfway convinced herself to sleep with half of San Francisco, had told herself she would rub it in their faces somehow. Lots of things. Fantasies of setting Wulf's fancy car on fire, or breaking every single one of Liam's video games, things like that. But she wouldn't ever actually do anything mean to them.

... would she?

6

KATYA WASN'T SURE WHO LOOKED MORE SHOCKED – HER, OR LIAM. SHE hadn't really allowed herself to think about what she was doing when she'd marched into his building. She hadn't been invited, and she was sure he hadn't been expecting her. At all. Probably ever again.

Even though it was afternoon, he looked like he'd just gotten out of bed. Owning and managing a night club-slash-sex club meant keeping strange hours. Noon was morning for Mr. Edenhoff. His hair was sticking up at right angles from his head, he was only wearing a pair of loose jeans, and he had a toothbrush hanging haphazardly out of his mouth.

"Uh …" he finally managed to grunt. She groaned and shoved past him, unwinding her thick scarf as she moved. His apartment was a mess – more so than usual. It made her feel a little better. Clearly, without her constantly nagging him about cleaning up and eating right and doing laundry, he couldn't lead a productive healthy life.

Good. Dysentery is still a possibility.

"We're not friends," she blurted out, kicking smelly socks and dirty pants out of her way as she waded through his living room. She glanced around. He'd had all the walls removed from his apartment, converting it into a wide open loft. With its high ceilings and faded yellow wallpaper, it very much embodied its owner's personality. Warm and larger than life.

"Is this like a reminder courtesy call?" he mumbled as he shambled into the kitchen. She listened as he spit toothpaste into his kitchen sink. She scrunched up her nose in disgust.

"You're a thirty-two year old successful business owner, yet you live like a nineteen year old frat boy."

"Seriously, did you just come over here to remind me of things I already know?" he asked, chucking the brush into the sink as well before turning around and leaning back against his counter. She looked away and wished he would put on a shirt.

"I came over because I wanted to ask you something."

"Alright."

He must have read her mind, because as he came back into the living room, he bent down to sift through the sea of t-shirts that were scattered about at his feet – he obviously wasn't too concerned with cleanliness. He finally found one he liked and he pulled it on before coming to a stop in front of her.

"If – and I really mean *if* – there's any chance you and I can be friends again, and *ONLY* friends, I need to know that you'll be honest with me. About everything. Anything. Things that happened, things that didn't happen, things that are going to happen. If you lie, I'll find out, Liam. *I will.* It's how the universe works. If you lie to me, I will never speak to you again. Worse than that, though, you will have to live with the knowledge that deep down, you are truly a horrible, hurtful, malicious person who only cares about himself," Katya finished in a rush, gasping for breath at the end.

Liam's eyebrows had raised throughout her speech, and by the time she finished, they were almost in his hairline. She knew he hadn't seen her mad very often. Just at the very end. No, only Wulfric had been lucky enough to be on the receiving end of her temper.

"Alright. I promise I will never -"

"I'm serious, Liam. Don't make a promise you're not sure you can keep."

There was another long pause. He took a deep breath, and for a moment, she thought he wasn't going to say anything. She wasn't sure whether she wanted to cry, or to feel relief. But then he rubbed his hand over the back of his neck and sighed.

"I'll never lie to you. I never should have. I only lied to keep from hurting you. Stupid, I know, but what can I say? Sometimes I'm a really stupid guy. But I can learn some things, and you definitely taught me a lesson. I won't ever lie to you again," he promised. She nodded.

"Good. Did you know Wulf was moving in?"

"Did I -, wait, what? With *you!?*"

"No, into the Hans' apartment."

"The who?"

"Jesus, the Hans! They live in the penthouse in my building, they've lived there for over ten years!" she snapped.

"Well, shit, how should I know that? I didn't even live here ten years ago. Wulfric is living with your neighbors?" Liam checked.

She took a deep breath and counted to ten. She wasn't being clear, she knew, and he had just woken up. He still had sleep creases on the side of his face and she didn't even have to look to know his bed was a mess.

At least it's empty. Jesus, this is Liam I'm dealing with – what if I'd walked in on him with somebody? It's almost more surprising that I didn't.

"No," she finally calmed herself down a little. "He found them a new place to live and moved them out last night, while you and I were at speed dating. He moved in this morning, I nearly got run over by his ridiculously over sized furniture. It just seemed … I mean, you just showed up at the event, and we were outside for so long, and then he just happened to get all his little deeds done at the same time. I'm not some toy you guys can play with, not anymore."

"I swear," Liam held up his hands. "I had no idea. I found out where you'd be through good old fashioned internet stalking, that's it. He can't do this, I'll tell him he has to move out."

Before he could turn to grab his phone, Katya stopped him.

"He said the same thing you said to me – he has a lease, and that you also signed an iron-clad contract allowing him to have total control over who he rents to. He won't even let me out of my lease. When I said I'd break it, he threatened to sue me," she explained.

"Seriously?"

"Seriously."

"God, that guy's a dick. And you fell for him instead of me," Liam growled, raking his fingers through his hair. Katya glared and before she could stop herself, she elbowed him in the stomach.

"I didn't fall for anybody – I was blindly manipulated into two separate relationships with complete and total assholes!" she yelled at him.

"I don't remember you being so violent, angel cake."

Katya snorted and turned around, heading for his front door. He jogged around her and blocked the exit.

"I just thought you should know about him moving in, and wanted to know if you knew. I'm done here," she explained, fighting with her scarf as she tried to wrap it around her neck.

"Not so fast. I feel like we're making progress here. What are you doing tonight?"

"Liam. Are you serious?"

"Too soon? How about this weekend?"

"Even if I wasn't busy, I still wouldn't be doing anything with *you*."

"Oh, busy, huh. Hot date?"

"Wedding."

"Wedding! Then you *need* a date," he smiled big at her. She smirked back at him.

"I already have one," she replied. He seemed shocked by her response and she took the opportunity to squeeze past him into the small hallway. The elevator was still sitting on their floor, so when the doors opened, she stepped right on. Unfortunately, Liam had gained his faculties by then and he followed her into the lift.

"Who are you going with?" he asked, trying to sound casual. Failing miserably.

"Just some sexy brunette," she told him, glancing down at his bare feet. There was a dinging sound and they got off on the ground floor.

"Please don't tell me it's someone you met at -"

"Katya!"

She looked up at the sound of her name, bracing herself. Prepared for Wulfric to be glaring at her. But it wasn't him. She smiled as Gaten Shepherd strode across the foyer.

"Hey, how are you?" she asked.

She was aware that Liam was looming over her somewhat. He was a tall, lanky guy, and usually his goofy smile and wild hair kept him from being intimidating, he could be when he put his mind to it. A glare combined with his size was usually enough to get the job done, but they had no effect on the other man. Gate walked right up to her and wrapped her in a hug.

"Doing good. We keep running into each other," he pointed out, chuckling a little.

"I know. Which reminds me! I know you do carpentry, but do you know anyone good with electrical stuff? My oven *still* isn't working, and the shitty management around here still hasn't gotten around to fixing it," she said, turning an icy glare onto Liam. He swallowed thickly.

"Hey, take it up with Wulf-man. I just own the place, I don't manage it," he said. She rolled her eyes.

"See what I mean? I should file a complaint," she managed a laugh. Gate glanced between her and Liam, then forced out an awkward laugh, as well.

"Could help. Or I do know a guy, I could have him come take a look. I'll give him a call, then I'll text you when I hear back," he offered. Katya smiled.

"Thanks, that would be awesome."

"Good seeing you again, Katya."

"You, too."

They shared one more hug – made more awkward by Liam stepping up so close, his chest was brushing both their arms – then Gaten got on the elevator. As soon as the doors slid shut, Liam groaned and followed Katya outside.

"You *cannot* be talking about him."

"About him, what?"

"*He's* your wedding date?"

She almost burst out laughing, then realized torturing Liam was kind of fun. She kept her giggles in check.

"Don't worry about who I'm going with."

"But he's like a hippy! I think he's in Green Peace, and he's always building shit, and he shops at Whole Foods. *Whole Foods*. You can't go with him," Liam insisted. They'd reached her building and before he could follow her inside it, she turned and pressed a hand to his chest.

"First of all – *I* shop at Whole Foods sometimes. Second of all – *it's none of your business*. Now go back home," she ordered him, pointing back at his building. He frowned and placed his hand over the one she had on his chest.

"Katya," he started in a soft voice. No. No, no, no, no, no. Not sweet, caring Liam. She'd never handled that aspect of his personality very well. "I know we did some really fucked up stuff to you. But my feelings for you were always real, I always told the truth about them. Even if you never return them, even if we never spoke again after this moment, I'd still care about you, and I can tell you don't like that guy. So don't do this."

Katya took a deep breath. Talk about hitting the nail on the head. It's what she'd been doing for the past two weeks – going out on dates, trying to feel better about herself by grabbing whatever random male attention she could find. And it certainly hadn't worked.

But he doesn't need to know that. He doesn't need to know anything.

"I'm only going to say this to you one more time," she said, her voice shaking a little. "What I do is *none. of. your. business.* If you can't handle that – if you think you're entitled to know everything that's going on in my life, then whatever it is we're starting here, it should just end right now."

She didn't give him a chance to respond. She just turned and hurried through the revolving door, praying that he didn't follow her.

Of course, the way her luck had been going, she halfway expected Wulf to be on the other side of the door. Just waiting to pounce and take away her last shred of sanity. Thankfully, he wasn't. The lobby was empty, all of his enormous furniture hopefully all tucked away in his new apartment.

Katya groaned as she rode up the floors to her place. Wulfric Stone, living two floors above her. Liam Edenhoff, still living one building away from her. Two men she'd been involved with, slept with, had deep, personal relationships with. Two men who'd empowered her and helped her grow and changed her very core. Two men who had used her and chewed her up and then spit her out.

And now both those men were her close neighbors.

Jesus, this brings a whole new meaning to "there goes the neighborhood".

7

THE REST OF THURSDAY PASSED WITHOUT INCIDENT, THANKFULLY. IT probably had something to do with the fact that she holed up in her apartment and refused to answer her phone or the door. Tori was able to come home early – she worked as a "bartender" of sorts. She was trained as a bartender, but she worked the private part of Liam's club. No liquor allowed. She doled out expensive water and soft drinks, as well as various brands of lubricants, condoms, and "personal massagers".

When the shit had hit the fan and Tori had found out Liam had been using Katya and basically lying to her, Tori had been ready to quit. But Katya knew the other girl really liked her job, and she never liked her jobs – hence why she'd had so many over the years. Rent wasn't cheap in San Francisco, and even on the good salary Katya made, she couldn't afford their nice, downtown, two bedroom apartment all on her own. She needed Tori to contribute.

Also, it didn't hurt knowing Tori liked regaling Liam with all of Katya's new dating habits. Really, it was amazing Liam hadn't fired her, yet.

"Why hasn't he fired you?" Katya asked, moving out of the way as Tori set the table.

"Because Jan said if he ever did for any reason other than poor work performance, Jan would – and I quote – '*rip his fucking head off and shove it up his urethra*'. Urethra, Kat. I almost pissed myself laughing."

"Well, better make sure you keep up the good work then."

"Please, they love me there. There are members who won't come unless I'm working, did you know that? Liam can't ever get rid of me. Besides, I think having me there, even being a bitch to him all the time, kinda makes him feel close to you," Tori said. Her voice was simple, as if she were prattling off the weather, but the sentiment was terribly sweet. Katya frowned and spooned beef stroganoff over the egg noodles that were waiting.

"I should tell you something," she sighed, turning around and setting the food on the table.

She explained everything. Running into Liam at speed dating. Bumping in Wulf downstairs. Using Gaten as jealousy-bait. Tori listened to it all without saying a word – which was somewhat of a miracle. She just kept nodding and shoving more food in her mouth. How she kept such a perfect figure, Katya would never know. She never worked out, never gained a pound, and had curves in all the right places. Grossly unfair.

"Wow," Tori said when Katya had finished speaking. "You've had a hell of a day."

"You're telling me," Katya groaned, poking at her remaining noodles.

"So now you get to pick."

"Pick what?"

"Whether you want my honest opinion, or would like me to say what you want to hear."

"Oh god."

Tori smiled big – "I knew you'd pick honesty."

"I'm afraid to listen."

"Look," her roommate sighed. "I'm not … I know my own track history with guys is not good. Or awful. Whatever. But that's me, that's what I do. You, though, I don't know … it's like all the good advice you always give me? The way you parent me and are so awesome? Well, when it comes to this dating stuff, it's my turn to be that way for you."

"Oooookay …" Katya let her voice trail off, still a little scared of what was going to be said.

"And while I'd like to say set all their shit on fire and key their cars, I think what you need to do is figure out what it is *you* really want. Just you. Not what Eden wants, and not what Wulf-man wants. Deep down, what you really, really want. If you want to forgive them and move on, then go for it – I've got your back. If you *do* want to set their shit on fire and key their cars, I've got a lighter in my back pocket. If you want to play your own game and push their buttons, then have fun, sister. Just make sure it's what *YOU* want to do," Tori urged, tucking her loose hair behind her ears.

While Katya absorbed all of that, let it roll around her brain for a bit, her best friend reached across the table with a fork and began eating the rest of the stroganoff.

"Just do whatever I feel like," Katya mumbled.

"Yeah. I mean, look how far it's taken you. This time three months ago, you'd be sketching right now. Or crocheting something. Or watching one of those cooking videos. Honestly, it was kind of sad. Now you're all '*I'm a vixen*', and '*look at me be a badass*', and … I don't know. Feels like you're finally …," Tori struggled to find the right words. Katya smiled.

"Growing into myself?"

"Yeah! Like you're finally becoming comfortable in your skin. Saying the shit that you usually keep bottled up inside. It's good for you! Sometimes screaming and throwing cake at a dude is good for you. And sometimes sleeping around and being selfish is good for you, too. But you know, like, in moderation," Tori amended her speech. Katya laughed.

"Gotcha. Alright – do whatever makes me feel good, as long as it's in moderation."

"Well, duh. What if you decide coke makes you feel good!? Moderation is key."

Katya laughed for so long, Tori had finished the last of the food by the time she stopped.

Friday afternoon. Katya had stayed late at the bakery, finally finishing everything for Lauren's cake. In the morning, she'd go down and put it all in place, then deliver the massive dessert to the event hall. She'd miss the actual wedding service while she went home and changed, but she'd be done in time for the reception.

On her bus ride, Katya thought a lot about what Tori had said. Thought a lot about how she felt, about the things she wanted for herself.

It was hard to be honest with herself – a common problem for most people, she knew. She kept a lot of things buried, too ashamed or embarrassed to admit them to herself. Right that moment, though, she decided to lay them all out in her mind, not caring if they were "right" or "wrong". All that mattered was how each thought made her feel.

Okay, so let's think about Liam.

Thinking about him caused a pain in her heart. It was strange, how much she secretly longed for him. How badly she wanted to call him and tell him some funny story from work, or to have drinks with him on her roof. In a short time, he'd become a very large, very important presence in her life. Almost invaluable. If she was being totally honest, she didn't want to picture her life without him.

He'd done something awful. Terrible. Unforgivable, really. But she wanted to forgive him. She wanted him to apologize – which he had, and she wanted him to mean it – which she was pretty sure he did. She wanted to cry, and she wanted him to hug her, and she wanted them to get to a place where they could be okay together. Maybe not that day, and maybe not the next. Maybe not for a while. The wounds were still too fresh. But maybe someday.

*Yeah. That's what I **really** want.*

She let out a rush of air so fast, the person sitting next to her glanced at her. Katya couldn't explain it, but again, it felt like a weight had been lifted. She'd been so ashamed to even admit to herself that she wanted to forgive Liam. Embarrassed, like she was letting down all of womanhood. But Tori had been right, she needed to do what *she* felt was right for her.

She felt so good about her decision, so proud of her self-analyzing abilities, that she barreled into the next thought without pause.

Let's do this with Wulf, now!

Her relief ran straight into a brick wall and she almost groaned.

If Liam was a pain in her heart, Wulf was a full body ache. She'd been closer to him in different ways, and his betrayal had cut a lot deeper. She'd shared her life with Liam; she'd shared her heart with Wulf. She could always get her life back.

A heart, though, wasn't as easy to recapture.

She was frustrated that she couldn't untangle her feelings for Wulf as easily. Forgiveness wasn't as simple, nor was being able to tell if she even wanted to forgive him. Keeping him at bay would be even more necessary than with Liam, but also harder. Wulf didn't like being told no, and he would never settle for being just friends.

She chewed on her bottom lip and stared out the window, watching cars slide by the bus. She didn't think she wanted to be Wulf's friend, and she certainly didn't want to date him ever again. She wanted … she wanted him to feel. Something. Anything. Feel a tenth of the pain he'd inflicted on her. Wondered if that was even possible. She wanted …

… I want him to love me the way he made me love him.

47

Shame, rolling over her in waves. Such a silly, girly revenge fantasy, but there it was – the stark, raving truth. She wanted him to fall in love with her, so she could look him in the eye and tell him she didn't feel the same way. That it was all just for fun, for laughs. She wanted him to know what it felt like to lose someone.

It was all ridiculous, anyway. She wasn't into playing games. She wasn't going to lure Wulf into any elaborate plot, that much she knew. But ... if he continued pursuing her, which she was sure he would, she could just let it all unfold however she wanted. Slam her door in his face one day, and invite him in for coffee the next. React in whatever way she was feeling in whatever moment. Keep him on his toes. Drive him crazy.

Wulfric Stone, crazy. It might be good for him.

She was so caught up in her little vengeance daydream, she almost missed her stop. She wasn't used to that bus route, so she hadn't been looking out for it. She wound up pulling the stop chord at the last moment, jumping up as the bus squealed to a halt. She hopped out onto the sidewalk and opened her umbrella, trying to protect herself from the down pour. Then, as she heard the bus roll away, she took a deep breath and turned around.

Wulf's apartment building.

She'd only ever been there once before – and on accident, at that. She hadn't been positive of the exact address, since he'd basically carried her there. She'd had to retrace her steps from that long-ago night, then use Google maps to track down the actual building.

It was well away from downtown San Francisco, and so tall, it looked like it was slicing into the sky. All dark metals and mirrored glass. Cold and ominous, exactly like the man who owned it.

She hurried across the street and into the building. A doorman held open the entrance for her, and as she shook out her umbrella over the marble floors, a man behind a desk cleared his throat.

"Can I help you?" he asked, smiling pleasantly at her. She smiled back.

"Yes – I'm here to see a friend," she explained.

"Of course. The elevators are on the right," he offered, extending a hand in their direction. She nodded.

"Yes, I know, but she's staying on the top floor."

"I'm sorry, which floor?"

Katya took a deep breath.

"Wulfric Stone's home. I'm here to see Genevieve Stone," she told him. She spoke in even tones, hoping to sound professional. Wulf's apartment was only accessible via a key card, and Katya didn't have Vieve's phone number. Her only way up was to hope the attendant would call and announce her.

"And your name?" he asked, tapping away at a computer that was hiding behind the desk.

Crap.

"Katya Tocci. She doesn't know I'm coming, so if you could just call and -"

"Ah! Ms. Tocci, I have you in here as an approved guest," he told her. Her jaw dropped.

"I'm … what?"

"It says here you are a pre-approved guest, to be allowed access to the apartment at any time. Did Mr. Stone not tell you that?" he asked. She gasped so hard she choked on air.

"No," she coughed out. "No, Mr. Stone did not. Can I, um, does it say when he put me on the guest list?"

"Of course, Ms. Tocci. Let me see … ah, yes, almost a month ago now," he told her, prattling off a date. Katya did some math – Wulf had given her full access to his home before they'd even gone to Carmel.

Why didn't he ever tell me!?

"Oh. Yes. I … uh … that's great. Um, I'd really love to go up there, but could you let Vieve -, erm, Ms. Stone, know I'm coming?" she asked.

"Of course."

A couple seconds later, and he assured her that Ms. Stone would be delighted to receive her. Katya was shuffled onto an express elevator and the man used his card to grant her access to the top floor. Then he smiled and stood stiffly while the doors shut between them.

As soon as the lift started moving, Katya sagged back against a wall. She wasn't sure how to deal with that new information. She had *begged* Wulf to take her to his apartment, and he'd always said no. If she'd ever gotten fed up and just shown up on her own, she would've been let right in, regardless of whether or not he was even home.

WHY WOULD HE DO THAT?

She couldn't figure it out. Wulf had always been hard to read, even when he'd been the grumpy teenager living next door to her while they'd been growing up. She'd been wrong more than once when trying to guess his thoughts and feelings.

Had it been a preemptive move? Give her access then, so he wouldn't have to bother with it later? Hmmm, didn't seem like him. Everything he did was calculated. If he'd given her access a month ago, it was for a specific purpose. Maybe … just maybe, even that long ago, he had been feeling something. Maybe he'd been starting to see her as part of his home, and so of course, he'd given her access to it. Not like he had to discuss it with her – he never discussed anything he did with anybody.

No, this is ridiculous. You are not now, nor were you ever, a part of his home. He was probably just hoping you'd show up in nothing but a trench coat, or something.

Before she could dwell more on that particular mystery, the elevator lurched to a stop.

Genevieve Stone was waiting outside the doors. She was only twenty-one, yet Katya had always been a little in awe of the other girl. While they'd never been best friends, they had been two girls of a similar age growing up next door to each other – they'd been to their share of slumber parties together. They'd gone to the same private schools. But after Katya had graduated, they'd only kept in contact through social media, and sporadically, at that.

Through her own mother, Katya had heard about Vieve going into med school. Turned out Wulfric wasn't the only one with brains in the family. Vieve had graduated high school a year early and had immediately gone to college. But after only one year, she'd dropped out. Apparently the Stone family had been rocked by that announcement, but not half as much as when they found out it was because she'd fallen in love.

Vieve got married three weeks after her eighteenth birthday. Katya had received an invitation, but school had prevented her from attending. Then, about six months ago, Katya's mom had mentioned that the man had passed away. Brain cancer.

Man, a widow by the time she was twenty-one. I can't even imagine.

And yet still, with all that in her past, Vieve stood there looking as cool and collected as could be. Despite the large age gap, she and Wulf could have been twins. They were both pretty tall, with fair skin and dark hair, which was all topped off with a matching pair of striking blue eyes. Wulf had been a swimmer, then had gone on to dominate the real estate industry in California. Genevieve had been a skilled equestrian, and there was no doubt in anyone's mind that she would've gone on to become an amazing doctor. Two peas in a pod. It made Katya feel small in comparison. Like if she stepped too close to the other woman, she might sully her with her presence.

"Katya, it's been so long!" Vieve breathed out, stepping up close and hugging her. Katya was a little surprised, but she hugged her back.

"I know, not since … wow, my graduation party, huh?"

"I guess so. Feels so long ago now," Vieve sighed, then stepped aside and gestured for Katya to enter the apartment.

It was hard being there. She'd only been there once before, and though it had seemed like a magical time, everything had come crashing down right afterwards. So the space made her feel

51

uncomfortable. In a short span of time, she'd made a lot of memories in that home. Ones she now worked very hard to forget.

"Yeah, but sometimes, it kinda feels like it was all just yesterday. So what brings you to San Francisco?" Katya dove right into her twenty questions. Vieve blinked her eyes in surprise, then quickly got control of herself and glided into the kitchen.

"I've been needing a change. A month or two ago, I had mentioned to Wulf that I was thinking of moving. He offered to find me a place. I was going to come here for a sort of extended visit, see if I liked it enough to relocate here," she explained.

"Oh. So you're thinking of moving here," Katya clarified.

"Maybe. I like it a lot, and it's nice to be close to Wulf. Is that why you're here? Were you hoping to catch him? He said he wanted me to have space, to really get a feel for living on my own here, so he's staying somewhere else," Vieve told her. Katya coughed out a laugh, maybe a little too forcefully.

"What, Wulf? Looking for him? No, no. I, uh, found out you were here, and thought it would be fun to catch up," she said quickly. Vieve smiled again. She had such a gentle smile, but it didn't quite reach her eyes. For someone so young, there was something about her that seemed so old. A person could just *feel* how weary her soul was; Katya wanted to wrap her up and take care of her.

"He told me about you two."

"He did?"

"Yes. When I called about looking for a place, he mentioned that living here would bring me closer to you. I was surprised he even knew you were in San Francisco," Vieve said, and Katya gave a genuine laugh. "He told me you guys had been seeing each other. I thought it was … nice."

"Yeah. Yeah, it was nice, for a while."

"He also told me it ended."

"It did."

"Do you … want to talk about it?" Vieve offered. Katya snorted.

"I don't think you want to hear it."

"I don't mind. I mean, he *is* my brother, so I'm going to love him no matter what. But that also means I know how difficult he can be."

"Difficult isn't a big enough word for what your brother is."

"Tell me about it. I lived with him, remember?"

Katya laughed again.

"He didn't tell you how it ended?" she asked.

"He mentioned that it didn't end well, and that he'd made some bad mistakes," Vieve replied.

"That's kind of downplaying it. Nothing else?"

"Not really. You know him, he's not a big talker. But then when I got here, after a couple days, I finally asked about you. He said not to worry, that you'd be speaking to each other soon. So that's why I assumed you were here for him," Vieve said. Katya groaned.

"No, I came here to see if you were in on his little plot to drive me bat shit insane," she explained.

"Oh. Um, that would be a no. I have not heard any plan for insanity. Maybe you should tell me what, exactly, is going on between you two."

"I really don't think you want to hear about all that," Katya waved her hand as she spoke. "I've been awkward enough, I should just go. I just … I don't know, like I said, I had to know that this wasn't all some Illuminati master plan to destroy me."

"Nope. I forgot to pay my Illuminati dues. But I'm an exceptional listener, and I like to help people, and I know Wulfric pretty well, I could offer some insight. It's not good to leave it all bottled up," Vieve insisted in that earnest way she had.

So Katya did just that – leaving out the dirtier and nastier details. She figured a sister didn't need to hear the kind of nasty language and activities Wulf was prone to. She also didn't want to make him out to be a monster to his family, Katya wasn't that mean.

She explained how she and Wulf had met, him tricking her into that first date, then just showing up at her house or job whenever he felt like it. Forcing his way inside her life. Into her heart. Then she glossed over the horrific train crash of an ending and wrapped it up with the current events.

"And then I walked downstairs yesterday, and found him moving into my building. He told me you were living here, and he was giving you space, so of course I kind of thought maybe you were working together," Katya finished explaining. Vieve nodded. She'd moved to sit on a stool next to Katya.

"We're not, uh, 'working together', but I have to ask you – if we were, if this was some elaborate plan for him to get you back, do you think I'd work against him and help you?" Vieve asked. It wasn't said with any malice or in any sort of tone, just a genuine question. Katya was pretty sure Vieve didn't have a mean or nasty bone in her body.

"No, and that's not what I'm here to ask or anything. I just wanted … I don't know, a heads up. To know where you stand. We're sort of friends, I'm sure we would've wound up in each others space at some point. I would hate to think someone else was keeping crazy secrets from me. It was … the worst feeling. If you're his new best friend, fine. If you don't plan on spending a lot of time with him, cool. I just want to know so I'm not caught in the middle again," Katya explained. Vieve smiled.

"I don't think Wulf's ever had a best friend, and if he did, it certainly wouldn't be me. There's no diabolical plan to get you back and I'm not keeping any crazy secrets for him. Though to be totally honest, I gotta say, I'm kind of rooting for him. He sounded … happier when he was with you. I hope things work out."

"That's very sweet. But if we're being honest, I don't. I hope that someday, someone makes Wulf feel as awful as he made me feel."

"IF THAT'S TRUE, THEN YOU'RE GOING ABOUT THIS ALL WRONG."

Katya gasped so hard, she almost fell off her stool. That wasn't Vieve speaking. Someone was in the living room, yelling to be heard from across the spacious apartment. A half wall separated that room from the kitchen, blocking the stranger from view. Katya got off her stool and leaned around the black marble structure.

She could see a pair of shoes propped up on the arm rest of a white loveseat. Leaning a little farther, she saw that the shoes led to a pair of legs belonging to a woman. A short girl, she fit fairly comfortably on the small couch. Her long dirty blonde hair was hanging over the edge of the cushion, almost brushing the floor. Her face wasn't visible, though. It was blocked by a ridiculously large smart phone, which she held up and continued playing with despite the fact that another person was approaching her.

"Um, I'm sorry … do I know you?" Katya asked. The other girl snorted.

"Depends on how you define *know*. Shit," she hissed, her thumb jamming down against the screen. "Lost again." She sat upright and Katya gasped. It was Brighton Stone, the youngest Stone sibling.

If Vieve and Wulf were cut from the same cloth, then Brie was from an entirely different bolt. She hadn't gotten any of the height or strong bone structure that ran through the Stone line. Brie took after her mother – dark blonde, on the short side, and curvy. She finally stood up and glanced at Katya with a pair of large, closed-off brown eyes. Then she raked a hand through her thick hair and strode into the kitchen.

"Brie," Katya finally managed, turning to follow her. "I'm sorry, I didn't even know you were here. I can't believe how long it's been, I barely recognized you."

"Yeah, long time, I know," the younger woman sighed as she rooted around in the fridge.

"Wulf didn't mention that you were here, too."

"Probably because he doesn't know."

"Uh …," Katya wasn't sure how to respond to that.

"I'm taking some time off school. Wulfy won't be happy when he hears that, he'll spout off to mom, she won't leave me alone till I go back, blah blah blah. I'm just over it, so I'm hiding out here," Brie explained as she popped the cap off a beer. Katya glanced at Vieve, who looked slightly embarrassed but still maintained a calm smile.

"Hiding out in his home? And aren't you, like, eighteen?" Katya double checked. Brie raised an eyebrow, then necked half the beer before responding.

"I'm nineteen, and do you see Wulf around this place? He won't come back as long as Vieve is here. I'm safer here than at home."

Katya wanted to keep asking questions, then stopped herself. She didn't know Brighton Stone, at least not anymore. And the girl seemed to have a wall ten feet thick out in front of her. *Don't fuck with me* rolled off her in waves, and Katya decided to heed them. She had enough problems of her own, she didn't need to get involved with an attitudey teenager.

"So what am I going all wrong about?" she went back to Brie's comment.

"*This.* You're mad at Wulf, right?" Brie checked.

"Uh, yes."

"And you want him to leave you alone, but you also want him to know you're pissed off at him."

"Um … sure?"

"Then coming here and whining to his favorite sister isn't going to do any of that," Brie finished. Vieve sighed.

"Brighton, I'm not -"

"You have to get his attention. Do some crazy shit. Then make him regret the day he ever met you," Brie talked right over her sister.

"You do know we're talking about your brother, right?" Katya checked. Brie shrugged.

"A man's a man. Not like he acts like a brother, anyway," she replied, then dragged her feet as she wandered back into the living room, disappearing from sight.

"Brighton," Vieve sighed, shaking her head. Then she fixed her smile back into place and looked at Katya. "She has some issues. With men. Our father left when she was so young, and then Wulf hasn't been around much, and then there was a boyfriend in high school."

"At least I'm not a widow at twenty-one!" Brie yelled from the other room.

Jesus. Katya had always assumed Wulf was the odd one in his family. Apparently, she'd been way off base. She got the feeling she could punch Vieve in the face, and the girl would smile and say thank you. And Brie seemed like "bitch" was her middle name.

They could probably get an amazing discount for some family therapy.

Before things could get more awkward than they already were, Katya grabbed her umbrella and started backing towards the exit.

"I've intruded long enough," she said, then held up her hand when Vieve went to argue. "I sort of came here on a whim. Thanks so much for being honest with me. It was great seeing you – both of you – again. We'll have to have lunch sometime!"

She kept rushing for the door, exchanging phone numbers with Vieve and shouting goodbye to Brie – who didn't respond. When she was safely in the elevator, Katya slumped against the wall and pressed her hand against her head.

I think I'm more confused now then when I came here. Why did I have to be neighbors with the Stones!?

8

FROM FOUR IN THE MORNING ON SATURDAY, KATYA WAS RUNNING AT TOP speed.

She left her dress hanging on the back of her bedroom door, and had her makeup prepped and spread out on her bed.

She took a taxi to work, put all the layers of the cake together, then put on the finishing touches. Then added some more accessories to it. Loaded it into the van for delivery, then rode in the back with it to ensure its safety, and to add a couple new elements she thought of at the last minute.

While the catering staff was moving the cake onto a trolley, they knocked the top layer askew. Katya's first instinct was to throw up, and then to kill everyone in the room. Then she remembered that she was a professional and she'd been through much worse, so she got out her baker's emergency kit and fixed the problem. By the time she had everything back in order and the cake was in place in the ballroom, she had twenty minutes before the wedding party was scheduled to arrive.

Cutting it close.

She felt a little better when she got to the apartment and found out Tori was running late, too. The other girl was running around in her underwear, attempting to curl her hair and brush her teeth at the same time.

Katya did her make up, helped Tori do hers, and then went to put on her dress, only to discover it had somehow acquired a huge stain on it. She glared down the hall in her roommate's direction – the stain was suspiciously the same shade as Tori's favorite lipstick.

The bride had a strict dress code for the reception – all white. Absolutely everyone was supposed to be wearing as much white as possible, with black pants and skirts being acceptable. Katya's closet wasn't exactly overflowing with white dresses. She'd bought her outfit specifically for the event. She yanked her hangers around and finally found one piece of mostly white clothing.

She frowned as she pulled out the dress. It was the one she'd worn on her second date with Wulf. To the small bar, when the sun had set everything on fire and they'd slept together for the first time.

She shook her head back and forth and yanked the dress off its hanger. She didn't have time for memory lane, or the massive cry fest that was lurking behind her eyes. She put on the appropriate underwear, slid into the dress, grabbed Tori, and was running to the elevator with high hopes of making it to the reception in time to see the cake cut.

"*Oh. My. God.*"

Katya was breathing hard, one hand pressed against her side. They'd literally ran down the block from their taxi. She wasn't as in shape as she liked to think, and while they stood at the entrance to the ballroom, she bent over and waited to catch her breath.

"What?" she asked, glancing at Tori. The other girl was staring across the room.

"You made that!? Like you. Little ol' you, made that … that … that piece of art!?"

Katya followed her stare and took in the huge cake. Sometimes, Katya forgot what she did for a living, even as she was doing it. It just became work. Like a puzzle. Something to figure out and create, like a Rubik's cube she built as she solved it. She knew she did good work, she could be objective enough for that, but art? All she saw when she looked at it was the massive amount of hours and stress it required. Hearing from someone else that it looked good, it meant a lot.

"Yeah, it turned out pretty okay," Katya sighed, resting her hands on her hips.

"Just okay!? Katya, it's phenomenal. Sometimes I forget how amazing you are. C'mon, let's go get shitty on expensive champagne and celebrate your frickin' awesome talent," Tori laughed, then dragged her to the bar. They had just received their glasses when Katya felt an arm wrap around her shoulders.

"You're here!"

Lauren, the newly-wedded bride, hugged Katya to her side. She looked stunning in her mermaid style gown and veil.

"Yes, finally," Katya laughed. "There were some complications, but we got here a minute ago."

"I hope this beast didn't cause you any problems. God, it turned out great. Thank you so much," Lauren breathed, looking over the cake again.

"No, thank you for trusting me with your special day. Everything looks beautiful, Lauren, and especially you."

"Oh, stop. I know, right? It turned out amazing. And you two look simply beautiful, I can't wait for …" Lauren's voice trailed off, then she burst out laughing. Katya and Tori glanced at each other.

"For … ?" Tori questioned.

"It's gonna be a fun night, I just can't wait till the drinks really start flowing. Just remember – no throwing *this* cake," Lauren teased Katya. "C'mon, let's go do the chicken dance."

Before anyone could say anything else, they were all forced onto the dance floor. Thank god the chicken dance wasn't actually playing, but Katya did get to witness Lauren and her husband reenacting the dance sequence from House Party.

After an hour or so of rocking out, the stress of the morning and afternoon drifted away. She did a shaky foxtrot with the bride's father, traded recipes with the groom's mother, and had to control the wandering hands of the best man. He eventually turned his attention to Tori, who loved playing games with drunk guys.

Katya laughed to herself as she watched them from across the room. Then she let her eyes wander around, taking in all the couples. A slow song was playing, and the candle light bouncing off all the white clothing and table toppings gave everything an ethereal glow. Hallmark couldn't have painted a more romantic picture.

Yet surprisingly, she didn't feel bad about standing there alone. In the past, when she'd gone to weddings or parties alone, she'd always felt a little conspicuous. A lady always had a handsome gentleman at her arm – that's how she'd been raised. But now she felt kinda good about being alone. Strong. She'd been having a great time, no male company needed. Who needed a man, anyway?

Of course, Katya should've known better. Whenever she was finally feeling better about her whole situation, the universe had a way of slapping her back into line.

"Care to dance, milady?"

She turned her head at the same time Liam stepped into her view. She gaped at him for a moment, then glanced around, looking for the hidden camera prank show. Then she looked back at him.

"What are you doing here? You crashed *a wedding?* That's low, even for you," she hissed. She was mortified. Lauren wasn't only a friend, she was a client. One that Katya had embarrassed herself enough in front of. She couldn't have Liam acting foolish at this wedding.

"Who said anything about crashing? I'm here under totally legit pretenses," he assured her.

"Oh, really. Like what kind of pretenses?"

"The legit kind."

"*Liam.*"

"The caterers," he sighed, gesturing over his shoulder to the elaborate set up on the other side of the room. "One of the owners used to work with me. I was able to wrangle an invitation through him. A *real* invitation, before you ask."

"How did you even find out what wedding I was talking about? There's like four others, at least, going on this weekend," she demanded.

"Tori was babbling about the fancy wedding she was coming to, I asked some questions. So where's the brunette?" he asked, looking over her head.

"Excuse me?"

"Your date, that guy, Fence or whatever his name is."

"Oh my god," Katya groaned. "His name is Gate, and he's not my date."

"But you said -"

"I said I was coming with a sexy brunette," Katya reminded him, all while pointing at Tori. The other girl was on the dance floor a couple yards away from them, laughing at her drunk partner.

"Ooohhh, I get it now. Funny. She is sexy," he agreed, and Katya watched as his eyes passed over her roommate. Tori was wearing a long, flowing white maxi skirt matched with a white tube top, both of which showed off her assets to perfection.

"Well. This has been super fun, but I have to go guzzle champagne directly from the ice fountain," Katya said, moving to walk around him. She didn't make it far. He grabbed her wrist and dragged her onto the floor.

"C'mon, just one dance. We never danced, did we? I'm a great dancer."

"Liam, I don't want to dance with you. I don't even want to -"

He didn't give her an option. It was funny, but it was easy to forget he was so much bigger and stronger than her. Before she knew it, they were in the middle of the crowd and he was wrapping his arms around her waist, trying to pull her close.

"Don't make a scene, angel cake. Just go with the flow," he suggested. She growled and pulled back, grabbing one of his hands and taking it up in a proper dance hold.

"Don't call me that. I thought I had made my feelings clear, Liam. I don't want to play games with you," she told him.

"I'm not playing games," he said. "I want to see you, Katya, but you won't see me. I'm willing to do whatever it takes. If you worked at a bank, I'd become a bank robber. If you worked at a McDonald's, I'd get incredibly fat. So if I have to steal an invitation to some swanky uptown wedding, then so be it."

"You *stole* the invitation!?"

"Um …"

Katya couldn't help it. She actually laughed. It was just so … Liam. And when he was standing in front of her, handsome in a white dress suit and white satin tie, smiling that goofy grin, it was actually hard to hold onto her anger. She still hurt over what he'd done to her, and she didn't think she could ever trust him again, but … Tori's and Brie's words were floating through her brain.

Just do whatever you want. Whatever feels good.

"You're such … such a dick," she finally sighed, smiling up at him.

"Yeah. But I live to see you smile, so I have some redeeming qualities," he pointed out.

"I wouldn't go that far. If you're here and Tori's here, who's running the club?" she asked.

"Hey! The club runs just fine without Tori there."

"Really? She told me about the trash can fire."

"Simple accident, could've happened to anyone."

"And the missing deposit."

"I would've found it on my own eventually."

"And the underage sting operation."

Liam paused for a while, staring up like he was thinking hard.

"Jesus, you're right. How did I run that place without her?" he asked. Katya smiled big.

"I told you to hire her, so you're welcome," she told him. He smiled back.

"It's good to see you happy, angel - … uh, Katya. Thanks for giving me this chance," he said in a moment of sincerity. Her smile faltered a little and she took a deep breath.

"Don't make me regret it," she replied. He nodded.

"I'll try my hardest."

The song ended after that, and when Liam went to lead her back to the tables, they bumped into the bride.

"Hello, hello," Lauren said, out of breath. "Who are you? I'd remember someone this cute being on my guest list."

Katya snorted and Liam laughed.

"Lauren, this is … my neighbor, Liam Edenhoff," she introduced them. "I hope you don't mind, he … I …"

"Mind! No, no, no. I'm excited to meet any neighbor of Katya's," Lauren laughed, shaking Liam's hand.

"Thanks," he laughed back.

"Good to meet you, Liam. Please, eat and drink *a lot* – I hate to waste money on this kind of crap. I'm so glad you both came. I'm just," the peppy blonde seemed at a loss for a moment. "I'm so excited you're here. Tonight is going to be *so fun!*"

Before they could question any of that, Lauren was whisked away by some other eager guests. Katya stared after her for a minute, then felt Liam's hand on the small of her back, guiding her off the dance floor.

"She's … interesting," he finally commented. Katya laughed, then stumbled against him as a crowd of people surged onto the dance floor. Sir Mix-a-Lot was blasting from the speakers, so she completely understood their enthusiasm.

"Yeah. I mean, she's always energetic, but she's like doubly so today."

"Sounds like a blast. So, what are you doing after this?"

He said it so off the cuff, Katya almost responded. It was what they did, after all. She'd explain how she had to go home and wash her hair and prep her outfit for the next day and balance her checkbook. He'd tell her she was ridiculous and inform her they'd be drinking margaritas and eating cookie dough. She'd argue. He wouldn't listen. And by one in the morning, they'd be wrist deep in chocolate chips, drinking sour mix and tequila straight from a pitcher.

But she caught herself, because that *wasn't* what they did – not anymore. Because he had ruined everything. It all came crashing back and Katya sighed, rubbing her hand across her forehead.

"I don't know, Liam, but I can guarantee it won't be anything with you. Baby steps," she reminded him. He pressed his lips together hard, then nodded.

"That's more than I hoped for," he finally replied. She managed to smile again.

"But I'm glad you came, I guess. Tori always gets distracted halfway through these things and I wind up fending for myself," she said, trying to get back to a place of at least fake-normalcy.

"Well, we can't have that. How about a drink? I'm dying in this thing," he said, pulling at his tie and loosening it up. She nodded.

"That would be great. I'll have -"

"Pinot gris or margarita, I'm on it."

She smiled and watched as he moved across the dance floor. Liam was in his element the most when he was in a crowd. He was a true people-person. He didn't know a single person in that reception hall, yet he smiled and laughed and talked with everyone as he moved. Twirled the mother-of-the-bride around and even dipped her. Flirted his way past a gaggle of twenty-something-year-old co-eds. She wished she had his ease, his self-confidence. She sighed and folded her arms across her chest.

"It's all an act, you know. He's piss-scared."

If Liam's voice had surprised her, then this voice froze her on the spot. She didn't turn her head, and the voice's owner didn't move into her line of sight. She could just barely see him out the corner of her eye.

"Is there anyone on the planet who *didn't* crash this frickin' wedding?" she asked through clenched teeth.

"I wouldn't know. *I* was invited."

Wulf didn't bother moving, and she was finally forced to turn so she could glare at him. He was wearing a black suit, with a crisp white shirt and matching pocket square. He could've been attending a funeral, but it worked for him. He looked severe and devastatingly handsome and more than a little dangerous. He had one hand in his pocket, and the other was holding an old fashioned glass.

"*You* got an invitation? How?" Katya asked.

"Well, I received an envelope in the mail, and inside it was an -"

"Shut up, you know what I mean. Why would Lauren invite you?" she demanded.

"Not sure. I sold her husband the building he runs his practice in."

"I didn't realize. I guess … that kind of makes sense."

"Oh, and I called and asked."

"What!?"

"I called her husband and asked to attend. He was more than happy to oblige," Wulf clarified.

"Why would you do that? You don't really know them, and you hate stuff like this," Katya pointed out. He finally looked down at her, cocking up an eyebrow as he did so.

"I do? Strange, I've been to lots of weddings. Never realized I hate them."

"*Shut up.*"

"You say that a lot, but then ask me questions. It's counter productive."

"I swear to god …"

"I asked because I knew *you'd* be here," he explained. Her jaw dropped for a second, then she regained her composure.

"How did you know that?" she asked.

"You told me."

"I did?"

"Yes. You told me about the cake you were designing – it looks amazing, by the way. You're very talented. And then in my apartment, when we talked about our cake fight. You explained who Lauren was. I remembered her name, and it wasn't hard to figure out the rest," he told her.

She was shocked. He was putting so much effort into … whatever it was he was trying to do. If he was trying to win her over, he was being kind of a massive dick about it – she preferred Liam's grovel-and-be-sweet method.

But stalking down the wedding information. Calling Lauren's husband and asking for an invite. Remembering tiny details from a conversation that felt like it had happened a lifetime ago. Oh, and moving his entire life into her apartment building. It was a little insane.

That's it. I've gone crazy. They drove me crazy and I'm hallucinating all this.

"But why? Why would you do that? Just because I'm here? What is going on!?" she demanded.

"You won't see me. This is grossly unfair – I should get my fair say before you cut me off," he told her.

Whoa. Deja vu.

She glanced across the room. Liam was walking back from the bar, laughing with one of the groomsmen.

"He's just as culpable as I am," Wulf said in a careful voice. "Yet apparently more worthy of forgiveness."

Katya took a deep breath. She really didn't want to get into it right then and there.

"I haven't forgiven him," she replied. "And you know what happened between you and I is leagues different than what happened between him and I."

"Do I know that? Because what I remember are promises being made, and then promptly being broken. I remember someone claiming to care about me, and then turning her back on me at the first sign of real trouble."

The tidal wave of emotions she felt was unlike anything she'd ever experienced before in her life. Anger and rage and betrayal and hurt and disgust and sadness and ... nausea? Did nausea count as an emotion? She wanted to simultaneously punch him in the face *and* vomit on him. But all she could manage to do was sputter and stare at him until Liam finally reached her side.

"Hey, they ran out of limes, so it's sweet and sour mix. I hope -"

Katya didn't wait for Liam to finish. She grabbed the glass out of his hand and downed the margarita-esque concoction in a couple gulps. Then, while gasping for air, she grabbed his drink and polished it off. She gagged on the last gulp. Bourbon, neat. She shoved the empty glass into his hand and worked hard to keep all the liquid in her stomach.

"Jesus, I hadn't realized you were so thirsty, I would've ... oh. Hello, Wulfric."

She took deep breaths and glanced between the two men. Wulf had fully turned to face them. Liam stood directly opposite him, and Katya was the only thing separating them. It was a surreal moment. Up until almost three weeks ago, she'd thought they hadn't known each other. She'd only ever seen them together once before, and it had been sort of a crazy moment in time. Lots of screaming and chaos and crying.

Now she took a moment to take it all in. How much taller Liam was than both of them. How much broader Wulf's shoulders were in comparison. Liam's dark tan next to Wulf's pale complexion. The laid back attitude meeting the control freak. She couldn't have found two more opposite people if she'd tried.

*And yet **they** found **me**, somehow.*

"Eden," Wulf finally replied, using the nickname everyone but

Katya used for Liam. The name hung in the air like an icicle and for a tiny moment, she wondered if they would fight over her.

"Oh god, just give me this!" she snapped, yanking Wulf's glass out of his hand and slamming that drink down, as well. She gagged and coughed almost immediately. Scotch, neat. What was it with these guys? Didn't they know the value of a good mixer!?

"So how did you get in?" Liam asked, shoving his hands into his pockets. In response, Wulf folded his arms across his chest.

"I was invited. How did *you* get in? Service entrance?" he guessed. Liam laughed, but Katya thought it might actually be true.

"Man, how I've missed these little meetings of ours," he sighed.

"Really? I can pencil you into my schedule, if you like. Take my lunches down at the club."

"I don't think anyone deserves that kind of punishment."

Their words were laced with venom and it was very clear they didn't like each other one bit. Yet the way they spoke to each other, it was still with a comfort and ease that said these were two men who knew each other. Knew each other so well, they knew which buttons to push and when the best time was to push them. She'd been in separate kinds of relationships with both of them, for a couple months, and had never realized that not only were they aware of each other, but they'd had a working relationship for years. Much longer than anything she'd had with either of them.

And I never ever once figured it out on my own.

"Just stop," she finally interjected. Liam glanced down at her. Wulf kept staring at him. "It's bad enough that we're all here – can you two not fight like children, just this once?"

"But I -" Liam started to argue.

"We still need to -" Wulf tried to say.

"No. I don't want to hear it. For the next hour, I'm Sally, and you're Harvey and Ted, and the three of us have never met before, got it? I'm pissed off," she said, then held her hand up when Wulf opened his mouth again. "At *both* of you. But this day isn't about me, and it sure as shit isn't about either of you. So keep your mouths shut and try to pretend like we all know how to be nice and have fun together, *understood?*"

The slightly psychotic edge to her voice must have gotten through, because Liam nodded and Wulf kept his mouth shut. She glared back and forth for a bit, then nodded and looked out onto the dance floor. Both men turned and stared into the crowd, as well. They maintained an awkward silence for maybe a minute before one of them cracked.

"I meant to say," Liam spoke. "You look really nice tonight."

"Thanks," she ground out.

"Yes," Wulf agreed. "I've always liked you in that dress, though it looked different the last time I saw you in it."

Flames raced across her face. She knew exactly what he was talking about, but she refused to respond. There was a brief pause, then on her other side, Liam let out a groan.

"Shit, I know what you're talking about. God, this is weird. This is so fucking weird."

"Yes," she let out a deep breath and grabbed two champagne flutes off a passing tray. "This is *so. Fucking. Weird.*"

And as if it wasn't already weird enough, Tori finally remembered she'd come with her best friend and she wandered over to where they stood.

"Can you believe that guy?" her roommate was laughing. "He was so drunk! I tried to find you earlier, but you were dancing with some tall guy. I hope ... *Eden!* I, er, ooookaay. I didn't know ... *holy shit, Wulf is here, too.*"

Katya was busy draining the champagne flutes while her friend spoke. When she finished, she leaned back and sat them down on an empty table.

"Yup, I am fully aware of that."

"This is awesome."

"Not the word I would've chosen," Wulf said, surprising

everyone. Katya barked out a laugh, then slapped a hand over her mouth. Tori's eyes bounced between everyone in the small group, then she grabbed her friend by the wrist.

"C'mon, you need to dance with me!"

Before anyone could argue, Katya was being yanked and pulled onto the dance floor. Some techno song was blaring, driving most of the dancers to their seats. Tori moved off rhythm to the awkward beat and stood close to her roommate's side.

"I have no idea what's going on," Katya cut her friend off before she could ask anything.

"They just showed up!?"

"Yes. First Liam, then Wulf. They didn't plan it together. At least I don't think so."

"Judging by the way they're glaring at each other like they want to have a knife fight, I'm guessing it was unplanned."

"I swear to god, if they give me any grief tonight …"

"Why would they? I mean, they're trying to like win your heart or whatever, right?" Tori asked, glancing back at the two men.

"They never mean to do anything, that's the problem. They just bumble around like jackasses, ruining lives and breaking hearts. I'm sure they spent exactly zero seconds thinking about what showing up here could do," Katya replied.

"Don't give them the chance, then," Tori suggested, bopping around to the music, forcing them to turn on the floor so the men couldn't see their faces. "You're in control here, girl. One word, and you can get them kicked out. One word, and it's restraining-or-der-city. You're the boss, and you don't even know it. If you just take charge a little, you could have both those dudes wrapped around your little finger."

Katya glanced over her shoulder, which caused her to almost stumble in her tall heels. Her drinking binge was catching up to her. She shook her head and tried to focus.

"My little finger, huh."

"Yup. You give them too much credit. They're just stupid guys. Fuck 'em. You're not here for their entertainment. *They're* here for *yours.*"

It occurred to Katya that her roommate was more than a little drunk. Katya must have been a little drunk, too, though, because the statement kind of made sense to her.

She'd been their play thing. Liam and Wulf's personal sex doll, practically tailor made. It wasn't fair. The way they could pop in and out of her life, screwing with her brain and her heart. Like they owned them. Owned *her*. No. She was her own master. She wasn't put on this earth for them, and she certainly wasn't at that wedding for them.

Take control. This doesn't need to be about them. It can be about you.

A new song had started, drawing a couple more dancers onto the floor. A raspy woman's voice sang about ex's and oh-oh-oh's. Seemed weirdly appropriate. She and Tori sang along loudly, dancing circles around each other and a couple bridesmaids who'd joined them.

Then Katya realized the guys were still watching her. Wulf with his usual stern look in place, as if he disapproved of her behavior. Liam's face was blank, his eyes following her movements, but not betraying any thoughts or feelings.

It wasn't fair that they got to stand there, both looking disgustingly handsome. Neither looking at all uncomfortable. Here she was, halfway ready to crawl out of her skin every time she glanced in their direction, and there they were, looking as if this was all old hat for them.

Not. Fair.

I want them to feel so uncomfortable, they'll never want to bother me again.

The liquid courage took over the controls in her brain and before she even knew she had a plan, she was dancing towards them. They both looked a little surprised, but stayed still as she moved around them. Liam smiled at her. Wulf kept a blank face, even as she wiggled between them, shimmying to the melody. She wasn't the world's best dancer, she knew, but she had rhythm. She could dance to the beat. And both men had seen what strip-aerobics classes had done for her, so she was confident that she had their attention.

Wulf was still feigning indifference to her, so she turned to Liam. Worked around so her back was to his front. She surprised him by dropping it low, then could hear him suck in air when she slowly lifted her hips, pressing against him the entire way up to standing. She couldn't hold it together, though. Being overtly sexy wasn't in her nature. She snickered, which caused him to laugh, so she grabbed his shirt and dragged him out onto the floor with her.

"Feeling good, angel cake?" he asked, almost shouting to be heard over the music. She nodded.

"Yes, but not good enough for you to call me that," she replied. He chuckled and tried to wrap his arms around her, but she kept squirming, rolling and weaving around him.

"I didn't realize you liked to dance so much, we could've been hitting up the clubs," he said. She snorted.

"You own a club, we could've danced there."

"I'm pretty sure we did, angel cake."

She went to snap at him, but when she looked up, it was Wulf who caught her eye. Any look of indifference he'd been wearing was gone. Now he looked *pissed*. Like just seeing Liam and Katya dancing was enough to make him see red.

It was a different sensation, realizing Wulf had never actually seen Katya and Liam together. No, he'd only ever heard stories. And hearing something was never like witnessing it in real life.

Clearly, Wulfric didn't like what he saw. Not one little bit.

Not so fun now, is it? Not when it's real and staring you in the face.

"Liam," she breathed, getting closer to him.

"Hmmm?" he almost purred.

"I don't want you to read too much into this, but ... it's been a *long* week, and I have been really stressed out."

"Okay."

Taking a deep breath, Katya grabbed him by the back of his neck and yanked him down to her height. He let out a surprised yelp, but then went completely silent when her mouth locked together with his.

It felt like it had been a *long* time since Katya had kissed Liam. Even as she shoved her tongue into his mouth, her brain wandered back over the weeks. On their first official date, he'd kissed her good night. But she'd been so keyed up and nervous, she'd barely registered what had been happening. Their last *real* kiss had been weeks before that one. So what … almost a month? A month since they'd locked lips?

She moaned as his arms came around her. She'd forgotten what kissing Liam was like – a little wild and out of control. Like a run-away truck on a hill. He took control quickly and easily, one arm wrapping tight around her waist while his free hand wandered over her back and side, fingers digging into skin where they found it.

He tasted like warmth and happiness. Good times and fun memories. But then a blanket of sadness covered everything, reminding her of why she'd stopped kissing him all those weeks ago, and why she shouldn't even be kissing him now. Before the feeling could turn the kiss bitter, she pulled away.

"Holy shit, Katya. I thought you'd never -"

She didn't wait for him to finish. As the the song hit a crescendo before heading into the bridge, she playfully pushed him away and danced her way back to Tori. Her roommate looked shocked, but when Katya shrugged, the other girl just laughed and kept dancing.

"Do you, sweetie!" she cackled.

"What's the other one doing?" Katya asked. Tori glanced over her shoulder, then her eyes got wide.

"Um, probably something you won't like."

"What do you mean?"

She never got to hear an answer. Wulf was at her side, grabbing her elbow and twisting her into him. She wasn't given an opportunity to accept his silent request to dance – it was more like a demand. An arm went around her waist and one of his hands held hers up, then they were moving together.

Liam danced like virtually any other guy in a dance club. He had rhythm, he could move, and he was a lot of fun. Wulf had grown up in a wealthy household and had attended the same private schools as Katya. He'd received the same etiquette lessons she had – which meant he also knew how to dance in a more classic sense. Something more fitting for the older half of the wedding party. So he was able to easily and effortlessly lead her across the dance floor, not even noticing that it took her a few seconds to catch up with him and remember the steps he was doing.

"How drunk are you?" he abruptly asked. She stopped staring at her feet and finally looked at him.

"I'm not drunk," she responded, glaring at him. He picked up the pace, weaving them through more and more couples as the dance floor grew crowded again.

"Alright, how *tipsy* are you?" he amended his question. She snorted.

"Just enough to tolerate your bullshit," she replied.

"Good."

He surprised her then by leading them into a tight twirl. Before they'd barely come to a stop, he was then dipping her. In time to the music even, her brain belatedly realized. Then he snapped her upright, startling a shriek of laughter out of her.

"I didn't know you could dance like that!" she exclaimed, shocking herself by smiling at him.

"There's a lot you don't know about me, Tocci."

She blinked up at him, lost in his stare. So lost, she didn't notice that he was leaning down to her. Didn't stop him from kissing her. Didn't care that the entire room had just witnessed her making out with another man literally one minute earlier.

Kissing Wulf was an entirely different sensation from Liam, equally wonderful and awful in its own way. He was slow and torturous, always dragging out the sensations, to the point it drove her crazy. Left her begging for more. His hands cupped the back of her head, holding her in place. Not touching her anywhere else, yet strangely feeling more intimate than when she'd had her whole body pressed against Liam's.

She sighed into him and ran her hands down the front of his chest. Remembered a time when she'd felt all those muscles without any clothing on them. That thought along with the sweet-sharp pain of his teeth cutting into her bottom lip brought her to her senses. This was a scary game she was playing. Messing with Liam was dangerous enough, but Wulf was downright bad for her health.

*Bad for **my soul***.

She yanked back with enough force that she stumbled completely out of his grip. She was breathing hard as she stared at him. He looked … almost a little sad. Then his lips quirked up into a little smirk and he reached out between them. Smoothed his thumb underneath her bottom lip, causing her to suck in a gasp of air.

"There. Back to perfection," he said in a soft voice.

Katya was halfway across the ballroom when Tori caught up to her side.

"Are you okay?" she asked, linking arms with her.

"Yes," Katya said, nodding her head. "Perfectly fine. You were right, you know. Doing whatever I want feels *great*."

"Uh … you sure about that?"

"Yup."

Before she could make it out of the room, though, they were waylaid. The bride all but leapt in between them and the exit. Katya stared as Lauren clapped her hands together.

"That was *amazing!* Admittedly, when I found out Wulfric Stone wanted an invitation, I was kinda hoping for another food fight, but honey, that little show was above and beyond my wildest dreams. I honestly didn't know you had it in you to be such a little vixen," she said.

"I, uh … I'm sorry, Lauren. I'm not usually so …" Katya struggled to find the right word. Childish? Slutty? Desperate? Weird?

"Amazing? Well, you should keep it up, then. I like seeing a woman handle her business – especially when it involves leaving two men like that with their jaws on the floor. Thanks for being a good sport."

Katya's own jaw was on the floor, but Lauren ignored it and stepped up close to give her a hug. Then she hugged Tori goodbye and thanked both women for coming before disappearing back into the crowd.

"You know," Tori said when they finally started walking again. "I always thought I was your weird friend. But that lady, I think she takes the cake. Literally *and* figuratively."

Katya laughed all the way to the taxi stand.

9

CONSIDERING THE AMOUNT OF ALCOHOL SHE'D SLURPED DOWN IN THE SMALL amount of time, Katya halfway expected to get home and go straight to bed. But she had so much adrenaline rushing through her body that it actually canceled out most of the alcohol. She changed into shorts and a tank top, then paced around the apartment while Tori ordered them pizza and broke out the white zinfandel.

"I've never done something like that before," Katya babbled. "I mean, kinda sorta dating two men at the same time had been 'wild' enough for me. But kissing two men, within like two minutes of each other, in the same room, in full view of everybody!? What girls act like that?"

"Uh, lots of girls. *This* girl. Any that have attended a frat party. I mean, have you seen The Jersey Shore?" Tori asked, following her into the living room. Katya kept moving, circling the coffee table.

"I thought it would be weird. I mean, I obviously didn't think about it at all when it was happening, I just did it. But if I'd thought about it, I would've thought it was weird," she said.

"And it wasn't weird?"

"No. It was kind of awesome. I mean, the look on Liam's face when we left. The look on Wulf's when I walked away. I didn't … I guess I didn't realize how much I affected them."

"Clearly. I told you – you got the power, honey," Tori told her, holding two glasses of wine in her hands while Katya kept pacing.

"I didn't know. I had no idea. I thought just letting it go would be the best. But this … I mean … it was actually kinda fun," she continued. Tori nodded, sipping at one of the glasses.

"Totally fun."

"God, that's so wrong. Isn't that wrong, though?"

"Uh, wrong is fucking you and then having secret slumber parties and talking about it, and then pretending not to know each other."

Katya stared at Tori for a moment, then nodded and marched across the room. She grabbed the other glass of wine on her way, then moved to stand on the couch. Once she got her balance, she held up her glass, as if toasting the room. Tori stared up at her, only wearing her tube top and underwear, her skirt somewhere in the hallway.

"You're right. I've been spending this whole time trying to take the high road, be the good person, act right, whatever. And it hasn't been working. It never works. So if they can fuck with me, then goddammit, I can fuck with them!" she proclaimed. Both women nodded firmly at each other, then chugged down their glasses of wine. While tilting her head back, Katya lost her balance and fell on her ass onto the back of the couch.

Well, maybe not just riding high on adrenaline. Did I really chug scotch!?

10

KATYA HAD TWO WEEKS LEFT OF HER "SABBATICAL" BEFORE SHE HAD TO GO back to work full time.

Two weeks to do whatever she wanted. She figured she should make plans, build mental defenses, all that jazz. Instead, though, fate delivered a plan right into her lap.

Early Sunday morning, her phone buzzed on her nightstand. She felt around for it without opening her eyes, then pressed it to the side of her face.

"Hello?" she grumbled, staying snugly under her covers.

"Hungover?"

She groaned at the sound of Wulf's voice.

"It's too early for this," she complained.

"Well, you're answering my calls, so either you're really hungover, or you've forgiven me."

"Neither," she sighed, pushing herself upright. "I just realized if I spent the rest of my life avoiding your calls, I'd probably go insane and have to give up phones."

"Took you long enough. We're going to breakfast, get dressed."

She burst out laughing.

"No, we're not."

"You don't kiss me yesterday and then act like nothing happened today, Tocci."

"Um, *you* kissed *me*, and I can do anything I want, *Stone*. Speaking of which, I have a message, I have to go."

"What? No, we're not done. We're going -"

Katya hung up on him. She stared at the screen for a minute, then laughed out loud. She could just picture his face. Incredulous, staring at his own phone, unable to believe that someone would have the audacity to hang up on him – let alone meek little Katya Tocci.

She really did have a message, so she thumbed open the app as she climbed out of bed. It was from Gaten, he'd spoken to his electrician friend and they were both able to come over that afternoon and check out her broken oven. She was typing a response when her phone started ringing again. Her thumbs kept moving and accidentally opened the call.

"Did you actually fucking hang up on me?"

Wulf's voice sounded exactly like how she imagined his face looked.

"Yes. I'm busy, Wulf, I don't have time to play with you right now," she told him, trapping the phone between her ear and shoulder as she rifled through her closet.

"Who the hell am I speaking to? Because you sure as shit aren't Katya Tocci," he said.

"Oh, yes I am. The new and improved Katya Tocci, specially modified by Wulfric and Liam. Don't like this new model? You only have yourself to blame," she sighed, yanking out a shirt and tossing it onto her bed.

"Cut the bullshit, I don't like playing games."

"That didn't just come out of your mouth, did it?" she laughed, settling on a pair of pants. "I'm not playing any games. I'm getting dressed, I have someone coming over at noon. I told you, I'm a very busy person."

"Busy my ass, Tocci. And who's coming over, on a Sunday of all days?"

"Just a neighbor."

"Oh jesus."

"Gotta go, Wulfy."

"If you ever fucking use that name again, I will -"

She hung up again and tossed her phone over her shoulder, onto her bed. She couldn't contain her smile and all but skipped into the bathroom.

———◆———

Katya sat back against her kitchen table, watching while Gaten Shepherd watched another man poke about her stove. They'd unplugged it and moved it out from the wall, and the new guy – Tad something or other – was examining it and using interesting gadgets to prod around.

"Yeah, it's not good," Tad sighed as he crawled out of the oven.

"Really?" Katya groaned. She'd been hoping it was just a heating coil or something.

Tad threw a bunch of technical jargon at her that she didn't understand. What it boiled down to, he finally explained to her, was that her oven was kaput. He could fix it, but it would cost less to just buy a new stove.

"Which your landlord or super can arrange for you," he finished. Katya snorted and Gate laughed.

"You would think," she grumbled. "Well, thanks for looking. How much do I owe you?"

Before she could even grab her purse, Gate stepped forward.

"Oh no, this was a favor from me. My treat," he assured her.

"No, Tad came all the way down here, I'd feel weird -" she started to argue, but both men held up their hands. She frowned.

"Seriously, it's fine. I didn't do anything except move your stove around. I do have an appointment at one o'clock, though, so I gotta get going if I want to beat traffic. Katya, great to meet you. Gate, see you at the game?" Tad checked, grabbing his jacket and tool belt as he headed into the hallway.

"Yeah, I'll be there tomorrow. Thanks for coming down!"

"Wait," Katya tried to argue. She didn't want to be indebted to some random dude. "Really, I should at least pay for some-"

The sound of the door shutting cut her off before she could finish her sentence and she was left staring after him. Gate chuckled and turned to face her.

"Sorry, that's the way me and my friends are," he said.

"I still feel weird, getting like an in-home check up for free," she replied.

"Okay, well how about you buy me dinner, and we call it even?" he suggested.

Katya's gut reaction was to say no. She had enough men problems, and as much as she liked Gaten, she wasn't about to add him to the equation. But just then, there was another noise from the hall. She thought maybe Tad had forgotten something and had come back for it. As she glanced out the kitchen doorway, though, she realized she wasn't that lucky.

"Call what even?" Wulf asked, adjusting his cuff links as he strode into the kitchen as if he owned the place.

"Oh, sorry, I didn't know you were expecting someone," Gate said quickly.

"I wasn't," Katya sighed. "Gate, this is Wulf – his company manages the buildings. Wulf, this is Gaten, he lives in the building next door."

Gate smiled and made a move like he was going to offer his hand, but when Wulf didn't move at all – didn't so much as twitch his lips – Gate held still.

"Charmed, I'm sure. Now Tocci, we're running behind schedule," Wulf continued speaking to her.

"Oh geez, I didn't mean to make you late," Gaten said, glancing between them.

"You didn't, I never confirmed. Besides, we're not done here. You said something about dinner?" she asked, turning her back on Wulf. Gate glanced at the other man for a second, then focused on her.

"Uh, yeah. I know a really relaxed place, not too far from here. I could pick you up after work?" he offered.

"I'll meet you there. Seven?" she took charge of the date.

"Sounds good. See you then. Nice meeting you, uh … wolf," Gate said, nodding his head before walking out of the kitchen. Wulf and Katya stared at each other until the front door opened and closed.

"Have you eaten?" he asked.

"How did you get in here?" she ignored his question and asked her own.

"I have access to the keys for every building we manage. Are you really meeting that *thing* for dinner?" he asked again.

"Okay, first of all, '*that thing*' is a seriously good looking, very successful, and ridiculously nice man – a man who has yet to lie to me and use me," she pointed out.

"Key word being 'yet.'"

"And second of all, I know for a fact my lease states you have to give me twenty-four hour notice before you just barge in here. If you come in again without my permission, I'm gonna file a complaint," she warned him. He laughed. Actually laughed. Something Wulfric Stone didn't do very often. She took a deep breath and looked away from his broad smile.

"Please do. I'll direct my HR department to hand deliver it to my desk so I can deal with it personally."

"Are we done here? I have things to do today that don't involve dealing with you," she snapped. He stepped closer to her.

"You might be even funner now than you were before."

"That's not funny, and if you can't realize that, then there is literally no hope for you."

"Ah, implying there *is* hope."

"Shut up."

"Feisty. I love it."

"I talked to Vieve," she blurted out. That finally stopped him.

"Oh, really," was all he said.

"Yup. Went to your place, had a cup of coffee with her," she said. That seemed to actually surprise him.

"You were in my home?" he checked.

"Yes. Apparently, I could've been spending lots of time there. Very generous of you to give me complete access," she said. He didn't react, though she noticed the tendon in the side of his neck was taut and straining.

"Yes, well, I've met you. I knew if you ever showed up, it would be a huge hassle with the front desk calling my office and you calling my cell phone and me having to drive across town. Was just easier that way."

"Sure. Okay."

"And how was the coffee? I have it imported."

Katya stared at the tight tendon for a moment longer. He was so good at putting on a false front, she knew. Looking calm and collected. After all, this was a man who ate million dollar real estate deals before breakfast.

But it was all fake. He was nervous. Deep down, she could tell. Being forceful was just his way of barreling through a problem he didn't actually want to deal with – he could just strong arm her into doing what he wanted. No unnecessary awkwardness. That was Wulf's M.O.

Yeah, well, my M.O. is to make him feel as awkward as humanly possible.

"I can't go to breakfast with you," she stated, brushing past him and heading down the hallway. He didn't hesitate to follow behind her.

"No shit, it's afternoon – it's too late for brunch, even. But that

Brazilian food cart is open for lunches now, we're going -" he started, but she waved her hand over her shoulder as she moved into her bedroom.

"I can't, I'm busy this afternoon. I have to go shopping for a new stove – don't worry, I'll have the bill sent to you," she joked, turning around and standing in the doorway to her room. He glared down at her.

"Don't be ridiculous. I'll talk to maintenance, we can get a new stove in by the end of the week," he assured her.

"Whatever. I have other plans."

"Tocci, I'm not -"

"But how about dinner?" she offered.

That seemed to shock him. He stood still for moment, his eyes wandering over her face. Obviously trying to figure out if she was lying. She offered him a big smile, and that just seemed to throw him even more off guard. He finally narrowed his eyes.

"If I make reservations, you'll be downstairs on time?" he checked.

"No," she shook her head. "But I can meet you there."

"Bullshit. You'll stand me up, and I'm not wasting my time, sitting around like an asshole waiting for you," he said.

"I won't, I promise. I have … a client I'm dealing with this afternoon. I don't know how long it will take," she told him.

"What about your dinner date with your darling handyman?" he asked. She shrugged.

"I'll figure something out, don't worry about it. I'll have dinner with you."

"You promise?" he checked, still glaring down at her. She nodded and ran her fingers across her chest in an X motion.

"Cross my heart."

"Fine. But don't fuck with me, Tocci. You won't like it if I have to come and find you. We have a lot to discuss," he informed her. She nodded.

"I'm sure we do. What's the dress code?" she asked. Wulf was a 3-Michelin-stars kind of restaurant goer when it came to dinner dates.

"A dress," he informed her, and then his gaze wandered over her shoulder. She had some clothes laying around on the floor, littered about on the bed. She was gearing up to do laundry. "If you'd like to try on some options, I'd be more than happy to sit and help."

Katya laughed and slid her hands up either side of the door frame. Wulf followed the motion with his eyes, which grew wide when she leaned towards him.

"Mmmm, that would be fun, wouldn't it?" she chuckled.

"Possibly."

"And it's been a very long time since you've been in my bedroom," she reminded him. He nodded.

"It has."

"And we never got to have any *real* fun in here, did we?" she sighed, glancing back at her bed.

"No. No, we did it not."

"It must make you wonder, though," she said, dropping her hands and stepping back into the room.

"Wonder what?"

"What kind of fun Liam and I used to have in here."

There was a split second where she got to see equal parts anger and shock ripple across his features.

Then she slammed the door in his face.

11

H AD SHE EVER TAKEN THE TIME TO THINK ABOUT IT, KATYA WOULD'VE
assumed she'd make a piss poor evil mastermind. She wasn't
malicious by nature, and had a tendency to think the best of
most everyone she met.

Yet she was finding it surprisingly easy to slip into the role of
evil genius, and even more shocking, she enjoyed it. It was a weird
sensation, sort of like waiting to open presents on Christmas, or or-
ganizing a surprise party.

No amount of huffing and puffing from Wulf had blown her
door down, so eventually he'd stormed off – after telling her the name
of the restaurant she would be meeting him at, of course.

As soon as he was gone, she finished doing her laundry. Then
made a couple phone calls – she wasn't a complete liar, she did go
over some design issues with a client. Then she scoured her closet
for the perfect outfit. One of her prized possessions, a dress she had
bought a month ago and been waiting for the perfect moment to
wear for Wulf, before shit had hit the fan.

It was a Herve Leger dress. Usually Katya favored light materials
and loose fits. Wispy designs with a fairy-like quality. But something

about this dress had called to her. Even in the store, its fit had been amazing, and she'd since had it tailored to fit perfectly. It was done in patches of black and beige fabric, all molding to her body from her bust to over her hips before it flared out in a short skirt. There were no straps, which just accented how well the garment presented her breasts.

She felt like an adult in the dress. Very powerful, and very sexy. She matched it with a pair of sky high stilettos, then worked some magic on her thick hair, coaxing it into an artfully mussy pony tail. A couple accessories and a lot of make up later, she finally headed downstairs.

She smiled as she walked across the lobby. Liam was standing by the exit, doing something on his phone and not paying attention. He was wearing an untucked dress shirt and a clean pair of fitted jeans – dressed up for him.

"Hi! C'mon, I'm running late," she said, walking right past him and out the door.

"Sorry, I didn't think you'd want me coming up there and grabbing you, so I … holy shit, what are you wearing?" he asked as he chased after her.

"This old thing?" she asked, holding out her arms and looking down at herself.

"Yeah, that," he said, unabashedly checking her out. "Jesus, I'm a little under dressed. Where are we going for dinner?"

After Wulf had stomped away and she'd come up with her evil little plan, she'd called Liam and had a brief chat with him. Asked him what he was doing that even, and when he'd said nothing, she'd told him to dress nice and that dinner would be on her. Of course, he'd accepted the invite without question.

Which was very, very good for her.

"It's a surprise," she said, then winked at him and stepped off the curb, heading to the cab she'd ordered.

They made idle chit chat in the car. It was awkward at first

– weeks without speaking to each other had done its damage. He would reach out to touch her, rest a hand on her thigh, brush her arm, then pull away abruptly. Obviously remembering that it wasn't allowed anymore, regardless of how she'd behaved at the wedding.

Not that her actions had gone unnoticed, though.

"So the wedding. What was all that about, anyway?" he asked, paying taxi driver while she climbed out of the car. Not an easy feat in the kind of dress she was wearing.

"I was just … I wanted to have fun, you know?" she offered, watching him as he got out behind her.

"Fun?"

"Yeah. I'm tired of being mad at you, it's exhausting. I was dancing with you, and we were having fun, and I wanted to have more fun, and frankly, I also knew it would piss Wulf off," she explained, standing still so he could hold open the door to the restaurant for her.

"Huh. So kissing him, was that to piss him off, too?" he grunted, glancing down at her. She smiled.

"Did that bother you?" she asked.

"It sure as shit didn't make me feel good."

"Oh, that's too bad. Then you're really not gonna like tonight."

"What? Why? Oh god, what do you have planned?"

But she didn't need to answer. She'd been striding through the restaurant, ignoring a hostess' plea to help her. Wulf wasn't hard to find, he'd stood up as soon as she came within sight of his table. Liam recognized him at the same time Wulf recognized who was following his would-be dinner date.

"You know," Wulf started, not bothering to look at her, only leveling a glare on Liam. "I'd figured you were gonna try to pull something, Tocci, but I have to admit, I'm impressed. I did not see this coming."

"Liam," she said in a prim voice, holding up a hand in front of him. "This is Wulfric Stone, we used to live next door to each other and recently ended a very strange relationship. Wulf, this is Liam Edenhoff – we currently live next door to each other and recently ended a very strange friendship."

"You're not funny," Liam said, glancing down at her.

"Really? Cause I'm having a hard time keeping from laughing," she replied.

Everyone stared at each other for a few long seconds. Then, when Katya went to pull out a chair, both men were jolted into action. Liam was closer, so he was able to help her get seated, but that also meant Wulf was given the chance to change seats. They were at a four top, and he'd been sitting opposite her chair. He switched it up, sitting in the chair to her right, no place setting laid out in front of him. Liam went to go take the empty chair to her left, but a waiter was walking by right then, and Wulf snapped his fingers.

"Yes, Mr. Stone?" the young man responded instantly.

"We won't be needing the fourth chair."

And just like that, Liam's chair was yanked away and was being carried off through the restaurant. He had no choice but to take Wulf's old seat – across the table. He glared as he sat down, then grabbed Wulf's left-behind wine glass and drained the contents.

"Now then," Wulf said as he adjusted his suit jacket. "What's the plan here? Are Eden and I supposed to fight? Challenge each other to a duel? Write you love poems?"

"Uh, that wasn't my plan, but now that you've said it, I would *die* to see the kind of love poem you'd write," Katya replied. He gave her a tight smile.

"You can go ahead and hold your breath while I write one."

"I'm sorry, angel cake, but I'm siding with Wulf on this one. What is your plan here? Because I don't feel like sitting through three courses with this asshole," Liam added his two cents. Wulf didn't even flinch at the insult.

"I thought," she took a deep breath. "This would be a good time to lay some ground rules."

There was a long silence.

"Ground rules?" Wulf finally asked.

"Yes."

"For what?" Liam asked.

"This."

"This what?" Liam glanced between her and Wulf.

"Us," she continued.

"Us … what?" Liam tried some more.

"What's going on," she said. Liam went to ask another question, but Wulf finally leaned forward.

"More bullshit. I told you before I wasn't going to come here just to waste my time," he snapped. "I don't have time for your games."

"Really?" she asked, turning in her seat to face him. "You had plenty of time two months ago. Days and days and weeks of playing games. But now you can't spare an hour? I guess it's not so fun when the other team gets to make the rules."

"*Truce!*" Liam called out before Wulf could snap back. "Alright, we're assholes, and we deserve any kind of torture you want to subject us to. But the sooner you can tell us what our punishment is, the sooner we can get to it."

"Okay then," she said, sitting back in her chair. "Wulf invited me to dinner. I assumed he meant as a date."

"You assumed correct," he said.

"And Liam, you've been trying to get me to go out with you ever since the big fight," she said, glancing across the table at the other man.

"Yes."

"You know, it's funny. You both worked out this whole big secret. All these lies and pretenses, when it was all unnecessary. Was it the thrill of lying that made you do it? It had to be, because I was completely open and honest about being with both of you. You could've admitted from the beginning that you knew each other and worked with each other, and it probably wouldn't have changed anything.

I still would have gone out with you," she said, staring pointedly at Wulf for a second before turning her gaze to Liam. "And I still would have slept with you. So. Now I'm going to give you two the opportunity you never gave me."

Both men glanced at each other briefly.

"I'm not sleeping with him," Liam said loudly. Wulf rolled his eyes.

"You should be so lucky."

Katya laughed.

"No. If you two want to see me, then you're both going to be fully aware of it. Both active participants," she explained.

"What, like … a threesome?" Liam asked.

"You wish," Katya snorted. "You two had so much fun playing around with me, think of how much better it will be this time around. You won't have to meet in secret to talk about our dates, we can have conference calls together, if you want."

"You want to date both us," Wulf stated. She shrugged.

"Sounds like both of you want to date me, and clearly you won't leave me alone until I agree to it."

"So …" Liam attempted to guess at her whole plan again. "This is like a real life 'The Bachelor' episode? Is one of us going to get a red rose at the end?"

"This is three people, having fun, but also being open and honest and fair about it. If I go out with Wulf, Liam will know, and vice versa," she said. "Basically, the same arrangement you had before, only this time, I'll get to be involved in the conversations."

"You don't think this is kinda weird?" Liam asked.

"Oh, it's totally weird. But also kind of exciting, and definitely sexy. Two men fighting over me?" she teased, pretending to fan herself. Wulf glared at her.

"Don't get ahead of yourself – nobody's fought, yet," he pointed out.

"That reminds me, though. No sex," she said.

"I'm sorry, what?" Liam looked like he'd short circuited for a moment.

"I won't be sleeping with either of you. I mean, geez, that would be gross, wouldn't it?" she laughed.

"Then what's the point?" Wulf asked. She pulled her clutch off the table and held it in her lap.

"If you honestly mean that, then I guess there's nothing else to talk about," she replied, staring right at him.

He looked angry. Beyond angry. Completely and totally pissed off. For a moment, she thought he was going to call it. Get up and walk away. But this was Wulfric Stone. He didn't take no for an answer, and he certainly never lost, and especially not to a man like Liam Edenhoff. He glanced at Liam, then went back to looking at her.

"Alright. You want to play games with us, then fine. We can play games. But I'm warning you – I'm much better at this than you," he told her. She nodded and slowly moved to stand up.

"True, but on the other hand – I learned from you, which is like learning from the best," she pointed out.

"Wait, wait, wait – what did we all just agree to here? What the fuck is going on?" Liam demanded.

"Little miss Tocci here wants to be part of the action. Thinks she can play in our big boy games, thinks she can teach us a lesson," Wulf explained. Katya glared at him, then placed her hands flat on the table, leaning low over it. Both men flicked their eyes to her chest, which caused her to smirk.

"We'll see how long you can last," she said in a soft voice, then glanced at Liam. "Both of you. You say all these great words. Make these big promises. But what happens when it's not so easy? When your prey isn't so weak and stupid and ignorant?"

"Katya, we never -" Liam tried to argue.

"You say you want to be with me," she interrupted him. "That I'm perfect for you." She turned back to Wulf. "That I'm all these

94

things to you. Is that still true?"

Both men were silent.

"What about when it's hard? Easy to say those things when everything is rosy and you're getting fucked regularly. What about when I'm a raging bitch and won't let you touch me?" she questioned. Again, both men were silent. "What about when I wear an outfit like this, and I remind you of how good that time in the shower was, or how incredible you were in the pool. Remind you of how long it's been since either of you saw me naked. What happens when it gets really, really *hard,* and I just walk away?"

She'd been dropping her voice while she spoke, and ended in a husky whisper. Her double meaning was not lost on anyone. Wulf was breathing slowly and heavily, not showing any emotion. Liam was staring at her with hooded eyes, looking like he was ready for dessert. She let the moment hang for a moment, then she sprang upright, grabbing her purse off the table.

"So you two can just think about all that and if you still want to see where things go between us, give me a call," she said in a cheery voice as she took a compact out of her clutch and checked herself in the tiny mirror.

"Where the fuck do you think you're going?" Wulf demanded. She laughed and put the mirror away.

"You didn't think I dressed up for *you,* did you?" she asked, then laughed harder when his glare turned homicidal and Liam looked like he wanted to strangle himself. "Oh no. No, no, no. I have a date tonight, remember? So while I'm off doing that, you two can just sit here and think about all the things I said, and the way I looked, and the fact that I'm not wearing one piece of underwear under this dress."

She wanted to witness their reactions. See Liam's jaw drop and Wulf's nostrils flare. Wanted to watch their heart rates increase. See if she could get at least one of them to beg her for sex by the end of the night. It was a real possibility with Liam, she knew. Wulf would be a much, much harder egg to crack. Begging was a long way off and would require a lot of effort.

Which is why when she turned around, she didn't look over her shoulder to see if they were watching her.

Besides, she knew they were.

12

WULF WATCHED KATYA WALK AWAY AND RESISTED THE URGE TO CHASE her down. To tackle her and hold her down and possibly choke her to death. Or kiss her. Have sex with her right there in the middle of the restaurant.

Goddamn she looks good. Has she ever worn that dress before?

"Is she really going on a date?" Liam asked. Wulf had almost forgotten the other man was still at the table.

"Yes."

"How do you know?"

"I was there when he asked her out. She told me she was going to cancel."

"She lied."

"Obviously."

"What are we going to do?"

Liam's voice came out as a heavy sigh, and when Wulf glanced over at him, it was to see that the other man had his head in his hands.

"Do you want her dating some random stranger?" Wulf asked. Liam jerked his head up.

"Of course not. I mean, you're bad enough, but at least I know what I'm dealing with," he replied.

"Exactly. I'm not happy about this, but if it's the only way she's willing to deal with me, then I have no other choice," Wulf said.

"Deal with *us*," Liam corrected him.

"You're just an obstacle," Wulf replied.

"Fuck you."

"Do you think she was serious about the no sex?" Wulf ignored the insult.

"Yes. She's a lot stronger willed than you think, Wulf. I've been on the receiving end of her frigidity. She can hold out through some, uh, *tough persuasion*," Liam assured him.

Wulf took a deep breath and counted to ten. It had all seemed like a game, in the beginning. Him and Liam laughing about their sexual conquest. But then they'd stopped talking about it, because it had stopped being a game. It was easy to forget that the whole time – beginning to end – Wulf had been seeing Katya, Liam had been there, too. Had been chirping in her ear, planting ideas in her head, worming his way into her heart, and apparently trying to seduce her via "tough persuasion".

"I think I might actually be ill," Wulf admitted out loud.

"Too late for me. Do you think she'll sleep with this guy?"

"For his sake, I hope not."

"Why?"

"Because I'd kill him."

He stood up after that, pulling out his wallet and taking out a hundred, throwing it on the table. He had to leave. Get out of there. Do something. He was getting that itching feeling under his skin. Like he wanted to crawl outside of himself. He had to run, or swim, or scream, or punch someone in the face.

"I just want you to know," Liam caught up with him once they were outside the restaurant.

"I'm not in the goddamn mood for a conversation, Eden," Wulf growled. Punching someone was suddenly seeming like the mostly likely outcome of the evening.

Far different from what I'd had in mind. Fucking Tocci, screwing up my life yet again.

"That's fine. But I just have to say – if that's what's really going on, if this is some sort of challenge, a way for her to make us prove our feelings for her, then game on. I'm not backing down, Wulf. You fucked her over just as bad as I did, which means I have just as good a chance at winning her back. Better even," Liam warned him. Wulf barked out a laugh.

"How are your chances better than mine?"

"Because you were just some guy she slept with," Liam said. "I was her friend. Maybe her best friend. That's harder to forget. I know her in ways you never did. I'm not gonna just let you walk away with this, not this time."

"What, implying you did last time?" Wulf was really laughing by then.

"No, I'm saying I backed down last time because I knew what we were doing was wrong, so I didn't want to hurt her any more than I already had by making her fall in love with both of us," Liam explained.

"Fine. Fine, Eden, if that helps you sleep at night, then fine. But I can tell you right now exactly why you'll lose," Wulf said, digging his car keys out of his pocket.

"Oh, really? And why exactly am I going to lose, oh wise and all knowing Wulfric?"

"Because you're still thinking of it as a game, and regardless of what she said tonight, she stopped being a game to me a long time ago."

13

L
IAM LAID IN BED AND STARED AT HIS CEILING. STREET LAMPS CAST A GLOW
through the windows, and the orange light stretched the entire
length of his apartment.

He'd removed all the walls, converting the penthouse apartment into a loft, because he liked space. Wide open spaces. He didn't like boundaries or borders. He didn't like being shut out of something.

It was basically an analogy for his entire life. He'd always been made to feel like he was second best growing up, but he'd never understood why. Sure, his twin brother had gotten better grades. Had been much smarter, which had afforded him more opportunities.

But why should that make Liam less worthy? Less capable of succeeding? That's how his parents had always made him feel, though. Landon Edenhoff was the golden child, could do no wrong, nothing could hold him back. The sky was the limit. For god's sake, he was a doctor in some charity hospital in Guatemala, or somewhere.

Poor little Liam, though, with his C grades. Sneaking off to surf instead of taking his SATs. Always being told because he wasn't smart enough, wasn't quick enough, wasn't sharp enough, he'd never succeed. It's bad enough having a successful sibling with a natural talent – but having that sibling be a twin? A carbon copy showing him up at every family gathering. And a real asshole, to boot.

So when Liam had gotten his management position, had done such a good job turning around the business, he had thought that would finally prove something. He was a success in his own right. Landon was having his own issues. A nasty divorce, problems at work. Maybe Liam had a chance to be the winner, for once.

And then enter Wulfric fucking goddamn "everything I touch turns to gold" Stone.

Liam had taken an instant dislike to him, but hadn't really cared, because he didn't have to deal with him much. When the twins in-herited the Twin Estates, Wulf had arranged a meeting. They'd signed paperwork, gone over some different management options. Then lat-er, Wulf had helped with the permits Liam needed to remodel his apartment. All strictly professional.

So when Liam had first gotten the idea to buy The Garden sex club, it had been a natural leap to think of asking Wulf for advice. And when Wulf had offered to invest in the club, to buy half of it and turn all the managing over to Liam, Liam hadn't seen a downside.

My biggest regret. Now I'm stuck with him.

It was like his childhood all over again. Wulf was an arrogant asshole who knew he was smarter than everyone around him. Knew he was richer and better and more talented. Knew he was all these things that Liam could never be.

They had a weird relationship that mostly involved attempting to one up each other. Hitting on the same girl at the bar, seeing who could get her phone number first. Seeing who she'd go home with first. It was a toss up, usually. Almost exactly 50/50, but that wasn't good enough for Liam. He wanted to win. Wanted to be better than Wulf at something.

That's why Katya had particularly stung. To really fall for that girl. To care about her and want good things for her, yet to have to watch her fall for the asshole. It was like confirming his worst fears.

That he was still that little boy who wasn't quite good enough for anyone.

It was right, and it damn sure wasn't fair. Liam was every bit as worthy of her love as Wulf. Hell, more worthy. He ran a successful business, he owned expensive property, he was funny as hell, he was sexy as fuck, and he was good in bed. He was every bit as good as Wulfric Stone.

I won't lose to him again.

14

"I'M SORRY, WHAT?"

Katya crept down the hallway, looking back over her shoulder.

"I said I want to go to the beach," Liam said, not creeping at all, just boldly striding ahead of her.

He's braver than I am.

"Okay. Have fun. You want me to water your plants, or something?" she asked, trying to remember if he even owned any plants.

"Angel cake, do I seem like the kind of guy who can keep a spider plant alive?" he laughed.

"Keep your voice down!" she hissed, swatting at his back as they stopped in front of a door.

"Why?"

"Do you want him to hear you? He'll murder you on the spot."

"I've given him much better reasons over the years than this, I'll be fine. Besides, I told you, Wulf isn't home," Liam said, flipping through a bunch of keys on a ring.

"Are you sure? I mean, positive? What if he comes home? God, why am I doing this?" Katya groaned, glancing over her shoulder again, expecting the elevator to open at any moment, revealing an omnipresent Wulf.

"Because it's exciting, and the new you seems to love danger and excitement. Are you really scared of the Wulf-man?" Liam teased, finally selecting a key and shoving it into the bolt lock. It slid open and he moved down to the door knob.

"I'm not scared of him," Katya responded instantly.

Liar.

"Liar," Liam echoed her thoughts. "I've never been to Wulf's house, though I've known him for years. You only went the one time, right? I'm curious. Let's go check it out. Let's be *bad.*"

Before Katya could argue, the door to Wulf's apartment swung open.

When Liam had called her and asked to go on a walk, she had figured it would be to a park or something, and that she'd be getting an earful about her behavior from the previous night. She was prepared to tell him that her "date" with Gaten had only been a ruse – even Gate had been aware that she'd only agreed to dinner to piss off Wulf, and the two of them had laughed heartily about it over fish and chips.

When it was clear Liam had no intention of going for a walk and had pushed the top floor on button the elevator, she thought he was going to try one of his seduction routines on her. But then he'd told her they were gonna take a tour of Wulf's apartment, and she'd been so thoroughly caught off guard, she'd just gone along with it.

Of course, she knew what they were doing was wrong. Like as in actually, literally illegal – not to mention an incredible violation of his personal space. Still. She knew Wulf would never invite her up on his own, and also, she didn't care about violating his privacy. Not one little bit. So she walked into the apartment and listened as Liam shut the door, locking it behind them.

It certainly wasn't on the same opulence level as his high rise penthouse. There was no hint of all the marble and black accents, and it was maybe a third the size. If that. She smiled to herself.

He must be miserable here.

It did have one thing in common with his old home, though. It was totally impersonal. No family photos or pictures, no artwork, no personal touches at all. He'd most likely had another designer set the whole thing up. The furniture was warmer, more homey, than his last place, though. She ran her hand along the back of the huge couch she'd watched his movers struggling with the other day.

"It's … nice," she finally said, looking over a ridiculously big television.

"If you like the idea of living in a hotel room, sure. It has about as much warmth as he does," Liam snorted from the other side of the room. Katya nodded as she moved into the kitchen.

"Yeah. Yeah, his other place is the same way."

There was almost no food, also like his other home. There was some fancy beer in the fridge, and a case of expensive water. Some Chinese take out, then just a quart of milk. The only pantry item was cereal.

How does he not have scurvy!?

"So we were talking about the beach," Liam's voice shouted from a different room.

"Uh huh," she replied, though she wasn't paying attention. She was being drawn through the apartment towards a large room in the back.

Liam kept prattling away, but she couldn't hear him as she entered Wulf's bedroom. It certainly wasn't as big as his other one, and there were no windows. Luckily, he'd left the light on in the en suite, and it caused enough of a glow for Katya to see her surroundings. For some reason, she didn't want to turn on the overhead light. Didn't want to disturb the scene more than she already had.

She was a little shocked to see that the bed wasn't made. Wulf was more than a little OCD, she had trouble picturing him leaving behind any kind of mess. Everything else in the room was in order

– just the covers on the right side of the bed were folded back, as if he'd yanked them off and never returned. She smiled as she took in the other side of the comforter, noticing that it was still in place from whenever the bed had last been made properly. Wulf slept primarily on one side. Even she didn't do that, preferring to stretch out in the center of her mattress.

She glanced over her shoulder, then stepped further into the room. She lowered herself to sit on the edge of the bed, in the spot where Wulf had probably been sleeping just hours earlier. On the nightstand next to her was a half empty glass of water, what looked like a datebook, and some sort of tablet or iPad.

Katya thought briefly about being a good person and getting up and walking out of the room. Then she decided fuck it, and she grabbed the tablet. She wouldn't go rooting through his social media files or anything, but was curious to see what he'd been looking at before he'd gone to bed, if he'd left it up on the screen. Maybe Wulf had some sort of kinky porn fetish she could use against him.

What she saw, though, when she unlocked the screen, surprised her more than any sort of weird kink. She held still as she stared down at the device, feeling a little short of breath.

"Did you hear what I said?" Liam's voice trickled into the room. She took a deep breath, but didn't respond.

She was looking at a picture of herself. Normally not a big deal – she took lots of pictures, had them all over her own apartment. On her own phone, the wallpaper was a selfie of her and Tori. Before that, it had been a pic of her and Liam. She was pretty sure Tori's wallpaper was a pic of herself and a famous basketball player she'd bumped into, and Katya knew Liam's wallpaper was a picture of him and her. Lots of people kept pictures of themselves or their loved ones nearby.

So to see it on Wulf's tablet was more than a little shocking. And it was more than just her picture being his wallpaper – it was knowing her picture was the *only* personal touch in his *entire apartment*.

It was very overwhelming. She almost wanted to cry. She sniffled and ran her fingers down the side of the screen.

It was from their trip to Carmel. They were in his car, at some overlook they'd stopped in for a moment. Wulf was in the driver's seat, barely visible at the edge of the picture. He was wearing a dark pair of sunglasses and staring down at his phone – the reason for the stop, some business popping up. He was always on his phone.

Katya was the one who'd taken the picture. She was sitting at an angle in her seat and leaning back, actually pressing against Wulf's shoulder so she could get him in the shot. She was smiling big with the tip of her tongue trapped between her teeth. Her hair was in a ponytail, blowing everywhere in the wind. She looked silly and young and messy.

How had he gotten the pic? He must have gone onto her Facebook profile, lifted it from there. A lot of effort for him. And she had to wonder, why that particular picture? She had lots of better ones, where she was dressed up. Even a few with him, where he was wearing his expensive suits.

What on earth goes on in your head, Wulfric Stone?

"You haven't been listening to me at all."

Katya let out a small shriek and dropped the tablet, startled as Liam entered the room. She'd forgotten about him. She caught her breath and picked up the device before she climbed to her feet.

"No, sorry, I got distracted," she replied, glancing down at the screen before sitting it face down on the night stand. It unsettled her, realizing Wulf looked at a picture of her everyday. At a silly, relaxed, cute, intimate photo of the two of them. Everyday.

"Find anything fun? Anal beads, ball gag, prostate massager?" Liam joked, moving around the bed to lay down behind her.

"No, he wouldn't have anything like that."

"Did you look? You never know."

"Um, actually, I think of all people, I *would* know."

"Gross, I hate when you remind me."

"You're the one who used to have pow-wows to literally discuss the sex he and I had."

"Gross, I hate when you remind me."

Katya grabbed the pillow next to her and swiveled around, smacking it across his face. He went to hold up a hand, but she continued to beat him with the goose down cushion. She got in a couple more good licks before he was able to grab her wrists. They struggled for a moment, her trying to make him eat the pillow, when he was able to shove her back onto the bed and hold her down.

"It hasn't been long enough for you to be cute about it," she growled at him.

"*You* make smart ass comments about it all the time," Liam pointed out, laughing as she struggled against him to no avail.

"*I'm* allowed to, I'm the injured party," she replied.

"You can only milk that for so long."

"I think I have a little longer."

"God, angel cake," he sighed, and she stopped moving. "I missed you so much."

Katya swallowed thickly, trying not to notice the look in his eyes as they wandered over her face and chest.

"Should've thought about that before," she replied in a soft voice.

"Hmmm. Do you ever think about it? Us?" he asked. She took a deep breath.

"More often than you could possibly imagine."

"You know, I thought it would be fun, sneaking around in here," he started. "Getting to see into Wulf's private world, and him not knowing I was here with you."

"Knowing that whenever you see him, he'll have no idea you did something that would piss him off," Katya laughed.

"Yeah. But now that we're in here, I have another idea," he said.

"And what's that?"

"Imagine how pissed off he'd be if we had sex in his bed."

Katya held still. On the one hand, he was completely right. Wulf would lose his goddamn mind. Probably kill them both, then burn his bed. On the other hand, she was never going to have sex with Liam. But on yet another hand, it was very empowering having Liam begging her for sex again. And one last hand – she could still use this situation to her advantage.

"Mmmm, that would be kinda hot," she agreed, shifting around underneath him so he could settle in between her legs.

"Seriously?" he was understandably shocked.

"I hadn't thought about that. Was this your plan, get me up here and have sex?" she asked, stretching her arms above her head. He was still holding onto her wrists, so he moved with the stretch, laying flat on top of her.

"No, but it's seeming like a really, really good idea."

"It would be so crazy," she breathed, lifting her head so her lips brushed against his as she spoke. "Can you imagine his face? When you tell him you fucked me in here?"

"I really don't want to imagine his face right now."

"Not to mention," she sighed, moving so her mouth was trailing down the side of his neck. "It's been a long time since you and I had sex together."

"A *loooong* time, angel cake."

"So long, I can barely remember."

"I could never forget."

"Really?" she whispered, slipping her wrists free of him and running her hands down his chest. "I find that surprising."

"Why?" he whispered back, his lips at her ear. She took a deep breath.

"Cause you've already forgotten what I said yesterday," she stated in a loud voice. He gave a start at the abrupt shift in tone, and she used that against him. She shoved hard at his chest, catching him off guard. With a shout, he fell to the side, bounced on the mattress, then slid to the floor with a thump.

"Jesus, Katya!" he snapped, rubbing his head where it connected with the baseboard.

"I told you – I'm not sleeping with you. What about that is so hard to get?" she said, climbing off the bed and straightening out her clothes.

"Now that I know that statement is backed up with physical violence, I'll be sure to keep my hands to myself," he grumbled, glaring up at her.

She laughed and left the room. She was still chuckling to herself, flipping her hair over her shoulder, when she thought she heard something. She went still in the living room, standing next to a huge stone coffee table that sat in front of the over-stuffed sofa. A jingling sound, near the door.

That would be keys. In a lock. Turning it.

"Oh my god!" she hissed. "Liam! Liam! What -"

The front door swung open and for a brief moment, Katya thought about making a break for it. Considered running down the hallway, locking herself in the bathroom, climbing out the tiny window, and shimmying down a drainpipe to freedom. But knowing her luck, she'd trip halfway down the hallway and knock out her front tooth or something. So she took a deep breath, stood up straight, and tried her best to act nonchalant.

Wulf came out of the entry way. He was holding a stack of mail in his hands, shuffling through the envelopes. A long, felt jacket was slung over one arm. He didn't look up as he moved, and was almost into his kitchen before he even realized someone was in his apartment. He stopped and stared at her for what felt like forever.

"Hello," he finally said in a simple voice. She smiled big.

"Hi."

"How are you?" he asked, setting his jacket and mail on the back of the sofa before walking around it.

"Good, good. And you? How was work?" she asked in return, sliding her hands into her back pockets. He moved until he was standing in front of her, the coffee table the only thing separating them.

"Same as always, busy. Tiresome."

He loosened his tie and slipped it free of its knot, tossing the length of silk onto the table. Next he slid out of his suit jacket, laying it carefully on the arm of the couch.

"You work too much. You should take a vacation," she suggested. He nodded while he undid his cuff links, rolling his shirtsleeves up to his elbows.

"I should. I suppose it's safe to assume you'd take care of my place while I'm gone."

"Of course. So," she took another deep breath, looking around the apartment. "Would you like a drink, or something?"

"Tocci."

"Sandwich?"

"What the fuck are you doing here? Breaking and entering is a crime, you know," he told her. She rolled her eyes.

"Please, I didn't break into anywhere. This is trespassing, or unlawful entry, at worst," she replied.

"I'm sure the police could easily explain the difference to us," he said, finally moving around the coffee table and stopping right in front of her. She smiled up at him, batting her eyelashes.

"Oh, c'mon, you wouldn't have me locked up," she said in a sweet voice. He frowned.

"Sometimes I think keeping you under lock and key is a great idea. Seriously, Tocci. What are you doing here? How did you get in?"

Luckily, she didn't have to scramble to think of something better than "we were curious", because right then Liam stomped out of Wulf's bedroom. He was yanking his shirt into place, grumbling to himself.

"If you had any idea what a prolonged erection does to a man, you'd -" he was complaining, and then he noticed Wulf.

"Ah. I see how you got in now," Wulf said simply. "You two don't have beds of your own?"

"Well, yours is a Tempurpedic. Better for back pain," she explained.

"I'm going to be sick. What happened to your no-sex rule?"

"See? At least *someone* has a good memory," she snapped, looking over her shoulder at Liam.

"Ignore her," he joked, wrapping an arm around her shoulders. "She gets cranky post-coital. I've told her time and time again, though – three orgasms is my limit. She has to work for it if she wants more."

Then he slapped her on the ass and walked into the kitchen. She stared at Wulf as they listened to the fridge being opened.

"Cranky, huh?" he finally broke the silence. "You never got cranky with me."

"Indifference isn't much better," she replied, and he barked out a laugh.

"What are you two doing in my apartment?" he asked again.

"Liam has a key," she explained, her mind racing for a suitable excuse. She didn't want him knowing that she was curious about him at all.

"So because he has keys, you thought it would a good idea to give yourself a tour? All you had to do was ask, I would've gladly shown you around," he told her.

"Oh, please. We all know that wouldn't have happened. It would've been a no, followed by a bunch of excuses, and then a couple more nos."

"Well, I guess we'll never know. I'm still waiting for a real answer, Tocci."

"We, um," she darted her eyes to the kitchen. Liam was humming as he moved around. What the fuck had he gotten her into!? What was she supposed to say?

Sorry for barging in, Liam wants to go to the beach, and thought he'd ask me to go with him from inside your apartment. What a nut! By the way, cute picture you've got on your tablet.

Thinking of the picture, though, set off a firestorm in her brain. Liam wanted to go to the beach. The picture on Wulf's tablet was of her and him, on their way to Carmel. Which had a beach. Her family was also in Carmel – her mother would *die* to see Wulf again, and she would also absolutely *love* Liam. Both responses would equally annoy both men. It would be *priceless*. And Liam and Wulf stuck on vacation together? She was having trouble holding in the laughter from just thinking about it. She took a deep breath and smiled big at Wulf.

"I thought you might be home, I wanted to talk to you about something. But then you weren't here, so we let ourselves in, so we could wait for you."

"Really. What was so important that you felt the need to break in?" he asked.

"I wanted to invite you back to Carmel," she said. He finally looked surprised.

"You want to go home with me?" he asked, and if she hadn't known better, she could've sworn he sounded hopeful.

"Yeah. See the home front. Spend a few days on the beach. Sun, sand, surf," she suggested.

"That … sounds interesting. And you're sure you want to do this with me?" he checked. Katya nodded and closed the distance between them.

"I think it could be really fun. Enlightening, even," she said, stepping so she was at his side and pressing her hand against his chest.

"And no sex," he clarified.

"Hmmm," she thought for a second. "How about – if you promise to go on this trip with me, I won't completely rule out sex."

"Deal," he said without hesitation. She cocked up an eyebrow.

"You sure? You *promise?*" she asked.

"Promise. I'll clear my schedule. Are you set on Carmel, though?" he asked, taking out his phone and tapping away at it with one hand. "If it's the beach you're after, I can rent a house in Malibu, we can -"

"You're out of mayo," Liam reappeared, holding a huge sandwich in his hand.

"Goddammit, I forgot about you," Wulf growled, not looking up from his phone.

"You ready to bounce, angel cake?" Liam asked. She nodded and headed to the front door.

"Sure. And guess what?"

"What?" he asked around a full mouth.

"Wulfy's coming to the beach with us!" she exclaimed, holding the door open. Both men's jaws dropped, Liam's while still holding food in it.

"Excuse me?" Wulf managed to ask.

"Carmel," she said again. "Malibu sounds awesome, but my mother and father are in Carmel, and besides, it has some pretty decent beaches."

"Wulf is *not* invited," Liam insisted.

"Wulf does *not* want to go," Wulf added.

"Wulf and Liam don't have a choice – if you want me to go to a beach with you," she said, pointing at Liam. "Then Wulf goes. And you," she shifted her point to Wulf. "Promised. Remember?"

There was another long silence, then Wulf cleared his throat.

"Yes. Yes, I did. I'll go to goddamn Carmel. But remember – you made a promise, too."

Katya smiled again.

"This is going to be a great weekend, boys. I can already tell."

15

TORTURE WAS FUN, KATYA DECIDED.

Getting to see Wulf and Liam squirm and fidget and generally be as uncomfortable as possible was the best thing ever. It did wonders to ease the pain that still sat in her chest.

They were driving to Carmel. Liam had rented an SUV for the trip – neither he nor Katya had a car, and Wulf's Mercedes was totally impractical. He bitched about their vehicle choice, but fell into a sullen silence after the first ten minutes.

It was only a two hour to drive down from San Francisco, and after half an hour of silence, Liam couldn't stand it anymore. He finally started chatting. He was excited to meet Katya's family, and curious about Wulf's. Then he talked about his own family.

"We should've stopped in Santa Cruz," he commented. "My mom lives there – she's dying to meet you, Katya."

"Me!?" she exclaimed. "Why me?"

"Because."

"Does she know Katya isn't your girlfriend?" Wulf asked, not looking up from his phone as he spoke.

"She knows I have a girl in my life who is a very good friend that I like a lot. That's all she needs – she's already picking out baby names. Sorry, angel cake," Liam replied, glancing in the rear view mirror. She shrugged.

"It's fine. My mother is the same way," she assured him. Wulf chuckled.

"I remember. She told me that you and I were going to have three kids, two boys and girl, and she thought at least one of the boys should be named after your father," he said. Katya groaned.

"Oh god, she didn't really, did she?"

"She did. We had a nice little talk over coffee. Your mother loves me."

"Only because she hasn't met me, yet," Liam pointed out, smiling big.

"She's going to die for you, Liam. Take it a little easy on her, I don't want her falling too in love with you when I'll only have to explain that we aren't anything," she explained.

"Well, who knows? Maybe by the end of the weekend, that'll change," he said. Wulf glared and Liam laughed. "So what about your mom? How is she? Hoping you'll marry the girl next door?"

"My mother doesn't care about my love life," Wulf replied.

"Really?"

"Yes. I'm pretty sure she thinks I'm indestructible, so she doesn't worry about me."

"That's kinda sad," Liam said a quiet voice. Katya cleared her throat.

"She doesn't worry because she thinks Wulf is a god," she explained. "You should see the way she looks at him – like a movie star is in her home or something. It's incredible."

"My mom cries every time I come home," Liam chuckled.

"Awww. Why?"

"She cries at the drop of a hat. When I'm happy, when I'm sad. When I got a new car, when I wrecked the new car. Sometimes we'll be sitting around the table, just telling stories and laughing or whatever, and she'll start crying at how sweet it all is," he laughed.

"Jesus," Wulf groaned.

"I think it's sweet," Katya piped up. "My mom isn't emotional, but she likes it when I'm home."

"I bet she's just like you," he guessed. She shook her head.

"You'd guess wrong. My mom is somewhat of a society matron. I had to go to etiquette classes, wasn't allowed to date until I was sixteen, had a curfew until I went to college. She's fun, don't get me wrong, just kind of prim and proper," she explained.

"So basically exactly the same as you used to be before we met," he teased.

"Oh god, you're right. I guess I am like my mom," she sighed. Wulf cleared his throat.

"You look like her."

Both Liam and Katya glanced at him.

"I kinda do," she agreed. He shook his head.

"More than 'kind of' – you could almost pass as sisters. Same hair, same height, same eyes," he continued.

"You're gonna be a hot old lady," Liam cracked up.

"Oh, shut up," she grumbled. Wulf smirked.

"He's right. Your mother is beautiful, and you're prettier than she is," he told her. "You're going to get even more stunning with age."

"Katya has a hot mom," Liam snorted.

"Okay, just calm down. My 'hot mom' is also happily married and wouldn't appreciate this conversation at all," she informed them, though she inwardly glowed at the "stunning" comment.

"Well, I for one am now super excited about this meeting," Liam said through a huge grin.

Mrs. Tocci didn't cry when she saw Katya, but she did hold her in a tight embrace for an almost awkwardly long amount of time. While that happened, Mr. Eugene Tocci introduced himself to Liam, smiling big and shaking his hand. Katya managed to pull away from her mom in time to see her dad shake Wulf's hand, exchanging an expression that spoke leagues, then he pulled the younger man into a fatherly hug.

"Good to see you, son," he said, letting Wulf go before turning to his only child. "But even better to see you, pumpkin."

"I missed you so much," she sighed, almost falling into his hug. She was close to both her parents, but since moving out on her own, she didn't get to see her father half as much as she saw her mother, so every time was special.

"Me, too. Lots to talk about kiddo. I'm building a gazebo!" he told her. She groaned and pulled away.

"Not again. Remember the shed?" she told him. He rolled his eyes and while keeping one arm around her shoulders, he led her towards the front door.

"That was years ago. This is different, it comes in a kit, I can't possibly screw it up," he assured her. She laughed all the way into the house.

Liam was given a tour and offered a room, but before he could accept, Wulf stated loudly that Liam would sleeping over at the Stones' house. No need to put the Toccis out more than they already were. Liam made a face like he'd chewed on a lemon, but he didn't argue. There was a round of goodbyes, then the men trooped back out the front door.

"It's good to be home," Katya moaned when she sank into the sofa in the living room. Her dad was in his study, working on a ship-in-a-bottle. He was an academic, but always needed to be doing something with his hands.

"It's good to have you home, dear," her mother sighed as she sat down, as well.

"Thanks for letting us invade," Katya continued, resting her head back and closing her eyes.

"Of course! You could bring home twenty people, you know that," her mom assured her. There was a pause, then she cleared her throat. "I was surprised, though. When you said Wulf would be coming."

Katya's eyes popped open and she stared at the ceiling. There may have been a slightly drunken, sobbing, confessional phone call made to her mother at an inappropriate time of night. They'd talked more about it since then, but never in too much detail.

"It's been a weird couple of weeks," Katya mumbled, finally looking at her mom.

"Sounds like it."

"I'm just ..." she searched for the right words. "Confused? Stupid? I don't know, mom. We're not together – for real, this time, so don't start anything or try to push us together," she said in a stern voice. Her mom held up her hands.

"I won't!"

"But he does feel bad, and I thought maybe ..."

Again, she had to rack her brain to think of what to say. "*I want to torture him and make him uncomfortable by forcing him to be in your presence*" just didn't sound good, no matter how well she could word it.

"Maybe your father could talk to him?" her mother suggested.

"Oh god, no. I don't want to get back together with Wulf, and I don't want Dad reading him the riot act, or even being mad at him. I'm an adult, and relationships end – but that doesn't mean anything bad has to happen to theirs," Katya insisted.

She'd had a lot of time to think about it – Wulf and her dad did have a relationship independent of Katya. Not anything too big, they didn't call each other or anything, but Katya knew that the few times Wulf had visited home during school, he'd made a point to stop by and say hello to Mr. Tocci.

Katya's dad had always looked in on the Stones after the divorce, taking special care to spend time with Wulf. Not a lot – Wulf had always been fiercely independent, not to mention busy with after school activities and jobs. But it was Mr. Tocci who'd taught Wulf how to drive a stick shift, and Mr. Tocci who'd surprised Wulf with a limo for his prom date, and Mr. Tocci who'd written Wulf a glowing recommendation letter for college.

So if her dad was the closest thing Wulf had to a decent father figure, and Wulf was the closest thing her dad had to a son, she wouldn't ruin that bond. Not for anything. Not even if she couldn't stand Wulf.

"Your dad wouldn't let that happen. He's concerned, about both of you. He was so happy when I told him about you and Wulf – he'd kind of secretly hoped it would happen, I think. So he was understandably sad when it went south. But he still loves you both," her mom assured her. Katya nodded.

"Good. Then that's all I want to say about any of it. It's just like I said – we were kicking around places to go for a weekend, and Liam wanted to surf, so we all decided to come here," she repeated their reasons for driving down. Her mother smiled and sat up straight.

"Of course, and we are so excited. I told your father about how much fun we had last time you were here, so we're going to have another barbecue. I've talked everything over with Wulf's mother, it's going to be a great time."

"Oh god," Katya groaned. The last barbecue was also a somewhat sore memory. Her ridiculous jealousy at Wulf talking to a pretty girl, then Wulf sneaking into her bedroom window. At least she knew that couldn't happen this time – at least not without Liam following behind him.

Talk about awkward.

"Oh hush," her mother slapped her on the knee. "It's going to be fun, and everyone is eager to see you again. So you will slap on a happy face and make nice with Wulfric for one afternoon, even if it kills you."

Whoa. Katya swallowed thickly and nodded. When she'd gotten her compliance, her mother smiled and stood up, smoothing her hands over her skirt. Then she informed her daughter that she and Mr. Tocci had dinner plans, so the "kids" would have to fend for themselves.

Katya jaunted over to the house next door, ringing the doorbell. She stood up straight and smiled as Ms. Imelda Stone opened the door.

"Dear, I was hoping you'd come stop by!" the older woman exclaimed, then she pulled Katya into a quick hug.

"Of course. How are you?" she asked.

"Oh, ticking along, like always. The boys are outside, if that's who you're looking for."

After exchanging a couple more pleasantries, Katya headed through the house. As she approached the glass door, she could see Liam standing in front of the pool. When she got next to him, she saw that he was looking down into the water.

"This thing is *huge,*" he mumbled, not bothering to look at her.

"Yup," she replied, sliding her hands into her back pockets.

"I mean, I knew he used to swim. That he was like an actual swimmer. But this is kinda insane," he continued.

"Hey, some people have parents who cry out of pure joy every time they see them. Others have parents who try to buy their love," she told him. He chuckled and looked over at her.

"Explains a lot about our pal Wulf. And what about you? What kind of weird stuff is normal for your parents?" he asked. She shrugged.

"They used to measure my skirts before I left the house," she threw out there.

"Holy shit. Your rebellion makes so much more sense now."

She biffed him in the arm.

"Where's Wulf?" she asked, looking around. He gestured over his shoulder.

"Some office or something," he explained.

"Uh huh. So. How do you feel about being roommates?" she asked, not resisting the shit eating grin that took over her face.

"Like it sucks. But his mom is super nice, and the room is

121

downstairs, far away from him. Which room is yours, again?" he asked, glancing at her house.

"The one on the … wait, why?" she was suddenly suspicious.

"So I know which room to sneak into later," he teased, wiggling his eyebrows at her. She looked away, praying her face wasn't turning completely red.

"My room is closed this weekend, sorry. My parents have planned a big backyard party thing for tomorrow, so looks like today is our only chance for the beach," she changed the subject.

"Sounds good, I'm good to go. His mom offered to roast a lamb shank. *Roast a lamb shank.* Do you just keep lamb shank in your freezer on the off chance family comes to town? You would think the fucking king of England was visiting, the way she treats him. She said she ironed his sheets this morning," he told her.

"I know. I think she's never stopped being amazed by him. I'm gonna go tell him the plans, then head back home and get some stuff. Fifteen, twenty minutes?"

"Okay, meet you out front."

Katya entered the house and slowly made her way to the office. She felt a little nervous. The last time she'd been in that office, they'd been getting ready for a date. The last time her and Wulf had been alone, they'd kissed. They hadn't really spoken much since the incident. So when she got to the office door, she took a deep breath and knocked once before walking inside.

"What did I say?" he snapped, not bothering to turn away from the desk. "Not to fucking bother me unless it involved you going home or dying of something, so please -"

"Are you five?" she laughed. "You seriously told Liam he couldn't speak to you while he's here?"

Wulf spun around in his desk chair, coolly eyeing her while he moved.

"No. I thought you were my mother."

It took her a second to realize he was joking.

"Liam said your mother wanted to defrost lamb for you," she said. He nodded.

"Yes. She put it back in the freezer when I told her we had other plans," he said, spinning back around and scribbling away at something on a piece of paper.

"I didn't think about that – I feel kinda bad, maybe we should stay and eat here or something," Katya said, walking up to the desk.

"No, bad would be telling her we're not going and making her feel like she does have to cook dinner for all of us. My mother doesn't particularly enjoy cooking, and she doesn't even like lamb," he replied.

"Wow. You're actually a pretty good son," she teased.

"Why are you bothering me?" he asked, flipping over the page he'd been working on and grabbing another one.

"Because it's so fun."

"I think you just like being in my presence," he said.

"You think wrong, then."

"Seriously. I was supposed to be in Malibu this weekend, closing on a property. I'm now trying to do it via e-mail and phone calls. So unless you have something important to stay, I'd appreciate it if you made yourself scarce."

"Malibu …" she let her voice trail off as something about that struck a chord. Then she remembered when she'd invited him. "That's why you wanted to take me to Malibu! You didn't want a romantic beach weekend, you wanted to close a deal."

"I didn't see why I couldn't do both," he murmured, concentrating on what he was writing.

Katya glared down at him. This was supposed to be her chance to mess with them. Make them feel awkward and embarrassed and just plain awful. Instead, Wulf was being pampered by his mother and continuing on with work as normal, as if nothing was out of the ordinary.

"Nice, Wulf. Nice to see you putting in a real effort," she said snidely, crossing her arms in front of her chest. He snorted.

"I'll put in a real effort when you stop playing games."

She was glad he was looking down, so he couldn't watch her face turn red as anger bubbled up in her veins. She sputtered for a moment, trying to think of a suitable comeback. Then she remembered what her roommate had told her.

You have the power here, not him. He can only get to you if you let him. Take a deep breath and let it go.

"You're no fun now," she sighed. "Liam and I are going to the beach, so have fun hiding in here, letting work run your life."

He spun around in his chair, but she wasn't standing near him anymore. She was striding out the door, not even waiting for a response.

Ha. Not so hard. Just gotta keep this attitude for the whole weekend and by the time we're done, neither of them will want anything to do with me anymore.

They had often joked about Liam's laid back personality – his "comfortable" style, his funny t-shirts, the way he slept in all day, every day. "Surfer" had been used to describe his attitude, but again, it had always been a joke. Katya hadn't ever thought he was really a surfer. It seemed like it would require too much energy and concentration.

So color her shocked when they got to the beach and he rented a board. He warned her that not only had he not surfed in months, but rental boards weren't the best to use. He wasn't used to the weight or the heft, it hadn't been waxed right, so don't judge him if he fell off immediately.

"Just get out there and shred a barrel, Edenherring!"

"Shred a barrel!? And did you just call me a herring?"

Katya had never known anyone who could surf. She'd grown up in California, near a beach, so of course the natural assumption was that she had spent all her weekends there, getting tan and developing a valley accent and chilling with cute surfers. But that wasn't reality, California was a huge state with lots of different cultures depending on where a person was from – she'd barely spent any time at the beach growing up and hadn't known anyone who was particularly athletically inclined, aside from Wulf.

So watching Liam slice through the water on a large piece of foam, she finally felt like a true California girl. She lost her mind, felt like she was watching a celebrity. She ran up and down the shoreline, screaming and cheering and clapping.

"Jesus christ, you would think you'd never seen a surf board before."

She rolled her eyes and looked over her shoulder, holding her wide brimmed sun hat on her head. The only dark rain cloud at the beach – Wulf had decided to join them, after all. While she and Liam had been loading a cooler and towels into the car, he'd sauntered out, shocking her with his shorts and polo shirt. Very laid back, for him.

But once they'd gotten there, he'd gone right back to work. Using a fancy tablet and writing things down in a folder. Why he'd even come, she wasn't sure.

Probably just to ruin my fun.

"I've never seen someone surf before," she said as he stepped up next to her. "It's so exciting!"

"I've never understood the appeal," he grumbled.

They stood side by side, watching as Liam climbed back onto his board. Katya smiled – he looked so happy. He didn't know any of the other guys out in the water, but of course he'd quickly made friends with them. A group of them floated around for a couple minutes, laughing and talking about something. Probably gnarly waves and a sick wipe outs, or whatever.

"Maybe it's not about you," she replied, glancing at him. "I don't understand why anyone would want to swim for miles, back and forth, never getting anywhere. And you probably don't understand why the thing I love most is standing in front of hot ovens all day."

"I get it, I get it." He paused for a while, and she thought that was it. Then he took a deep breath. "But it's all part of his thing."

"What thing?"

"You love to bake because it's part of who you are – I love to swim because it's part of who I am. Eden surfs because it's another way to distract himself from the fact that he doesn't have anything," Wulf explained. She frowned.

"That can't be true."

"It is. He has no real sense of self," Wulf explained. "Why do you think it's so easy for him to smile at you while lying to your face?"

That stung. It just reminded her of how stupid she'd been. Also, her instant reaction was to defend Liam, which she couldn't even do. Wulf wasn't say anything that wasn't true.

"Maybe," she agreed. "But … I mean, he has things. He likes his job."

"Because saying he owns his own business makes him feel important – being a business owner isn't his life passion. I don't think he knows what it is, and that makes him bitter," he said. She glanced at him.

"Real easy to be so judgemental of someone else. What makes *you* so bitter?" she snapped. He smiled tightly.

"Father issues."

Liam was paddling back in, so Wulf returned to his spot on the beach. Katya smiled big and clapped for the returning surf hero.

"You're amazing!" she laughed. He rolled his eyes and chuckled.

"I was shit for a while," he chuckled. "But it always comes back."

"Well, *I* thought it was amazing. It looks like you're flying when you're out there. When did you learn?" she asked, falling into step with him as he headed back to the board rental shack.

"Oh god, like when we were ten? Eleven? My dad got Landon and I these ridiculous boards, huge. I thought it was the coolest thing ever – broke my nose on a rock, first time out. Landon wasn't as into it, but he eventually got into it. Surfed religiously through high school," he recounted.

"Back when dinosaurs roamed the earth?"

"Hey, not that long ago."

"You were surfing while I was in elementary school."

"God, when you say it like that, I kinda want to barf."

She laughed loudly.

"Seriously," she finally said, catching her breath. "You looked relaxed out there. Like you were having fun. You looked … good."

He glanced down at her as they waited in line, his board shielding them from the people ahead of them.

"Thanks. I think you look good, too," he complimented her, his eyes wandering over her body. She was wearing the tiny orange bikini she'd bought last time she'd been to Carmel – the one that had been meant as a surprise for Wulf.

"This old thing?" she laughed, glancing down at herself. "It's a little too much, huh."

"Your body is a little too much."

She glanced up, but he was still staring at her skin. The way his eyes ate up her line and soft curves, she could tell he was falling back into memories. Going back to silly mornings spent wrapped up in sheets and hot moments under hotter showers. She took a deep breath and stepped closer to him.

"I've been exercising," she said softly.

"Really?"

"Mmm hmmm," she nodded. "No job and no men equals a lot of free time. Gotta stay in shape."

"Any time you need help stretching out, just feel free to give me a call," he offered, not once looking up into her eyes.

"I don't know, my work outs are pretty hard."

"Angel cake, you don't even know what hard is."

"Oh, I think I do," she whispered, almost closing the gap between them. He was finally forced to look her in the face. "I think I have a very good idea of what *hard* means."

She watched as he took a deep breath. Struggled to keep his eyes on her face. He licked his lips, went to speak, thought better of it. Licked his lips again. Then opened his mouth.

"I think I'd like to *show you* what 'very hard' means."

Katya threw back her head and laughed. So loud, everyone in line turned to look at them. Liam was startled so much, he stumbled backwards a couple steps. She finally lifted her sunglasses and wiped at her eyes.

"I think," she snickered and gasped for air. "I've seen all you've got to show, and once was enough, thank you very much."

Liam looked stunned at first, then a little bit pissed off. He stepped back up to her, obviously ready to speak his mind, but someone else beat him to the punch.

"Good for you, girl," a middle aged woman from the front of the line spoke up. "Don't you take no sexual harassment from some sandy piece of ash."

Katya started laughing all over again, bending at the waist and pressing her hands to her chest. Liam just grumbled and moved along with the line, leaving her to snort and wheeze all by herself.

They spent the rest of the day sunbathing and generally ignoring each other. It was clear that Katya's skimpy bikini was making the men uncomfortable in all kinds of ways, but Liam was still angry at her, and Wulf was trying to act like he didn't care. She smiled to herself and stretched out a couple feet in front of them, giving them a nice view while she got a nice tan.

She went up to a snack bar at one point, grabbing a hot dog, and came back with a friend. Some guy who'd struck up a conversation with her while waiting in line. She'd made it very clear from line one that she wasn't there to meet guys, but he seemed nice enough and didn't hit on her, so they talked about growing up in Carmel, different restaurants and parks they liked. He walked her back down the beach, laughing about a mutual acquaintance it turned out they both had. By the time they reached her towel, though, her two companions had turned into watch dogs, and were standing at the ready. Arms crossed, glares visible through sunglasses, wide stances. Her friend made a hasty goodbye and all but ran down the beach.

Katya didn't even acknowledge Wulf and Liam, just skipped past them and sat down, enjoying her snack.

To her San Francisco acclimated self, Carmel felt warm. But as it shifted into evening, it dropped down into the fifties. Still not terribly cold, but when combined with a stiff breeze that started rolling in off the ocean, Katya was shivering soon enough. Wulf was the one who finally called it and told them to start packing up – Liam could've stayed there all day, it seemed like. He really was a beach bum.

They loaded up the car, but still didn't head home. Surprising them all, Wulf had been productive during his down time at the shore and he'd found them a place for dinner. Almost a pub – which shocked Katya – with a whole outdoor terrace, complete with large heaters. She put on a huge maxi skirt and a long sleeved, tight crop top over her bikini and then followed the men into the restaurant.

"This is actually nice," she sighed, pulling her hair up into a high ponytail as the waiter walked away with their drink orders.

"Yeah. I'd never been down here before," Liam commented, glancing around the area. "A friend and I drove to Manhattan Beach once, but that's really the only other place in Cali I've been, besides home and S.F."

"Wow!" Katya was surprised. She continued messing with her hair, piling it into a messy bun.

"I'm not surprised," Wulf replied, tossing his menu to the side.

"Shut up. The entire time I've known you, you've never even left the state," Liam snapped. Wulf cocked up an eyebrow.

"I've gone plenty of times – when you fly in a private plane, you can go and come back from just about anywhere in a day. In May, I spent every weekend in New York."

Sensing a "who's got the biggest dick" competition, Katya cleared her throat.

"Favorite vacation," she spoke loudly. "Mine was when I was twelve – my parents took me to Spain, and we did this whole mutli-country backpacking trek. My dad was super into that kind of stuff, back in those days."

Liam smiled big and sat up straight.

"Favorite vacation – summer camp, when we were thirteen. My mom shipped us off to this Christian bible camp. You know, like we had to go to chapel once a day and sing songs, learn how to make friendship bracelets and brush down a horse, that kind of jazz."

"*That* was your favorite vacation?" Katya was skeptical.

"Yup. Sandra Clement. She was fourteen, we'd known each other a couple years through the camp. A big tomboy, I always picked her for capture the flag, dodgeball, stuff like that. We got in trouble one time and they made us muck out the stables. She totally took my virginity in the hay loft, and for the rest of the summer, we'd sneak off whenever we could and had sex just about everywhere in that camp," he chuckled.

"You lost your virginity at thirteen?" Katya scrunched up her nose. Both Liam and Wulf laughed at her.

"Yeah, and to an older woman. Talk about bragging rights. Also two full years before Landon – I still won't let him live that down," Liam said with pride.

"When did you lose your virginity?" Wulf interrupted, staring at her. She shook her head.

"Uh uh, we're talking about vacations. What's your favorite?"

"When I came to Carmel with you last month."

It was like he'd dropped a bomb. She stared at him and Liam stared at her. She refused to react, though. She didn't believe him, and wasn't about to dissect that comment right there in front of

Liam. She took a deep breath.

"I was seventeen," she blurted out. Both men glanced at each other, then back at her.

"When you went to Carmel?" Liam checked. She crossed her eyes at him.

"When I lost my virginity," she replied.

"I want details," he insisted.

"I want to know with who," Wulf added, speaking slowly. She wouldn't look at him, though. She was still reeling from his comment, plus she was pretty sure he'd know the guy.

"It was with a boyfriend," she replied. "We'd been dating since I was fifteen. It was totally stereotypical – he was a senior, we went to his prom. It was held in a fancy hotel in Monterey. We'd talked about it, he got a hotel room for the night, there were rose pedals everywhere. I cried after he fell asleep, and I was *positive* my mother was going to know just by looking at me. Ha! She thought I was a virgin till my third boyfriend."

"That is … kinda boring," Liam sighed. She threw a piece of bread at him.

"Who was it?" Wulf asked again, and she finally glanced at him.

"You probably don't know him, he would've been five years younger than you," she pointed out. He shrugged.

"Then it won't hurt to say his name."

"Kelsey Hochstein."

"Hochstein?" Wulf's eyebrows shot up. "You went out with one of the Hochsteins? Actually had sex with one?"

"What's so bad about them?" Liam asked while Katya groaned.

"Nothing. Nothing at all – their dad is a surgeon, and their mom is a therapist. Great family, nice boys. He was very sweet, and it was actually really good the second time, and it got better from there on out," she insisted. Wulf snorted.

"Did he need to step on a stool to kiss you?"

"He wasn't that short."

"They're *all* short."

"Like how short are we talking?" Liam asked, looking between them.

"Not that short," she insisted.

"Extremely short," Wulf spoke over her. "As I remember it, the oldest kid was around five-foot-four."

"So he was shorter than you?" Liam chuckled. She rolled her eyes.

"You know what? Yeah, he was. But he was also amazing in bed and is now worth more than both of you combined, so *shut up*."

There was silence for about three seconds, then Wulf cleared his throat.

"Wow, you really missed the boat, Tocci."

Liam burst out laughing and Katya couldn't even be mad. It was pretty funny, and it was also sort of amazing – the three of them, sitting together, and all smiling. All having a pretty good time. She would never admit it out loud, but it was kind of … nice. It made sense, she supposed. She'd gotten along immensely well with both of them in the past, so it stood to reason they'd have a good time now. So long as they all conveniently forgot just how fucked up their little threesome was.

Their drinks were eventually delivered and they ordered dinner, but after the waiter left, Liam realized his cocktail had gotten screwed up. Instead of waiting for their server to return, he decided to head to the bar on his own to get it remade. Katya smiled as she watched him go. He cut across a large dance floor, moving in between people, flirting with girls, stopping to even twirl one.

"He has so much charm, it should probably be illegal," she laughed, finally looking at Wulf. He wasn't watching Liam, though. He was watching her.

"Come dance with me."

"What, now?"

"No, tomorrow. *Yes,* of course now."

He didn't give her a chance to accept or deny, Wulf just grabbed her arm and hauled her to her feet. She stumbled onto the dance floor behind him and before she could kick up a fuss, he had his arms loosely draped around her waist. She frowned at him, but eventually put her arms around his shoulders.

"Tell me something," he started talking after they'd been moving around for a minute. Katya glanced up at him once, but standing so close to him made her nervous, so she leveled her gaze to just over her shoulder.

"What?"

"What are you getting out of all this?"

She chewed on her bottom lip for a moment. Could feel him staring down at her.

"Closure?" she offered finally.

"Hard to get closure when you're the one prolonging it all."

"I'm having fun," she snapped, finally looking him in the eye. "Seeing you and Liam having to interact with each other, knowing he's going to be sleeping down the hall from you. Watching you both fall all over each other for something that will *never happen*."

"Hmmm, never. That's a bold statement. Almost seems like a challenge," he said.

"No," she replied quickly, shaking her head. "It's closure. If you two can feel a small modicum of what you made me feel, then I will have *closure*. Get it?"

He didn't look annoyed or intimidated or crestfallen, like she'd kind of hope for – no, he still had that annoying smirk on his face. His eyes still looked at her like he knew about her little scheme than even she did.

"Do you really think it's that simple?"

"Yes."

"It didn't work so well for Eden or I when we decided to have fun with someone," he pointed out. Wow, she hadn't been expecting that, at all. She finally looked away.

"Well, there's a big difference between the two situations," she said.

"And what's that?"

"With you two, the end goal was me," she reminded him. "But with me, the end goal is just to be left alone."

"See, I don't think that's true."

"Oh, really?"

"Yes."

"And why's that, Mr. Stone?" she asked in a bored sounding voice.

He suddenly stopped moving, surprising her a little. She glanced around, but there were still surrounded by other people dancing. They were near the edge of the terrace, which was lined with tiki torches. The flames danced off Wulf's face, making him actually look a little warm and inviting as he stared down at her.

"Because at that wedding," he said.

"Huh?"

"You were challenging yourself, when you kissed Eden," he informed her. "But with me, you didn't do anything. *I* kissed *you*. And you couldn't handle it. And do you want to know why?"

She refused to look at him. She stared into a flame until she felt his hand on the side of her neck, his thumb pressing underneath her jaw. She took a deep breath and closed her eyes, trying to fortify herself against him.

"Because despite everything," he spoke softly, moving closer to her. "The fighting and the lying and the game playing," his lips were actually brushing against her. "You still feel … exactly … the same … about me."

A person could stand as strong and steady as they wanted, but they were no match for something made of stone. He bowled her over, always. Knocked her down and suffocated her and boxed her in. She gasped against his mouth, moaned as both hands moved to cup the back of her head, tried not cry when his entire body came into contact with hers.

He's not right. **He's not right.** *He **can't** be right. Please, god, this isn't right. I don't want to care about this man anymore.*

"See what I mean?" he sighed when he pulled away, his fingers massaging her scalp lightly.

Disgustingly, she felt like crying. For a moment, she really thought she was going to. But she refused. *Refused* to let him see that he'd gotten to her. She took a huge breath, held it in for a second, then blew it out quickly.

"Mean about what? A half rate kiss in the middle of a cheap bar? Geez, Wulf, I expected better from you."

Without waiting to see his reaction, she turned around and strode back to the table, her skirt sweeping along behind her.

———————◆———————

The rest of dinner had just been an awkward shit show. Any of the joviality from before had been swiftly murdered by Wulf's kiss. When she'd gotten back to the table, Liam had been standing there, looking like a wounded puppy. She'd actually felt bad for a moment, but then she remembered that none of this was her doing – it was all them. If they had just been decent goddamn human beings, none of them would be there and she would be at home, prepping for work the next day.

And basically being the most boring bitch that ever lived. I hate everyone.

Wulf ate without any outward sign that he was bothered by the uncomfortable tension. Liam and Katya pushed their food around, refusing to speak unless absolutely necessary. Eventually, Wulf got up and paid for everything, then their depressing group marched out to the car.

She reminded them of the barbecue the next day, then she hurried into her house and went straight to her room and changed into her pajamas. Then she walked around and double checked that every window was locked. No surprise visits that night!

She was about to lay down when she realized the pool was reflecting light into her room. Casting memories onto her walls. So she went around and lowered all the blinds.

Then she laid in bed and stared at the ceiling. Her new favorite past time. She tried to distract herself, going over outfit choices for the next day in her mind, but her thoughts eventually wandered back to the last time she'd visited home. When she'd been in bed, feeling antsy and disturbed. When someone had crawled through a window and fulfilled a long standing sexual fantasy. She was squirming around under the blankets, remembering the way Wulf had touched her and talked to her, remembering that kiss from the dance floor, when her phone dinged.

When she picked it up, she saw that it was almost one in the morning, and that it was Wulf who'd texted her. She grimaced, and debated whether or not to open it. Figuring it was probably some excuse to get out of the party the next day, she finally slid her thumb across the screen, reading the message.

I know exactly what you've been thinking about, and yes, it makes you a very, very bad girl.

She didn't fall asleep for a long time.

16

"THIS IS ACTUALLY FUN."

"See? You just need practice."

"Let's not get out of control, angel cake."

Katya laughed and wiped at her forehead with the back of her wrist, glancing over at him. They were making crescent rolls together. His looked a little ... *unique,* but she didn't mind. She appreciated the help, and he was right, it was actually a lot of fun.

He'd turned up early in the morning, shocking both her and her mother. She'd been in her pajamas and her mother had been in a housecoat – it was only seven, after all. While Mrs. Tocci scampered off to make herself descent, Liam had asked about what they were doing so early. When Katya explained that they were prepping stuff for the party, he'd rolled up his sleeves and joined them.

She was impressed, Liam peeled potatoes, helped set up tables and chairs, and received a lesson in table setting from her mother – who was, as predicted, completely in love with him already. He teased her and flirted harmlessly with her, making her blush and giggle. It cracked Katya up, seeing her mother all red and fidgety.

I really do take after her.

Most of the food was prepared and ready by the time guests started showing up, but her mother had nearly had a breakdown over the fact that she'd forgotten crescent rolls. Why the simple baked good was a necessity, Katya wasn't sure, but there had been crescent rolls in Mrs. Tocci's vision for the barbecue, so goddammit, there was *going* to be crescent rolls!

"It's been a good party," she commented, wiping her hands down the front of her apron and glancing out the kitchen door out to the back yard.

"It has. Your parents are awesome, Katya," he told her, sliding the last rack into the oven. He spun the timer, then they both trooped into the pantry, where there was a large utility sink.

"Thanks, they're pretty okay," she laughed while they washed the flour and dough out from under their fingernails.

"I honestly thought this weekend was going to be awful," he said, grabbing a towel and drying off his hands. "But the beach was fun, and then today has been nice. I guess I haven't taken a weekend off in a long time."

"Liam, your entire life is a weekend," she teased him. The towel was thrown in her face.

"Shut up," he laughed. "I work, and you know it. That club doesn't run itself."

"I know, I know, I just like to give you a hard time," she snickered while she wiped off her own hands.

"You like it too much," he said, then walked past her. He stopped at the end of the counter by the door. "What is this?"

She turned and watched as he picked up a large mixing bowl. He lifted the large towel that was covering it, then let out a moan.

"Oh, I made that earlier, but then my mom decided she wanted something more 'exotic' – that's why I made those rosewater short-bread cookies," she explained, standing next to him and looking down into the huge batch of chocolate chip cookie dough that inside the bowl.

"So what, you're going to just let this go bad!?" he asked, sounding offended at the very idea. She shook her head.

"No, I was going to bake them after everyone left – I know how you are about your cookies, I figured you could take them home with us," she assured him.

"Good girl, solid plan."

She gasped when he stuck his finger into the bowl, swiping up a chunk of the batter. The she swatted him in the arm when he shoved the finger into his mouth.

"Stop it! That's so bad for you," she hissed. He glanced at her, then put his finger back in the bowl.

"Are you kidding? If eating cookie batter meant certain death, then I would go with a smile on my face."

"You're an idiot."

"You cannot tell me you don't sample cookie dough as you make it," he said, eating more chocolate chips and dough.

"No."

"Honestly?"

"Well … not when I'm at work," she was honest. "And I try not to when I'm at home – it really is bad for you. You could get E. coli, or any number of other – *stop it!*"

She cut herself off when he started shoving a dough coated finger into her face. She pressed her lips hard together and grabbed at his wrist, trying to hold it away from her face.

"Oh, c'mon, it's delicious. Eat it," he urged, laughing as they tripped around the room.

"No! That finger was just in your mouth! I don't want it in mine!"

"Uh, angel cake, you've had way more interesting parts of my body in your mouth before – a finger isn't that bad, in comparison."

Katya burst out laughing and he used it to his advantage, shoving the dough into her mouth. He was right, of course – she loved eating cookie dough, if the truth was told, and she moaned as she curled her tongue around his finger.

"Okay, okay," she mumbled when he'd pulled his hand away from his face. "It's good."

"Sooooo, good," he sighed, moving to pull the towel back over the bowl.

"Oh, you're done now? You sure you don't want anymore?" she asked, jumping forward and swiping up her own fingerful of the uncooked dessert. "C'mon, it's good! Totally not gross!"

She laughed while she turned the tables, jumping to try and force her finger into his mouth. He shook his head and backed away from her, easily swatting her hand away.

"No way, I don't know where your finger has been."

"*My* finger!?"

"Yeah. I mean, you did date Wulfric," he pointed out, then made gagging noise.

The struggle became real after that, with Katya digging her hand into the bowl and trying to shove a whole hand's worth of dough into his face. He laughed and held onto her wrist, twisting her around and away from him. Her back connected with the door, knocking it closed, and then he shoved her up against it.

"Okay, okay," she laughed, squirming as he forced her own hand closer to her face. "I give up! I give up. Truce. *Truce!*"

They were both laughing and breathing hard, Liam still holding her hand up near her face. Then without warning, he leaned down and wrapped his lips around two of her fingers. She stopped laughing as he worked his mouth all the way down to her knuckles. She felt his tongue swirling around, then he slowly pulled the digits free.

"Delicious," he murmured, staring down at her.

Katya swallowed thickly, staring back at him with wide eyes.

When he kissed her, she wasn't as shocked as when Wulf had done it, but she was a little taken aback with the strength of the kiss. He fell against her, sending them crashing sideways into the counter, knocking the bowl of cookie dough over. She tried to catch her breath, but when she opened her mouth, his tongue quickly invaded, taking up the space.

They'd gone from playful banter to a scorching hot kiss in zero seconds flat. What was going on!? She was acting on autopilot and moaned, standing on her toes and curling one arm around his shoulders. Her free hand she held aloft, trying to keep the sticky dough away from them.

"Did I ever tell you that I love your goodies?" he mumbled, his lips moving along her jaw as he started yanking at the apron strings behind her back.

"Liam," she breathed, trying to catch her breath.

"Baked goodies, of course," he chuckled, sucking at the sensitive skin under her ear. She shivered, then licked her lips, trying to focus.

"Liam, stop," she whispered, then bit back another moan when his hands ran up the back of her shirt, his palms hot against her skin.

"Okay, okay, *all* your goodies," he corrected himself, his tongue making a course for her collarbone.

You are in your parents' home – get it together!

"Stop," she said loudly, pressing her clean hand against his chest. He finally heard her and he backed away, one of his hands gripping her hip and the other shoved down the back of her pants.

"What? What's wrong?" he tried to catch his breath.

"Well, first of all, we're in my parents' kitchen," she pointed out.

"So?"

"So, even if I hadn't made a solemn promise to never, ever have sex with you," she reminded him. "I certainly wouldn't in the middle of the day, in a pantry at my parents' home, with fifty of their guests just a couple feet away."

"Ug," he groaned and dropped his forehead to her chest. "I forgot about your stupid rule."

"Yeah," she agreed. "It does feel kind of stupid right now."

"Well, I guess that makes me feel a little better," he sighed, standing upright.

"Why?"

"If you agree that it's stupid, then maybe later we can discuss breaking it entirely," he pointed out. She went to argue, but he dropped his head down again and licked another finger clean of cookie dough. Her breath caught in her throat at the motion, and she bit her lips between her teeth, refusing to make any sort of noise.

When he finally stood upright again, he winked at her. She wanted to defend her rule, or at least claim she had no intention of ever breaking it, but he didn't give her a chance. He swooped in and kissed her hard, then pulled her away from the door, swatting her on the butt before heading out into the kitchen.

Katya stood in the pantry for a while, trying to catch her breath. Trying to get rid of the excess blood in her cheeks. Then she moved back to the sink and washed her hands again. When she was drying them off, she noticed they were shaking a little, and she took a moment, trying to collect herself.

Seriously, get your shit together, Katya Tocci. This weekend was supposed to be about making them feel uncomfortable and unfulfilled – so why are you the one having all the problems!?

"I have a plan," Katya's dad mumbled near her ear. She looked up at him.

"I'm listening," she whispered back.

"I fake a heart attack," he continued in a low voice. "You shout that you're a nurse and you'll drive me to the hospital. We spend the rest of the day playing mini-golf."

"Won't work," she shook her head. "Everyone here knows I'm a baker."

"So say nursing is your hobby."

She cracked up.

"It's not so bad, Dad," she laughed. "Everyone is having a great time, and they love your gazebo project."

They were standing side by side at the edge of the patio, looking over the Tocci's backyard. It was filled with friends and neighbors and colleagues of both the Toccis and Stones. Katya's mother was in her element, moving among her guests and passing out appetizers. Liam was off in a corner, laughing with some guys he'd made friends with, and she hadn't seen Wulf yet.

"I spoke to Wulfric when he first came in this morning," her dad said casually, seemingly reading her mind.

"Tell me you didn't say anything embarrassing."

"Me? Embarrassing? Never."

"Oh god, it's even worse than I thought."

"No, no," he chuckled. "You didn't even come up. I asked him how he was and how his business was doing and told him that if he ever needed an ear to bend or a shoulder to lean on, I was always here."

"That's really nice, Dad. Thank you. I'm sure he appreciated it," she said honestly.

"I would hate to see you unhappy, pumpkin," he continued talking. "And if you tell me that boy broke your heart, I will gladly go break his legs."

"Dad!"

"You always come first with me. But that Wulfric ... he's never been a happy guy. That's all I ever wanted for him. You know, his dad wanted him to be an Olympian, and to graduate with honors, and to buy and sell the world. Took a toll on him. I tried to show Wulf that all he really needed in life was to be happy. Kills me that he hasn't learned that yet," her father finished talking.

"That's very sweet, Dad, but he's a complicated man, and he doesn't listen very well. He'd rather be the one doing all the talking," she said.

"Don't I know it. He's already tried to tell me what I'm doing wrong with the gazebo!"

"Did you tell him it was from a kit?"

"Yes – he said that was the main problem."

Katya laughed at her dad, then excused herself. She hadn't spoken to Wulf yet, and she didn't want him thinking he'd scared her away with his saucy little text.

She found him near the gate to his yard, talking with his mother and a woman whose back was to Katya. She waved her hand as she approached, trying to catch his attention. He finally glanced at her once, then looked back and watched her walk up to them.

"I thought you were going to avoid me all day," he commented.

"Really? And here I thought you were avoiding me. We still have a lot of dishes that need to be done," she joked. The mystery woman turned around and Katya was shocked to see that it was his sister, Genevieve.

"Oh, Wulfy doesn't do dishes," Ms. Stone said quickly. Vieve smiled.

"It was the chore he hated most," she added. "He always made me or Brie do it."

"Because I wanted to teach you responsibility," he pointed out. Katya rolled her eyes.

"I'm sure that was the only reason. Vieve, I didn't know you were coming this weekend, it's good to see you again," she said, leaning in and giving the other girl a quick hug.

"Yes. My mother called and told me about it. Sounded like fun, so I dragged Brie into the car and drove down. Been a long time since all of us were here, together," she pointed out. "We only got here about an hour ago, I came straight over."

"I know! Is Brie here, too?" Katya asked, glancing around.

"No, she didn't feel up to a party," Vieve explained. Wulf snorted.

"She's pouting," he corrected his sister. Katya raised her eyebrows. "Because I found out she took off from school in the middle of the semester," he added.

"Oh boy. And I'm sure you handled that with delicacy and grace," Katya sighed.

"Her grades are already in the toilet – she can't afford to be running around on the beach for two goddamn weeks. I want her back in class, *now*."

"Please!" Ms. Stone raised her voice. "Can we not discuss this here?"

There was a brief awkward moment, and Katya felt guilty for engaging in such a private conversation. She desperately tried to think of something to say, but then was saved.

"Hello, hello, who is this?" Liam asked, appearing at her side and turning his magnetic smile on Vieve.

"Genevieve," she introduced herself.

"Nice to meet you," he said, then he turned and looked at Wulf's mom, taking her hand in his. "Wulfric, you didn't tell me *both* your sisters would be coming today, or that they were so gorgeous."

Laughter from all the women.

"Think very carefully about how you behave over the next few minutes," Wulf warned him.

"I'm sorry you haven't met our little sister yet," Vieve explained as Liam turned and shook her hand, as well. "She's catching up on her beauty sleep."

Wulf snorted.

"She's *lazy*. There's a difference."

"You dealt with *that* the entire time you were growing up? You poor, poor thing," Liam sighed dramatically, making Vieve laugh again.

"He's not as bad as he pretends to be," she tittered.

"Yes, he is," Wulf and Liam responded at the same time.

Katya was about to join in with the witty banter when Liam shocked her by coiling his arm around her waist. The move wasn't lost on anyone – least of all Wulf.

In another lifetime, the move wouldn't have bothered her all that much. She would've teased him and he would've flirted with her and they would've gone about their day. But too much had transpired between them since those days and now it just wasn't okay, regardless of whatever happened behind closed doors between them.

Also, the tension between him and Wulf was palpable. It was like the air was vibrating with it. Maybe leaving them alone in the same house had been tempting fate – they never could stand to be around each other too much. Maybe they'd reached their limit.

When Liam's arm grew tighter, pulling her closer, she knew she had to do something. She laughed at something Vieve was saying and tried to pull away. He held tight. Katya held onto her smile, gritting her teeth while laying her hand over the one Liam had on her hip. She dug her fingernails into his skin, causing him to pull back, but he just used the move to his advantage and he grabbed her hand, linking their fingers together.

This is my fault. One steamy kiss, and suddenly he thinks all his forgiven. Never again will I ever eat raw cookie dough, goddammit.

"Oh, wow, I totally forgot the napkins!" she suddenly gasped. "C'mon, help me carry them."

She all but dragged Liam through a back door into the garage. The whole way she tried to yank her hand loose, but he clung to her like glue. When they were finally standing next to her father's work bench, she jerked herself free of him.

"You should've told me you wanted to get me alone," he teased, stepping close to her. She put her hands on his chest.

"That's not what I want," she said sharply. "What are you doing? That's my family out there."

"What do you mean?" Liam seemed genuinely concerned.

"You can't just do that, come up to me and hold me and grab my hands. That's not how this works," she informed him. He frowned.

"Let me get this straight – we can kiss and you can make out with me whenever you want, but I can't hold your hand?"

"Um …"

Wow, it sounds really shitty when he puts it like that … but then again, he was a pretty shitty person to you.

"We've been having a fun time, right?" he asked, laying a hand over one of hers. "I thought things were better between us."

"Better does not mean you just get to touch me any old time you feel like it, Liam. Not like that," she informed him. His frown devolved into a glare and he stepped away from her.

"You know, I've really been trying, Katya," he told her. She nodded.

"I know. I do, and I appreciate it."

"Really? Cause I'm getting some pretty big goddamned mixed signals."

"Hey, I told you what it would take for me to spend time with either of you again. I said there would be no-sex, repeatedly. I wasn't the one shoving my tongue down someone's throat in that pantry, Liam. If it's too much for you, I'll understand if you want to walk away," she assured him.

No, I won't. Because after everything you did to me, I'm still here.

"No. No, that's not what I want," he sighed, raking his hands through his hair. "It's just … this is hard for me, angel cake. Really, really hard. I'm in uncharted waters. I've never … I'm trying to change, okay? But you gotta grade me on a curve. I'm gonna fuck up and make mistakes. Just trust that I'm trying."

Awww, okay, maybe he's not so shitty.

"I get that. I do, Liam."

"Then you're more gullible than I thought."

Katya groaned as Wulf walked into the garage, shutting the door behind him.

"What's that supposed to mean?" Liam snapped.

"I think we both know exactly what I'm talking about," Wulf replied. Liam instantly bristled and Katya could see that this time, he wasn't just going to let things go.

"Guys," she moved so she was standing between them. "C'mon. We've been having a pretty okay weekend, for the most part. Let's just keep rolling with it and -"

"No," Liam's voice was serious, stern. He stood up to his full height, head and shoulders taller than Katya, and at least two inches over Wulf. "I *have* been 'rolling with it', *and* taking the jabs, *and* kissing ass."

Katya gasped, a little shocked at how upset he sounded, and a lot angry at the things that were coming out of his mouth. Wulf didn't look at all surprised, though. He looked … *amused*.

"Okay. Okay, well, *I'm* going to let all *that* roll off me, because we are at *my parents' house* and we are *not going to make a scene,*" she hissed at him.

"No, no, I think we can talk like adults," Wulf interjected. "I want to hear what Eden's got on his mind."

"Oh you would love that, wouldn't you," Liam snapped. "Looking like the good guy while I throw a fit."

"Hey, if the temper tantrum fits …"

"Knock it off!" Katya snapped. Liam finally looked down at her.

"No," he shook his head. "I thought I could do this, I really did. I wanted another chance, and if the only way was to take shit from Wulf and get treated like garbage, I was willing to do it. But I think it's gone far enough."

Katya burst out laughing. Both men looked at her like she was a little crazy, but she couldn't help it.

"I'm sorry," she struggled to catch her breath. "Far enough. You said … it's gone far enough. It's been … a week. An entire week. And you couldn't hack it."

"I didn't say I -" he tried to argue.

"You two screwed with me for almost two months. Laughing and having a grand old time. I do the same thing to you, but to your face, with you fully aware of what's going on, and you can't handle a week. How can you not see that that's funny?" she was still chuckling.

"This isn't a joke, Katya."

Everyone fell silent and she wiped at her eyes.

"I know that, Liam. I didn't find it funny when you did it to me, either."

"Then how can you keep doing it to me?" he asked. He seemed to have forgotten that Wulf was standing behind her. For a moment, she struggled with how to answer. Then she decided to be honest.

"Because you deserve it," she answered simply. He hunched down so he was looking her in the face.

"What I did to you was fucked up," he said, staring her very directly in the eyes. "And wrong on so many levels. And I really am willing to do whatever it takes to be forgiven, but I'm not jumping through all these hoops if it's only for you and Wulf's entertainment, before you two ride off into some sunset."

"So let me see if I have this straight, if I'm reading between the lines right," she took a deep breath. "You're willing to do whatever it takes for me to forgive you, so long as I only like you and pay attention to you and never forgive Wulf."

Liam frowned and seemed to struggle for a moment. Not for the first time, Katya thought he should take poker-face lessons from Wulf. Liam's emotions were always printed across his features. It was clear that he'd meant everything he'd said exactly as she'd interpreted it, and was just now realizing how bad it sounded.

How did we go from kissing and cookie dough, to yelling at each other in a garage? What is it about kissing me that makes men want to yell and use dessert as a weapon?

"No, not just that, I just wanted ..." he searched for words.

"You're just a spoiled brat," she spit out. "It's fun to mess with other people, but when they do it to you, you want to stomp and pout and cry about it."

His confusion turned to anger.

"You know what, I'm sick of this," he snapped. "You act like you're so innocent in all this – like Wulf and I are the fucking devil."

"Care to explain to me how I'm wrong?" she offered, throwing up her arms and glancing over her shoulder. Wulf was being smart – he had his mouth shut, though he was watching Liam through narrowed eyes.

"*You* went looking for a good time, angel cake. You didn't want to be with me, fine, whatever, but you *used me*. You always seem to conveniently forget that," Liam told her. She gasped.

"What!?"

"Yeah, yeah, I'm an asshole because I lied to you, but you know what? You're an asshole because you didn't care about what you were doing. Fucking laughing on the roof, sex in the shower, bringing me food. I was good enough for a fun time – good enough to learn from so you could share it all with *him*, but not good enough to be with you. You were fine doing all that, stringing me along and teasing me, yet I'm the devil. You should look in a mirror," he informed her.

Technically, everything he was saying was true. Katya had struggled with those thoughts, herself. But having him yelling it at her, after everything he'd done, after the kind of weekend she'd had – she was not mentally prepared for it. Rationality left the building and blood red colored her vision.

"She's right, we all need to take a step back, and you need to calm down and watch how you speak to her," Wulf finally tried to talk some sense into everyone.

"Screw you," she growled, ignoring him entirely and directing all her anger at Liam. "At least I was always honest with you. You knew every step of the way how I felt about you and how I felt about him. If it upset you, you should've said something. I'm an asshole because I couldn't read your mind!? Grow a pair, Liam, jesus."

"Grow a pair!?" he yelled, then stepped up close to her, getting in her face. "Get fucked, angel cake."

"Hey!" Wulf snapped, stepping around Katya and planting his hand on Liam's chest, shoving him back. "Calm the fuck down and remember where you are and who you're talking to."

"Screw you, too. This is all a fucking game to her – neither of us are going to win, you realize that, right? She's using us for her own entertainment, the way she used me, and maybe you're okay with that, but I'm not. Not this time," Liam said.

It was one thing for Katya to think of it as a game – something she could play and use to torture them. It was another thing to hear that he was still thinking of it as *his* game – that she was a prize to be won.

"Not this time?" Katya was shouting over Wulf's shoulder – he was holding out an arm to keep her behind him. "As opposed to the last time, when you *lied to me every single moment we spent together?*"

"Yeah, yeah, keep milking it. Maybe the next group of guys you fuck will -"

He never got to finish his sentence because a right hook from Wulf shut him up. Katya was stunned. She'd never seen a fight before, not in real life. Her jaw dropped as Liam stumbled to the side, slamming into her dad's work bench.

"I told you to watch what you fucking say to her," Wulf said in a calm voice. He stood still, his arms hanging loosely at his sides. But his shoulders were drawn back, his muscles stretching taut under his shirt.

"Are you fucking kidding me!?" Liam exclaimed, spitting on the floor and rubbing at his jaw. Katya finally regained brain function and she cleared her throat.

"Okay, things just got really out of hand. All of us need to apologize or maybe we need to take a couple minutes and -"

She shrieked when Liam launched himself off the workbench and dove into Wulf. He led with his right shoulder, like a linebacker, and tackled the other man into the car that sat behind them. They slammed into the fender, Liam briefly lifting Wulf off his feet.

Though he was a couple inches shorter, Wulf was actually the bigger of the two – broader shouldered, and with more muscle mass. He was back on the ground in an instant, driving his elbow into the side of Liam's head.

What have I done? Again, this is all my fault. Everything is always my fault.

151

"Stop it!" Katya yelled, running up to their side and grabbing someone's, anyone's, arm. "Stop it, that is my parents car you're scratching and denting! Stop being ridiculous!"

She managed to wiggle in between them, through she wasn't sure she was helping matters. She got jostled around as they all stumbled all over the garage. She yelped and shouted, pushing at chests and pulling at clothing. Having absolutely no effect at all, though at least being in the way seemed to make it harder for them to throw anymore punches.

The way my luck has been going, I'm going to get hit in the face.

Luckily, she didn't have to wait for that to happen. She was aware of someone shouting, then Wulf was abruptly yanked away from the mix. Liam had wrapped an arm around her at some point, and he held on tight, keeping her from falling over.

When she looked up, she was shocked to see her father there. Standing behind Wulf, one hand gripping his arm, the other the back of his t-shirt. He looked equal parts shocked and pissed off, his eyes bouncing between all of them.

"I don't even want to know what's going on, but it ends right now. You two are guests in my home," he growled through clenched teeth. "I won't tolerate this behavior."

"I'm so sorry, Dad. I -" Katya started, but her father shook his head, silencing her.

"Not right now. Right now, I'm too angry to talk about this. All three of you need to go separate ways," he informed them. Katya pulled herself free of Liam, skittering away. When no one else moved, her dad took a deep breath. "I said *NOW.*"

Humiliated at not only being treated like a child, but at having acted like one, Katya felt her face turn bright red. She nodded her head, but it was Liam who moved first. He stormed out of the garage, striding out of sight around the door frame.

Wulf was guided by Mr. Tocci's hand through a side door into the house, and Katya was left alone. Feeling small and embarrassed and ashamed of herself. She waited a couple minutes, then she went through the door to the house, too. Slowly made her way through the living room, hurried down the hallway, then dashed up the stairs. When she got to her room, she slammed her door shut and leaned back against it. She was breathing so hard, she was almost hyperventilating.

"What just happened?" she whispered to herself. "What the hell am I doing? *What am I doing!?*"

17

LIAM STRODE ACROSS KATYA'S BACKYARD, IGNORING ALL THE STRANGE LOOKS he was getting. He didn't like being rude or making people uncomfortable, but if he stopped to smile, or tried to talk, all the rage that was still rushing through his veins would come pouring out his mouth.

He wound up circling around the house till he came to a glass door that led into the kitchen. He wasn't sure where he was going – he was now surrounded by middle aged women drinking wine. He smiled tightly at all of them, then remembered his moment with Katya in the pantry, a couple hours earlier. It was a good sized room off the very back corner of the kitchen, next to a stack of recycling tubs.

He headed into it, slamming the door shut behind him. Then he leaned over the large utility sink, taking several deep breaths. As he looked down, he saw that his knuckles were bleeding. A misplaced punch had landed squarely on Mr. Tocci's Lexus. He hissed and turned on the water, running his hand under the stream.

"That looks bad."

Liam spun around so quickly, he knocked over a bucket and

mop, causing them to slam to the ground. He glanced down at them, then back up at his intruder.

A woman was sitting at an odd angle on a step ladder in the corner, her hands behind her back. She must have been there the whole time – he'd intruded on her, actually. He didn't recognize her, hadn't met her over the course of the barbecue. He assumed she was a friend of Katya's.

"Sorry," he finally grumbled. "I didn't know anyone was in here."

"I'm hiding out. Looks like you're doing the same thing," she said, nodding at his hands.

"Yeah. Just needed … a moment," he managed to say, reaching over and grabbing a towel.

"Not a fan of family functions?" she asked. He chuckled while he dried off his hands.

"This isn't my family, and no, I'm not the biggest fan of this function."

"Tell me about it. Need to relax?" she asked. He glanced at her, raising up an eyebrow.

"Uh … what did you have in mind?" he was curious. She smiled and moved her hands to her lap. She had a joint between two fingers, a thin trail of smoke curling up from one end. He'd interrupted her little smoke fest.

"The way you came bursting in here, I thought you were busting me," she said, then took a long drag from the joint. As she inhaled, she stood up and turned around, picking up a purse from the floor. Since she'd been sitting down, he hadn't realized how small she was – she had to have been a foot shorter than him. But goddamn, she had the most amazing ass he'd ever seen. He was openly staring at it when she turned back around. She was holding her breath and holding the joint out to him.

"You know what? Yeah, fuck today," he sighed, then he took a hit. She nodded and puffed out the smoke.

"Tell me about it. Some days just can't end soon enough," she

155

groaned, shoving her hair over her shoulder.

"I *was* having a good time, till this," he said in a tight voice as he held the smoke in his lungs. He held up his bloodied hand, then exhaled.

"How'd that happen?" she asked.

"Hit a car."

"What did the car do to you?"

"Nothing. I was trying to hit an asshole," he explained, taking one more drag from the roll before handing it back. She smirked at him and delicately ground out the cherry on the joint.

"Looks like you missed," she told him, dropping the roach into a small canister before shoving it into her purse.

"I'll get my chance again later," he assured her.

"Let's hope you have better aim by then."

He frowned. At first glance, she had seemed nice. At second and third glance, she had definitely seemed sexy. But now she was coming across as kind of bitchy, and bitchy was the quickest way to look ugly, in his opinion.

"Look, I didn't mean to intrude, Miss …" he fished for her name.

"Halsey," she answered.

"Your name is Halsey?"

"*Miss* Halsey," she corrected him. "So who was the asshole?"

"Some guy," he sighed. "Wulfric Stone."

She rolled her eyes.

"Oh god. My next question was gonna be did he deserve it, but now I know the answer."

"Not a fan?"

"He's pretty much the biggest asshole I know. We go back a long time, though we haven't seen each other in years," she told him, pulling a phone out of her back pocket and glancing at it.

"So if you don't like Wulf, and don't like parties, what are you doing here?" Liam asked. She ignored him, scrolling down her screen. "Are you Katya's friend?" More silence. "Did you go to school with

Wulf?" Nada. He sighed. "You know what? I've had a bad fucking day, and I'm all full up on dealing with assholes, so if you'll excuse me, I've got a revenge fight to plan, and a girl to beg forgiveness from, so thanks for the toke."

"You want to get revenge on Wulfric?" the girl – Halsey? – finally spoke again.

"I want to strangle him slowly, then rearrange some of his better features, yeah," he replied, tossing the bloodied towel into the sink. She slid her phone back into her pocket and finally looked at him again. He was struck by how gorgeous she was, with a round face and wide eyes. He couldn't quite place her age – she was wearing a lot of make up. She had to have been Katya's age, or maybe a little older, twenty-five even. Was probably another neighbor, some long class-mate from yester-year. God, Carmel just made hot people, it seemed.

When she cleared her throat, he realized he'd been staring a little too long. He coughed and looked back into her eyes. She was glaring, but she always seemed to be glaring, so he wasn't sure if she was offended or not. She abruptly dropped her purse to the floor and she sat back down on the step ladder, leaning back a little. The pose forced her chest out, making it almost impossible not to stare at her tits, while she stretched her shapely legs out in front of her.

"Want to a take picture? Might be easier to stare at," she offered in a nasty, sarcastic tone of voice. Liam groaned and rolled back his head till he was staring at the ceiling.

First I get the run around from Katya. Then I get punched in the face by Wulf. Now I'm getting hassled by some stranger. I should've stayed at the fucking beach.

<hr />

"What the hell is going on!?"

Wulf took a deep breath, then yanked himself away from Mr. Tocci's grip. He didn't want to offend Katya's father, but he also was about two seconds away from completely losing his shit and tearing the whole goddamn house down.

First I will smooth things over with the Toccis, then I will take about eighty deep breaths, and then I will fucking shove Eden's head up his goddamn asshole.

"It was an intense moment, I reacted poorly," Wulf said by way of an answer.

"No kidding," Mr. Tocci sighed, leaning against his desk. "I know we haven't spoken in a long time, Wulf, but *I know* you know better than this. For god's sake, you're a grown man! What are you doing brawling in my garage?"

"It wasn't something I planned on."

"So what happened. Make me understand this before I have to deal with my wife. She won't be happy when she sees that dent on our car."

"I'll pay for the damages, of course," Wulf said.

"I don't care about the car, Wulfric. What is going on?" Mr. Tocci asked in a carefully modulated voice.

Wulf stared at the other man for a moment. He'd never once thought of Mr. Tocci as his father. No, Wulf had a father, even if the man was a cold hearted bastard. Mr. Tocci was something else – he was one of the first people Wulf had ever truly respected, and to Wulf, respect meant much more than any sort of fatherly affection. He hated to admit it, but he didn't like the idea that he might have disappointed the man.

"Words were said," Wulf finally answered. "And I didn't like what I heard."

"Not good enough," Mr. Tocci shook his head.

"I'm sorry, but the rest isn't really any of your business. I'm sorry I lost my temper at your party, and I'm sorry for any damages caused. Of course, I'll pay for -" Wulf began to say.

"What happened to you, Wulf?"

There was silence for a moment, the two men staring at each

other. Then Wulf took a deep breath.

"Well, I went to school, got several degrees while opening a business that's been thriving ever since, all while taking care of my family and putting my sisters through school," he snapped.

"I know all that, but when did you turn into an absolute dick-head?" Mr. Tocci asked.

Wulf was stunned for a moment, then he barked out a laugh. Before that moment, he'd never once heard Katya's father use a curse word. Mr. Tocci chuckled as well, then both of them were laughing away.

"I'm not sure," Wulf laughed. "Probably around eighteen."

"Ah, graduation year. Crazy time for you."

"Don't remind me."

"I have your mug shot in my scrap book."

"Seriously?"

Two minutes later, Mr. Tocci produced a large photo album and found a page towards the back. Sure enough, there was a mug shot of him in black and white. He hadn't looked at pictures of himself in a long time, and it was kinda surreal looking at the eighteen year old Wulfric Stone. The young man in the photo was glaring, his hair wild on his head, sticking straight up. He was bleeding from a cut on his lip, and his left eye was already starting to swell shut.

"You still owe me bail money," Mr. Tocci chuckled. Wulf rubbed a hand across his mouth.

"I can't believe you kept this. Wow, what a night. Drunken and disorderly, breaking and entering, assaulting a police officer," Wulf recalled his graduation party. Things had gotten a little wild. Youthful exuberance and whatnot.

"I know. When I got that call at three in the morning, I nearly had a heart attack. Katya was at a friend's house that night, and I was so sure it was her, that something had happened to her. Imagine my shock when they said it was the county jail calling."

Wulf frowned. His mother had been doing a double shift at a

restaurant, she'd never even known about the arrest.

"No, Katya never would've done something that would land her in jail," Wulf assured him.

"I would hope not. She was twelve at the time."

They both laughed.

"At *any* age."

"Maybe. But I don't know, sometimes I don't think I know my daughter as well as I thought I did," Mr. Tocci said in a careful voice. Wulf glanced at him.

"I'm sure you do, you two were always close while I was growing up," he said. The other man nodded.

"I know. But I'm not around now. I have to admit, when Elena told me you and Katya were seeing each other, I was happy. Happy knowing someone I respected and trusted was looking after my baby girl."

It took a lot to make Wulf feel bad. About anything. But Mr. Tocci seemed to have a magic key straight to Wulf's nerve center. He winced as he listened to the words coming from Katya's father. Felt guilty that he'd ruined everything, and for more people than just him and Katya. Funny, when he'd first decided to have his fun with little Katya Tocci, it hadn't even occurred to him that it would effect their lives back home.

Sometimes, being self-centered isn't such a good thing.

"I'm sorry things didn't work out," Wulf finally managed to say. "I made some mistakes."

"People do. But if you're trying to win her back, punching out the competition isn't the way," Mr. Tocci insisted.

"That wasn't what I was doing," Wulf chuckled. "Though I mean, it had occurred to me before."

"Then what the hell was the fight about?"

"Let's just say 'the competition' had some unflattering things to say about your 'baby girl' – and I didn't think that was okay," Wulf explained. Mr. Tocci's eyes got wide, then he slowly nodded.

"Well then. I hope you got in more than one hit."

Wulf laughed again.

"I got in a couple."

They both chuckled for a while, then fell silent.

"Okay, okay, I'm not your father, I can't keep you here," Mr. Tocci sighed and stood upright, leading Wulf towards the door to the living room. "Just know that I'm rooting for you, son. I hope you and Katya can work stuff out."

Wulf felt warm at hearing that, and he nodded as he followed the older man out of the study.

"Thanks. That means a lot," he said in all honesty.

"But," Mr. Tocci continued. "If you make my daughter cry again, I swear to god, I will beat you unconscious with one of my textbooks, and then I'll back over you with my car."

"Jesus, okay."

"You think I'm being facetious, but you forget that I have friends who teach forensic pathology at Quantico. I know how to make it so your corpse isn't distinguishable from a rotting pig's."

Wulf didn't laugh that time. He stared at the other man, then nodded.

"Understandable. If I knew someone was making her cry, I would feel the same way."

"Would you?"

There was a tense moment while they stared at each other.

"I would."

"Good, glad to know I can count on you to take care of her. Now get out of here before Elena finds out about the fight and starts looking for you. Hell hath no fury like my wife when someone misbehaves," Mr. Tocci faked a shudder.

"Thank you. And ... thanks, for bailing me out that night," Wulf added at the last minute. Mr. Tocci smiled, adjusting his glasses at the top of his nose.

"Any time, son."

18

KATYA DIDN'T SEE WULF OR LIAM AGAIN. WHEN SHE FINALLY GOT HERSELF together and went back down to the party, both men were gone. Her mother seemed none the wiser that anything had happened and her father was keeping silent. He gave her a stern look, but didn't say anything while they had guests.

It wasn't till she was helping her mom clean up that Vieve came over to help. She also explained that the boys had left. They'd already headed back for San Francisco. She seemed surprised that Katya didn't know anything about it, and informed her that Wulf had arranged for Vieve and Brie to bring her back.

Katya was a little stunned that no one had said anything to her. Sure, things had taken a super weird turn, but she'd driven down there with them. Had basically planned the whole trip. What if Vieve hadn't been there? And to not say *anything* – Wulf was a quiet man, but this was taking it a bit far. And what about Liam?

It wasn't till she went back upstairs that she realized she'd left her phone up there all day. She had dozens of missed messages and voicemails from Liam, all explaining that he was embarrassed over his actions and didn't want to make her family more uncomfortable than he already had; he'd felt it was best to leave, and apparently, Wulf had agreed. Had even been willing to call a truce on their little fight so they could drive home. She learned all that just from Liam – there was only one message from Wulf.

Remind your father that I'll be sending a check for his car.

The drive to San Francisco felt like it took an eternity. Vieve owned a huge black Cadillac Escalade, it was kind of ridiculous for a single woman. Brie, who Katya hadn't seen once over the weekend, had made her grand entrance when they were leaving. Wearing sunglasses that covered half her face and a tank top paired with yoga pants, she'd climbed into the back seat, stretched out, put her earphones in, and never said a thing.

Vieve made small talk, and Katya managed to join in a little, but she didn't really pay attention. She kept going over the weekend in her mind. Her own actions, Liam's outburst, Wulf's reaction. She was embarrassed, and not just because she'd acted like a fool in front of her family, but because she'd been making some extremely bad choices. Tori had said to do what felt good, but none of it was feeling very good anymore.

Oh yeah, sure, so funny taking them home. Hilarious. It didn't occur to you that by embarrassing them in front of your parents, you might also potentially embarrass you parents!? You're no better than the two of them.

By the time they were driving down Katya's street, she'd pretty much decided to give everything up. If the men wanted to pursue her, fine, but she didn't need to engage them. She didn't need to react to everything and provoke them. Liam was clearly on edge – she hadn't realized how much he was being effected by everything. He was usually so laid back and easy going. If anyone was going to have a meltdown, she would have guessed it would be Wulf. He had, after all, shoved a handful of cake into her face and smeared it all around last time she'd pushed him too far.

When they pulled up in front of her building, Vieve actually got out of the car and came around to the back, helping Katya grab her small weekend bag. Brie didn't say anything – she was still lounging across the back seat, her feet sticking out the window. Katya leaned over the trendy shoes and waved at the young woman.

"It was fun, Brie," she said, though she hadn't spoken to her once all weekend. Brie had never bothered to stop in at the Tocci's party.

"Super duper fun," Brie said, pulling one earphone away.

"Must have been fun to see Wulf again," Katya tried again. She couldn't help it, she had the strongest urge to crack through Brie's prickly exterior.

"Fun isn't a word I would ever use to describe my time with Wulf."

"Huh. Well, did you like Liam? He's a blast, everyone thinks he's fun," Katya pointed out. Brie sighed and picked her earphone back up.

"I went out with some friends, didn't get home till around four in the morning," she replied before plugging back into her music. Conversation over. Katya frowned. It was really Brie's loss, because even though he was somewhat of a bumbling idiot, Liam really was a lot of fun, especially when someone first met him.

"I had fun," Vieve offered, stepping up next to her and smiling that smile that didn't quite reach her eyes. "I went over to see why everyone had disappeared, and Wulfy was pouting in his room and Liam was sitting at the table, nibbling at an apple, looking so sad. So I made food and we had dinner together. He's very nice."

Katya was a little shocked. Calm and cool and perfect Genevieve, sitting down to dinner with loud and raunchy and deviant Liam. It had probably been adorable.

"Good, I'm glad. Well, it was definitely an interesting weekend, that's for sure. It was good to see your mom again. Have you decided whether or not you're going to stay in S.F.?" she asked.

"Yeah," Vieve nodded. "I think I'm going to. I've got a couple job prospects, and of course Wulf would find me somewhere in one of his companies. Since I'll be here for a while, maybe we could have lunch sometime?"

Katya was caught off guard by the desperation in Vieve's voice. It was just under the surface of her words, barely noticeable, but there all the same. It suddenly dawned on Katya that Wulf's sister didn't really have any friends.

"I would like that. I go back to work this week, but call me sometime and we'll get together. I'll bring my roommate Tori, you'll love her," Katya said.

"Whoa, whoa, whoa," a voice said from behind her. She looked around to find Gaten Shepherd approaching them. "Don't tell lies about Tori, now. Love is a strong word."

Vieve looked startled, but her smile was carefully plastered onto her face. Katya chuckled and held up her hand.

"Vieve, this is Gaten, he lives in the building next door. Gate, this is Genevieve Stone – her brother owns the company that manages the buildings," Katya introduced them. Gate grinned and reached out, enthusiastically shaking Vieve's hand.

"Good to meet you. Are you moving in?" he asked. She seemed flustered and worked to pull her hand away.

"Oh, no. No, I live … somewhere else," she stuttered.

"Vieve and I used to be neighbors," Katya took over the conversation. "We grew up next door to each other. She's just moving to San Francisco now."

"Fun! You'll love it here. Nice meeting you. Katya, always good to see you. We'll have to do dinner again sometime soon," he said, pulling her into a hug. She laughed and patted him on the back.

"Soon," she agreed.

"It was nice meeting you, too," Vieve said, holding out her hand again. Gate waved her away.

"C'mon, you know you want a hug, too," he teased, leaning close and hugging her as well.

Katya almost burst out laughing as Vieve's entire face turned red. She was so fair, a blush was impossible to hide. It wasn't nice to snicker, but Katya couldn't help it. She was glad she wasn't the only one who had trouble hiding it when she felt awkward or embarrassed.

He finally pulled back and walked away, waving goodbye to both women. When he'd jogged across the street to his car, Vieve finally cleared her throat.

"Is he your new boyfriend?" she asked nonchalantly. Katya laughed again.

"No. No, I think me having a boyfriend is a dangerous idea. Gate's just a friend, I've house-sat for him when he's gone out of town, he's fixed some stuff around my apartment. Super nice guy. Too nice – since I've lived here, he's had one girlfriend after another who's treated him like garbage. This is the first time since I've met him that he's been single," she explained.

"Oh, that's too bad. I hope he finds a nice girl," Vieve sighed, still watching after the man.

Hmmm, pity I'm so shitty at relationships, or I'd seriously consider playing Cupid for those two.

But Katya didn't want to screw up anyone else's life. She'd done a thorough enough job screwing up her own. So she said another goodbye to Vieve, promising to call at some point, then she stood back and waved as the big car pulled away from the curb.

After the Stone sisters had disappeared around the block, Katya sighed and turned back towards her building. She stared up for a moment, bracing herself for all the questions Tori would ask, then she took a step towards the door.

"Katya."

She froze and looked over. Liam was stepping around the corner of the building, offering a grim smile. He stopped a couple feet away from her, his hands shoved deep into his pants pockets. He looked upset and nervous and like he was going to be sick at any moment.

She took a deep breath and sat her bag down on the sidewalk.

"Katya, I'm so sor -"

She cut him off by leaning in and wrapping her arms around his torso. She let out a sigh as she hugged him tightly, pressing her face into his chest.

"Me, too," she whispered, trying not to cry. He was stunned for a moment, then his arms came around her shoulders.

"You don't have anything to be sorry for," he said in a low voice. "I completely lost it. I … I didn't mean any of it. I was just so angry and … stupid. I'm a stupid, stupid guy."

"No," she shook her head. During her drive home, she'd thought a lot about the things he'd said. "You were right – I'm not some perfect angel. What you did was horrible, and you're still kind of an awful person, and if you ever talk to me like that again, I will punch you in the throat," she started to threaten. He chuckled.

"You'd have to jump to reach."

"But I guess I kind of forgot about your feelings, too. I knew … when it was all happening, I felt bad about the way I treated you. And then I was so angry at you, I convinced myself it didn't matter if I'd done something bad. But that's not right, I'm not that kind of person. And I'm really sorry," she finished.

"Not as sorry as I am."

"Good."

He barked out a laugh, then she felt his lips against the top of her head.

"I don't deserve someone like you in my life," he whispered. She nodded and felt a tear slip down her cheek.

"Probably not. Pity you're impossible to get rid of," she whispered back. He laughed again, then rubbed her back.

"You really could've worked this moment, angel cake. I was literally ready to get down on my knees," he told her. She snorted and pulled away.

"Who says I'm done? The day is still young."

He smiled, then reached out and wiped at her face.

"You are a good person, Katya Tocci."

She sniffled.

"You're an okay person sometimes, Liam Edenhoofernanny."

He burst out laughing, and it broke the tense moment between them.

"I give up. I'm going to legally change my last name to Eden, just so you can pronounce it," he told her. She nodded and picked up her bag.

"Good, it will make life easier."

"Are we really okay?" he checked. She shook her head.

"No. But how about if I promise to treat you better, you promise to *be* better," she offered. He nodded.

"I can do that. That's all I want – to be a better man for you."

"Why?" she asked, and it seemed to surprise him. "I mean, there's lots of women out there, Liam. Women who quite literally throw themselves at you. What you and I had was special, but … is it really worth all this to you?"

He stepped up close to her again.

"Yes. You're so worth it, Katya. I never … you see, before, you were so into Wulf. From the beginning. And that was my fault, it was all a game to me, so I never really tried for you. Not until it was too late and we were in the lie too deep and I was so scared of losing you. But even before it all ended, it was only you, angel cake. The only girl I've ever wanted to spend every moment with," he told her. "The only girl for me."

Wow. She'd never heard him talk that way before – not in so many words, at least. It was still hard to fathom how deep his feelings ran for her. She really hadn't been paying attention. Only her? The only girl?

"Liam," she shook her head. "That's very sweet, but I'm sorry, I just find it hard to believe. The only girl for you? You once told me it felt like if you didn't orgasm twice a day, you were going to explode.

And you and I certainly weren't having sex twice a day."

"Okay, well, no, we weren't," he started stumbling over his words.

"That's part of why I always thought we were casual," she continued. "I was dating Wulf, and I assumed you were still seeing other women."

"Well, I mean, of course I was," he agreed. "Jesus, you've slept with me, I couldn't just let all those women go cold turkey."

Katya laughed.

"See? And that was always in my mind. Even if I was sleeping with you and dating someone else, I knew if it ever got serious with Wulf, something would have to give. Despite everything I've done, I'm still an old fashioned, one-guy-one-girl kinda chick," she told him.

It was kind of eye opening to realize they'd never talked so honestly and openly about their relationship. She'd always been obsessing over Wulf, and Liam had always been laying low, biding his time, playing his game. It should have felt awkward, but it didn't. She felt … *relieved*.

"I can be that way for you," he said quickly. She smiled sadly.

"I don't think I believe that, Liam."

"No. No, I can, and I have – when I say you're it, I mean it. You don't have to make any promises, and if you don't return my feelings at all, fine. I can handle that. But if the only thing holding you back from me is me sleeping with other girls, then you don't have anything to worry about," he assured her, speaking fast.

"So you're saying you haven't slept with anyone since me?" she cocked up an eyebrow. He swallowed thickly.

"Well, uh …" he glanced around the sidewalk, as if the answer was written in the concrete.

"If you're going to start this new-you off with lying, then this is pointless," she stated. He nodded.

"Okay. I did sleep with other women when you and I were sleeping together," he was honest. She nodded.

"See? I get that you think you feel a certain type of way, but you can't just say things like 'you're the only one'," she told him. "You say things, and I believe them, and then I catch you in a lie, and it's the same thing we've been doing, over and over."

"I'm not lying. Since that date we had, right before shit hit the fan," he took a deep, deep breath, "I knew you were it for me. And you've been it ever since."

Katya watched him carefully for a moment. He had lied so convincingly to her for such a long time, trust was tentative at best between them. He was looking at her, his eyes wide and pleading. His lips pressed into a hard line. He was begging her, pleading with her, through his gaze.

"Okay," she said softly. "I'm trusting you – but I'm warning you, this is a big thing you're saying to me. Something you don't even have to lie about, Liam. I won't hate you, I won't be mad at you. But I will feel both those things if I find out you lied to me again."

"You won't," he said quickly. "I mean it, angel cake. I want ... I *am* the man for you, I know it."

"And don't get ahead of yourself," she held up her hand. "I'm still confused and angry and hurt. You may think you're my one and only – that doesn't mean I do."

"*Yet*," he corrected her, finally smiling big. She couldn't help it, she laughed. He was impossible to resist when he was in one of his silly modes.

"Maybe," she agreed. "Possibly. God, what the fuck am I saying? And I'm still not having sex with you!"

"Yet," he said again. She snorted and lightly punched him in the chest.

"I'm all full up on meaningful talks today, I'm going to take a bath and a nap," she told him, heading towards the door to her building. She stopped for moment, then turned back to him. "I haven't talked to you at all today – have you just been lurking out here, all morning, waiting for me to show up?"

"Uh … no," he said, rubbing at the back of his neck. "I got a guy on the inside, you could say."

"Tori," she groaned.

"Yeah. I asked if she knew when you'd be back."

"Did you happen to mention why you came home before me?"

"No. I value my balls, thank you very much."

"Better hold onto them," she warned him as she pulled open the door. "She's going to find out what went down, and she won't be happy."

"I'll prepare myself. Can I call you tomorrow?" he asked, standing at her side. She shrugged.

"Sure, why not, who knows what's going on, anyway."

"And hey, if you change your mind about that no sex thing, I'll be next door all day."

"Okay. You go and hold your breath and wait for me."

Before she could slip through the door, he grabbed her arm and yanked on it. She let out a squeak, then gasped when he kissed her hard. Before she could wrap her brain around what was happening, he let her go, smiled at her, then strode off towards his own building.

Her head was still spinning when she hustled into the building, so it took her a second to realize she'd walked into yet another awkward scenario.

I need to start making some girl friends, jesus. All these men, no wonder I'm always getting into trouble. Maybe I should go move in with Vieve and Brie.

Wulf was standing in the lobby, his arms crossed in front of his chest. He was back in one of his suits, obviously on his way to or from work. He was looking very stern and nodding along as some woman talked to him. Talked to him and laughed at him and kept touching him. His arm, his chest, his shoulder.

While trying to swallow any sort of jealous feelings she might have, Katya looked over the other girl. She lived on the second floor, had long blonde hair, pretty blue eyes, and really big boobs. She also drove some sort of expensive looking car and only wore designer clothing. That was all Katya knew about her.

… that, and now I know she's apparently attracted to rich looking handsome men. Slut.

She took deep breath and shook her head. She was the one playing silly games, she was the one who had said no sex, and she was the one who kept making it plain that she had no intention of getting back together with him. So she had absolutely zero right to get jealous. Less than zero. The way she'd been acting, she should be congratulating him.

Yuuuuup, I'll get right on that.

She tried hugging the left side of the lobby, hoping to get by unnoticed. But of course, life wasn't that kind to her. He saw her before she could sneak behind him and turned in her direction.

"Tocci," he barked out. "You never answered my message."

"Uh …" she responded articulately.

"Vieve messaged me from the road – I've been waiting down here for fifteen minutes," he informed her, as if they'd had plans to meet or something. She stared at him, not sure how to respond, when his new friend joined the conversation.

"Oh, you're the baker! You live upstairs!" the woman gushed. Katya glanced between them and Wulf slowly smiled.

"Yup, I do. Katya Tocci," she said, walking over to join the pair.

"Lana Tisdale," blondie introduced herself. "So nice to meet you! You know our fearless leader here? Mr. Stone manages the building."

Katya looked back at him. His smile had gotten a lot bigger.

"Yes, we're acquainted. How are you, Mr. Stone?" she asked.

"Surprisingly good. Like I said, I was waiting for you to get home when Ms. Tisdale introduced herself – she'd gotten her key stuck in her mailbox," he told her.

"And can you believe it, he got it unstuck. Magic fingers on this one," Lana Tisdale giggled. "So I'm taking him to lunch to say thank you."

"I figured you'd gone to lunch with Vieve," Wulf explained. Katya let out a dramatic sigh.

"I'm happy for both of you. If you'll excuse me now, I have a shower that's calling my name. Have a good time," she said, scooching around them while she talked and then making a beeline for the elevator.

"Tocci."

She made a face as the doors slid open, then looked over her shoulder at Wulf.

"Can't avoid me forever," he said, still giving her that shit-eating grin.

On the elevator ride up to her floor, she ground her teeth together. Stupid blonde. Stupid Wulf. Stupid lunch. Stuck key? Ridiculous. And the "can't avoid me" sign off – she wasn't avoiding him! He's the one who ran away at the crack of dawn!

She didn't know how much more she could handle. First her break through with Liam, and then a run-in with Wulf. As she let herself into her apartment, she thought again about what she'd realized over the weekend – her little torture plan wasn't working so well. She wasn't getting back at anyone, and she was just making herself – and apparently Liam – miserable in the process. Wulf, however, was rebounding better than she would've thought. Stupid lunch date with a blonde, gorgeous, ridiculous, horri-

Katya gasped and dropped her bag, coming to a stop in the middle of her kitchen. At least, in what used to be her kitchen.

Gone were the scratched counter tops and old cupboards. The ugly sink and ancient fridge. Her thrift store table. Even the light green tile floor was nowhere in sight. All of it, just gone.

Sometime since she'd left Friday morning, her entire kitchen had been gutted and replaced. She was staring at laminate wood floors and granite counter tops, with a matching island standing in the center of it all – complete with four bar stools in front of it.

She hurried around it and came to a stop in front of a state of the art propane stove. Five burners and a huge oven, with a second oven built into the cabinets next to it. Everything was stainless steel and brand new, complete with the tags and protective film still on them.

How had this happened!? She'd only been gone three days! She peered into the new sink – a large, farmhouse style in a brushed satin finish. Deep enough to hold her huge cooking pots, with a long necked faucet that was perfect for filling those pots.

She was turning a circle, taking it all in, still shocked. She'd asked for a new oven – not an entirely new kitchen. This was amazing. How had it gotten done so fast? Was this Liam's doing, more apologies for his behavior?

When she'd turned back to the stove, she saw something she'd missed during her first pass through. A folded card was propped up at the back of the appliance, resting against a subway tile back splash. She plucked it off the counter, noticing that there was now recessed lighting built into the bottom of her cupboards, and opened the card.

You can say thank you in the form of something short and lacy. I expect dinner at six o'clock promptly.
—W

Red. So much red, clouding her vision. A nuclear bomb of anger went off in the back of her skull, and the note got crumpled in her fist. First she had to witness him flirting with some random chick, then rubbing the whole lunch date in her face, and now she finds out he was trying to buy her forgiveness and/or sexual compliance via a new kitchen. What, he was going to go bang some blonde chick during lunch, then have Katya for seconds?

I am NOT seconds.

She was storming off the elevator into the lobby before she even realized she was moving. She took out her phone and texted Liam, hoping he'd answer right away. But by the time she'd reached his apartment, he still hadn't answered. She groaned and knocked once on his door, then burst through it. He was in the kitchen, hidden behind his open fridge door.

"We need to talk!" she snapped, letting the door slam shut behind her.

"Huh?" he called back, his voice muffled.

"I think we should have sex, right now," she said, pacing back and forth by his couch. He finally stood upright, letting the fridge fall shut.

"I'm sorry … what?"

He sounded so caught off guard, his voice was even different. She glanced at him, noticing that he was only wearing a towel wrapped around his waist, then she kept pacing.

"Sex. I know I said no sex, but what the hell, it's been a long time, and I'm *really* pissed off, and everything is fucked up anyway," she growled, pounding her fist into her palm. There was a pause as she made her way to the front windows, then she heard footsteps behind her.

"You want to have sex with me, like right this minute," he double checked. She looked over her shoulder, then went back to the view.

"Yup. You showered really fast – it's only been like five or ten minutes," she commented, staring down at the street. A white Mercedes was parked at the curb in front of her building. She glared down at it.

"What can I say, I'm fast. So are we doing this, or what?"

He still sounded strange, so she turned to face him. She frowned as she looked up at him. He was standing at the other end of the long couch, smiling back at her. Something seemed off, but she couldn't quite put her finger on it.

"No," she sighed. "I'm just … I got my feathers ruffled. Did you know he was going to do that?"

"Who?"

"Wulf?"

"What wolf?"

"Uh, that asshole you hate – *that* Wulf," she repeated herself. He thought for a second, then his eyes got wide.

"Ooohhh, yeah. Yeah, that Wulf. Okay. Yeah. Asshole. No. No! What did he do now!?" he exclaimed. She shook her head.

"What's wrong with you? Have you been drinking?" she checked. He shrugged.

"Maybe a little."

"Jesus, Liam, it's ten in the morning."

"Hey, it's six at night in London," he countered, smiling big at her. "So about that sex. Maybe we can just try it, for old times sake, and you can tell me -"

Before he could finish, though, he was cut off by the sound of the front door opening. There was a rustling sound as grocery bags were kicked through it.

"Sorry, I decided to stop down at the corner store. That dickbag is always short changing me, I had to fight to get my five bucks back."

Liam was striding into the apartment, scooting bags with his feet, his arms full of other bags.

Katya's jaw dropped open and she stared at him for a second. Then stared at the Liam that was standing in front of her. Then back at the other Liam. Her brain short circuited.

Why is it someone can say they have a twin, and you know what an identical twin is, yet it's still shocking when you meet them.

"You're Landon," she blurted out, pointing at the man in the towel. Liam finally glanced up from his grocery scooting.

"Hey, I didn't know you were here," he said.

"I … I …" she stammered, her eyes still bouncing back and forth between them.

"She was just graciously offering to have sex with me," Landon said. "But I told her I couldn't, since I'd just taken a shower."

Both men laughed.

She couldn't stop staring. She knew she was being rude, but it was amazing. Two Liam's, standing in front of her.

Though the more she stared, the more she could see the

differences. Landon was a different kind of tan – super dark, the mark of someone who'd spent *a lot* of time in the sun. He was also more weathered, making him look just a tad bit older. His hair was longer and liberally sun streaked, and was being held back by a head band, she noticed for the first time. And where Liam had a silly, goofy kind of grin always at the ready and a good natured feel to his attitude, none of that was present in Landon. His smile was more cunning, and his tone of voice was like someone who was laughing *AT* her, not with her.

But other than that, they seemed to be carbon copies of each other. Same height, same eye color, same bone structure, same body – Katya was very familiar with Liam's naked torso, so it was kind of shocking to realize she was also intimately familiar with Landon's. She had to force her eyes to not dip down to his towel.

"I'm sorry, what?" Liam scratched his head.

"I … I thought he was you," Katya stammered. "I didn't know he was here."

"Oh god," Liam groaned. "I'm sorry, Katya. What did you say to her, Landon?"

His brother shrugged.

"Probably the same stuff you would say if a gorgeous girl burst in on you and demanded to have sex. Katya, it was a pleasure. Hopefully next time we meet, I'll be wearing more clothing, or you'll be wearing less," Landon said before nodding his head at her. Then he walked back into the bathroom and shut the door behind him. Liam hurried to her side.

"Sorry – when I got home last night, he called me from the bus station. He flew to L.A. from Mexico City, then took Greyhound here. I would've warned you, but you and I had our own shit to deal with, and I didn't think you'd be coming over," he told her. She held up her hand.

"It's fine. I barged in, he was just messing with me. You said identical, but it's so …" she searched for the word. Liam smiled.

"Overwhelming?"

"Yes. That's a lot of male-ness, for one room," she told him, and he laughed at her.

"Thanks, I'll take that as a compliment. We get a lot of attention if we ever go out together."

"I'm sure. How long is he staying?"

"He's sort of avoiding home right now," Liam said, rubbing at the back of his neck. "I think he's gonna be around for a week, maybe two."

"That's … nice."

Katya suddenly felt awkward. There was no privacy in Liam's studio-esque apartment, they wouldn't be able to get away from Landon, and she didn't want to discuss any of her problems in front of him.

Luckily, Liam seemed to sense all that, and a huge grin spread across his face.

"Hey, I have a great idea. Come with me."

He left all the groceries on the floor, except for a six pack of beer. As he scooped it up off the ground, he hollered to his brother that he'd be back later. Then he grabbed Katya's hand and led her back to her building. Up all the floors in the elevator. Out onto her rooftop.

She hadn't been back up there since their fight. She hadn't been able to bring herself back there – too many memories with him, and she didn't trust them. Which were real, and which were calculated and fake? She frowned as he dragged her across the roof and deposited her on the love seat.

"Is this okay?" he asked, glancing at her as he unscrewed the lid from one of the bottles.

"Um … I guess it had to happen at some point," she replied, glancing around.

"You don't want to be in my place while Landon is there. He's … special. He takes getting used to," he told her.

"He seems like it. He's a doctor?"

"Yeah, but also a massive asshole."

"Ah."

"And I don't want to go to your apartment until you invite me, so I figured this was a nice halfway point," he explained. She finally smiled at him.

"Thank you, Liam. For being understanding."

"This is good, right?" he asked, handing her a beer and then reaching down to grab one of his own. "I think we're going to be … better."

He spoke tentatively, not with any of the boldness he'd been displaying over the past weekend. The cocky, overly confident, competitive Liam really seemed to have taken a break. She was glad – she didn't like that version of him as much as she liked him being natural.

"Yeah. Yeah, I think maybe so," she agreed with a laugh. "Maybe you should've called me a bitch who used you a lot sooner."

"I didn't mean that," he grumbled, taking a long drink from his bottle.

"No, you did. And you were kinda right. I *was* using you, sometimes. I can remember thinking it and feeling bad about it, yet I never did anything about it. Pretty bitchy."

"Well, if you're saying it …"

"But you also used me – not to mention lied to my face, manipulated me, violated me … should I go on?" she snapped. He shook his head.

"Nope. I think I've got it," he assured her.

Katya nodded and sipped at her own beer while she looked out over the neighborhood. She'd always enjoyed their little rooftop jaunts. Liam didn't allow other people to come up there, she was the only one with a key, so the space really did feel special. Somewhere he'd only ever been with her; somewhere she'd never shared with anyone but him.

"So am I going to have to watch you make out with Wulf in front of me anymore?" Liam suddenly blurted out. She snorted, almost choking on her drink.

"I don't think so," she said. "I thought … I don't know, I thought it would be fun to make you guys feel like shit. Sort of play you against each other. But *I* just wound up feeling shitty."

"Me, too."

"Wulf three, probably."

"I doubt he even has normal human feelings," Liam pointed out. Katya frowned.

"You'd be surprised.".

"Can I propose a deal?" Liam suggested. She glanced back at him.

"What kind of deal?"

"How about – I say I'm sorry, for everything. I promise to tell you the truth from here on out. And I try my hardest to prove to you that I care about you, every bit as much as he ever did," he laid everything out. She took a deep breath.

"Okay."

"And in exchange, we start over."

She stared at him for a long second, her lips pressed into a hard line. It was a difficult decision. Part of her screamed "*yes, please god, just let all this bullshit end*", yet another part of her whispered "*no, what they did is unforgettable – how can you trust him*", and she wasn't sure which voice to listen to, which way to turn.

But he was staring at her, looking past her eyes and straight into her soul. Pleading with her again. And god, how she'd missed him. How she'd needed him, the last couple weeks. She blinked back tears and slowly nodded.

"Okay," she whispered, then cleared her throat. "Okay, you promise and you try, and I accept your apology, and we start over."

He smiled. It was small and it was sad, but it was genuine. Then he sat up straight and held out his hand.

"Hi, I'm Liam Edenhoff," he introduced himself. She smiled and wiped at her eyes before shaking his hand.

"Hi Mr. Edenhofferhana, I'm Katya Tocci," she laughed. He chuckled and squeezed her hand between his.

"We can work on the name," he told her. "I'm a thirty-two year old ex-surfer who generally enjoys doing as little as possible while eating as many tacos as possible. I own two buildings in downtown San Francisco, and I own a successful sex club."

"Sex club, huh. Sounds crazy. Way too wild for a simple little baker like me," she said.

"I bet you'd surprise yourself. You'll have to come check it out sometime," he offered.

"Maybe I will, Liam."

"Or," he took a deep breath. "You could go out on a date with me."

She lost her smile.

"I don't know. I don't think I'm in the dating market right now," she said slowly. He nodded.

"Okay, I can respect that – but if you ever decide to dive back in again, I hope you'll think of me. I think I could show you a really good time," he said, staring at her again.

"I'm sure you could, Liam. I'm really, really sure you could."

19

THEY SPENT THE REST OF THE DAY AND HALF THE NIGHT ON THE ROOF — ONLY leaving to grab a pitcher of margaritas from Katya's apartment. He called into his club, telling Tori that she was in charge of the downstairs bar for the evening.

Though part of her still felt like a traitor to herself and to the female sex in general, she was happy that they'd moved past his betrayal. It felt good to be laughing with him again. In the short time they'd known each other, they'd really forged a bond together. And it felt better now – there were no secrets between. No wolf lurking in the shadows – literally. They could talk openly and freely, about anything and everything.

"*Tell me about Landon.*"

She'd waited a while to ask that – there was a tension between the brothers that wasn't necessarily obvious, but she could still feel it. She'd been surprised to learn his twin would be staying with him, and she wondered how Liam was handling life with a roommate.

She learned that Landon was technically the older of the two, and he seemed to take that title very literally. He'd always been serious – quite a contrast to Liam's laid back personality, especially since they were twins. Landon had thrown himself into school and college and his work. Gotten married, then gotten divorced. Then he'd shocked everyone by joining an aide group and traveling to South America.

There was a lot of bitterness in all that information. Liam felt like the second-best twin. The also-ran, the after-thought. There was Landon, acing everything he put his mind to, traveling the world, helping people, saving lives. And there was Liam, struggling in school, inheriting his living, needing Wulf to help him get the club.

Even worse was the fact that Liam felt like everyone was idolizing a sham. Landon may have been a doctor, sure, and he may have seemingly selflessly dedicated his like to an aide group, okay. But that didn't all translate to him being a good guy. Liam was privy to Landon's darker side, something the other twin kept hidden from the rest of his family.

A serial dater with more women under his belt than even Liam, he also had a problem with drugs that stemmed back all the way to high school. On top of that, he just wasn't a very nice person – his shame at his addiction and his lofty position as a doctor had turned him into a nasty, snobby, vindictive person. It killed Liam to see his family worshiping this man who had lied to them, stolen from them, and hidden himself from them.

But he let Landon stay with him because even though they had their differences, he said, that was still his twin. It was hard to look into what was essentially a mirror and say "no" – plus, Liam knew if he did, it would come back to haunt him. Landon would go home and claim that his brother wouldn't let him visit, or something. Liam didn't want to deal with a dozen phone calls from his family that would just result in him caving and letting Landon stay, anyway.

"*Don't trust him,*" Liam had warned. "*And don't listen to him. He'll either treat you like you're stupid, so you'll let him get away with anything, or he'll lie to you, try to get you to do anything.*"

"*Jesus, being a lying shit hole seems to run in your family.*"

"Watch it, angel cake. We called a truce, remember."

Around two in the morning, Katya had to call it quits. She'd gotten up early to drive in from Carmel, and the day had taken an emotional toll on her. Dealing with Liam and coming to an understanding with him, then meeting his twin and dealing with all those issues. And of course, as always, running around in the back of her mind was Wulf.

She not only hadn't made him dinner, she hadn't bothered answering her phone when he'd called. No doubt he'd stopped by her apartment, and of course she hadn't been there. He'd be pissed.

Added to that, she still wasn't sure how to feel about him. She'd somewhat forgiven Liam, so it stood to reason that she should extend the same courtesy to Wulf. But his betrayal felt different from Liam's, she wasn't sure if she was ready to forgive Wulf. Wasn't sure if he was ready to truly apologize. She couldn't imagine him breaking down on a street sidewalk and begging her to forgive him with only a look.

So when she said goodnight to Liam, she was still thoroughly confused about how to move forward with the two men in her life. She changed into pajamas and brushed her teeth and climbed into bed, then got to her new favorite hobby.

Staring at the ceiling.

It was all so different. Knowing the two men knew each other, knowing she'd slept with them both and they both not only knew about it, but had talked about it. Discussed it. Before, she'd never considered Liam a contender because he'd never tried. Now, it was at the forefront of his intentions. Did she want to consider dating him? Could she ever forgive Wulf?

I'm going to be glad when I go back to work – I'm ready to have other things to concentrate on.

"Wait, wait, wait," Tori practically yelled, slapping her hands down on the kitchen island as she turned to face Katya. It was noon the day after Katya had come home, but the first they'd seen each other.

"I know what you're thinking, and don't -" Katya tried to cut her off.

"There's *TWO* of them!?"

"- get excited."

"Two Liams. Two! I mean, wow. I can't even imagine. And you saw him? Are they really identical?" Tori asked. Katya had made the mistake of mentioning Liam's brother.

"I did see him, and yes, they're almost indistinguishable. I was talking to Landon for a while before Liam walked in and I realized it wasn't him," she replied.

"I have to meet him."

"Well, don't hold your breath. They don't get along too well, and Liam says his brother is kind of a jerk. I don't think he'll be coming around the club, or anything."

"Whatever. What about this kitchen, huh? Isn't it amazing?" Tori asked, switching the subject abruptly and smoothing her hand over the granite island top.

"Yeah, about this kitchen – why didn't you mention it in your texts?" Katya asked, putting her hands on her hips. She and Tori had texted back and forth throughout the weekend, but there had been no mention of a new kitchen being installed in any of the messages.

"I thought it was supposed to be a surprise," her roommate shrugged. "These workers showed up Friday, right after you left. They had copies of your maintenance requests, and a whole letter from the management company, signed by your Wulf-man, so I just stepped aside and let them in. They were almost done by Friday night, and then when I got home Saturday night, everything was in place."

"He's crazy," Katya sighed, rubbing her fingertips across her forehead. "I can't believe he did this. And then he expected me to make him dinner while he was out eating with that blonde bombshell from the second floor."

"Ouch."

"Tell me about it."

"Sounds like being a heart breaker isn't working out so well," Tori said in a careful voice.

"This was your idea!"

"Um, no it wasn't."

"Yes, it was! You said to do whatever I wanted!"

"Yeah, I did. And you did that, and it was good that you did, and now you're going to do something else. That's how it works," her roommate explained. Katya blinked her eyes a couple times.

"I'm pretty sure that made no sense," she pointed out. Tori smiled brightly.

"Good. Gotta keep you on your toes. So break this down for me – you and Liam are officially friends again," she checked. Katya frowned, but nodded. "And you and Wulf are …"

"Confusing?"

"Sounds about right. Got any plans with either of them for to-night?" Tori asked, dancing around the island and opening the large fridge.

"No, not as of right now. I'm gonna take it easy today. First day back is tomorrow," Katya reminded her friend.

"Ooohhh, right. Exciting! I bet you'll be glad to get back to the shop, huh?"

Katya nodded, twisting a hank of hair around one finger. She was excited to get back to work, but she'd also started thinking more and more about breaking out on her own. Having her own shop would make it easier for her to set her own hours – not to mention, she could make her own rules, set her own prices. She had a lot of freedom at Fondant's, and she loved the owners, but still. She was long overdue to branch out on her own.

Katya left Tori alone to make a lunch and went to take a shower. When she was done, she wrapped her thick hair up in a towel and scampered into her room. She didn't plan on going anywhere, so she slipped on a comfy pair of jeans and a simple tank top. Barefoot and not wearing any make up, she made her way back to the front of the apartment.

"Did you try the stove?" she asked, bending at the waist and vigorously rubbing the towel over her head. "I haven't cooked a meal on propane in so long. We should think of something yummy to make for dinner."

"Sounds good to me. I like my steaks rare."

She snapped upright, her hair falling all over her face. Liam was in her kitchen, leaning back against the island while playing with his phone. Katya glanced around, but Tori was nowhere to be seen.

"How long have you -"

"About thirty minutes."

"And where is -"

"She was making something that smelled like burning, then threw it away, then said she was gonna go to that place you went that one time, and she'd see you tonight, after she got off work," he answered, standing upright and finally slipping his phone into his back pocket.

"Oh. Okay. What are you doing here?" Katya tried a new line of questioning.

"I don't usually go into work till after two," he said, which she already knew. "But Lan is passed out on my couch, so I didn't want to be there. I figured I'd see what you were up to."

It took Katya a second to catch on that *Lan* meant his brother Landon.

"I didn't really have any plans for today," she replied.

"Sounds like we have the same plans, then. So what happened in here? I don't remember all this," he commented, turning around and taking in the new kitchen, as if he'd just noticed it.

"That's why I came over to your place the other day – Wulf had all this done, while we were in Carmel. I asked for a new oven. He took my request a little too seriously," she explained.

"Damn, he really did. It looks nice," Liam mumbled. She nodded.

"It's gorgeous."

"You like it?" he asked, glancing back at her.

"Yeah, what's not to like? Lots of counter space, two ovens, state of the art appliances," she said. He frowned.

"Have you seen him since he did this?"

"No. Haven't talked to him at all. He left a note, saying I was supposed to make him dinner last night, but ..." Katya let her voice trail off. Liam's smile returned.

"But you spent last night with me," he filled in. She nodded.

"I did."

"Good girl, good for you. Stick it to the man. C'mon, let's get cooking."

It was actually pretty fun. Liam always managed to shock her a little; it turned out he wasn't a half bad cook. It shouldn't have surprised her, really – when Liam liked something, he threw himself into it, and Liam *loved* food.

Even though it was only the afternoon, they made a full meal. Asparagus with a hollandaise sauce, steak, rice pilaf, and even a batch of chocolate fudge cupcakes. While the desserts were cooling on a rack by the sink, they carried their food into the living room and sat at the coffee table, an eighties movie playing on the tv in the background.

"Wow, you can really cook, woman," he mumbled through a mouthful of food. She smiled, nibbling at her asparagus.

"Thanks. Baking is my thing, obviously, but I like all kinds of cooking," she said.

"You can cook for me *anytime*, angel cake, and I really mean that."

"You couldn't afford my hourly rate."

He didn't say anything after that, just licked his plate clean. Then he groaned and laid back into the couch. She smiled and ate a couple more bites, then shoved her plate aside and put her elbows on her knees, her chin in her hands.

"It was so good, Katya. Thank you," he sighed, rubbing a hand over her back.

"You're welcome," she said, rolling her head around on her shoulders. His hand moved, working its way under her hair and rubbing at her neck.

"I haven't seen your hair down in a long time," he commented. She groaned and sat upright, leaning into his touch a little.

"Yeah, I guess not," she said, tilting her back to him so he could rub harder.

"Looks good."

"Okay, enough," she laughed, laying back and forcing him to move his hand. "No flirting, Edenhoff."

"Oh my god!" he all but yelled, sitting upright. She put a hand to her chest, shocked by his outburst.

"What? What!?"

"My name!" he laughed, looking down at her. "You got my name right. For like the first time ever."

"Oh jesus," she groaned. "Liam, I've always known your name. You're just fun to mess with."

He playfully glared, then poked her in the side.

"And I'm the bad guy, huh? All this time, I didn't think you cared enough to remember," he grumbled, continuing to poke her all over as she laughed and squirmed.

"That's awful!" she gasped for air. "Of course I cared, I just thought it was fun to annoy you!"

"Exactly," he said, using both hands to tickle her. "You're an awful, awful girl."

"Well, I learned it from you, Edenhooferhasslehoffer."

They were all but wrestling at that point, Liam leaning over and following her as she squiggled down the couch. She kicked his plate off the coffee table, which caused her to shriek with laughter. He pinned down her legs after that by straddling her thighs, which left her pretty much at his mercy.

"I'd forgotten," he was panting for air when he finally stopped.

"What?" she gasped.

"How stunning you can be," he said in a soft voice.

She choked on air for a minute, struggling to shove her wild hair out of her face. She felt him move, then one of his hands was in her hair, helping her. He tucked the still damp strands behind her ear, then he left his hand against the side of her neck.

"You can't just say stuff like that," she whispered. He smiled.

"But I said I wouldn't lie anymore."

She was working that over in her brain when he leaned down and kissed her. She blinked a couple times, unable to focus on him because he was so close. Then she softly moved and let her eyes fall shut.

This is a bad idea. Stop him. Stop this. This isn't what you want.

Instead of saying all that, though, she moaned. He shifted around, bracing an arm on the side of her to hold himself upright, then his tongue was in her mouth, causing her to gasp. Both his hands were in her hair, pulling lightly as he kissed her harder.

They'd shared a kiss in Carmel, and he'd kissed her on the street, but it wasn't the same. It had been a long time since they'd been intimate together in any real way. She'd almost forgotten what it was like – how warm he was, the way he smelled and tasted. How his hands were bold as they wandered over her body, but also gentle.

Katya was a red-blooded woman who hadn't had sex in a long time, and Liam Edenhoff was a stupidly sexy man who was very good at what he did, seduction wise. She got lost in the moment, lost in his heat. Gasping and moaning underneath him, arching her back so she could feel his chest against hers.

When he bit into her bottom lip, she also felt his hand on her breast. It startled her a little, the long ignored nerve endings suddenly receiving so much attention. It reset her brain a little, shocked

190

her into the here and now. As his hand wandered farther down, she opened her eyes again. Sucked in a deep breath of air while his teeth cut into the side of her jaw.

"Liam," she breathed his name.

"God, you feel so good," he groaned in response as he shoved her tank top so it was scrunched up under her breasts.

"Liam," she repeated herself while trying to clear her throat.

"A long time, angel cake," he continued talking, and she felt his hand moving between them. Fumbling to undo his belt buckle. "I have been dreaming about this for a long time."

"Stop," she said more forcefully, placing her hands over his before he could shove his jeans down.

"What?" he asked, finally lifting his head, seeming to realize for the first time that she wasn't an active participant anymore.

"I ... I'm sorry, I can't," she whispered, blinking up at him.

"Oh. Oh god, I'm sorry," he started speaking fast. "You said you weren't ready for anything, I wasn't even thinking. You just ... I just ... god, I'm sorry."

He started to move off her, but Katya felt bad. She'd kissed him back, she'd been moaning and whining and rubbing against him. She was just as guilty for starting something she couldn't finish, so she made him stop. Wrapped her arms around his shoulders and forced him to lay down flat on top of her.

"Don't be sorry," she told him, combing her fingers through the back of his hair. "It was nice – so nice, I forgot what was even happening."

"Thanks," he mumbled into her neck.

"I just don't want to use you again, and I still don't know what I want. I don't want to do something we'll both just regret later," she said softly. There was a long pause, then his arms wiggled their way around her waist.

"I could never regret sex with you," he informed her, and she barked out a laugh.

"Good to know."

"Do you want me to leave? I don't want you to feel uncomfortable," he asked, letting her go and pushing himself upright.

"No, you don't have to go. Unless *you* feel uncomfortable," she told him.

"Um, I'm *extremely* uncomfortable," he laughed. She could tell – she could feel the bulge in his pants against her thigh. "But I'd like to stay. If that's okay."

She nodded and scooted to the edge of the couch. He fell into place against the cushions, spooning her from behind. She got comfortable, resting her head on his bicep as he stretched his arm under her neck. He draped his other arm across her waist, his fingers brushing against the exposed skin above her pants.

"This is definitely okay, Liam. Thanks," she sighed, focusing on the tv.

"Thank *you*," he breathed in her ear, making her shiver.

Good idea or bad idea, this feels pretty damn good.

––––––––––◆––––––––––

Wulf usually thought of himself as a smart man, but sometimes, he got confused. It seemed to happen a lot around a certain baker. So he would switch tactics. Try different things to try and keep her on her toes. Maybe confuse her for once.

Like playing along with her game.

Or installing a new kitchen in her apartment while they were gone.

Even trying to annoy her with his demand for dinner.

Then there was the run in with their ridiculous blonde neighbor, that had been rather fortuitous. Katya's face had been priceless.

Now, though, he was realizing he was kind of an idiot. All those things had just riled Katya up, and a riled up Katya was more like a hurricane than a rational person. It emboldened her and caused her to react rashly. Then after setting all that into motion, he'd given her thirty-two hours alone. Time to ruminate on what he'd done and retaliate.

And, he realized as he stood in her living room, time for her to reconnect with Eden.

When he'd discovered that her front door was unlocked, he'd let himself in, expecting to find her poking around her new kitchen. Instead, he'd found her asleep. She was on her back on her sofa, breathing heavy, her hair absolutely everywhere. He couldn't remember the last time he'd seen it down, it was a lot longer than he'd remembered.

He also didn't remember her having a tumor, but she seemed to have grown one. A six-foot-two, one hundred and seventy pound tumor. Liam was was on his side, his face buried in her hair, one of his arms draped across her stomach, one of his legs stretched across both of hers.

They were both deep asleep, Liam even snoring lightly. It looked like they had been that way for a while. There was a plate half full of food on the coffee table, and it was all cold to the touch. Most of the lights in the apartment were off, just the tv was on and the lights in the kitchen.

Wulf stayed completely silent and let his eyes wander over them, trying to figure out what exactly had gone on. Had they had sex? If they had, how would he handle that? Not well, he was sure. No, if he found out they'd slept together, he was pretty sure he was going to put his fist through something. Most likely Liam's face.

But he didn't think they had slept together. A glance down the hall showed that Katya's bed was made and free of wrinkles. Both of them were wearing all their clothing; Liam even had his shoes on. If he had to guess, he would say they'd had a meal together, then they'd cuddled up on the couch to watch a movie, falling asleep after a long enough time.

He took a deep breath and tilted his head to the side, cracking his neck. Trying to lower his blood pressure. He couldn't get mad. Wulfric Stone didn't get mad. Getting mad didn't help anything – it just ended in people fighting in a garage, or throwing cake in a reception hall. So even though he was seething angry and he wanted to commit murder and it felt like part of his soul was dying when he looked at another man touching Katya, he schooled his features into a mask of neutrality. Then he cleared his throat. Loudly.

Katya's head twitched, then she yawned and stretched out, raising her arms above her head. He cleared his throat again, and then counted to ten in his head when she rubbed her hand up and down Liam's arm.

"You're snoring," she murmured. Liam snorted.

"*You're* snoring," he grumbled back.

Wulf full out coughed.

"What time is it?" she yawned again, struggling to sit up a little. "I can't believe we fell asleep. You're so late for -"

She completely froze when her eyes locked onto Wulf. No hint of sleepiness remained and while he watched, she swallowed thickly and began tapping Liam's arm.

"When I said you had to make dinner," Wulf finally spoke. "I meant *for me*."

"This is not what it looks like," she spoke quickly. He rolled his eyes.

"Don't be cliché, Tocci."

"*Liam!*"

A solid punch to his shoulder finally brought the other man out of his sleep. He snorted again and pushed himself up, then wiped at his jaw.

"How long were we out for?" he asked through a yawn. Katya slithered out from under him, falling onto the floor.

"We have company," she replied, ignoring his question and all but leaping to her feet.

"Tori's supposed to be at work," Liam mumbled, finally shifting into a sitting position. He stretched his arms above his head, then finally looked around the room. He paused when his eyes landed on Wulf, then he slowly smiled. "*Oh.* Oh, this is too good."

"Please, Liam," Katya groaned. "Don't make this worse than it already is."

"Don't have the time," the other man sighed. He climbed to his feet and made a big show of buttoning his pants and putting his belt back to rights. Wulf arched up an eyebrow and glanced at Katya. Her face was beet red, her lips pressed into such a hard line, they weren't even visible.

"Please, don't let me interrupt anything," Wulf said. Liam chuckled.

"Don't worry – you're *too late* to interrupt anything."

Katya's jaw dropped at that statement, but Liam didn't give her a chance to argue or deny anything. He leaned down over her and pulled her close, kissing the top of her head before ruffling up her hair.

"I'll call you tomorrow. Thanks for dessert."

With a wink and pat on Wulf's shoulder, Liam left the apartment. The door falling shut behind him was loud in the quiet space, almost seeming to echo. Katya stared at Wulf for a long time, looking like she was caught somewhere between nervous and angry.

This should get very interesting, very quickly.

This is going to get very ugly, very quickly.

Katya stared at Wulf for what felt like an hour. His face was completely blank, not one thought or emotion showing on it. That made her even more nervous – like the calm before the storm.

"Um …" she finally spoke. "What, uh … what are you doing here?"

"You missed dinner last night," he replied. "I wanted to see what

195

you were up to tonight."

"Oh."

"Apparently, you were very busy."

"We watched a movie and we fell asleep," she said quickly. He nodded.

"Of course, obviously. I often undo my pants in order to enjoy a good show."

"Don't be ridiculous. Do you really think I was banging Liam on my couch just now?" she asked, throwing her hands up. He shrugged.

"Honestly, I don't know what to think about you anymore."

She glared at him, then bent over and grabbed Liam's plate from where she'd knocked it onto the floor. She placed it on top of her own and carried them into the kitchen.

"You know what? Screw you. You could've walked in on me blowing him, and it's okay, because not only are you *NOT* my boyfriend, but this is *MY* apartment, which you shouldn't be walking into, *PERIOD*," she informed him while she scraped her left overs into the trash.

"Are you really going to lecture me about coming in here uninvited?" he asked, standing on the other side of the island. "I find that hilarious, considering I caught you walking around my apartment the other day, when I wasn't even home."

"Don't even try to make me feel bad about that – you never ask before you do anything, why should the rest of us be any different?" she asked, tossing the plates into the sink.

"Is that a serious question?"

"Screw you. What do you want, Wulf?"

"I told you. Dinner."

After she'd rinsed the plates off, she turned around to face him, folding her arms across her chest.

"I am not making you dinner," she told him.

"I guess I got here too late. Tomorrow?" he asked.

"Not then, either."

"I spent a lot of money on this kitchen, Tocci. Pick a date that's good for you," he told her. She shook her head.

"I didn't ask for a whole new kitchen, *Stone*. You can't buy my forgiveness, or my love, or whatever it is you're trying to do," she said.

"Oh really? Then tell me what Eden did. What kind of lie did you believe this time, so I can know what kind of bullshit to spout off to get you to forgive me," he replied.

"I don't get you. You talk to me like I'm the stupidest person you've ever met. If that's how you feel, then leave," she snapped, pointing at the exit.

"I can't help it when that's how you *act*," he snapped back.

"This is unbelievable. You're jealous because you saw me napping with another man, so you're throwing a temper tantrum. What about blondie this afternoon!?" she yelled at him.

"You don't get to be jealous, Tocci," he growled, and then slipped off his jacket while he spoke, tossing it onto the back of one of the stools. "You forfeited that emotion."

"What are you even talking about?"

"*You* cut me out!" he yelled, shocking her a little and pointing his finger in her face. "You wouldn't talk to me, you wouldn't answer your phone. You want to play your little games, and you refuse to forgive me. So I've done everything you've wanted. I've been nice to you, I've apologized to you, I have watched you kiss another man and sleep with another man. I've even played along with your game, *just like you wanted*. How can you possibly be jealous!? *You* don't want *me*, so clearly, you can't be jealous."

"I *did not* sleep with him," she hissed, leaning forward and slapping his hand away. "And I never said I was jealous, and besides, you lied to me! You lied, over and over again, and you treated me like garbage."

"Not always, Tocci. You love acting like it was the worst thing ever, but there were some pretty good goddamn moments. But apparently, they're not worth remembering. Only Eden's memories are good enough for you," he said.

That actually hurt. It was ridiculous, she knew, but a pang of guilt cut through to her core. She knew his actions had ensured that she never needed to feel guilty about anything ever, but she couldn't help it. The heart reacts how it reacts, and to hear him say he thought she didn't care about her memories with him, it *hurt*. She shrank back, bumping into the counter behind her.

"How can you say that?" she asked. "*You* ruined all those memories. Do you have any idea how hard it is, just standing in a room with you? You ruined everything, and what, you just expect me to go back to like it was? It's not that simple, Wulf."

"But it is with Liam."

She took a deep breath.

"Maybe it is."

There it was – a crack in his demeanor, finally. White hot rage, flashing across his face. For a moment, she thought he was going to explode. Lash out, maybe kick a chair or punch the counter top. But that was silly, this was Wulfric Stone. He took a deep breath and grabbed at the knot in his tie, yanking it loose.

"If that's true," he growled. "Then that makes you a liar. That means you lied every bit as much as I did, if not more. That means you're an even worse human being than I am."

Katya was suddenly so tired. Of going in circles. Of not knowing what she wanted, and not knowing how to explain that to Wulf. Of not being to give him what he wanted. She turned away abruptly and her hand bumped into the cupcakes that had been left to cool. She sighed and began piling them onto a serving plate.

"Maybe I am, Wulf. Just go home," she said in a soft voice, picking up one of the desserts and peeling the wrapper from it. She heard him move, and suddenly he was at her back.

"No. Be a fucking adult and look me in the face and tell me it's him over me. That your decision is made and final," he said in a stern voice.

"Would it even matter? Would that stop you?"

There was a long pause.

"No."

"And if I told you I still didn't know – that I might not ever know, that I might not ever forgive you. What then?" she asked, picking chocolate cake crumbs up off the counter.

"Then we do the same goddamn thing tomorrow. And the day after. And every day, until you realize the right choice."

It must be wonderful to be so confident in oneself.

"I have to go to work tomorrow," she sighed again, turning away and heading back into her living room. "You need to go."

"We're not done here," he said, following right at her heels.

"*I'm* done, Wulf. I was done a long time ago."

"Well, I'm not. Because you may not be in love with me any-more, but I'm -"

Katya was so shocked at what she thought he was about to admit, that she went to whirl around to face him. Her heel landed in something slippery, probably from Liam's plate when it had been on the floor. Her foot went out from under her, threatening to send her to the ground. Wulf latched onto her elbow, yanking her upright, but it also caused her to spin around. She threw out her hand to help keep her balance and wound up planting it solidly in the middle of his chest. It wasn't till after she'd made contact that she realized she was still holding the cupcake.

"Oh ... no," she breathed, staring at the mess that was coating his tie. The cupcakes had a pudding filling, which was now dripping down his chest.

"Are you fucking serious?" he said in a low voice. She glanced up at him, but he was still staring at the dessert catastrophe. She tried to contain it, but couldn't stop herself – she let out a snicker. Managed to swallow a laugh, which resulted in her snorting.

"I'm sorry," she managed to choke out. "It's just so ..." she cut herself out, she started laughing so much.

"You're right. This is done," he suddenly growled, letting go of her and stomping back into the kitchen.

"No wait!" she yelled, hurrying after him, shaking cupcake bits off her fingers. She grabbed a tea towel and wiped at her hand while chasing him into the hallway.

"Want another cake fight? This is a fucking joke to you. *I'm* a fucking joke," he stated, reaching for the door knob. "A goddamn game. You only want to play games."

"No! I swear, I didn't mean to -"

But he was beyond listening – he had red lined in the anger zone, and clearly didn't want to be in her presence anymore. He didn't even look at her as he started to yank the door open, and somehow she knew. She knew if he walked out the door, that would really be it. There would be no going back. They would have damaged each other too much to come back from it. It was one thing to walk away from Wulf when he had knowingly, intentionally, hurt her. It was quite another for Wulf to walk away from her over what was a simple accident involving dessert. That could not be the reason for their ending, she wouldn't allow it.

So without thinking about what she was doing, Katya leapt between him and the door, throwing her weight back against it. The door slammed shut, the knob yanked out of his hand. He glared down at her.

"Move," he hissed, grabbing for the knob again. She slapped his hand away with the towel.

"No," she stated. "I didn't mean to hit you with a cupcake – it wasn't some elaborate plan to humiliate you, or part of my game, or anything like that."

"I don't really care at this point. *Move.*"

God, he was mad. He had been about to confess something big, she was sure of it. Something very important to him. And he had thought she was laughing at him. She knew exactly how that felt, and she felt kind of terrible for making him think it.

"Just calm down," she urged, pressing the towel and both hands against his chest.

"I said move."

He grabbed the knob again and jerked hard. She didn't weigh much and he was very strong, the door opened fairly easily, throwing her into his chest. But before he could manually move her out of his way, she pushed off him again, forcing the door shut. She moved herself so she was in front of the knob, blocking him from it.

"I've dealt with your bullshit for months!" she yelled at him. "You can at least deal with mine for one evening!"

"Bullshit I can handle!" he yelled back. "Jerking me around is something else."

"I'm not jerking you around!"

"That's *all* you do. You were telling me to get out five minutes ago!"

"I changed my mind!"

"Well, so have I," he snapped, grabbing the side of her hip and trying to shove her. She quickly grabbed onto the knob behind her and held tight, refusing to budge. "So you and Eden are welcome to each other."

"See!? Jealous. Like a little girl. Little girl lose her favorite toy!?" Katya snapped in a snide voice.

"Don't overestimate your value, Tocci."

"You're the one who put the price tag on me, Wulf."

"*You wanted me gone!*" he yelled, slamming a flat palm against the door above her head. "So I'm trying to go!"

"I didn't want it like this!" she shrieked back at him.

"Fine. I'll *make you* move."

His arm was around her waist, lightning fast, and he actually picked her up against him. She was jerked away from the door and with his free hand, he was already turning the knob. But she'd locked it behind her, so it uselessly spun back and forth for a second, buying her some time.

"I tried to say I'm sorry," she grumbled, pushing against his hold. "Just listen to me!"

"Doesn't feel good, does it? When someone refuses to listen to you, and all you want to to do is apologize?"

He dropped her and she almost fell on her butt. He started to undo the knob lock, so she did the only thing she could think of and she reached out, grabbing his cupcake smeared tie. She yanked on it, hard, causing him to stumble forward. He bumped into her and she stepped back into a pile of shoes.

Katya lost her footing and with a shriek, she fell to the side. She still had a hold of his tie, though, so Wulf went with her. Her back hit the wall and she slid sideways, taking coats down off their hooks. His arm was back around her, trying to stop her downward fall, but gravity had already grabbed a hold of him, too. They crashed into a side table, sending picture frames and knick knacks and a vase to the floor.

"I'm sorry," she breathed quickly, still trying to get her feet back under her. "I'm really, really sorry."

"Just stop moving," he said, bracing one hand against the table top.

She held still and he hoisted her upright. The hallway was dark, though, like most of the apartment. The side of her head connected with a wall sconce, causing her to yelp in pain and the bulb to break inside the frosted glass. Wulf stopped moving and his hand went to her head.

"Are you okay?" he was quick to ask. She groaned and he felt around for the wound.

"No," she chuckled. "I have a concussion."

"Please," he laughed as well, massaging the spot where the light had hit her. "Your skull is too thick for any serious damage."

"Shut up, I'm injured. I could sue," she joked, finally looking up at him. He was smiling down at her – a real smile – for what felt like the first time in a long time.

"Go ahead. My lawyers love a fight."

"Shocker."

They smiled at each other for a second longer, then it was like there was a crackle in the air. A snap of electricity. A blink of an eye, and suddenly he was diving into her. She gasped right before his tongue filled her mouth, then she groaned around it. She still had her hands wrapped around his tie, so while she kissed him back, she yanked the knot apart and threw the material to the ground.

He pulled her back away from the wall, crushing her to his chest. They stumbled across the hall, then they moved forward again, stepping haphazardly to the side. Her back connected with the side table again, but Wulf kept pressing into her. She wiggled around, standing on her toes and moving so she was sitting on the table.

She was on autopilot, she didn't even think about what was going on. All she knew was her blood was pumping in her ears and his skin was so hot and how long had it been since she felt like she was on fire? While he moved between her open thighs, she quickly worked at unbuttoning his shirt, yanking it free of his pants.

"Off, off, off," he was breathing hard and pulling at her shirt, as well. She finally lifted her arms and her tank top went sailing over her head, landing on the ground somewhere behind him. Then he was kissing her again and she was scratching at his back while she shoved his shirt away from his shoulders, letting it flutter to the floor.

"Oh god," she moaned, letting her head drop back when his lips moved to her neck, his teeth biting down hard.

Then his hands were on her ass, pulling her off the table. As soon as her feet hit the ground, he was shoving her backwards, forcing her down the hall. They rammed into her door jam and paused for a moment. His hands were pressing down on her skin, moving heavily over her body while she struggled with his undershirt.

"You wear too many layers," she growled. He chuckled, then started pulling his t-shirt off. She leaned close, running her tongue up the center of his chest.

"Noted. I'll be naked next time we decide to fight," he replied, his hands briefly slipping down the back of her jeans before sliding around to the front. He pulled the button open, then slid down the zipper before pushing at the material.

"I don't want to fight anymore," she said, shifting her hips side to side, allowing the denim to fall at her feet.

"You love to fight," he whispered back.

Then he was picking her up again and she went willingly, wrapping her legs around his waist.

It was dark in her room, just a lonely street lamp from outside casting a glow into the space. He stumbled over a purse that had been left on the floor, almost sending them both to the ground. But he managed to maintain his balance, tripping across the room. He didn't stop kissing her for a second, not even when they fell into her drafting table. He sat her on the edge of it, then kissed a trail down her chest.

"God, what are we doing?" she suddenly said, raking her hands through her crazy hair.

"Shh, you ruin things when you talk," he replied, both his hands spanning her rib cage and gently pushing her so she was laying flat.

"But we're mad at each other," she kept talking. "I'm mad at you. This is such a bad idea."

"So angry," he breathed, his breath hot against her stomach. "Can't even see straight. Not aware of what I'm doing even."

"Nice try," she almost laughed. "You're always aware -"

Her breath caught in her throat when he folded down the top of her panties and blow a stream of cold air against sensitive skin. Then she gasped when his mouth moved lower, his tongue finding other more sensitive body parts as her underwear was worked down her legs.

"So mad," he spoke against her, sending vibrations along every nerve ending she owned. "I think you deserve to be punished."

"Yes, please, god, whatever," she chanted, willing to say anything he wanted if it kept his lips on her.

It didn't work, though. He moved away for a second, making her moan at the loss of body heat. Then her panties were yanked clear of her feet. She opened her eyes just as he stepped close again and his hands were back on her ribs, yanking her upright.

She moved easily, coiling her arms around his neck. Letting her hands wander along his broad shoulders, his smooth skin. It had been *so long*. She hadn't realized how much she missed touching him.

Bad idea or not, she was beyond caring. Beyond rational thought, even. Definitely beyond stopping. Both their hands were between their bodies, pulling his belt apart, shoving his pants down. Before she could touch him, though, he was grabbing her hands, forcing them over her breasts.

"Take this off," he growled, curling his fingers over the top of her bra cups.

She was heeding his command, both hands behind her back to undo the clasp, when she felt his erection between her legs. While she was flicking the eye-hook apart, he was pushing inside her. She sucked in a deep breath, letting the straps slide free from her arms, and she fell back against the table.

God, had he always been that big? That thick? She squeezed her eyes shut tight, trying to remember how to breathe as he pumped back and forth, in and out. He wasn't giving her time to adjust, just immediately thrusting into her hard and fast. Like he knew if he moved to slowly, her brain would catch up with what they were do-ing and put a stop to it.

"Oh my god," she whispered, raising her arms above her head and pressing her palms flat against the wall. "Holy shit, Wulf. *Oh my god.*"

"Jesus, was it always this good?" he asked, raking a hand down her chest.

"Yes," she said, then cried out when he started pumping harder.

"God, so good. You're so good."

Suddenly she was yanked upright. She let out a squeak as she was pulled off the table. He had to kick free of his pants as he moved them across the room. Then he dropped them onto the bed, his full weight almost driving her through the mattress. She shrieked, impaled on his hard on.

"This was always going to happen," he whispered, his lips moving over her breasts, his hands following close behind. "What the fuck were you thinking, trying to shut me out?"

She was seething and writhing underneath him, so full and so desperate for friction. She needed him to move, needed him to cure the ache that was growing deep inside of her.

"I don't know, I don't know. Please, Wulf, please," she pleaded. It was like he'd taken every nerve ending to the height of pleasure, and then pushed pause. It was almost painful. Could someone die of pleasure overload?

But what a way to go.

"Now she begs," he chuckled, his hand briefly wrapping around her throat. "Tried to kick me out half an hour ago, and now she begs me for more."

"Yes, yes, yes," she whispered. The hand left her throat and worked its way into her hair.

"Is this what you wanted? To pit us against each other? See how we stacked up against each other? Did he get this far?" he asked. She frowned and put both hands against his chest, trying to create some space between them.

"No. No, please, don't, I don't want to -"

The hand in her hair pulled tight, causing her head to snap back. He finally answered her prayers and started moving again, pumping his hips slowly a couple times. But then he pulled away completely.

"I know what you want. *Turn around.*"

The hand in her hair was pulling even harder, setting her scalp on fire, and his other hand was between her legs, keeping her blood boiling. While long fingers slid in and out of her, she slowly rolled around onto her stomach.

He used both his hands to yank her hips into the air, dug his fingers into her flesh as he fucked her from behind. She started moaning again, clutching her bedspread between closed fists. When she started pushing back against him, urging him faster, one of his hands went back to her hair, pulling her up again.

"Please, Wulf, I'm so close," she cried, reaching out and trying to grip the top of her bed frame. He was fucking her so hard the bed posts were slamming into her wall and she couldn't keep hold of it. It didn't matter anyway, since he kept tugging on her hair. Her back was forced to bend, her spine arching until the back of her head was touching his jaw.

"You have no idea how close you are," he hissed in her ear, then she felt his teeth on her earlobe, biting down hard.

"God, I need you. Please," she all but sobbed, reaching over her shoulder and trying to touch him, combing her fingers through his thick hair.

"Of course you do. No one can make you feel this," he whispered, his tongue trailing along the side of her neck. He finally let go of her hair and she managed to nod.

"No one," she agreed. His free hand moved from her head down to her breasts, briefly toying with her nipples before continuing its southward journey.

"I want you to think about that," he growled, his fingers diving into her slick heat. A thousand different muscles clenched and pulsed, forcing another shriek out of her. "Next time you think you're confused. Think about what I'm doing to you right now, about how I make you feel, next time you're with *him*."

This is a bad, bad, so monumentally bad, idea.

But it was too late. She was shrieking in time to his thrusts, crying out as his fingers strummed faster, coming hard while he continued fucking her. She couldn't remember the last time she'd had an orgasm that big – it had probably been with him. She moaned as her whole body went into spasms, everything falling apart, inside and out.

Again, she needed space. She needed time, her body wanted to crash. But Wulf didn't care. He just kept fucking her, keeping her locked in the orgasm. She was shaking so much, she couldn't do anything, couldn't hold onto anything. He finally moved his hand away and she fell forward, pressing her face into the blankets as her arms stretched out limply at her sides.

"See what happens when you listen to me?" he said, breathing hard as his thrusts turned almost brutal. She could barely pay attention to what he was saying – her ears were ringing and her eyes were rolling back in her head. "You get everything you want. *Every. Single. Fucking. Thing.*"

Each word was punctuated with a slam of his hips. Accompanied by a shriek from her throat. Then he was hunching over her, gripping her rib cage so tightly, she thought he was going to break something. He hissed curse words as he came hard, his hips twitching against her ass.

Finally. I can breathe again.

When he eventually let go of her, it felt like he had to work his fingers out from between her individual ribs. Katya groaned and slid down flat on the mattress, stretching her legs out behind her when he moved away.

She was in orbit. In a different galaxy. She folded her arms up at her side and just laid there, gasping for air, her hair a wild mess all around her. She was vaguely aware that he was moving around, but she couldn't lift her head to see what he was doing. He'd fucked her into a pool of orgasmic goo, stolen every single one of her bones.

Maybe stole a little more than your bones …

"Jesus," she finally croaked out. From somewhere to her right, he chuckled.

"Close. You owe me a tie, Tocci."

She frowned. She didn't care for his tone of voice, not one bit. Flippant and cold, almost snide. It reminded her of how he'd been on their first date, when he'd been so rude to her in that fancy restaurant.

She managed to pull herself into a sitting position, shoving her hair out of her face. She grabbed a large pillow and held it against her body, then she looked around for him.

He was by the door, and she was shocked to see that he was halfway dressed. He'd already gotten his shoes, socks, and pants on. His undershirt was draped over his forearm while he worked his belt back into the loops on his slacks.

"What are you doing?" she asked in a hoarse voice, then she rubbed at her throat.

"I came here for dinner," he said, glancing at her once before shaking out his t-shirt. "I'm starving."

"Oh," she frowned. She was confused. What was going on? "I mean, I guess I could cook something -"

"I have reservations," he interrupted her, pulling the shirt into place and tucking it into his pants.

"Reservations?"

"Yes. When I realized you weren't going to cook for me, I had decided to take us out for a meal. But you had other plans," he replied, combing his fingers through his hair. Then he turned in a slow circle, staring at the floor around him. He finally spotted his dress shirt, laying in the hall, and he strode out to it.

"You're leaving!?" Katya exclaimed, climbing onto her knees and hugging the pillow tightly to her chest.

"Of course," he said, slipping his arms into the sleeves.

"But … but …" she stammered. While he buttoned up the shirt, he headed back into her room.

"But what? You told me to get out, remember? So I'm going," he said in a calm voice. His dress shirt was finally tucked in, and to look at him, it was almost impossible to tell he'd just fucked the life and bones and soul out of someone.

What the fuck is going on!?

"Wulfric!" she snapped his name. "I think we've moved beyond our stupid fight!"

"We certainly have. We just worked out some very pent up aggression – thank you for that, by the way."

"Are you serious right now?" she asked. He nodded and moved to kneel on the mattress in front of her.

"Yes – my reservations were half an hour ago. I would invite you, but you're a mess right now," he teased her. She glared at him.

"*Not funny.*"

"It's hilarious. We'll have to do this again soon," he informed her, smoothing his hands over her hair. She gaped at him.

"What we just did was -"

"Was something we could've been doing all along," he suddenly whispered, leaning down close to her. She swallowed thickly and stared up at him. "How fun are your little games, now?"

"This isn't a game," she whispered back. He smiled his shitty little smirk.

"Nice try," he chuckled. "Cuddles with Liam? Sex with me? I hope you're keeping score somewhere, because I just hit a home run. But next time, please, spare my clothing? No more food fights."

She was shocked. He thought it had all been a ploy. That having Liam over that afternoon had been part of her stupid challenge, and then sleeping with Wulf had just been upping the ante. Of course, why would he think otherwise? She'd never told him it was different.

Her mouth was still hanging open when he closed the gap between them and kissed her. She held completely still, her mind reeling, while his arms wrapped around her and his hands smoothed over her bare back. Then he slapped her on the ass and pulled away.

"See you soon, Tocci."

Her mouth was still open, and she continued gaping as he walked out of her room. Strode down her hallway. Slammed the door shut behind him as he left.

Then she let out a shriek and fell forward, screaming into her mattress.

*Such an idiot. I am **such** an idiot, thinking I could play in the same league with these guys. Shit, what do I do now!?*

20

KATYA RUSHED FROM THE KITCHEN ONTO THE BAKERY FLOOR, CARRYING A tray full of desserts. A customer squealed in excitement, they both set about picking which one the woman liked best for fiftieth wedding anniversary party.

Then she had a very private meeting with a semi-famous reality star about his engagement party – an engagement the press knew nothing about, and he wanted to keep it that way. They were able to settle on two cake designs, one for him and one for his fiancée.

Immediately after that, she was whisked downtown to go over designs for a massive cake that was being commissioned by the mayor's office for his annual Christmas ball. Measurements even needed to be made, and at one point they asked her if she could use real gold in some of the decorations.

She loved every moment of it all. In the midst of her personal drama, it was easy to forget how much she enjoyed her job, and how good she was at it, how proud it made her feel.

Yet at the same time, every moment also drove home all the thoughts she'd been having lately. She had to work within the constrictions of her bakery, and the owners would still get a huge cut of the profits from the cake. Obviously, that was completely fair, but Katya wanted bigger. She wanted to set her own hours, take on her own commitments. Bigger projects and less of them – freeing up more time for herself, and allowing her to really challenge her talent.

She was going over her busy schedule with one of the intern bakers, assigning different details to the young man. She was only halfway through November when the door burst open, letting in a gust of air. Katya glanced up and was surprised to see Tori standing in the shop.

"Hey!" she said, smiling and handing off her clipboard to her coworker. "This is a nice surprise."

"I wanted to see how your first day back was going," Tori said, unwrapping a scarf from around her neck and glancing around the cases.

"Busy, good lord."

"Too busy for a cup of coffee?"

"I'd love one – I worked through lunch."

Katya leaned into the kitchen enough to holler that she'd be stepping out for fifteen minutes, then she grabbed her coat off a rack and followed Tori out the door. A small tempest was blowing through town, carrying moisture through the air and making her shiver.

"So it's good?" Tori asked once they were seated in a tiny cafe, sipping at americanos.

"Yeah. Feels different, after all this time, but it's good. I missed it," Katya responded.

"Good. That's good. Now we can talk about way more important stuff."

Katya went still. Her roommate didn't know about her less than decorous behavior the night before. She hadn't seen Tori since the morning before, since the girl had gone to straight to work from downtown. Katya had left her room long enough to tidy up the crazy scene she and Wulf had left in the hallway, then she'd taken a second shower before going to bed early.

She most definitely didn't deserve dessert, not after the bad things she'd been doing with him. She was embarrassed with herself, that she'd caved so easily. That she'd been so desperate and needy. God, she'd begged him. *Begged.* It was a little humiliating. And then she hadn't said anything, done anything, to stop him from walking out the door.

"Like what?" Katya asked carefully. Tori started digging around in her jacket, then pulled a long piece of material out of a pocket.

"Like what the hell is this?" she asked, dropping it on the table.

Katya groaned as she realized what it was – Wulf's tie. The one she'd clobbered with the cupcake. It must have gotten tossed or kicked into the kitchen. She'd only cleaned up the hallway. She frowned and picked up the offending piece of silk, looking over the dried and caked on chocolate filling.

"Um, this is ..." she mumbled, trying to think of a plausible lie.

"That is sex," Tori said loudly.

"Shhh!" Katya hissed quickly when a table of old ladies glanced at them. "It's a frickin' tie, Tori. That's it."

"Yeah, okay," her roommate snickered. "Just an expensive silk tie, that was probably ripped off in a fit of passion and thrown across a room, right before some brooding jerk boffed your brains out."

"I will get up and leave, and you will never hear the story," Katya warned her. Tori sighed and leaned back in her chair.

"Alright, alright. I'll keep it down. So what happened?"

Katya gave a watered down version of the evening – a surprisingly cozy dinner with Liam, cuddling on the couch. Waking up and being stalked by an angry wolf. She didn't give all the gory details, but enough to get it across that yes, some brooding jerk had indeed *"boffed her brains out"*.

"Please don't make it into a big deal," she whispered at the end, rolling up Wulf's tie and wrapping it in a napkin before shoving it into her own pocket.

"How can I not!? For weeks you've been moping around about

these dudes – now you're finally back where you were before. Isn't that a good thing?" Tori asked. Katya shook her head.

"No – before I was caught between two men. Now I'm back in that same position, only the men are much, much worse in my eyes. I still don't fully trust either of them, and Wulf still thinks it's a game. He just walked out afterwards, laughing about the whole thing. *Laughing.* I wanted to die a little, I was so angry."

"Okay, so drop the jerk and go with Liam."

"It's not that easy. I don't want to … how did this turn into a choosing thing!?" Katya suddenly exclaimed. "I was supposed to be using them. Torturing them. Now it's a contest for which prince can climb my tower and win me over."

"Climb your tower, huh. That's a new one on me. Is that like when one of them eats you -"

"*Tori.*"

The other girl cackled and downed the rest of her coffee before sitting upright.

"Well, on the bright side, at least you're not angry at them anymore, right?"

"… well, I guess so … kinda …"

"And a little sex never hurt anybody."

"*Wrong.*"

"You look more relaxed, so there's that."

Katya didn't feel relaxed. She felt hot and bothered. Caught between being raging pissed off at Wulf, and so incredibly turned on she wanted to drive to his work and fuck him right at his big desk. She felt worried and guilty, because while he was still playing some stupid one-up-manship game, Liam was pouring his heart out and making a real effort.

I have to tell him.

"I have to tell Liam what I did," Katya sighed, rubbing at her temples.

"Are you going to sleep with him, too?" Tori asked. Katya barked out a laugh.

"I didn't want to sleep with Wulf, it just happened. I don't know. I don't think so? God, I don't know," she groaned again.

"Look, it's like I said," Tori sighed, climbing out of her chair. "Just do you. Keep doing what feels right, and eventually, it'll lead you where you need to be. It's how the universe works."

"And what about you?" Katya asked, leaning back so she could look up at her friend. "How come we never talk about your love life? Who's boffing your brains out?"

"God, I wish. I'm all about that cash nowadays. Liam's promoting me to night shift manager downstairs, comes with a big raise."

"That's amazing, Tori. Good for you!"

"Thanks. I've been working really hard for it. I know I'm still pretty new, but I'm the best he's got down there. And you know, I think it's better this way. Keeping busy, focusing on work. No offense, but I don't want your boy problems," she laughed. "I went through all that before on my own, and no thank you. I think lil' Tori just needs to take a well deserved break from men."

She was smiling and she was laughing while she spoke, but Katya got the feeling her friend didn't feel like doing either of those things. In fact, she felt like Tori almost seemed a little sad. Like she was covering something up with all the big grins and talk of hard work.

"Are you *sure* you don't have anything you want to talk about?" Katya asked. Tori shrugged and began wrapping her scarf back around her neck.

"Lots of things. Like bears. How weird is hibernation? Not peeing for months on end? How do they do that?"

Katya rolled her eyes.

"You know that's not what I meant. What's going -"

"Would love to talk, gotta run, gotta bar to manage. Kisses!" Tori called out as she strode for the door, blowing kisses over her shoulder. Then with the tinkle of a bell, she was gone, leaving Katya blinking in her wake.

Hmmm, I am going to have to tie her down and get the truth out of her, eventually.

---◆---

She threw herself into her work for the rest of the day, ignoring her phone entirely. Liam was really back to his old self, sending her silly messages and pictures through the afternoon. Wulf texted once, just one line, like normal. Something vaguely smug and slightly dirty. Enough to piss her off even more *and* turn her on more.

Asshole.

Luckily, both men turned out to be too busy to harass her any further. Liam was gearing up for a huge party at his club – The Garden was turning ten years old, four of which had been spent under his direct management and ownership. They were going all out for it. While they'd been in Carmel, she'd reluctantly agreed to go to the party, but only under the condition that Wulf would be there, too. It had seemed like a funny joke at the time, because Liam hated it when Wulf was in the club.

Now it wasn't funny at all. Wulfric, in a sex club, and around her, and her around Liam, knowing she'd just had sex with Wulf, but not with Liam – Liam, whom she'd had sex with in the club once before.

Think about how many times you just thought the word sex, and re-prioritize your life, you sex fiend.

The party was on Saturday, and she'd long since scheduled that Sunday off, even before her little sabbatical. She wondered if she should cancel. Tell Liam she was simply too busy catching up at work. But then he sent her a really sweet text, telling her how much he appreciated the chance to start over again, and she knew she had to suck it up. He was really putting in an effort to be a good friend and a better man. She could at least hold it together for a couple hours at his party.

Thursday was more of the same at work, but also with classes mixed in with her regular duties. The bakery was one that interned bakers from a local college – it was how Katya had found her current position. So once a week, she took them all to learn special techniques or to different seminars or expos.

She was so caught up in at all, she hadn't noticed that she'd missed several phone calls throughout the day. On the train ride home, she finally pulled out her cell and was surprised to see that Wulf had called her three times. While she stared at the screen, he actually called again. She took a deep breath and brought the phone to her ear.

"Tocci."

He barked out her name like a drill sergeant. Like he was about to give an order.

"Stone," she said back in a comically deep voice.

"Where the hell have you been?" he demanded.

"At this little place called work," she laughed at him.

"Oh, so they decided to take you back."

"No thanks to you."

"Hey, you threw that first piece of cake."

"And the last, technically."

He snorted and she felt proud of herself. She'd had many a pep-talk with herself, prepping for the next time she would see him. If he could treat mind blowing sex like it wasn't a big deal and just walk away from her, then she could do the exact same thing. Or at least, she could act like she could.

"Watch it. I was calling to remind you – you still owe me dinner," he stated. She chewed on her bottom lip and clutched the rail in front of her as the train rocked.

"I don't owe you anything," she reminded him.

"After the gift I gave you the other night, you owe me *a lot*."

She felt her face burn red, but she refused to let her nerves come through in her voice.

"That's adorable that you think that," she replied. "Because from my point of view, seems like you left me *wanting a lot* the other night."

A man standing nearby glanced down at her and she rolled her eyes.

"*That's* adorable – you probably couldn't walk for the rest of the evening," Wulf chuckled.

"You think too highly of yourself."

"Because I know I'm that good."

"If this whole conversation is going to be this annoying, I'm going to hang up," she warned him.

"Dinner, seven o'clock sharp. I'm thinking seafood," he told her. Her mind raced around for an excuse.

"I really can't cook for you tonight," she insisted.

"Why?"

"Because …"

"It's okay, take your time. I've got all evening to wait for you to make up a convincing excuse."

Hear that sound? That's your sanity that he's bending and snapping in half.

"Okay, fine – you want to know why I can't?" she snapped. "Because I'm going out with Liam. I didn't want to hurt your feelings, that's why I wasn't going to tell you, but since you apparently don't give two shits about mine, there it is. I can't cook you dinner because I'm going to be too busy screwing Liam into next Saturday!"

Now every person standing around her looked at her. She sent a glare around to the crowd, then shoved her way to a door as soon as the train stopped.

"Oh. I see. So apparently I wasn't that good," he spoke in a carefully modulated voice.

"I told you – your ego is going to be the death of you," she told him as she stomped down the street.

"Most likely. When you realize how unsatisfied you are by a boy like Liam, call me."

He didn't say goodbye, just hung up on her. She growled and

shoved her phone into her pocket.

Okay, it wasn't her finest moment. She had absolutely no intention of sleeping with Liam any time soon, and using him to make Wulf jealous wasn't okay on *any* sort of level. Guilt rolled over her and with a heavy sigh, she pulled her phone back out. Stabbed at a contact and held it to her ear.

"I was just thinking about you," Liam's warm voice filled her ear. She grimaced.

"Awww, that's sweet. I was just talking about you," she replied.

"Hopefully it was all flattering. Lots of money, big penis, that kind of stuff."

She laughed out loud.

"I was talking to Wulf."

"Oh god."

"Yeah. He was being kind of a jerk, so I did something bad," she told him.

"Like what?"

"Well, he was demanding I cook him dinner, so I told him I couldn't because I was too busy having dinner with you tonight," she was semi-honest.

"Naughty girl, angel cake," he laughed.

"I'm really sorry, I just blurted it out. He makes me so angry sometimes, I just ..."

"It's okay – I would've paid to have seen his face. You can use me any time to piss Wulf off. Now, what are you going to make me for dinner?" he asked, and she could practically hear how hard he was grinning.

"Uuuggg, I bake all day, and then you people expect me to cook," she grumbled.

"Shut up, you love it. Come bring me food."

"Okay, okay. Tacos?"

"Always. See you in a few."

"Bye."

She stopped at home for a bit, changing her clothes and setting up some sketches on her drafting table. She tried not to blush when she remembered what had happened on it the night before – how it had gotten that far, so fast? *So fast.* One minute they'd been fighting, the next they'd been ripping off each other's clothing.

She shook away the memories and headed out. She stopped in and grabbed a bag of tacos from his favorite spot, then was off to Liam's club.

She hadn't been back since their big fight. Just walking down the alley to it, she felt like she was going to break out in hives or something. Too many bad memories. Or fake memories. She wasn't sure which feeling was worse. Ever since that first evening together, it had been planned. Premeditated. She took a deep breath with ever step she took, bracing herself.

She made small talk with Jan the bouncer. She'd seen her hero a couple time since he'd saved her from her two personal demons. He'd come home with Tori a few times for a late night meal. He was scary to look at, but he was actually a big teddy bear in real life. She gave him a hug before she headed inside.

She'd texted Tori ahead of time so the girl could be waiting upstairs for her. Katya wasn't mentally prepared to deal with the rest of the staff. Most of them had witnessed her epic freak out and resulting race through the club. The whole situation was still embarrassing and sore.

Her roommate greeted her inside the door, then lead her downstairs. She chattered about what preparations were being made for the coming weekend and what kind of music there would be and what she was going to wear. Katya got the feeling it was more filler, that her friend was trying to avoid talking about anything real. But before she could even get a word in edgewise, she was at the hallway to Liam's office and Tori was scampering back to her bar.

Before Katya got to the door, voices filtered out to the hallway and froze her in place. Knocked her down and hurtled her through space and time.

No no no no no, not again.

"… all your fault," Liam was saying.

"I didn't tell you to use her," Wulf's voice said.

Katya started breathing fast, feeling lightheaded.

"You gave me her number!"

"Her card, there's a difference."

Wait, what?

"She's like a goddamn nazi."

"That's going a bit far."

I am not a nazi! Am I!?

"She's taken everything and basically called me stupid."

"Well, she's not exactly lying."

"I just wanted someone to do my accounting – I didn't want some tiny bossy lady taking over my entire office."

Katya felt the oxygen returning to her lungs.

"Ayumi is a CPA – she originally worked for me in accounting. She's excellent at this, just let her do her thing. Do you have my check?"

Katya almost laughed. Ayumi Nakada – Wulf's assistant. They were talking about Wulf's assistant. Not her. Ayumi, who apparently was also a CPA. She pressed a hand to her forehead and walked up to the door, gently knocking on it.

"What!?" Liam snapped. She took that as an invitation and pushed open the door. Both men stared at her for a moment and she managed a smile.

"We've got to stop meeting like this."

Her voice lacked any kind of strength to drive the joke home, but both men chuckled. Liam hurried around the desk and grabbed the food bag from her while guiding her to a chair.

"Sorry, I tried to get him out of here before you got here," he grumbled, shooting a glare at Wulf. The other man smirked at both of them.

"Is that dinner I smell? Wonderful, I'm starving," he said, sitting in the seat next to Katya.

"No, no, no, this is a private intimate dinner for two," Liam informed him. Wulf rolled his eyes and shrugged out of his jacket. She noticed that he wasn't wearing a tie, and when she looked up at him, his smile got bigger. She frowned and looked away, grabbing the bag off Liam's desk.

"It's fine, I got enough to choke a mule."

"Which means barely enough for me," Liam groaned, but he sat down in his desk chair and wheeled himself out so he was sitting with them.

It was an awkward dinner, for sure, but nothing could keep Liam quiet for too long. He eventually started talking, telling old surfing stories from his early twenties. Katya pointed out that she was still in her early twenties, which made everyone chuckle.

Wulf said that his early twenties hadn't been very fun. Completing grad school, building a business, taking care of a family. They both stared at him in silence for a moment, then Liam cleared his throat.

"You're kind of a downer, bro."

When Katya finished her food, she realized Wulf was staring at her in a way that made her very uncomfortable. Liam still had a lot of hours left at the bar, so she made her excuses and went to leave. He gave her a big hug and kiss goodbye, adding to the uncomfortable feeling. She tried to hurry out without saying anything to Wulf, but of course, he never let her get away with anything.

She was sliding her jacket on and hurrying down the hallway when she heard him closing in behind her. She glanced over her shoulder, then groaned before turning up the stairs to leave.

"I don't have time to deal with you, I have to get up early tomorrow," she told him. He walked so close behind her, she could feel his body heat. He stayed that way clear through the whole club, all the way until they were outside. Jan gave him a nasty look, but didn't say anything as they headed out of the alley.

"You sure about that? I'm still hungry, I could go for some dessert," he said, and she nearly choked on air.

"Are *you* sure about *that?* It might wind up all over your smug little face," she warned him.

"It didn't last night."

She lucked out and a taxi was letting someone out at the curb right next to them. She hurried down and grabbed the door, then turned to face Wulf. He'd stayed right on her heels and she almost wound up with her nose in his collar.

"Not for lack of trying. Speaking of which, I have something for you," she said, pulling his messy tie out of her pocket. She unfurled it and wrapped it around his neck.

"That mess better come out, this was very expensive," he told her, leaning down close as she wrapped her hands around the ends of the tie.

"You know what else costs a lot?" she whispered, standing on her toes and meeting him halfway. His eyes were on her lips, following their movement.

"What?" he whispered back.

"*My time.* Stop wasting it, Wulf."

She abruptly let go of the tie and dropped into the taxi's backseat. She slammed the door and waved at him as she gave an address to the cabbie. Before Wulf could say a witty comeback or get into the car with her, the cab was sailing off down the street, with Katya laughing the whole way.

21

"How're things, kiddo?"

Katya balanced her phone between her shoulder and ear while she moved around her kitchen. To celebrate Tori's promotion, Katya had made her roommate's favorite foods and dessert. Her dad had called right in the middle of it all.

"Good, busy. Work has been insane," she said, kicking the dishwasher door shut with her heel before hurrying over and peering into the oven.

"That's good to hear, glad your back at it. Your mother's got me on this low-sodium, low-carb diet. I think she's trying to kill me," he chuckled. She laughed.

"Good for you, you need taking care of."

"Speaking of taking care – how are your two boys?" he asked in what she was sure he thought was a nonchalant voice.

"They're not mine, and they're fine."

"No more punches?"

"Not yet, but we're all going to a party on Saturday," she told him.

"Sounds nice. I know I was angry, but Liam did seem like a really nice guy, pumpkin," her dad said. She paused as she held a pot over a strainer. Where was this coming from?

"He can be, when he puts his mind to it. He feels really bad about how everything went down," she replied.

"I know – he sent your mother flowers. She's embroidering 'Mr. & Mrs. Edenhoff' on pillowcases."

"Oh jesus."

"I know! It was my car that got scratched, where the hell are my flowers?"

"I thought Wulf was paying to have that fixed?"

"Sweetie, he did more than pay for it."

"What do you mean?" she asked, tossing the now empty pot into the sink and putting her hands on her hips.

"Let's just say Daddy's got a new toy."

"Excuse me?"

"Remember that motorcycle I had when you were eight?"

"Oh my god, he did not send you a motorcycle!"

"We'll have to take a ride on it when you come down."

"No. This is not happening. I'm going to tell him to take it back."

"You'll have to pry it from my cold, dead, fingers first. You don't have to ride on it – he had the car fixed, too."

"Dad," she took a deep breath. "You're over fifty. You're glasses are basically coke bottles. You should not *ever* be on a motorcycle."

"You underestimate your old man. It's like riding a bike. Get it? *A bike*," he laughed at his own joke.

"I'm really not okay with this, Dad. I don't like the idea of you cruising down the freeway on a motorcycle," she whined, using her little girl voice that usually got her anything.

"Relax, sweetie. I've only ridden it twice, around the block. It's sitting in the garage under a cover right now," he assured her.

"Good. Good, okay, thank you. He shouldn't have done that. Why would he do that!?" she groaned, rubbing her hand across her forehead.

"Well, I think he felt bad, too."

"He could try saying he's sorry!"

"Maybe that just is his way of saying sorry. Not everyone operates the same way you do. Wulf's always been special, I always found it was best to let him do things his way. Box him in, and he just gets resentful."

Hmmm, I get the feeling we're not talking about expensive gifts anymore.

"Dad, what are you trying to say?"

"I'm trying to say that Thanksgiving isn't too far away, and we would love it if you to brought a date – but only *one* date."

"And you want my date to be the kind of guy who gifts motorcycles," she grumbled.

"No, I want your date to be the kind of guy who treats you right and you like," her dad countered. "I know those two boys are twisting you up inside. I want you to figure out what it is *you* want, and just go for it. I like motorcycles, sweetie, but I also love weekends at the beach and learning how to surf. Or hey, even just spending a holiday alone with my baby girl."

Katya sighed and leaned against the counter.

"Thanks, Dad. I mean it. What you think … it means a lot to me. Thank you for being understanding. I know none of this is what you'd like for me," she said in a soft voice.

"Of course not. I wanted you to be a doctor."

"Daddy!"

"Gotta go, sweetie. Mr. Tunt across the street wants me to race against his Harley."

"Please tell me you're joking, I don't want -"

"Love you lots."

"Love you, too."

And then her dad was gone. Katya frowned and started moving around again when Tori wandered into the kitchen. They worked together to put the meal on the table and laughed and talked through the night, but her mind was always halfway thinking about her conversation with her father. When she'd gone home with Wulf a month or so ago, her mom had impressed her with how understanding she was about the whole two men situation. Now her dad was blowing her away with his level of understanding.

Jesus, maybe I'm the one who isn't very understanding.

Katya knew she was stalling. It was so easy to say, or even think, *just make a choice.* Wulfric, or Liam. Or hell, neither. It just wasn't that simple, though. If it was, she already would've made the decision.

Starting out, she'd had the strongest emotional connection to Wulf – an almost physical pull on her soul, tying her to him. But he'd ruined it and damaged that connection. It wasn't as electrical as it used to be, she didn't trust him, so she kept pushing away any potential feelings for him. How could she choose him? And worse, if she didn't choose him, was she prepared to never see him again? Because she was pretty sure he wouldn't be interested in "staying friends" afterwards.

Her bond with Liam had been different, and maybe even stronger in some ways. She'd seen him almost every day. He made her laugh and feel good about herself, but back then, there hadn't been that spark. She'd never even contemplated it, because she'd been focused on Wulf. Now, though, things were different – he was putting in the effort, apologizing and trying. Making her feel special. Was she willing to lose that kind of special person if she chose Wulf?

Maybe I should be alone – this is a stupid problem to have.

Just to complicate things more, Liam showed up around ten o'clock with a bottle of champagne. The three of them dove into the lemon soufflé Katya had made for dessert, a sort of specialty of hers that she didn't the opportunity to make too often.

Tori surprised them all by begging off early, cracking jokes about having to go to work early for her ball busting boss. Liam chuckled, but after she'd gone into her room, he mentioned to Katya that Tori didn't need to be at work till two in the afternoon.

"I wonder why she's going to bed so early?" Katya mumbled as she followed Liam up the stairs.

"Maybe she has a boyfriend," he suggested, fumbling with the keys to the rooftop door.

"What, hiding in her room?" Katya laughed, hugging a blanket tight to her chest as he opened the door.

"Maybe. Tied up in her closet," he joked, leading the way to the worn loveseat. They skirted the kiddie pool he'd brought up there so many weeks ago. All the water had long since evaporated.

"Ooohhh, maybe an online boyfriend!" Katya gasped. It was possible. Right out of high school, Tori had driven clear to San Diego for some guy she'd met through a chat room.

"I hope not. She's too good for that," Liam said, holding out a hand.

She handed off the blanket and they both sat down, rearranging the fluffy blanket around them. When she was settled back into the cushions next to him, he sat a plastic bag on his lap and pulled out a bottle of wine and a box of desserts. She laughed and grabbed the box.

"What are these?" she asked.

"You've never had a Choco Taco!?" he gasped, staring down at her.

"No. No, I have not."

"Oh my god, they're amazing. Ice cream and chocolate and cone. I figure you're always making stuff for all of us, I should try to do something. But I can't bake for shit," he laughed, opening the box for her and pulling out one of the treats.

"It just takes practice. Holy shit, these *are* good," she commented after she'd taken a bite.

"I know. Also, I forgot to grab glasses."

The wine was screw top, at least, so they took turns passing it back and forth, drinking straight from the bottle. They both ate their desserts, Liam polishing off four before coming to a stop.

"Where do you put it all?" she asked, looking over his body

when he finally leaned back in to the couch. "You're so trim."

"I know, right? Always been this way. Can pretty much eat whatever I want."

"Lucky."

"Says miss skinny minny. You're like a bird. A tall, skinny, bird," he said.

"I think you just compared me to an ostrich," she laughed.

"Nah. Your butt's not big enough."

"And I can't eat whatever I want. Notice I almost never eat my own desserts? I gained forty pounds while I was in school. I learned real quick to never eat as I baked," she laughed.

"I can't imagine that."

"Tori, though, she's like you. She can literally eat and drink as much as she wants, and she always looks the same. She's looked like that since the eighth grade," Katya said.

"Jesus, she had those tits in eighth grade? She must have been really popular."

"Nice, Liam. Real nice."

"Aw, don't be jealous, angel cake," he teased, cuddling in close to her. "You have nice breasts, too."

It was a nice moment. Feeling comfortable with him again, being in their special place together. She loved that no one else had never been up there. Not Wulf, not even Tori. It was the one place that only belonged to her and Liam.

"I'm glad we're friends again," she sighed, looking across the rooftop.

"Me, too."

"You sure?" she asked, glancing at him. "Even if I only ever want to be friends?"

"I'm sure," he said, then his hand was sliding into her hair, gently pulling her close to him. "But I'm still not positive that's what you want."

"*I'm* not even positive what I want," she replied.

"That's good. Take your time. Figure things out," he suggested. She smiled at him.

"Thank you."

"Aaaand ... maybe I can help you a little," he offered.

"Oh really? And how do you -"

He was kissing her. Of course he was. And it was nice and lovely and she felt warmth blooming in the center of her chest. But tainting the whole thing was her dirty secret. The feeling that what she was doing was very wrong.

"Liam," she breathed, pulling away. "I have to tell you something."

"Something about love, devotion, free meals for life," he mumbled, rubbing his nose along the side of her neck, breathing her in.

"No. I want us to be honest with each other, always."

"I know, that's how you know I'm telling you the truth when I say you're the one for me," he chuckled, then his teeth were nipping at the tendon in her neck.

"Yeah, soooo .... I should be honest, too, and I feel like I need to tell you something. It's about Wulf, he -" she tried to confess, but Liam backed away suddenly. Two fingers were pressed over her lips, effectively silencing her.

"I don't want to know," he said simply.

"Hhhmph?" she mumbled.

"I really don't. This isn't about him – he doesn't matter to me, not when I'm with you. I don't care what he's scheming or how many kisses he's stolen, or whatever. This is about us, right now. I don't want him to ruin it," Liam insisted. She frowned and pushed his hand away.

"That's very sweet, but I really feel like -"

He leaned back in and kissed her hard, forcing her to swallow her words.

"I don't care," he whispered, moving so both hands were in her hair. "This is us. Just be here with me."

She wanted to be insistent – to argue and demand that he listen, so the situation couldn't come back to haunt her. But she couldn't get another word out, his tongue was taking up all the available space in her mouth.

———◆———

Though Liam had pulled out some of his best moves while kissing her, Katya managed to escape the roof unscathed. Her father's words were still strong in her mind – she needed to make a choice. Sex would only confuse things more than it already had, and she didn't want that; she didn't want to string these men along.

She tied up everything neatly at the bakery before heading home the next afternoon. She wouldn't be going in the next day, which was okay because Sunday was typically slow, anyway. She went home feeling guilt free about taking a day off so soon after her sabbatical and tried to get excited about the party that evening.

Since she'd only gotten to wear it for such a brief amount of time, she changed into the Herve Leger dress she'd worn to her dinner with Wulf and Liam. The black and beige fabric clung to her body in a way that probably should've been obscene, but fell just short of it and stayed nicely in sexy.

She went to pull her hair up into a bun, then paused as she looked at her reflection. She thought for a second, then smiled and started digging around under the sink, searching through Tori's enormous supply of make up and hair products.

Almost an hour later, she'd blown out, flat ironed, and put waves into her dark auburn tresses. Definitely a different look for her, she felt like it even changed her face. It really highlighted her apple cheeks, her narrow chin. She did her eye makeup a little darker than normal, but stuck with a pink gloss for her lips. Happy with the over-all look, she grabbed her special-events-only Burberry trench and made her way downstairs before ordering an Uber.

When she walked into the club, she was a little blown away. It

232

looked like a New Year's party was being thrown – there were fancy gold and black balloons everywhere, coating the ceiling. She was shocked to see that the door to the super private downstairs bar was propped open, and Timmy the bartender explained that for the party, all illicit activities had been put on hold.

It was only around seven at night, but the party was in full swing. A lot of people had turned out for the event, she was happy to see. Liam had pumped a lot of money into marketing the party, and the chance to be in a real live sex club had been too much for most people to resist their curiosity. When she got downstairs and walked around, she saw people giggling and pointing at the private apartments that had all been opened up, and gasping over the sex toys that were for sale behind the downstairs bar.

"*Kitty Kat!*"

She turned around at Tori's high pitched voice, then gasped as her roommate approached her. Tori normally dressed super sexy for work, but she'd really outdone herself that evening. She wore a black sequin pair of underwear – "*they're booty shorts!*" – with a black jewel encrusted push up bra. Her wavy brown hair had been pinned away from her face, but fell in curls down her back. Knee high boots, fishnets, and fingerless leather gloves completed the look.

"What do you think?" she laughed, turning around and shaking her very perky, and very exposed, butt at Katya.

"Uh … I think you look like a prostitute," Katya was honest. Tori just laughed harder.

"Thanks a lot."

"I mean, the sexiest one I've ever seen. Probably like super expensive," Katya tried to fix her comment while she took off her jacket.

"I take that as a compliment. The more tit I show, the bigger my tips. Eventually I'm gonna talk Liam into letting me wear pasties," she joked.

"I'm pretty sure if you just say 'pasties', he'll say yes."

"Right!? That man, oi vey. C'mon, you can stash your jacket in his office."

After they'd hung up Katya's precious coat, Tori made her way back behind the bar, flirting every step of the way. Katya hung out near the entrance to the hallway, looking around the crowd. She didn't recognize anyone at first, and while she was sociable, she wasn't particularly good at striking up conversations with people she'd never met. Luckily, her eyes landed on a small knot of people across the room and she smiled before making her way over to them.

"Hey! I didn't know you guys would be here!" she exclaimed, stepping up between her neighbor Gaten Shepherd and Wulf's sister Vieve. Brie stood across from them, absorbed in her phone.

"Yeah, Wulfy invited me. I gotta say, the idea of coming to a sex club for a party made me nervous," Vieve laughed. "But he assured me it would be rated PG-13 for the evening."

"I saw a flyer in our lobby," Gaten explained. "I remembered you saying something about that guy in my building owning the place. Then when I got here, I recognized Genevieve from the other day, so I came over and said hello."

The way he was smiling at Vieve, it made Katya's mind begin to wonder. Obviously, he had probably assumed Katya would be there, and Katya and Vieve were friends – had he come hoping to bump into Vieve? That would be so sweet.

Vieve, however, seemed oblivious to the attention she was getting. She smiled at everyone and nervously fingered the pearls around her neck.

"And you?" Katya asked, directing her question at Brie. "I really wouldn't have thought you'd be here."

"Is that an actual question?" Brie asked back, not bothering to look up.

Vieve may be a carbon copy of Wulf looks-wise, but Brie opens her mouth and it's like listening to him.

"I meant, it doesn't really seem like your scene," Katya explained. Brie finally put her phone away into a tiny crossbody purse.

"Um, there's free alcohol and there's good looking men – *rich* men. It's my scene," she assured her.

"Oh. I guess that's as good a reason as any."

"Besides, Wulf said his partner would be here. I'm curious to meet anyone who can drive my brother insane," she commented, her eyes scanning the crowd. Katya turned to look around as well and spotted the object of their discussion leaning against the end of the bar, laughing at something Tori was saying.

"He's right there – I'll go see if he can come say hi. Excuse me."

Katya wormed her way through the thickening crowd and popped up at Liam's side. He did a double take at her, not recognizing her at first. Then his eyes grew wide and he turned to face her.

"Holy shit, angel cake. You look … incredible. Your hair," he said, his eyes wandering all over her.

"Normally I hate to wear a dress to two events so close together, but I really do love it," she laughed.

"So do I."

"Me, too," Tori chimed in while she shook a cocktail shaker up and down. "Does amazing things for your ass."

"Uh, not as amazing as what those sequins are doing for yous," Katya laughed back.

"An excellent point. Your ass is defying gravity tonight, Tori," Liam agreed.

"Hush, I take sexual harassment in the work place very seriously," Tori said.

"Really? Then why do you keep flirting with me?" he asked.

It had clearly been meant as a joke, and Katya even started to laugh, but she was surprised to see Tori blush a little. Tori never blushed. Her eyes bounced between Katya and Liam before a grin was fixed into place.

"Because *you* keep flirting with *me*. Go away now, I'm super busy because SOMEONE decided having liquor down here for the night would be a great idea," she huffed out, then she skipped down to the other end of the bar.

"She has no concept of authority, does she?" Liam sighed, his eyes following Tori's movements.

"No, not really. C'mon, Wulf's sisters are you – you met Vieve, now you can meet Brie," she offered, linking her arm through his and turning him to face the crowd.

"Oh lord, I can't even remember the one, and now you want me to meet the other? Where are they? Are they just like him?" he asked, searching the crowd.

"Brie kinda is," Katya snickered, then she pointed to the other side of the room. "They're standing over there."

Under her arm, she felt Liam tense up. She glanced up and saw that he was frowning a little. Gaten was laughing at something one of the girls had said, Vieve was playing with her necklace again, and Brie was back on her phone.

"Those are Wulf's sisters?" Liam double checked.

"Yeah. You met Vieve, remember?" she asked.

"I … I guess I don't. It was a crazy weekend, and I took a punch to the head," he said in a low voice, his eyes never leaving the other group.

"Well, the tall one who looks just like Wulf is Genevieve – she's the older one."

"Oh, close to Wulf's age?"

"No, she's only twenty-one."

"Oh god."

"Don't worry," Katya laughed. "She acts more like she's forty, totally low key, super sweet and polite. Brie is the one you have to worry about."

"Uh … why?"

"Because she's only nineteen, thinks she's smarter than everyone, and pretty much hates the world. C'mon, let's go say hi," she urged, trying to walk forward. He refused to move, though.

"I can't, angel cake," he said, pulling his arm free from hers. "I have to go upstairs, there's a raffle going on that I have to announce. Then I have to check on a missing case of champagne, and then a million other things. Maybe later."

"Oh, okay. Maybe later."

She watched in surprise and confusion as he jogged up the stairs. Surely, he could've spared two seconds to meet the Stone girls. Of course, he didn't care for Wulf, so maybe he wasn't interested in getting to know Wulf's family. She supposed it made sense. She shrugged off his weird behavior and rejoined her friends.

It really was a great party. A band had been set up against the back wall, playing jazzy versions of modern hits. Gate twirled her around the floor a couple times, then she convinced Vieve to go out and dance with him. And by convince, she more like shoved the other woman into his arms.

"I think he likes your sister," Katya laughed, folding her arms as she watched the pair awkwardly dance together.

"Bummer for him," Brie grunted.

"What do you mean? He's a nice guy, she's a nice girl."

"Exactly – he's nice and normal. Vieve isn't normal at all."

"Could've fooled me."

"Again – exactly. It's what she does best. Now if he were to get hooked on drugs or develop cancer or lose a leg, she'd be all over him like white on rice," Brie said in a casual voice. Katya finally turned to look down at her.

"What's that all supposed to mean?" she asked.

"It means my sister has to feel needed. Indispensable. She has to be saving someone. She only feels like she's worth something if she's taking care of someone. Why do you think she's always mothering us?" Brie pointed out.

"Wow. I had no idea."

"Why do you think she married a guy with terminal brain cancer?"

"She knew he had brain cancer? Before they got married?"

"Try before they even dated. Whatever. She's a head case. I'm gonna go get a drink," the younger girl sighed and dragged herself to the bar.

Katya stared out at the dance floor, watching Genevieve Stone carefully. The other woman did look normal. All her dark hair had been swept up into a sleek, fancy ponytail. She wore a strapless jump-suit that showed off her delicate bone structure perfectly. She was stunning, really. How could she have such esteem issues?

Of course, that logic didn't make much sense. Katya looked back at Brighton – a gorgeous woman in her own right, yet she seemed to have a whole truck load of issues. Crazy, to be so young and so maladjusted. So hateful on the inside, yet so beautiful on the outside.

She was wearing a bodycon dress that showed off her curvy body to perfection. It had long sleeves and a high neck and went clear to her mid-calves, but the light peach color paired with the fact that it was painted on her body gave the illusion that she was naked at first glance. Her long, thick hair had similar waves to Katya's, and she was wearing so much makeup, she was hard to recognize. Highlighter and bronzer and contouring and false eyelashes. Katya almost felt under dressed in comparison.

"Jesus, what is she wearing?"

Katya whirled around to find Wulf standing behind her. He was glaring poison darts at his little sister.

"I think she looks nice," Katya offered.

"She looks like a Playboy Bunny."

"Well ... they usually look nice, too," she tried again.

"And is she getting a drink!?" he demanded.

"Um, I hate to tell you this, but a lot of nineteen year old's con-sume alcohol. She's been living alone at a dorm for the past year, I can guarantee she's had a drink before, and would bet money that she has a fake ID," Katya pointed out.

"I don't give a fuck – she's nineteen and Liam is wandering around here somewhere, she's not fucking drinking," Wulf growled.

Katya barked out a laugh.

"What does Liam have to do with it?"

"Get a few drinks in him and he tries to fuck anything with tits. I will murder him if he so much as breathes wrong in her direction," Wulf warned, then he started for the bar. Katya put herself in front of him.

"Whoa, calm down! He is *not* like that, and it's insulting *to me* to say so. Besides, Brie seems more than capable of taking care of herself. Have you actually met her? She's got a black belt in making people regret they've spoken to her. You're being ridiculous," she snapped, putting her hands flat on his chest.

"I don't care, she's my sister."

"Oh my god, Wulf. You're protective of your baby sister!" Katya started laughing again. He finally looked down at her.

"Of course I am. What's funny about that?" he demanded.

"It's just … it's kind of adorable. I didn't think it was possible for you to be adorable," she teased him.

"Shut up, Tocci."

"C'mon, clam down," she urged. "Brie's a big girl and besides, is Tori even serving her? My roommate's good at her job."

They both looked back at the bar and sure enough, Tori and Brie were getting into it. A heated exchange took place for a minute and ended with what Katya assumed was a fake ID getting tossed to the floor at Brie's feet. She held up her middle finger as she retrieved it, then she stormed across the room and disappeared up the stairs.

"She shouldn't even be here," Wulf said in a low voice. "Vieve just lets her get away with anything."

"Brie's an adult, Wulf. Not you and not Vieve can stop her from doing anything she wants. When was the last time you actually spoke to her?" Katya asked. His frown got worse.

"A while."

"Have you even seen her since she's been staying here?"

His frowned disappeared and he looked shocked for a moment.

"What do you mean, staying here?"

Oops, I think I just spilled the beans.

"Um …" she glanced around, looking for a way to escape.

"Cut the shit, Tocci. What are you talking about?" he demanded.

"She's been staying with Vieve, at your place."

"Why the fuck isn't she back in school!?"

"Because maybe she needed an extended break?"

"She doesn't get a fucking break, not when I'm cutting the checks."

"Well, maybe she would take it more seriously if she knew you were paying for it," Katya pointed out. He looked like he wanted to curse some more, but he managed to keep his mouth shut. "Hard to get mad at her for keeping secrets when you never tell her anything."

"You can shut up, any time now."

She laughed again as he stomped up to the bar.

She mingled for a while after that, chatting with some of the employees and meeting their significant others. She was pleased to see Vieve and Gaten sticking close together, even sitting close in one of the booths.

It was a while before she saw Liam again. When she spied him standing in a corner, talking to a group of three gorgeous blondes, she snuck up behind him. Smiling big, she tapped him on the shoulder.

"You've been hiding all evening," she teased as he turned around. She blinked up at him for a moment, then recognition kicked into gear.

"I'm beginning to think you have a crush on me," Landon Edenhoff smirked down at her.

"Sorry," she laughed. "I'm sorry. You just …"

"Look just like him?" he offered.

"God, that sounds stupid. I'm sorry," she babbled. Talking to him was disconcerting. Someone who looked so much like Liam, but had none of his warmth and ease. Landon had a tendency to stare her very directly in the eye while he spoke, which further unnerved her.

"It's okay, we're used to it. You know, you've seen me naked, and I don't even know your name," he pointed out. She blushed a little.

"You weren't really naked," she said quickly. He quirked up an eyebrow.

"Yet still, you've seen me naked."

Realizing he meant that having seen Liam naked, she'd effectively seen him naked, her little blush turned into full on tomato face.

"Well … uh … congratulations?" she finally blurted out. He burst out laughing.

"Oh, I think you and I are going to get along just fine," he said, stepping up close and draping his arm around her waist. The three blondes shot her death stares. "Now, how about you tell me your name, and we can discuss what *you* look like naked."

"I don't believe we've met."

Usually, Katya was annoyed by Wulf's habit of popping up out of nowhere and just speaking out of turn. That time, though, she was thankful for it. He appeared at her elbow, a martini glass in his hand and a stern look on his face.

"Dr. Landon Edenhoff," Lan said in a smooth voice, holding out his free hand. Wulf shook it.

"Wulfric Stone."

It was crazy, standing between them. It was like watching two lions meet for the first time. Two alphas, trying to decide whether or not to rip each others throats out. As cocky and condescending as Landon was, though, she was still pretty sure Wulf would come out the victor. His ego was deep seated, part of his genetic make up at this point. Lan's felt forced, a facade put in place for god only knew what reason.

"Ah, Richard Mason," Lan laughed, using Wulf's business pseudonym. "The bane of Liam's existence. The pleasure is most definitely all mine. I like anyone who can give my brother so much shit. He needs someone to keep him in place."

Wulf didn't laugh in return.

"I think with a successful business that has thrived under his ownership, Eden doesn't need anyone to keep him in place, least of all an arrogant sibling. Tocci, a word?"

He could've broken into an Irish jig, slapped one of the blonde women, or started singing opera, and Katya would've been less shocked. Had Wulf just defended Liam!? Her jaw was brushing the floor as he gripped her elbow and walked her away from the small group.

"Did you just do what I think you did!?" she asked.

"Yes, and if you breathe a word of it to Eden, you won't like your punishment," he warned her, stopping them at the end of the bar. A tray of champagne glasses was sitting there, all of them full, so he grabbed one and handed it to her.

"Why would you do that? You hate Liam," she pointed out.

"I don't hate him. I just don't like him. Fortunately for him, I like presumptuous cocky assholes even less."

"Uh, I feel like that's the pot calling the kettle black," she snickered. He narrowed his eyes.

"Don't start with me, I'm not in the mood tonight."

"Are you ever?" she laughed.

"I was the other night."

She stopped laughing.

"*That* was a mistake," she informed him, slugging down some of the champagne.

"Tocci, that night was as close to perfection as you've been in a long time," he laughed loudly at her. She frowned.

"Maybe that's your opinion, but don't count on it happening again," she told him.

"Oh, so you can flirt with Eden and threaten to sleep with him, but I'm suddenly not good enough?" he asked.

There it was again – "not good enough". Usually Liam was the one with large and in charge insecurities over feeling second best, but now it was twice that Wulf had made mention of not being good enough. Had she finally managed to make him feel nervous? Unsure of himself? The very idea made her feel confident and a little bit powerful.

"You know, I have to admit," she said in a slow voice. "Seeing you jealous is pretty hot."

"Is it, now? Don't get used to it."

"Why?"

"Because it's only a matter of time before you make the right choice."

Confidence and power, gone. To be reminded that she was even in this ridiculous situation put a damper on her evening. Made her feel silly and dramatic. She frowned and put her champagne glass down.

"You know," she said, smoothing her hands down her dress. "I told Vieve I'd meet her for brunch tomorrow, so I think I'm going to call it a night. Thanks for a lovely time, as always."

She turned and headed down the hallway, not one bit surprised when she heard his footsteps walking after her.

"Can't handle the tension?" he asked. "You always run to Eden when things get too hot."

"Which would be very telling if it was true, but it's not. My jacket is in his office," she replied.

"Uh huh. Nice dress, by the way."

She felt his fingers grazing her skin at the top of her dress, right over her left shoulder blade. Then his hand pressed flat and ran clear down to her hip, leaving a scorch mark in its wake, she was sure.

"You've seen it before," she told him, swatting at his hand. He moved it to her lower back.

"It looked nice then, too."

"Stop it, Wulf," she growled, pushing at his hand again.

"And this hair. A new look for you, Tocci. Who are you dressing up for, hmmm?" he asked. She swung around, slapping his arm away forcefully.

"As hard as it may be to believe, I dressed up *for me*," she hissed.

"That is hard to believe. Sure it wasn't for someone special?" he checked, fingering a lock of hair.

"Of course. There's no one special here."

He tugged on the strand, coiling it around his finger.

"No need to be rude, Tocci. Covering up your insecurities by being a smart ass isn't very attractive."

"Again, Wulf, and I really want to beat this into your thick skull – not *everything* is about turning *you* on."

He let go of the lock and moved his hand to push the heavy fall of hair over her shoulder. His fingers lingered in the auburn strands, his thumb moving in circles just under her ear.

"See, that's where you're very mistaken. What time is brunch tomorrow?" he asked. She glared and shoved at his wrist.

"Early."

"Pity. Tell Vieve to pick you up at my apartment, that way you don't have to rush back to yours."

She burst out laughing and gripped his wrist between her hands, trying to jerk it away. His fingers just clenched tighter in her hair.

"I'm seriously not in the mood, *Wulfy*," she growled. "I won't be going to your apartment tonight, or ever."

"I can remember a time when that's all you wanted to do."

"Yeah – a long time ago, before I knew what an … an … an awful human being you are," she swore.

For some reason, that simple insult seemed to get to him more than anything else she'd said so far. He narrowed his eyes, glaring down at her.

"Is that what you really think? That I'm an awful human being?"

"Yes!"

"Worse than Eden?"

"*Yes!*"

She glared right back at him, shooting sparks out of her eyes, she was sure. The hand in her hair clenched all the way into a fist, and she dug her fingernails into his wrist. He could make her so angry, it was almost impressive. So mad, she couldn't see straight. So mad, she couldn't think straight. So mad, she wanted to punch him in the face and stomp all over his unconscious body.

So why, about one minute later, they were stumbling up against a wall with their mouths attached to each other, she didn't know.

"You have a lot of pent up aggression, Tocci," he chuckled in her ear as he wrapped his arms around her waist. She worked her hands underneath his jacket.

"I wonder why, *Stone.*"

"I'm not complaining. *I like it.*"

She was very aware that they weren't being very tactful. They were about thirty feet from Liam's office door. At the other end of the short hallway, people were wandering in and out of the plush rental rooms. It was a matter of time before someone came upon them.

"Oh my god," she groaned while he kissed along her neck, his hands cupping her breasts. "We have to stop. This is … this is not good."

"No, stopping would be very, very bad."

They were still moving around, sliding around on the wall, when they bumped into a door jam. Wulf fumbled with the knob, yanked the door open, then shoved her into the room. She fell across the floor, ramming into something solid and tinny. Wulf had already shut the door and it was incredibly dark in the space. She felt around her and realized she was leaning against a huge utility sink.

"I can't see anything," she hissed, turning so her back was against the sink and reaching her arm out.

"Pity."

She yelped and jumped a little – his voice was right next to her. She turned her head and her nose brushed against his chin, startling her again. She jerked back a little, but then his hands were on either side of her face, holding her still so he could kiss her.

Of course, Katya normally kissed with her eyes closed, like a lot of people did. So most of her kissing had technically been done in the dark, but *literally* doing it in the dark was a new experience for her. She was nervous as she reached her hands up and gripped onto his lapels. Held still while he kissed her thoroughly.

"This is weird," she breathed when he pulled away.

"Why?" he spoke softly, moving his hands to her hips and pulling her closer to him. She stepped hesitantly, afraid of knocking into anything. She kept her eyes squeezed shut tight, as if that would help some how.

"I don't know, it's so dark. I'm scared of the dark."

He chuckled at that, and she got prepared for him to make fun of her.

"Don't be scared," he whispered. "I'm here with you in the dark. You never have to be scared with me."

When he kissed her that time, she felt her fear start to flow away. Excitement and endorphins took its place. She pressed her tongue against his, moaned when his hands moved to her ass, squeezing hard before sliding up her back and into her hair once again.

He pulled gently on the strands, forcing her head back so he could move his lips over her throat and down to her collar bone. She smoothed her hands along his shoulders, then combed her fingers through his hair. She was feeling so good, she even opened her eyes.

She was shocked to find that she could see. There was light. Only a little, more like a glow. A soft, orange glow, originating from the wall by the door. She finally found the source – one of those scented plug-ins that doubled as a sort of night light. It wasn't enough to fully see everything, but she could get the basic idea of their surroundings.

It was a supply room. Shelves lined the walls on either side of the narrow space, and they were filled with bulk packages of paper towels and toilet paper, cases of glasses, promotional displays, tons of dish towels, napkins, all kinds of random odds and ends a bar might run out of that they'd want close at hand.

"Wulf," she moaned. "We can't have sex in here."

"I beg to differ.""

As if to drive his point home, he yanked on the zipper at her back. In one fell swoop, he had it all the way down. The material fell away from her chest but the dress was tight enough to stay clinging to her hips.

"I've never done something like this," she whispered.

"Good, then I get to be your first," he said, pushing at the dress, causing it to fall around her feet.

"This is so screwed up. We can't just have sex every time we get into a fight. This isn't … isn't right," she stressed as he finally stood upright and looked down at her.

"No. No, what isn't right is the fact that I've never seen you in something like this before," he breathed, stepping back so he could look over her whole body.

She glanced down and realized she was standing in only her sheer bustier, a pair of satin black panties, and her strappy black heels.

"It's only underwear," she replied, gripping the sink behind her.

"Katya," he sighed, stepping close enough to touch her. He traced a finger from the hollow in her throat down through her cleavage. "You are too beautiful to sell yourself so short. You, Miss Tocci, are a work of art. Pure perfection."

*Why can't he talk like this **all** the time? It would make everything so much easier.*

She had his tie and jacket off in record time, then he was shoving her up against the shelves next to them, running his leg up between hers. They kissed with passion and tongue and biting teeth, her fingernails clawing at his shirt while his hand dove into her underwear.

No foreplay there – her eyes crossed as two fingers began thrusting in and out of her. She whimpered and dropped her forehead to his shoulder for a moment, trying to catch her breath. Then she bit into her bottom lip and worked shaky hands down his chest, managing to undo the buttons on his shirt.

Everything was happening so fast. She couldn't have stopped it if she wanted to – the room was loud with the sound of their panting, the air growing hot from their body heat. She whimpered and mewled and cried out at everything his lips and fingers were doing to her.

But she didn't stay idle. Once his shirt was unbuttoned, she went to work on his other clothes, yanking his belt clean out of the loops before almost ripping apart his button and fly. Then her hand was down his pants, wrapping her fingers around his dick and making him hiss.

"God, it feels like it's been forever since you've touched me," he panted, pulling his hand free of her underwear.

"We just had sex the other night," she reminded him. He snorted and placed his hand on his crotch, wrapping his fingers around hers through his pants.

"We didn't do *this* the other night," he replied, stroking up and down, setting the speed and pressure. Both of them groaned.

"Then yes. Yes, it's been forever," she replied.

"Too long."

His forehead was pressed against her chest and he let go of his crotch, raising both his hands to squeeze her breasts. She struggled to catch her breath, squirming under his touch.

"Wulf," she breathed. "Wulf, please."

He jerked upright, startling her and causing her to let him go. Then his hands were on her ass, squeezing tight and pulling her up. She was lifted off the ground, her legs forced around his hips, and then he held her up, pressing her into the shelves.

"Too much. You're too much for me, I swear," he was whispering, struggling to use one hand to shove his pants down a little.

"Not enough," she replied. "I don't think I've ever been enough for you."

He didn't respond, too busy with shoving the crotch of her panties to one side. She was sliding her hands over his shoulders when he was suddenly very much inside her, so fast it shocked her. She gasped and dug her nails into his muscles before raking them down his chest.

"Too, too much," he grunted, slamming his hips hard against her.

God, they were making so much noise – she hoped he'd been able to lock the door behind him. A box of napkins tumbled to the floor, breaking open. The shelves were rattling and shaking, shifting against the wall behind them. She was moaning at first, then was kissing him, aggressively and sloppily.

"Jesus, why is it always like this now!? So intense. Too intense," she gasped when she finally pulled away, stretching her arms out to the side and gripping the shelves. It took some of her weight off him and he was able to free one of his hands, which he immediately ran up her body.

"Because," he groaned. "If we're slow … you'll think too much … and make a mistake …"

"A mistake? I – *AH!*" she cried out, throwing her head back when he leaned down and bit at one of her nipples through the material of her bustier.

"Yes," he said when her cry turned into another moan. "Because stopping something like this would most definitely be a mistake."

"Don't stop," she gasped, looking down at him. "Don't ever stop."

"Never," he replied as her hair fell around them like a curtain.

Nerve endings were firing off like canons in the pleasure center of her brain. It was amazing, gravity was pulling her down every time he thrust up, allowing him to hit places she hadn't known existed. Within just a couple minutes, she was shaking and moaning and absolutely falling to pieces all around him.

"Oh my god," her voice was even shaking. She let one arm drop away from the shelves and wrapped it around his neck, pulling him as close as possible. "Please, Wulf, please. I'm going to … I need to … I want to …"

"God, I love it when you beg," he groaned, pressing his forehead to hers. "Again. Do it again."

"Please," she whimpered. "Please, Wulf."

"So close, yet can't say the right words," he teased. She groaned in frustration.

"Please, *please*, make me come. Please."

He kissed her then, his tongue halfway down her throat and distracting her from the fact that his hand was now between their bodies. She was moaning into his mouth when she felt his fingers sliding between them, strumming and pinching at swollen, sensitive flesh.

She understood why he'd kissed her so suddenly, because when she came, it was so hard she actually screamed. The sound was absorbed by his mouth. He started thrusting harder against her and she was reduced to just one long, continuous groan. He finally moved his lips to her throat and she let her head fall back again as she cried out in time to the electric pulses that were shooting through her body.

She wasn't sure how long she rode that orgasmic wave. It felt like forever because the harder he fucked her, the more it regrouped and spread further throughout her body. She was useless by the end, almost halfway unconscious. She suddenly realized she'd been staring at the ceiling for some time, gasping for air. She felt his hand back on her breast, pulling at the bustier material and trying to drag it down her chest.

"The best," he was grunting. "The best, the best, the best, Tocci."

"Yes," she sighed, fully stepping back into reality. "This is the best."

"You better goddamn remember that," he growled, his tongue running up her cleavage.

"I will," she whispered, combing her fingers through his hair.

"Remember who makes you feel this way, next time your with him. Remember who's the best, when you're tallying your points."

It was like a bucket of ice water was tossed over her entire body. She completely froze in place. Here she'd been, having a moment with him. Sure, it had started out as an anger bang born out of a silly argument, but it had moved into something lovely – him telling her never to be scared with him. Then something sensual – him telling her she was a work of art.

She hadn't been thinking about any game, or any choices, or any Liams. There had only been the two of them in that moment, just Wulf and Katya. If he hadn't said a word, she would've walked out of that room holding his hand, ready to go home with him and create even more naughty memories.

But the whole time, he'd been thinking about winning something. About beating Liam. She actually felt sick to her stomach, and she couldn't even be mad at him. She'd done this to herself. She'd set it up this way, she'd never been fully honest with him, so why should he think it was about anything else?

*Because I want him to just **feel** what I'm feeling when we're in these moments. Maybe that's hoping for too much, though.*

"Stop," she said loudly, her voice flat.

"What?" he panted for air, slowing to a stop. She started pushing at his chest.

"Let go of me, get off," she insisted, shoving at his shoulders.

"What's going on? What happened?" he asked, stepping back and slowly lowering her to the floor. His arms were still around her, though, and she started pulling at them.

"I said let go," she grumbled.

"What's wrong? Are you okay, did I hurt you?" he asked, still out of breath. He started moving his hands over her body, rubbing up and down her sides. Trying to comfort her. A sweet gesture, really.

Goddammit, DO NOT cry right now!

"I'm okay, I'm fine," she said, trying to hide a sniffle as she pulled herself free of his embrace. He gaped at her as she made her way back to her dress and stepped into the puddle of material.

"Tocci, what the fuck is going on!?" he demanded as she wiggled back into the dress.

"I have to go, I have to get out of here," she replied, struggling to work the zipper up her back. He looked stunned for a moment, then he hurriedly put himself back together and zipped up his pants before stomping over to her.

"We were kind of in the middle of something," he growled, then he whirled her around and zipped up the dress for her. "So don't tell me everything is fine."

She didn't respond. If she didn't start moving, she really was going to start crying, so she hurried to the door. She was able to get back out into the hallway before he caught up to her. He draped his loose tie around his neck before going about buttoning up his shirt.

"I didn't say that," she finally replied to his statement. "I just ... I don't want to be here anymore."

She burst into Liam's office without knocking. She'd halfway hoped he'd be in there – Wulf most likely wouldn't cause a scene in front of the other man. But unfortunately he wasn't there. She strode across the room and grabbed her trench coat and purse off a rack.

"Katya!" Wulf snapped, grabbing her arm and pulling her to a halt. "Jesus christ, talk to me here. What happened?"

She refused to look at him. She dug around in her purse instead, searching for a hair tie. Once she found one, she quickly combed her fingers through her tousled locks, yanking everything up into a messy ponytail. Then she struggled to put on her jacket. Her hands were shaking so bad, though, she couldn't get the first button through its hole.

"Tocci." She felt his forefinger under her chin and he forced her to look up at him. "Talk to me."

Her lips shook for a moment, but luckily he didn't notice. He was staring right into her eyes. He looked confused and angry and still somewhat shocked. His hair was mussy and worked over, his clothing wrinkled and out of order.

He's beautiful.

"It's just ..." she spoke in a strained voice, then she cleared her throat. Took a deep breath. "I think we need to have a long talk some day soon."

"Fuck that," he snorted. "We're talking *now*."

"No. I'm not doing this here, at some party, in Liam's office. I just … can't," she said.

"You can't leave me like this and just say 'we'll talk sometime' – you owe more than that," he insisted.

"I know," she held up her hands, wishing she could magically make him disappear. "What just happened … it was a mistake."

"It wasn't a -"

"*Yes,* it was. It was a mistake because … because it's not like that anymore. *I'm* not like that anymore," she said.

"I'm sorry, not like what? The kind of chick who'd have sex in a broom closet? Because I hate to break it to you, but clearly you are," he laughed. She glared and slapped his chest.

"This isn't a fucking joke to me!" she yelled at him, then she shoved him out of the way and stormed out of the office.

"Wait, wait, wait," he called out, chasing her down. "Okay, I'm sorry. Bad joke."

"It's all a joke to you," she hissed, trying to yank free when he pulled her to a stop.

"Enough!" he snapped. "Tell me what the fuck is going through that brain of yours."

"This," she said, gesturing between them. "Is not a joke. Not a competition. Not some game. What happened in that room? That was a big deal to me, and you … you acted like it was a game of black jack."

His eyes grew wide for a moment, then he narrowed them.

"So what, I'm the bad guy because I can't read your mind?" he demanded. She shook her head.

"No, I know that, that's why I had to stop it, I knew -"

"And if it's not some goddamn game to you, then why are you jerking me around? Fucking around with Eden to piss me off?" he snapped. She let out a small shriek and shoved him hard enough to knock him up against the wall.

"*I'm not fucking around with anybody!*" she yelled. "I spend time with you! I spend time with him! I'm confused and I'm upset and I don't know anything anymore and it's all a fucking game to you!"

"It was never a game to me – it's a game *to you*. A game that *you* started, and that *you* wanted us to play. So I did that for you, I did exactly what you wanted. *I did everything you wanted.* Jesus, if that wasn't what you wanted anymore, why didn't you say anything?" he demanded. "Again – I'm not a fucking psychic."

She was beyond angry. Angry, humiliated, confused, and *so fucking pissed off*. She stepped up close to him, got in his face.

"I didn't ask you to be one," she said. "I just hoped you'd be a little more sensitive to the situation."

"Are you serious? Have you met me?"

"God, I just want to go home," she moaned, turning away from him. Once again, he grabbed her arm and pulled her to a stop.

"You can't get angry at us for not knowing what's going through your head, Tocci," he pointed out. She struggled with his grip.

"There's no '*us*', Liam already knows it's not a game anymore," she told him. His glare grew more severe.

"Oh really? And I suppose he knows you had sex with me?"

"I tried to tell him," she insisted. He barked out a laugh, a harsh sound that cut her down.

"Sure, okay. Still sounds like a game to me, only this time instead of being a victim, you're just playing one."

Enough.

She slapped him across the face. It surprised him enough that he let go of her and she stepped out of grabbing range.

"Leave," she insisted, pointing down the hall. Wulf's eyes burned with anger as he stared back at her.

This was why she hadn't wanted to discuss the issue there – it was too intense. At home, they could hash it out. Misunderstand and miscommunicate and get angry. Shout and yell and get confused and cry, and hey, maybe even come to some sort of resolution. Maybe even laugh and be better afterwards. But not now. Now words were left unsaid and feelings were hurt and if she didn't stop them, it would spiral even further out of control.

"I have more of a right to be here than you do," he said in a low voice.

"Want to test that theory?" she threatened, standing up straight.

He stared at her for a long moment, obviously weighing his options. He could refuse, could continue following her and fighting with her. Create a scene in the middle of the party. But that would just get Liam and Jan the bouncer involved, and they would always take Katya's side. Worse than those two, though – it would get Tori and his sisters involved. Katya didn't want that, she wanted to leave with what little dignity she had left.

"I have tried, I want you to know," he started speaking at the same time as he began tucking his shirt back into his pants. "I tried giving you space. I tried giving you time. I tried being myself. I tried being nice. I tried playing your game, and tried playing the villainous part you cast me in. Obviously, I just don't know what it is you really want from me, Tocci. I'm beginning to wonder if I ever did."

By the time he was done, he'd put his clothing all to rights and even reknotted his tie. Before she could respond, though, he was striding out of the hall. Disappearing into the wild crowd that was dancing in front of the bar.

She sucked in a gasp of air and pressed her hand to her mouth. The tears refused to be held back any longer and it was like a faucet behind her eyes was turned on. She turned away and stumbled to the end of the hall, leaning against a door before the turn towards Liam's office.

She'd fucked it all up. So many awful things, perpetuated by two dastardly men, and in the end, it had been her who'd screwed it all up. Her who'd been an asshole. Playing games, what the fuck? Why couldn't she have just kept her distance? Or why couldn't she have been truly honest with herself – that deep down, she just wanted to forgive and forget?

But no. She'd stubbornly held onto her anger and had let it transform her. Had let it control her, leading her from one bad decision to another. Now one man she cared about was in the dark, and the other was raging pissed off at her.

Was possibly planning to never speak to her again.

Was that a goodbye? What that speech a kiss off?

She took several deep breaths and wiped at her face. Maybe it was, and maybe it wasn't, but she wouldn't know until she at least tried to talk to him again. No more assuming things – she was a serial assumer, and it had done nothing but gotten her in trouble. She would do what he'd done for her, and she'd give him some space. Some time. And then she would sit down with him and at least ... talk to him. Even if nothing came out of it, she could at least explain what had gone on in that utility room.

Still feeling like shit, but less like a jackass, she stood up straight and smoothed her hands over her dress. Patted at her hair. It was beyond time to leave the party, and she thought maybe she was finally ready.

But as she turned to walk away, she heard a noise through the door behind her. A sort of groaning sound. She was in a sex club, so her first thought was that someone was sex. Then it happened again, though, and it didn't sound like a sexy time groan. It kinda sounded like someone was in pain. She leaned against the wood and listened closely, heard someone coughing and wheezing.

"Hello?" she called out, knocking loudly on the door. "Hello, are you okay in there?"

As if to answer her, there came a loud crashing sound. Breaking glass and something heavy hitting the floor. There was a brief shout, then another long groan. She bit down on her bottom lip and grabbed the knob, throwing the door wide open.

For a moment, sheer terror gripped her. It looked like Liam had collapsed through a glass coffee table. But she was getting better at spotting their tiny differences, and she quickly realized it was Landon laying on the floor in front of her. He was moaning and trying to pick himself up, but he was only wiggling around in broken glass.

"Oh my god," she breathed, hurrying into the room and kneeling near him. "Stop, you're going to cut yourself!"

"I can't … my face … wow …" he spoke in a slurred voice, almost like his tongue was too big for his mouth.

"What happened? Can you talk?" she asked, gripping his arm when he reached out for her.

"No … muuuhhh … woosaaaaw," he garbled, clutching at her bicep so tightly it made her wince.

What had happened? Was he really, really drunk? He didn't seem like it, though – maybe a stroke? Did thirty-two year olds have strokes!?

"Somebody!" she yelled out while she looked around the room, trying to figure out what had happened. "Hey, we need help in -"

Her voice cut off when her eyes landed on an end table. Katya was more than a little naive sometimes, she knew that; she'd grown up in a gated community, had strict parents, and had gone to private school. So things that other people just seemed to know about, she was still oddly in the dark about.

Like drugs. She'd never done a single drug in her life, had never even seen any up close. So when she saw all the random paraphernalia laid out on the little table, she couldn't be positive what it all was. A baggy of white powder, a baggy with pills. Some rubber tubing, and some kind of pipe. Whatever it was, it all equaled up to something very, very bad. That much she was sure of.

"Oh god, are you OD-ing? Please don't OD here!" she shouted, shaking his arm. He was slumping back to the ground, face down in the glass. "Hey! *Hey!* Wake up! You're a doctor, tell me what to do!"

Clearly, that wouldn't work. Not ready to watch someone die in front of her, she shook off his arm and started digging around in her pockets for her phone. Once she pulled it out, she immediately started hitting keys.

Holy shit, I've never done this before. 9-1-

"Fuck."

She glanced up at the hissed swear word and found Liam standing in the doorway.

"I found him like this," she said quickly.

"Goddammit! Fucking shit goddammit, Lan!" he continued swearing as he rushed over and dropped down next to his brother.

"I'll call an ambulance," she said, looking back down at her phone. She was startled when it was swatted out of her hands.

"No!" Liam yelled. "No, no ambulance, they'll call the cops."

"But Liam! He's turning blue!" she yelled back.

"He's fine, I know how to handle this. Just get out," he said, then he wrapped his brother's arm around his neck and jerked him up to his feet.

"Are you serious!?" she exclaimed, slowly standing.

"Yes. This isn't a new thing for him, I've dealt with it before," he said through clenched teeth as he gently sat the other man on a loveseat that was against the back wall. Katya sighed and started taking off her jacket.

"I think this is a really, really bad idea. You should -"

"What do you think you're doing!?" he demanded, finally looking at her again. She froze while holding her coat wide open.

"I'm staying," she said. "I want to help you."

"No. I said leave," he said, pointing at the open door.

"Liam! You can't do this alone, please. Just let me -"

"I said get out!" he shouted at her. She was shocked. Liam so rarely got mad, it was always flooring when it happened. "You're not part of this! This is between me and him, *not you*. This is family, this is private. Just go."

She felt like a child who'd been chastised. She let go of her jacket, but didn't move towards the door.

"I know I'm not family," she said softly. "But I'm your friend, I want to be here for you. Please, let me help you. You need help."

If she had been shocked by him yelling at her, she was completely blown away when he stormed over, grabbed her by the arm, and forcibly removed her from the room.

"I didn't ask for your help," he said, and she could tell he was working hard not to yell again. "And I don't need it. This doesn't involve you, I don't want you to be a part of it."

"Liam, I -" she said after she'd been shoved into the hallway.

"Seriously. We're fine without you."

And with that, the door was slammed in her face.

What. In the ever loving. All that is holy. FUCKING FUCK!?

Was it a full moon out? Was she hallucinating? What on earth was going on that night!? Sex in a bathroom, a break-up-level fight with Wulf, an overdose, and Liam kicking her out and shutting her out.

Maybe if I'm really lucky, when I walk home I'll get hit by a bus.

22

WULF SAT IN THE DARK ON HIS SOFA IN HIS APARTMENT. HIS NEW apartment. His way too small, awfully located, and in a horrible building, new apartment.

He hated it there. Not nearly enough windows, too many closed off rooms. He could see why Liam had converted his apartment into a large studio. In its original layout, the apartment felt like each room was its own closet. Wulf liked natural light, and lots of it. Hence why his own penthouse was full of floor to ceiling windows.

But he stayed, and he waited. He tripped over hidden rules and bumped into confusing emotions. He sat silent went he wanted to rage, and he spoke softly when he wanted to shout. He'd tried doing it his way, then he'd tried doing it her way. What other way was left?

He took a deep breath and worked his head side-to-side, cracking his neck. Maybe she really didn't know what she wanted. Maybe she wouldn't ever want him again. Good sex was, after all, just good sex. It didn't matter how it made him feel right before, during, and after.

No, she feels it, too. She all but admitted it back there, when I fucked everything up.

Not that she was completely innocent. Of course, when he'd cooled down enough to think of everything she'd said to him, she hadn't been acting innocent, really. She was acting like she was upset with herself. If they continued fighting and continued having sex, it would just lead to more confusion and more distance and more *everything*. When did it all end?

And fuck, if this was happening between the two of them, what was happening between her and Liam? Whenever Wulf was around her for too long, it seemed like they inevitably ended up fighting. From what he'd seen and heard, it wasn't like that with Eden. They laughed, and they got along. Talked a lot – which even Wulf had to admit, talking was more productive then having angry sex.

He closed his eyes and leaned his head back, clearing his thoughts. He was a smart man, a logical man. He just had to stop for a moment and think it through. If she was confused, at least that meant she hadn't fully made any sort of decision yet. It may not have been a game anymore, but she was still struggling with whether or not she wanted to be with either of them. Sex clearly wasn't helping that problem, either.

Shit, is she having sex with Eden? Please god, no.

Okay, so she was struggling with her feelings. She was on the fence. Pushing her too far might send her into Liam's arms, but not pushing enough could keep him trapped in this loop. Trapped in her confusion and her warped emotional state. Granted, he'd helped to put her in that state, but that didn't mean he enjoyed being stuck in it with her. Neither of those things worked for him, so what was the alternative?

Let her go. End both their misery. He just seemed to cause her pain. He'd always known he wasn't built for long term relationships. Too emotionally stunted, too bitter, too aggressive. He'd compared Katya once to a garden, and it felt like all he'd done was cause her to whither and slowly fade away. Maybe she'd be better off without him. Maybe the truly good thing to do would be to just … *let her go.*

*But it's not that simple. It's beyond that now. What is good or right isn't an option anymore. It's moved into the realm of need. I **need** her, so much. She belongs with me, we belong together. So however long it takes, that's how long it takes. I can play the part of a stone and wait her out. It's what I was born to do, after all.*

He groaned and rubbed his hands over his face. Why did it all have to be so complicated? This was his punishment, for being an awful human being. She'd been right, that's exactly what he was – goddamn awful. And maybe his punishment was to chase her around for the rest of his life.

Well then, okay. That's what he would do. He would chase and he would push and he would press his attentions. He would jump through hoops and throw her off her guard and sweep her off her feet. And he knew – had to *believe* – that in the end, she would find her way back to him. She had to, she'd made promises, after all. He would hold her to them.

You said you would fight for me. You said you would believe in me. You said you would bring me back from hell. Time to get to work, Tocci.

23

LIAM STOOD OUTSIDE KATYA'S APARTMENT, TAKING DEEP BREATHS. HE KNEW he had to talk to her, but he wasn't quite prepared yet to start the conversation.

Last night had been beyond fucked up. So many shitty things happening all on the same evening. One catastrophe after another. He'd managed to drag his brother to his office, and once there, he'd tossed him into his private bathroom. He had a small shower stall, and he'd shoved Landon under the spray.

It wasn't a true overdose, but it had been close. Landon had drug problems – had for a long time. Liam was the only one in the family who knew, that's why everyone's hero worship of his brother stung so much. Everyone looked up to a sham. No one even knew that he'd almost lost his license to practice medicine, and that's why he'd decided to join the traveling doctor group. Being in a third world country made it slightly easier to get away with examining patients while high.

None of that was Katya's business, though. Liam felt bad about the way he'd spoken to her, but it had been a critical moment and she hadn't been getting it. They were very close, sure, but not as close as Liam and his twin, regardless of their issues. It had been a private moment between siblings, she would have to understand that.

Please be understanding, I'm so tired of apologizing.

He took one final deep breath and knocked on her door. There was no response. He frowned and knocked again. She was supposed to be home – Tori had told him that she'd taken Sunday off from work, just in case she'd had too good of a time at his party.

Which he knew she hadn't, because after he'd assured himself that Landon wasn't going to die, he'd gone looking for her. That guy, the one who lived in Liam's building – Fence? Gate? What kind of fucking name was that? – had told him that she'd left in a hurry. Liam would've gone after her, but it was his business' anniversary party, and it was in full swing. He had to be there, for whenever the next inevitable fuck up happened.

So he'd waited till the next day, then after getting up and shaving and giving his brother an earful, he'd jogged over to her building.

Maybe she went to the store …

He took out his phone and texted her, hoping for a quick response. She was hit or miss – sometimes she texted back right away, other times he had to wait a day or two. Luckily, his phone pinged just a few seconds later.

If you're home, angel cake, open the door. It's me out here.

Can't. Too tired. Later, okay?

Uh, no, not okay. Pleeeeease? I'll be nice, I swear.

I'm not mad. I'm just tired. Tomorrow.

I will knock on your door for an hour straight if you don't

open it right now.

She didn't respond, and for a moment he thought she was calling his bluff. He raised his arm, fully prepared to knock away, but then he heard the bolt lock turning. The chain lock was next, and finally the door was creaking open.

"Please, Liam. I'm not in the mood today. Tomorrow," she begged. He frowned as he looked over her face.

"Geez, are you okay?" he asked, pressing his hand against the door.

She looked ... almost sick. She was wearing her pajamas, yet it was almost noon. Not normal for her. She had dark circles under her eyes, which were also bloodshot and looked a little puffy. She was paler than normal, and kinda looked like she wanted to throw up.

"Yeah," she sighed, opening the door farther and leaning against the frame. "Just a late night. Great party, by the way."

"It was okay," he chuckled. "Could've done without some of the surprises."

"Is he okay?"

"Yeah. I mean, no, not really – he's a fucking drug addict. But he's back at the apartment now, hogging the tv," he told her.

"I'm sorry that happened. It looked bad," she said.

"I've seen him worse."

"Then I'm even more sorry."

"Look," he smiled as he spoke and leaned over her. "How about I go get you breakfast? I can bring it back and we can go cuddle on the roof. It's supposed to be warmer today, not so windy. I'll even lend you my hoodie."

She finally smiled back at him, and even seemed to brighten up a little. But then she sighed and shook her head.

"You are too good to me, Liam Edenhoff."

"Ah, there it is again, my last name. Poetry when you speak it right," he teased.

"I would love to, but seriously, I'm exhausted. I already switched my brunch date with Vieve Stone to lunch tomorrow. Rain check?" she asked.

"Always, angel cake. I have to meet Wulf's assistant chick to go over some accounting issues tomorrow, but I'll be free later in the afternoon," he told her. She seemed to perk up.

"Okay, I can meet you after lunch. Say four o'clock?"

"Four sounds good."

"Meet me here," she said. "I have some things to tell you. I'll make margaritas and we can still go hang out on the roof."

"I'll bring the hoodie. Four o'clock," he confirmed.

"Thank you. Really, thank you, Liam. You've been so ... wonderful, lately. I know I act crazy sometimes, but I really appreciate it. After everything we've been through and everything that's going on ... I just wanted you to know that," she babbled.

"Awww, shucks, you're gonna make be blush," he teased her some more. "And it's easy to be so nice when you're so sweet."

He leaned down and kissed her then. He tried to kiss her every time he saw her – mainly because it was Katya. Kissing her always felt good. But also to constantly remind her of who she was dealing with, what kind of man was standing in front of her. How good he was for her, and how much better he was than Wulfric goddamn Stone.

When he pulled away, she wasn't smiling. She was staring up at him with very wide eyes, almost looking nervous. He smiled, though, hoping to ease any stress she was going through. Then he brushed his thumb down the side of her cheek.

"Call me if you need me, okay? If you need anything. Anything at all," he told her. She nodded and managed a smile.

"Okay. I will."

He walked home with a skip in his step, whistling a tune. He spent the afternoon playing video games and arguing with Landon.

Then he stopped down at the club and flirted harmlessly with Tori for a bit before getting distracted by other things. He didn't come home till almost one in the morning, and he crawled straight into bed.

Katya didn't call once.

24

S HE FELT A LITTLE BETTER THE NEXT DAY. SHE GOT UP EARLY AND TOOK A walk, bringing home fresh bread for her and Tori. Her roommate was wickedly hung over – apparently the bar had shut down after a certain time and Liam had relieved her of her duties. She'd partied it up with Brighton and Gaten, then she and Gate had shared a taxi home.

Katya had no messages from Wulf, which she decided to not think about – it wasn't worth it to worry about something when she didn't have any clue as to what was going on. She was done making assumptions.

While she got ready for her lunch date with Genevieve Stone, she got some messages from Liam. He reminded her of their own rooftop date at four o'clock, and she assured him she'd be there. She was hoping to have a very frank, open conversation with him. No more of his witty banter and no more of her being a weenie.

At two o'clock, Katya was being seated inside a very fancy cafe. She was glad she'd taken care to dress nicely. She'd wanted to be somewhat on par with Vieve, who always dressed up, but she hadn't realized she'd be eating somewhere so nice. She sat and sipped at sparkling water until the other girl showed up.

"So sorry I'm late," Vieve breathed as she hurried up to the table. Katya stood up and leaned in for a brief hug.

"Please," she laughed. "It's been five minutes."

They both sat back down and then a very observant waiter hurried order, taking their drink orders. Katya ordered a lemonade, but was a little surprised when Vieve ordered a mimosa.

"So how was the party after I left?" Katya asked, smoothing her napkin over her lap. "It seemed like you and Gaten were having a good time."

Light pink stained the tops of Vieve's fair cheeks and she polished off the rest of her mimosa.

"It was a lot more fun than I expected. I thought … I don't know, it was a sex club, in a big city. Leather and whips?" she offered, and Katya burst out laughing.

"It's never quite been like that, even when it's operating like normal. But you and Gate, I -"

"Katya," Vieve sighed. "I appreciate you introducing us, and he was a very nice guy. Super good looking, polite, seemed intelligent. But I'm just not in the mood to date anyone right now."

Katya's first instinct was to argue. She always wanted everyone around her to be happy and thriving in some way. That's why she never cared what kind of job Tori had, whether it was in a law office or slinging drinks in a sex club. As long as she was being productive and it made her happy, that's what counted. It seemed like Vieve was a little sad and a little lonely, and Katya just wanted to help with that.

But she stopped herself, realizing that she was making assumptions *again*. Just because Vieve seemed one way, didn't mean anything. Katya ultimately didn't know the other girl very well. So she smiled politely and nodded, then changed the subject to Vieve's job hunt.

They ate watercress salads and cucumber finger sandwiches, laughing about how silly Liam was and how different he was from his twin. Neither ever brought up Wulf, which Katya thought was a little telling in itself, but she was also thankful.

By the time their plates were being cleared away and they both shared a plate of fruit for dessert, Katya still wasn't sure why they'd met up. Maybe Vieve had really just wanted to go to lunch with someone. Seemed strange, since they really weren't that close.

"This was a lot of fun," Katya said, wiping at her mouth as a waiter took away their credit cards.

"Yes, it was," Vieve agreed. "We haven't really gotten to spend any time together, just the two of us. I thought it would be nice."

"Oh. Well, thank you for that," Katya replied, not sure what to say.

"And I just … I wanted you to know, I hope … it would be nice, if you and Wulf ever got back together. I won't lie, I think it would be really nice. But I'm not hoping for it or counting on it or even necessarily rooting for it. He's a difficult man, it would require a lot of compromise and hardship to be with him, I'm sure. So no matter what happens between you two, I wanted you to know I'd understand, and I would also … I'd really love it if you and I could be friends. Outside of your relationship with him," Vieve laid everything out.

Katya was a little surprised. She'd never had some request to be friends with her, it almost seemed silly. Was definitely very sweet. Was also easier said than done. If she and Wulf were really over, if they never fixed what had broken between them, could she stand to be around Vieve? A constant reminder of him? Would Vieve really want to be around the woman responsible for making Wulf even more miserable than he already was?

But that was ridiculous. Who knew how it would go? Would she let potential fall out stop her from rekindling a friendship? Also, Vieve didn't know anyone in San Francisco outside of Wulf and Brie – she'd be all alone.

"That would be great, Vieve," Katya said, smiling big. "You should come over for dinner next week. Tori and I are gong to make huge pitchers of margaritas and a feast for her birthday."

It looked like the other girl let out a deep sigh of relief.

"I would really, really like that. You know I didn't really have a lot of friends growing up, and then I was so busy, getting married and with everything that happened, and Brie takes up a lot of my time. Part of why I moved here, I just wanted to get away a little bit. Wanted to … I don't know, feel like a grown up. God, that sounds stupid," Vieve chuckled, turning pink again and starting to collect her stuff.

"It doesn't," Katya insisted, leaning back as a waiter showed up and sat their credit cards on the table. She grabbed hers, then stood up and grabbed her jacket. "I always feel like I'm two steps behind everyone."

"But you have a career!"

"Yeah, and you went to med school," she teased. "Doesn't make a difference, I still feel so young compared to almost everyone. I think we were too sheltered growing up."

"Yes. So much yes to that," Vieve groaned.

"Well, you'll get to hang out with Tori next time, and she can broaden anyone's horizons," Katya laughed. "God, I remember this time, she made me break into a …"

Her voice trailed off before she finished. Her phone had started ringing and when she looked down, she was a little surprised at the number on the screen.

"Into what?" Vieve asked, holding open the front door.

"Sorry, just a second, I need to answer this," Katya replied.

As she stepped out onto the sidewalk, she gave the other girl an apologetic smile. Then she lifted the phone to her ear and answered the call.

Liam angrily paced up and down the hall outside Katya's door.

It was well after four. Hell, it was actually closer to five, now. He'd double checked with her about meeting at four – he'd rearranged his work schedule around it. He'd also tried calling her and texting her.

He'd known she'd taken off around two to meet up with Genevieve Stone, Wulf's sister. That made Liam very, very nervous. What had the two women talked about? Was Vieve telling all kinds of stories? Saying anything to advocate for a beloved older brother?

Bullshit. Liam had put in the time, put in the work. He had earned this win. He *deserved* to win, to finally beat Wulfric Stone at something. Just the idea that he couldn't get a hold of her because of Wulf was enough to drive Liam insane.

What the fuck do I have to do to come in first!? Why am I always second best!?

He paced for a while longer, texting her increasingly annoyed sounding texts. He even tried texting Tori, but she wasn't answering her phone, either. Finally, when it was a quarter after five, he gave up. He growled and stormed into the elevator, all while banging out one last text to Katya.

This was important to me. I thought it was important to you. The least you could do is answer me, let me know you're okay.

He was frustrated. He was annoyed. He was tired of feeling like he wasn't good enough. And, keeping it completely honest, he was a little hard up. He'd been looking forward to their little meeting on the roof. They'd been sharing a lot of hot kisses, and he had figured it was the perfect time to end their dry streak. He could still remember how she'd looked in her dress the other night, with her hair long and sexy around her face. So incredibly hot, he hadn't been able to get the image out of his head all night.

Now he was left hanging for over an hour, which no excuse or apology forth coming. He leaned back against the elevator wall, stewing and letting his imagination run wild. He pictured her lunch date with the Stone sister, imagined Wulf showing up. It would be just like the other man to use his family to weasel his way in. It wasn't fair, Liam didn't have a super sweet sister to use to his advantage. Maybe he could call one of his cousins …

When he finally got out at the lobby, he stood off to the side, try-ing to calm down. He was over reacting, he knew. More than likely, she'd just gotten caught up with her old friend. Probably reminiscing. Still. It always felt like he was an after thought. Always getting pushed down and pushed aside. Not returning phone calls, not answering texts, canceling plans. The feeling was getting pretty fucking old.

"Hey, I know you," a voice broke into his thoughts.

Liam glanced to his right and saw a pretty blonde woman. She had clear skin and pink lips and big blue eyes – almost a walking, talking, real-life Barbie. He'd seen her around, she lived in the build-ing he was pretty sure.

"Yeah. Yeah, I live next door. Liam Edenhoff," he introduced himself, holding out his hand to her.

"Lana Tisdale," she gave her name through a big smile and placed her hand into his. "I live upstairs."

"Ah, I thought I recognized you."

"Really?" she gasped, taking her hand from him and pressing it to her chest. "I can't believe it. I've seen you around for ages, but thought you'd never noticed me."

"Oh no," he laughed. "You'd be hard not to notice."

He wasn't lying. If he'd had to guess, he would've said she was from Los Angeles. Long blonde hair – that shade that isn't found anywhere in nature. A forehead that was smooth and completely de-void of any lines, even when she raised her eyebrows. Breasts that were far too perfect, and a body that looked like it had been sculpted by a professional. A professional who had been very good at his job.

"I met the building manager the other day," she continued. "Mr. Stone?"

"Ah, yes. Good ol' Mr. Stone. He lives on the top floor."

"Yes, we went to lunch. He mentioned that you owned the building," she said. Liam's smile got tight.

"Did he, now?"

"I mean, of course it doesn't matter to me," she said quickly. "I just wanted to thank the owner in person for providing me with a home, a roof over my head and four walls."

"And you are very welcome, Ms. Tisdale."

"Oh, Lana. Always Lana," she insisted, squeezing his arm affectionately.

He stared down at her for a long moment. She wasn't subtle at all, that was for sure. He'd told Katya once that he'd had female residents offer to fuck him in exchange for reduced or free rent. He hadn't been lying. He wouldn't be shocked to find out she'd made the same approach to Wulf. She said they'd had lunch together – what else had they done together?

And if Wulf had done more than just have lunch with this chick, then he wasn't the good guy that Katya seemed to believe he was. Maybe this was Liam's opportunity to get some real dirt on Wulf. Something that would finally put Liam over the top and help him win this stupid contest, once and for all.

He finally smiled big again and fully turned to face her.

"Well then, always-Lana," he teased. "How about we think of an interesting way for you to thank me?"

"You're bad!" she giggled. "I would love to invite you up for a drink, but my roommate is doing an online yoga class today, boo. But you live right next door, right? Top floor?"

"I do, in fact."

"I just love the views from the top floor."

"Do you? Unfortunately, my brother is visiting at the moment, and he's not feeling very well," Liam sighed, glancing around.

"That is a shame. I was so hoping to get to know you."

He didn't really want to go to some bar somewhere, it would be too hard to have an intimate conversation with her. He stared back down at her again, trying not to look at the impressive expanse of cleavage she was showing or how long her legs were under her skirt. His mind started spinning quickly, coming up with an idea.

"Me, too. Maybe we still can …"

25

"KATYA? KATYA!"

Vieve had all but screamed her name, but Katya hadn't heard a thing. She'd stood on that sidewalk, staring into the street as she'd dropped her phone. She also hadn't realized she'd started sobbing uncontrollably.

The things that happen when panic strikes you.

Vieve had grabbed her phone off the ground, then she'd wrapped an arm around Katya and hauled her down the street. By the time they got to the parking garage where Vieve's car was, Katya was almost on the ground. An attendant ran over to help them, offering to call an ambulance. She managed to shake her head, though, and she was loaded into the large SUV.

While Katya had continued sobbing, Vieve had spoken into her phone. Made sounds of sadness and understanding. Then she'd made another call while she'd pulled out of her spot. By the time she got to her home – Wulf's home – she'd hung up and she helped to cart her friend inside. She laid Katya out in Wulf's bed, then she'd shut all the curtains, shrouding the room in darkness. Before she'd left, she'd forced Katya to take three smalls pills. She wasn't sure what they were, but they calmed her down a little. Made her brain foggy. Made everything feel like she was in a dream.

That's what this is. A dream. A waking nightmare.

It had been her parents' neighbors on the phone, the Tunts. The man who had a Harley that her father wanted to race against. Just the other day.

Daddy ...

Her father had been in a car accident. On their street, just a couple houses down from home. When she'd heard that, Katya's first thought was it had been that stupid motorcycle Wulf had given him. But no, he'd been in his car, in the Lexus. It had been someone from a couple blocks over, a drunk driver. Doing around seventy miles an hour in a residential neighborhood. He had broadsided Mr. Tocci's car, ramming full force into the driver's side door and sending the car rolling onto its side. It had skidded across the street, hit a tree and spun around before finally coming to a stop.

Her mother had gotten to her father before the ambulance. They said she had to be sedated. Mr. Tocci had been pulled from the wreckage still alive, but they were sorry to say, they weren't sure he would live through the night. They were doing everything they could for him, and in the mean time, could Katya come down, please, so she could help take care of her mother. It was never said, but she got the feeling they also wanted her to come down to say goodbye to her father.

But I'm an only child. It's only us. I can't lose my dad. I just can't.

She curled up in the large bed and just sobbed. Cried into the mattress for a long time while the pills kept her wrapped in a fog. She couldn't imagine a life without her father. Couldn't think about anything else. What was she going to do? *How was she supposed to handle this!?*

She had no clue how long she laid in that bed for – it felt like seconds, but when she finally sat up, she saw that almost two hours had passed. Vieve had come in and out, bringing her water and wiping at her face. Even cuddling up behind her for a bit. She had a vague memory of Brighton stopping in and saying she was sorry.

I can't be here. I need Tori. I need Liam. I need Wulf. I need my mother. I need … **my daddy.**

"I have to go," she said in a hoarse voice, wiping at her face as she finally emerged from the bedroom.

"Of course," Vieve said, jumping up from the sofa. "I've spoken to my mother – she's gone over to your parents' house, made some meals for you and tidied up, locked all the doors and took home the keys. She said you are welcome to come stay with her, if you go home."

"Thanks. I have to …" Katya's mind was everywhere. She felt like she was stoned. "I need to go to my apartment. I need to get a bag, and Tori. A car. I need …"

Her chin started shaking. She was going to start sobbing again.

"We can go right now. I can stay with you, I can drive you down there," Vieve offered, grabbing her purse and leading the way out of the penthouse.

"No, no," Katya coughed to clear her throat as they got onto the elevator. "You have things to do here, interviews, everything. I'll go alone."

"No. That is a very, very bad idea. I … I hope you don't mind, I called Wulf."

"He was kinda close to my dad," Katya whispered as they got out at the lobby.

"I know. He's in Los Angeles right now."

"I didn't know."

"An emergency meeting, an issue with a property. He flew down this morning and was coming back tonight. He said … he said he was so sorry," Vieve told her.

"That's nice."

They were silent when they got in the car and Katya leaned her forehead against the glass. She closed her eyes, letting the vibrations from the vehicle give her a headache.

When they got to her apartment, Vieve walked her inside and waited while she drank an entire bottle of water in one go. She offered more of her magic pills, but Katya declined. She needed to be alert. She needed to be present. She needed to get her ass in gear.

"So much to do," she whispered.

"Let me help you," Vieve offered, but Katya held up her hand.

"No. No, I really, really appreciate your help. I can't even tell you how much. But honestly, I just want to be alone," she said.

Most people would've argued, she knew. Not Genevieve Stone, though. As a woman who had seen her fair share of disaster and pain, she seemed to know that when someone said that – they really meant it. She gave Katya a big hug, crushing her to her chest. Then she asked to be kept informed as she finally left the apartment.

The moment the door was shut, Katya started crying again. She leaned against the island and wrapped her arms around herself, trying her best to hold herself together.

*What to do ... what to do ... you need to go. You need to go right now. He's dying, they said. He won't last the night, they said. You have to go **right now.***

But she couldn't go alone. She knew she physically could not make that drive by herself. She felt half a step away from fainting. Someone would have to go with her, would have to drive her. It wasn't terribly far, but it was asking a lot so late in the day – whoever it was would probably have to stay the night.

Wulf was out of the question. Even if he got on a plane right that moment, he wouldn't make it into San Francisco for at least another hour. She couldn't wait that long. She tried calling Tori, but the other girl had made a bank run, and had apparently left her phone behind the bar. Katya asked if Liam was there, but they said no, he'd taken the afternoon off.

I was supposed to meet him at four.

She glanced at her watch. It was almost six o'clock. If he wasn't at the club, he might still be at home. She tried calling him, but got no answer. Still. He could be playing video games or dealing with his brother or doing laundry. He was her best bet.

She tore around her apartment, tossing the first articles of clothing she touched into an overnight bag. Then she slung it and her purse over her shoulder before hurrying downstairs. She didn't even bother waiting for the elevator in Liam's building, she ran all the way up the stairs to his apartment. She banged on his door with one hand while wiping at her face with the other. She prayed that he would answer, but that day wasn't her luckiest of days, it seemed.

"*What the fuck!?*" Landon Edenhoff yelled as he ripped open the door. "Is there a fire!?"

"I'm sorry," she gasped. "Is Liam here?"

He looked ready to tell her to go fuck herself, but then he paused. Seemed to take in her disheveled state. Crazy hair and glassy eyes and tear streaked face. He frowned and relaxed his demeanor.

"No, I thought he was with you, he left for your place a while ago. Are you okay?" he asked. Her lip started trembling and she shook her head.

"My father was in a really bad car accident and I … I just need to talk to Liam," she said quickly, barely holding the tears at bay. He was an asshole, but Landon was also a doctor, so she figured hearing about a medical emergency must mean something to him.

"I'm sorry, car accidents can be some of the most unforgiving. Did you try his phone? I haven't heard from him," he said, pulling out his own cell and checking it.

"I did, but no answer. We were supposed to meet and go up to …"

The roof. God, maybe he was waiting for her on the roof. If she hadn't been at her apartment and she hadn't answered his messages, he just might have gone up there to wait for her. She was ridiculously late – would he still be up there? She hoped he was, and also hoped he wasn't drunk on margaritas already.

"Good luck!" Landon yelled after her as she raced back to the stairwell.

Katya was running on pure adrenaline. She took the elevator up to the top floor in her building, then ran up the last set of steps. The stupid door was locked, of course. She had a key, luckily – one of only two, with Liam owning the other. She fumbled with her key ring and dropped it, swore out loud, then scooped it up and found the right key. Shoved it into the lock and burst out onto the roof.

When she saw him sitting on the loveseat, it was the first feeling of relief she'd had since she'd gotten the awful news at lunch. She hurried towards him.

"Liam, I have to -"

She froze mid-step, not quite sure what she was seeing, at first. It had already been a surreal kind of day. Maybe she was hallucinating. Could acute and sudden stress bring on hallucinations? She would have to ask Dr. Edenhoff when she had a chance.

Because if she wasn't hallucinating, then she was witnessing Liam getting a blow job from some blonde chick. On the loveseat. On the roof. On *their* roof. Their special place.

Why is everything nothing like it seems?

"I'm sorry," she breathed. "I didn't mean … I'm sorry."

He was gawking at her, looking completely shocked. As she started walking backwards, he began shoving at the blonde woman. Oddly, Katya's first thought was *"how rude"*, and she almost laughed.

"Katya, wait," he said, stumbling to his feet and knocking the poor woman over. "I can explain. *Wait.*"

"Hey!" the other woman yelled. "We were gonna talk about my back rent!"

Katya didn't care. Not even one little bit. It was all so stupid. Her father was dying in some hospital. All alone, while his wife was under sedation and his daughter was caught up in some stupid drama. It was unacceptable. She turned and walked back out the door.

"Wait! Wait, wait, wait, I really can … I'm sorry," Liam was rushing his words as he ran up next to her. Katya held up her hand.

"I know. It's okay. It's really okay," she said, stabbing the elevator button repeatedly.

"Jesus," he groaned, tugging at her elbow and following her onto the lift after the doors had opened. "Please. I don't know … fuck, why am I always fucking things up!?"

"I'm serious, Liam. It's okay, I'm not even mad," she told him, running her fingers under her eyes as the tears started falling again.

"God, please don't cry, angel cake. Please don't cry over me," he begged, moving so he was standing in front of her.

"I'm not. My dad was in a car accident," she said quickly. "That's why I couldn't make it this afternoon. I have to go to Carmel. I just … I wanted you to know that. I'm leaving."

"Holy shit," he whispered, staring down at her. "I thought … you didn't answer, and I thought … I thought you were with him."

"My dad?"

"Wulf."

She laughed. It sounded loud and scary, like a sound a psychopath would make.

"Wulfric. When I didn't show up or call, you thought I was with Wulfric, so you brought some girl up here to give you a blow job?" she asked.

"No. I mean … yeah, but … fuck, it sounds so bad. I was just angry! It's like you never notice me, and I'm a man, Katya, I can't just wait around forever, and I don't … I'm just really sorry," he babbled.

"Liam," she sighed, rubbing her hands over her face. "I don't … I don't really care. We weren't dating. We weren't exclusive. I've slept with Wulf since we got back from our trip."

"I'm sorry I – wait, you have?"

"Twice. I tried to tell you the other night, when we were up here," she said. "So I don't care if you need to fulfill your needs. I don't care if you go bang every chick in San Francisco."

"I didn't … I guess I didn't realize that," he mumbled. The

elevator dinged to a stop and they moved into the lobby.

"What I do have a problem with is you lying to me, again. *Continuously*. I think you have a serious problem with that. 'You're the only one for me, Katya', saying you hadn't been with anyone since us. How many chicks have you slept with since that date we had, honestly?" she demanded. He frowned.

"Um … like … four?" he answered, but his voice was shaky.

"Okay, so I'm just gonna go ahead and double that number, then round up, cause I can tell you're lying to me *right now*. And on the rooftop, Liam!? That's low, even for you. I never took anyone up there, not even Tori. *Not even Wulf*," she growled.

"I'm just … I'm really sorry," he said in a soft voice.

"You don't know what that words means. And do you want to know how I know that?" she snapped, whirling around on him before they could exit the building. "Because what you did up there? It doesn't matter. Like I said, line women up and have them suck your dick right out there on the street. Have fun, go to town. But doing it to get back at me, because you're angry at me? Angry at something you *thought* I *might* be doing? That right there is the worst thing you've ever done to me."

She was fully crying again, gasping for air as she shoved her finger into his chest, trying to drive her point home.

"My father is alone, and he's in pain, and he needs me, and what am I doing!? Standing here fighting with Liam Edenhoff, once again, over some fucking lie! *Some other fucking lie!*"

She was almost screaming, shoving him in the chest. He grabbed her hand, trying to get her to hold still.

"Stop, Katya. Stop," he whispered, trying to reel her in.

"No! *You* stop! You have *no business* being someone's friend until you learn how to be *a goddamn friend! Do you hear me!? Just stay away from me until you figure shit out!*"

She didn't wait for a response. While still sobbing, she yanked away from him and almost fell through the door. She could hear him behind her, knew he was still trying to talk to her, but at that same moment someone was getting out of an Uber at the curb. She all but fell into the backseat and slammed the door shut.

The Uber driver wasn't very happy at first, what with a random stranger falling into his backseat and a strange man yanking at the door handles from outside. But when Katya managed to gasp out her sob story, the kindly older gentleman offered to drive her anywhere, free of charge.

By the time they pulled up to the alley where Liam's club was, Katya had pulled herself together a little. What Liam had done was awful, but she wasn't thinking about it at all. He could've set all of her stuff on fire, and she'd already be over it. She had bigger problems. New priorities.

She managed to get downstairs without really saying anything to anyone. The place was slow, the employees taking it easy after the festivities from the night before. Tori was behind the bar downstairs, laughing at something a man in a suit was saying to her. She only took one look at Katya, though, to know that something was up.

"Hey, what's going on?" she asked after she'd led her friend into Liam's office.

The waterworks started immediately. Katya explained about her dad, how bad the accident was, and how she had to get home. Like right then. But she didn't want to go alone, didn't think it was safe for her to drive.

She hadn't even finished talking, though, and Tori was already pulling on her jacket and grabbing her purse.

"Wait," Katya asked, sniffling and hurrying to catch up as her roommate rushed through the bar. "Don't you need to call Liam? Ask for time off, find a cover?"

"I will, as soon as we're on the road."

"I don't want you get in trouble."

"I don't care if I get in trouble. Some things are just too important."

Within half an hour, they'd rented a car and were on the road.

Tori didn't even bother going back to the apartment and getting clothing, insisting she could just borrow something from Katya or buy something in Carmel.

After what felt like an eternity, they finally pulled up to the hospital where her father had been taken. While Tori parked the car, Katya ran into registration and asked about her parents.

Her mother was fine, but was still asleep, so she asked if she could see her father. She couldn't, she was informed, because he was in emergency surgery. She was told what floor and what wing, and to head to a waiting area there and a doctor would see her soon. She texted all the info to Tori, then she went up to wait.

It was another forty-five minutes before anyone showed up to speak to her. Tori had turned up by then, saying she'd called Liam and had a bizarre conversation with him. But she was good to be gone for as long as she needed.

"Do you want me to call Wulf?" she offered, wrapping an arm around Katya's shoulders.

"No," she sighed. "His sister called him, he was at some big meeting in Los Angeles. He's probably on a plane home right now."

"I'll call in an hour, see if -"

They didn't get a chance to discuss it right then, because a tall, very serious looking doctor showed up.

All sorts of things were explained to Katya, most of which she didn't understand. Contusions and concussions and fractures and compounds. Swelling brains and punctured lungs and inflamed organs. Transfusions and oxygen levels and erratic heart beats.

His face had actually hit the door frame – he must have been looking out it when he'd been hit. His left cheekbone had basically shattered, it was more than likely he would lose both eyes, and his skull was fractured.

They'd already amputated one leg, and they weren't sure they could save the other. It would have to wait, anyway. His body was in such a state of shock, it made all non-emergency surgery too dangerous. His heart had stopped beating twice already.

That was the other thing. He'd been deprived of oxygen for several minutes one of the times. Clinically dead for three whole minutes. If he survived his injuries, and if he regained consciousness, there was also a chance he wouldn't be the same man she'd grown up with; he might have amnesia. He might have severe mental problems. He might need to relearn how to talk and eat and speak.

She was ready to faint again by the time the doctor was done speaking, but he said there was some good news. Her dad's heart was beating steady again, and his vitals were starting to improve. He was still in the danger zone, anything could go wrong between then and the morning. He was still listed as critical, and they could only wait and pray for the time being.

There was nothing else they could do. She wasn't allowed to see him, not while he was in post-op. She went down to see her mother in her room, which they were allowed to go into and sit down. She held her mom's hand while a nice nurse explained that Mrs. Tocci was fine, but she would sleep through the night. It would be best if Katya and Tori went home. The hospital would call if anything happened.

But she couldn't go home. She couldn't go to that place, not without her parents. Not knowing that her father might never be there again. So they got a room at the closet hotel and dragged themselves up there.

By the time she laid down on the bed, Katya felt fifty years older. That morning, her life had been about baking cookies and worrying about stupid boys. One moment. One phone call. Suddenly her entire life had changed and she realized just how superficial everything was in comparison to how precious her family was to her.

"It's going to be okay, Katya," Tori assured her while she changed into some cheap t-shirt she'd bought at the hotel's gift shop.

"You don't know that," Katya said in a voice that was hoarse from crying.

"I do. I really do," her roommate said, curling up on her side next to her.

"How? How can you possibly know that?"

"Because – no matter what happens, you will get through it. Your parents are amazing people who raised an exceptional daughter. I'm not saying it'll be easy. It's going to be the worst thing ever," Tori explained, starting to cry, as well. "But I know that in the end, whatever happens, you will be okay."

They fell asleep holding onto each other and for a brief moment, right before darkness took over everything, Katya thought to herself, *"looking to all these stupid boys for strength and love – I forgot that nothing beats a best friend in those departments."*

26

IT WAS OVER A WEEK BEFORE KATYA AND TORI CHECKED OUT OF THE HOTEL.
Miraculously, her father didn't die. Defying all odds, he actually woke up. After four days of a medically induced coma, they stopped the drugs and waited to see what would happen. A day later, he opened his eyes.

He couldn't talk because they had a lot of tubes down his throat. But using his fingers to squeeze a doctor's hand in response to questions, he was able to indicate that he could hear, that he knew what year it was, and he knew his own name.

It really felt like a miracle. There were still a lot of hurdles to overcome. They had managed to save one leg and one eye – but he would need to be in a wheelchair for a long time before he could learn to walk with crutches or a prosthetic limb, and his eye was still seriously damaged. He could see a murky sort of grayness, he told them, but that was it. They couldn't guarantee he'd ever see more than that.

Katya got to see him, but it didn't go so well. She cried so hard she couldn't walk over to him. The whole thing upset him so much, she had to be removed. It was Tori who went into the room and assured Mr. Tocci that though his family was upset, they were holding it together. She promised that she would take good care of his wife and daughter, and that he'd be back home before he knew it.

Mrs. Tocci was not doing well, unfortunately. She'd moved into the hotel room next door to the girls, and even after she'd been told her husband would survive, she wouldn't leave. She had to be right next door, she had to be five minutes away, she insisted.

Tori suggested they go home. Get the house ready for whenever Mrs. Tocci decided to come back, clean out the fridge of old food, things like that. Katya finally agreed, and they headed to her parents' house.

"God, I haven't been back here in years," Tori sighed as they drove through Katya's old neighborhood. Tori had lived on the other side of town, and since graduating, her parents had moved to another city.

"Hasn't changed much," Katya said, watching the houses roll by.

"No. Not at all. Look!" Tori laughed, pointing at a huge home with big pillars. "Remember that kid!? He was in love with you!"

"No," Katya chuckled. "He was using me to get to you."

"Get out of here!"

"Yeah. He had a huge thing for you, wanted me to tell you he was a good kisser."

"Why didn't you?"

"Because he was an asshole."

They both laughed.

"Look at you, feisty even back then," Tori teased as she pulled the car into the Tocci's driveway.

"Hardly feisty. I think he kissed me once, no tongue, and I nearly peed myself. He wasn't even that good, he – *holy shit*," Katya leaned forward in her seat for a second, then she leapt out of the car.

The house had looked normal, at first glance. But when they'd come to a stop, she noticed the inside of the garage. There was a long white ramp leading up to the door to the house, complete with railings. When she turned to look at the front of the house, she saw that a similar ramp had been built there, but painted in colors to match the exterior paint.

"Did you arrange this?" Tori asked, coming around the car and putting her hands on her hips.

"No, I didn't."

"Your mom must have -"

"No," Katya shook her head. "This morning, before we left, she was talking about how we'd have to get it done. She asked me to look into it. I figured we had a month or so before even thinking about him coming home."

"Then how did this happen?" Tori asked.

They went into the house and were in for more of a surprise. An electronic chair lift system had been built into the stairs. Emergency pull cords had been installed in all the bathrooms, the kitchen, and in her parents' room.

In fact, the entire home had been made handicap accessible. It was amazing, as if someone in a wheelchair had always lived there. She couldn't believe it. It must have cost a small fortune. Who could've done something like that!?

Who do you know who could afford something like this?

"Wulfric," she whispered.

"Huh?" Tori asked as she headed into the kitchen.

"It had to have been Wulf," Katya said, following her friend. "He's the only one who could have afforded all this, and his mother has a key to the home."

"You really think so? Have you heard from him at all?" Tori asked.

"No, but I've barely been checking my phone."

"Do you think he's here?"

"I have no idea. I've talked to Vieve a lot, she didn't mention anything."

"If he did do all this, *I'm* going to marry him," Tori threatened, and they both laughed.

A thorough search of the kitchen showed that they didn't need to do any kind of cleaning. Any food that had grown old since the house had been empty was long gone. Fresh food filled the fridge and lined the cabinets. In fact, they almost over flowed with it. The pantry was fully stocked, too. Lots of water and cans of food.

And, she noticed, lots of ingredients for baking all sorts of different things. She almost cried as she looked it all over. Brand new pans and pie tins and molds lined a whole shelf. He'd gotten her stuff to bake with, because he'd guessed she would be there for a while, and Katya always had to be baking.

"Hey," Tori interrupted her thoughts as she poked her head into the pantry. "I have an idea. You call and check on your mom, and I'm going to run out and get us a shit ton of Chinese food and some cheap beer. We'll have a mini-celebration, in honor of your dad."

"Yeah. Yeah, that sounds awesome."

Tori skipped out of the house and Katya dialed her mom's number. She was on the phone for about ten minutes when the doorbell rang. Figuring Tori had forgotten the house key, she trapped the phone between her ear and shoulder and yanked open the door.

Of course, she wasn't expecting to see Wulf standing out there. He always popped up when she wasn't at all prepared for him. She stared up at him for a second, then she grabbed at her phone.

"Mom," she said, stepping out of the way and letting Wulf walk inside. "I was just calling to tell you that the house is good and we got here okay. Glad to hear Dad is still doing good. You'll call me if anything happens, or if you need anything?"

"Of course, dear," her mother sighed.

"I don't care if it's three in the morning, Mom. You call me."

"What would I be doing at three in the morning?"

"I know you and your partying ways."

"You're so silly. I'm so glad you're here, honey."

"Me, too. I'll talk to you in the morning," she said, shutting the door and following Wulf into the living room.

"Love you, sweetie."

"Love you, too."

Katya hung up the phone and slid it into her back pocket, then she finally looked up.

He was standing at the other end of the sofa, one hand casually shoved into his pants pocket. She felt like she hadn't seen him in a long time. Much longer than a week. Almost like she was looking at him for the first time since they'd been neighbors. When her father was whole and she wasn't broken.

"How are you?" she asked, moving to stand in front of him.

"I'm good. How are *you*?" he asked in a cautious voice.

"Good. I mean, you know, awful," she managed a laugh. "It's been pretty awful. But he's alive, and that's what matters. He knows who we are and who he is, thank god, so I'm happy."

"Good, I'm glad."

"Do you want to go see him?" she asked.

"I have," he told her, nodding his head. "I usually wait till you and your mother are gone."

"I had no idea," she said, honestly surprised.

"I didn't want to interrupt anything. This is about your family. I knew you'd want to be alone with them," he told her.

She held it together for about a second longer, then she fell against him. She wrapped her arms around his torso, hugging him tightly while she squeezed her eyes shut tight. Didn't matter, though, the tears got out anyway.

"You're his family, too," she whispered. His arms came around her and he hugged her back.

"No, I'm not. I'm a Stone."

"Wulfric, he cares about you as much as he cares about me. He would want to know you were there at the hospital. He'd be glad to know you're here now. *I'm* glad you're here," she told him.

"I was worried," he whispered, smoothing his hand over her

hair. "We didn't part on the best of terms, and I didn't want to upset you in any way. But I had to come. After I got off the phone with Vieve, I flew from L.A. straight to Monterey and then drove here."

"You probably got here before me."

"I did. Since I'm not family, though, they wouldn't tell me anything at the hospital. Wouldn't even let me into see your mother. So I came back here and waited. Vieve started passing along information so I started making calls about your house. I hope you don't mind," he said in a slow voice. "I wanted everything to be perfect for whenever he came home. I didn't want you or your mother to have to worry about anything."

"I don't mind. Thank you. Thank you so much."

"And you really won't have to worry, ever. He's going to get the best physical therapy I can find, the best doctors. I don't care if I have to fly him to Sweden or Thailand or South Korea. I don't care if he can't ever come home – I'll build you a new house next door to the hospital," he said in a fast voice. She laughed a little and pulled back to wipe at her nose.

"I don't think we'll need that, but thank you. You don't have to do any of that," she told him.

"I do, Katya."

"Why?"

"Because, I …" his voice trailed off, and she noticed he wasn't looking at her. His head was turned, he was staring out a window, looking at his own home.

"Because you're family," she finished for him.

He was silent for a long second, frowning hard. Then he visibly swallowed and nodded.

"Your father has been a very good man to me," he said, his voice barely above a whisper. "I owe him a lot. I can only hope to repay some of it."

They held onto each other for a while longer. She pressed her cheek back to his chest and closed her eyes, listening to his heartbeat for a while. So strong. First he'd carried his family on his shoulders, now he was offering to carry hers. Offering? Hell, he already *was* – he'd had their home practically remodeled in a matter of days.

I almost feel bad. Just what he doesn't need, more stress in his life. More responsibilities. More people to take care of.

But like he'd said, this wasn't about him, and it wasn't about them – her father needed the help, so she couldn't turn it down. They would need all the help they could get, and as long as he was willing to give it, she would have to take it.

"I'm sorry I wasn't there," he finally broke the silence.

"Excuse me?"

"San Francisco. I should've been there. I should've driven you home, been at the hospital the whole time," he said softly.

"Wulf, you couldn't have possibly known."

"I know, but still …"

They didn't get to discuss it anymore, though, because Tori walked through the front door. Wulf stepped back and Katya dropped her arms. Her roommate chattered as she moved through the house, dropping the food and beer onto the breakfast bar. Then she turned and noticed Wulf for the first time.

"Oh, it's you," she said, in typical Tori manner.

"It's me," Wulf agreed, nodding his head. She put her hands on her hips and walked right up to him.

"Did she tell you?" she asked, nodding her head at Katya.

"Tell me what?"

"About our engagement."

"Whose engaged?"

"You and I," Tori said, gesturing between them. "We're getting married."

"Oh. Glad to know. Have we set a date?" he asked, and Katya laughed at them both.

"You just tell me when."

"Okay, well, I hope the proposal was romantic."

"Baby cakes, you outfitting this house for papa Tocci was the pro-posal. I hope you're ready for me, I'm way freakier than this chick," she teased, winking at Katya before turning back to the kitchen.

"Some how, I doubt that."

Tori laughed, but he'd said the comment while looking at Katya. She smiled back at him. It was so different seeing him without all the bullshit between them. Nothing like a near loss-of-immediate-fami-ly to put things into perspective.

"Well," he sighed. "I should be going. I just wanted to check on you."

"No. No, stay," she insisted, grabbing his hand as he walked by.

"I shouldn't. My mother's also upset, and the girls are coming home tonight. I think I should be there when they get in," he ex-plained, squeezing her fingers.

"God, I feel awful, I should've gone over to see her," she said.

"No, you've been where you're needed. She understands. Have a good night, relax, take it easy," he instructed, opening the front door.

"Will do."

"And Tocci," he stopped before he could step off the porch. "If you need anything, you can call me. You know that, right?"

"Of course."

He gave a curt nod, then he was heading off towards the house next door. His mother's home. *His* home.

"Soooo ... does this mean *you're* going to marry him?" Tori asked. When Katya turned around, she found the other girl licking orange sauce off a chopstick.

"I don't think so," Katya replied.

"Pity."

"Why?"

"Because you're going to be so bummed when you hear about all the crazy sex he and I are going to have."

It was another week before Katya's mother came home. By then, their extended family had started to trickle in – Katya's mother's sister, from Connecticut, and her family. Her aunt and uncle from Massachusetts, and her father's uncle.

Though Liam insisted that Tori should stay in Carmel, Katya convinced her friend she was free to go home. She'd given up over two weeks to be there for her, but she did have her own life. She knew Tori would stay forever, for however long it took to tie things up at the Tocci household, but Katya didn't want that happening. So she sent her on her way.

Katya even spoke to Liam a couple times. Very brief conversations, but enough to keep him informed and to tell him not to come down. She didn't hate him, she assured him, and she wasn't angry, she promised. She had so many other things to worry about that honestly, he was nowhere close to even being on her radar.

Her mother was doing much better, but was by no means running at 100% – it was Katya who mainly dealt with doctors and nurses, relaying information to her mother and the rest of the family as she got it.

And though she didn't see him much, Wulf had really stepped in to deal with all the bills and insurance. Katya'd signed him off as someone who could receive sensitive information, and after that, he took over the monetary side of everything.

Her father was doing as well as could be expected. He had good days and bad days. At the beginning of the second week, he got a nasty infection in his lungs and had to be put back into the ICU. Then it got cleared up and he was doing better again, slowly improving. He got frustrated, of course, and sometimes even angry at people. But there were times that he smiled, even laughed, and that's how Katya knew that somehow, everything would be okay. It may never be the same again, but it would all be okay.

"I feel like we should do something," her mother said, late one night. They were sitting on the couch together, both zoning out to the television.

"What do you mean?" Katya asked, taking her mom's hand and squeezing it.

"Well, everyone's here, and so many people have done so much for us. The Stones and the Tunts. The Patels. We have enough food to last us for a whole year," she chuckled. "I feel bad, I haven't seen anyone. I feel like a thank you is in order."

"Well, we could make thank you cards. You love doing that," Katya pointed out.

"Yes, we could, but it seems so impersonal. I mean, look at this place, look at what Wulf did for us. A thank you card? I would feel so guilty."

"Then I'm not sure what you want."

"I think maybe a small gathering," her mom suggested.

"Mother, no. You are in no condition to make appetizers and pass them around at a cocktail party, I forbid it," Katya said sternly.

"Of course not," her mother said quickly. "Lord, I don't even have the energy to do the crossword in the morning. No, I was think-ing something small. Just close friends and our family, that's it. We can hire a caterer, you and I won't have to do anything more than make a phone call."

"I still think it's too much. The accident just happened, no one expects you to be doing a song and dance for them," Katya said.

"Honey, I'd like to do this for me," her mom finally spoke with some strength in her voice. "Every time I go to the store, or step outside, someone is asking me a question. This way, we can answer everyone's at once. Tell them how Daddy is doing, and show them that we're doing good, and that we appreciate all they've done for us. I'm no help to your father if I continue falling apart. It's time to do something, be productive."

It was clear this was something her mother had thought about a lot, and something she really wanted. Katya couldn't bring herself to talk her out of it, so she smiled and nodded.

They went through Mrs. Tocci address book, picking out potential caterers they would call the next day. They made a list of who they'd invite, and a tentative menu. It was the kind of stuff her mother lived for, and by the time she went to bed, she actually seemed a lot happier.

While Katya laid in bed, she held still and kept quiet. Strained her eyes and listened to the sound of water lapping in the near distance. Though the nights got kind of cold, she kept all her windows open. That way, when Wulf went for a late night swim, she could hear it. She didn't watch him, and she didn't go to see him. But it was comforting listening and knowing he was out there.

———————◆———————

They had the gathering the following weekend. Everyone who was invited showed up. It was morbid to even think it, but Katya kind of felt like she was at a wake. She wore a simple A-line dress, black and sleeveless. Then when she went downstairs, she saw that her mother and most of the female guests were also wearing black. There was only maybe a dozen or so people in the house, and they were all speaking in hushed tones. Whispering. Frowning and casting sad glances at Mrs. Tocci.

This is so depressing.

The weeks of stressing were finally catching up to her. Keeping strong for her father, taking on all the household duties for her mother. She'd told the bakery she was quitting – she didn't see herself going home any time in the foreseeable future. How was she going to pay her half of the rent? Liam wouldn't make her, of course, but still.

And of course, ever present, was the worry about her father. Would he really be okay? Would he ever regain his happy-go-lucky nature? Would he be in constant pain, would he be depressed? He loved his job – would he be able to do it anymore? He liked working with his hands – would they stop shaking long enough for him to make things? How was he going to deal with all of that while relearning how to use his now heavily damaged body, navigating a world that was murky gray? ***Would he ever be okay?***

"I'm so sorry, dear," Mrs. Patel said, squeezing Katya's hand.

I swear to god, if one more person says sorry one more time, I'm going to scream. Literally, actually, scream.

"Katya, I'm -"

She whirled around, ready to let loose with an ear-splitter, but stopped when she saw Vieve Stone standing behind her. She took a deep breath and pressed her hand over her heart.

"Sorry, you startled me," she chuckled.

"Oh no, I'm sorry," Vieve said quickly. "I wanted to come over sooner, but didn't feel it was right. How are you holding up?"

"Good. Okay. Sort of," Katya managed a laugh. "I never got to really say it, but thank you, for being there that day. I don't know what I would've done without you."

"Oh, please. I wish I could've done more," Vieve insisted.

"Don't be ridiculous. You were amazing. I hope you do become a doctor someday – your bedside manner is amazing," she said, and the other woman smiled big.

"Wow. Thank you, so much."

"You're welcome. Hey, my mom would love to see you again, she's in the kitchen."

"Oh, of course. I'll talk to you later?"

"Definitely."

Katya managed to hold onto her smile while the other girl walked away, then she turned on her heel and strode outside. She could only manage pleasantries for so long before she felt like her head was going to crack open.

She stood in her backyard and took deep breaths of fresh air. There were a couple people on the patio, talking quietly and nibbling at food. Other then that, it was quiet outside. She glanced around. If Vieve was there, where were Wulf and Brie? She'd seen Ms. Stone inside already – where were the rest of her kids?

Not wanting to go back into the party, Katya decided to go find them. She made her way through her backyard and into theirs, then marched right through the open sliding glass door that led to their den.

There was no one in the room, but she could hear raised voices. Not yelling, but someone didn't sound happy. It was a voice she didn't recognize, a man. She made her way to the front of the house, following the noise.

Brighton Stone was standing in the grand entry way, her back to the stairs. A man was standing in front of her, pointing down and speaking fast. Katya stared for a second, a little shocked. She'd never met him before, but she immediately recognized him.

*Wow. Wulfric looks **just like** his father. A little taller, a little broader, but that face. Those eyes. Mr. Stone and his son could almost be twins.*

She was so in awe at seeing the mysterious Mr. Stone, that she didn't clue into what he was saying for a minute. When it started cutting into her thoughts, she frowned and looked back at Brie. The girl looked small, and embarrassed, and even a little … scared.

"… drop out!" Mr. Stone was yelling. "No child of mine will be called a drop out! Do you have any idea how humiliating that is? To tell people that!?"

"I'm sorry, Dad. It just wasn't for me. I really -" she started, but he slashed his hand through the air.

"Not good enough! Wasn't for you!? You're a spoiled brat. Between Wulf and your mother, they've ruined you. Look at you," he sneered, his eyes wandering over his daughter's form. "You look like a tramp."

Again, Katya had led a somewhat sheltered life, never getting exposed to much violence or trouble. So hearing a parent speak to his child that way was flooring. How could he speak to her like that?

"I'll change," Brie insisted. "I can go upstairs -"

"Changing your clothes won't change who you are, Brighton. A degenerate drop out. I'm embarrassed that you share my name."

Katya's fuse was lit, burning down, and an explosion was imminent. How dare he. *How fucking dare he.* Her father was laying in a hospital bed, missing an eye and a leg. Katya had come close to only having one parent. One member in her immediate family.

And here this man was, berating his youngest daughter, maliciously hurting her, casting her aside. Had *already* cast her aside, many years ago. Had cast them all aside. Thrown Brie away, like trash. Thrown Vieve away, like she was broken. Thrown Wulfric away, *like he wasn't good enough.*

"*How fucking dare you.*"

She'd spoken without realizing it. Both Brie and her dad whipped their heads towards her and watched as she stomped into the room.

"Who the hell are you?" he demanded, standing up straight.

"Someone who actually knows Brighton, *unlike you,*" Katya snarled, standing between him and his daughter. He narrowed his eyes and pointed at her.

"I know you, you're that girl from next door," he said.

"I'm that girl who has spent more time with your family than you have," she spit out at him. "Get the fuck out of her house."

"How dare you speak to me like this! I bought this house!" he yelled at her.

"*Wulfric* bought this house," she corrected him. "And *Wulfric* raised your daughters, and *Wulfric* sent them to college. So you know what? I don't think you're fucking welcome here!"

There was a gasp from behind her, and Katya suddenly remembered that Brighton hadn't known any of that. Wulf had always allowed the girls to believe that their mother had been taking care of them all these years.

Well, good. They need to know.

"I don't know who you think you are," Mr. Stone snarled, stepping up close to her. She didn't move an inch, just glared right back at him. "Probably just another tramp, like her. Why are you even here? For her, or for Wulf? Well, don't you worry, I would never allow some little tramp to ruin everything my son – *AH!*"

He let out a shout as he was yanked backwards, almost off his feet. Both Katya and Brie shrieked, with Katya backing into the other girl, shielding her. It took her a second to realize what had happened, though, and then she watched with wide eyes as Wulfric dragged his father back by the collar of his jacket.

"*Never* call me that," he was growling as he shoved his dad up against a wall.

"What do you think you're doing!?" Mr. Stone demanded.

"I am *not* your son," Wulf continued, pinning his father in place. "Get the fuck out of *my house*, and don't you ever fucking come back."

"You can't do this to me! I came here because your mother -"

Wulf didn't wait to hear the reason. He yanked his father around by his suit jacket, dragging him to the front door. Once he had it open, he shoved his father out onto the porch.

"Don't come back here," Wulf said, out of breath as he pointed as his father. "And don't *ever* speak to Brighton again. Or Vieve, for that matter. If I hear about you contacting them in any way, so help me god, *you will regret it.*"

"Wulfric, please. Be an adult about this," his dad insisted, keeping his voice calm as he straightened out his jacket.

Instead of responding, Wulf shut the door in his father's face. They all stayed silent, listening as Mr. Stone banged on it for a minute. Katya held her breath, watching Wulf. He was almost trembling with rage. She could tell he wanted to open the door and *end* his father, but she got the feeling he was holding back because she and Brighton were in the room.

Speaking of Brighton ...

"Oh my god," she breathed, turning around as soon as they heard Mr. Stone huff down the front walk. "Are you okay!?"

Brighton was flat against the wall, tears streaming down her face.

She wasn't wearing a stitch of makeup and she looked young. Much younger than nineteen even. She didn't look at Katya, just stared at her brother.

"How could I not know that?" she finally asked. Wulf stayed facing the door till they heard car tires peeling out of the driveway – Mr. Stone finally leaving.

"What was he doing here?" he asked, ignoring her question as he headed towards them.

"Mom called him, told him about Mr. Tocci. Begged him to come," Brie explained, wiping at her nose and face.

"Goddammit," Wulf growled, squeezing his eyes shut tight for a moment. "Why the fuck does she do that!?"

"*Why does everyone lie to me!?*"

Brighton was screaming. Katya hurriedly stepped away, giving the brother and sister some space.

"Brie," he sighed. "We didn't lie, we just …"

"Never told me anything! Does Vieve know?" she demanded. There was another pause.

"She found out a little while ago, yeah," he was honest.

"God! You all think I'm so stupid! I always thought mom was paying for college. Paying out of child support from *him,*" she sobbed. "You all wonder why I never talk to you! Now do you see why!?"

"Brie, just calm down, and let's talk about this."

"No! No, you all are always leaving me out! I'm like the ugly step-sister, you might as well have just chained me up in the basement!" she shouted. He looked bewildered.

"What are you talking about?"

"Not as pretty as Vieve," she was sobbing. "Not as smart as you. You never talk to me, Mom never notices me. Dad hates me. Jesus, I hate this fucking family!"

Stunned at her outburst, neither Katya nor Wulf moved when Brie ran across the room. She was out the door before Wulf could take a step, and driving down the street by the time he got to the door.

"*Goddammit!*" he roared, slamming the door shut so hard the chandelier above them rattled.

"I'm sorry," Katya spoke quickly, walking over to him. "I'm so sorry. I just heard him, the way he was talking to her, and I … I didn't even think."

Wulf didn't respond. He turned and walked straight up the stairs, surprising her a little. She hesitated for a moment, then followed him. Stayed a couple steps behind all the way to his room, then she lingered in the door way.

"Come in," he finally said in a gruff voice.

She stepped softly into the space, looking around. As a teenager, she'd often fantasized about going into Wulfric Stone's bedroom. But with the way things were, it almost felt wrong to be there now.

It had long since been made over, there were no signs that a teenager had ever inhabited the room. It wasn't the master bedroom, but it was huge, with a spacious walk-in closet and its own sitting area. Wulf walked in there, straight to a bar that was set up against a wall. He poured himself a couple fingers of scotch, slammed it back, then poured another glass.

"Here," he said, offering her the glass. Katya didn't drink scotch, but she didn't argue. She took the glass and sipped at it while he made up another one for himself.

"Are you okay?" she asked in a soft voice. He shrugged.

"Just as okay as I ever am," he replied, then he swallowed all the scotch in one go again. "And you? Are you okay?"

"I'm fine."

"When I heard him talking to you that way," he started in a soft voice, staring at the wall in front of him. "Talking to Brie … I wanted to hurt him."

"I know," she nodded.

"*You have no idea,*" he whispered.

"It's okay. It's okay to feel that way," she assured him, struggling

304

to keep calm.

"It's always like this," he suddenly said, and she shrieked when the glass in his hand broke. He'd squeezed it so hard, it had shattered. "Whenever I come home."

"Oh my god, Wulf, you're bleeding," she gasped, hurrying over to him and setting her glass down.

"This is why I stay away from the girls, I just ruin things," he kept talking while she searched the bar area. There was a small sink, and underneath it she found some bandages and towels. She wet one of the towels and grabbed his hand, dabbing at the small cuts.

"Stop it," she said, throwing the towel aside and opening one of the bandages.

"And you," he continued. "Look at what happened with you."

"I said *stop*," she urged, smoothing her fingers over the large bandage, sticking it into place.

"And right now," he kept going. "You don't need to be part of this bullshit. Your dad ... Mr. Tocci. I can't imagine, Katya."

She nodded, stepping back and wiping at tears.

"It's bad," she agreed. "It's pretty shitty fucking awful. But you know what?"

"What?" he asked, frowning at her.

"At least ... at least I don't have *your* dad."

His eyes got wide and she startled a laugh out of him. She laughed as well, and for a few moments, nobody frowned. But she couldn't stop crying and eventually they fell silent again.

"I'm so sorry, Katya," he sighed, reaching out and wiping her tears away with his thumb.

"You don't have to be sorry," she told him.

"I'm sorry I was the wrong man for you," he said. She held still for a moment, then started shaking. She chewed on her lips for a moment before taking a deep breath.

"Not wrong ..." she whispered, and he smiled sadly.

"But definitely not right," he whispered back, moving his hand to cup her cheek. "I'm sorry I'm not a very good person. I'm sorry I broke you."

"Me, too, Wulf."

When he kissed her, she cried harder. When he tried to pull away, she clung tighter to him. Wrapped her arms around his shoulders and never wanted to let him go.

He kissed her lips and her chin and her eyelids. Wiped away her tears and whispered to her soul.

"I'm sorry. I'm so sorry. Forgive me."

She didn't want to go home. She didn't want to go back to San Francisco. She didn't want to be Katya Tocci, the baker, and she didn't want him to be Wulfric Stone, real estate mogul. She wanted them to be the kind of people who wouldn't hurt each other. Who could just love and hold each other and take care of each other.

They bumped into his bed before she even knew they were moving. It was so quiet in the room that when he pulled down the zipper on her dress, she felt like the sound echoed around them.

The dress and her shoes disappeared when she laid down on the bed. His shirt was gone by the time he laid down on top of her. Her bra was removed while she pushed at his pants with her hands and feet.

"I don't want to hurt you," he whispered, his lips trailing across her chest while his finger curled around the top of her underwear.

"You can't," she whispered back, holding still as he removed her panties.

Maybe it was wrong. Maybe it was awful of them. But they were both so broken and hurting, and there was nowhere else she wanted to be at that moment. She wanted his touch to heal every pain he'd caused. She wanted to kiss away all the hurt he'd experienced in his life. She wanted to be in that moment with him, where they were the only things that mattered to each other.

Sex between them had rarely been overly emotional, but something powerful happened when he entered her. She took a deep breath, feeling every inch of him every inch of the way. She pressed her head back, straining her body away from him even while she pressed her hips closer.

"No one else," he breathed as he slowly moved over her and inside of her. "No one else has ever been like you."

"No, no one," she agreed, hugging him close and whispering in his ear.

"I never stopped," he said.

"Stopped what?"

"Looking at you like you were Christmas. Even when you were angry. Even when you thought you hated me. Even when you were with him. You've always been a gift to me."

"A gift," she whispered, pressing her face to the side of his as she started crying again.

"Thank you, Katya. For being the best present I ever got."

She was never, ever going to stop crying. Her heart would always be breaking for this beautiful man, but if she had to to be hurting, then Wulfric Stone was very much worth it.

He abruptly rolled them over, startling her. He handled her like she was weightless, settling her on top of him, her knees on either side of his hips. She moaned shakily, having trouble breathing because he filled her to the point overflowing.

"I want to see you," he breathed, brushing her hair out of her face. She nodded and started moving her hips.

"You do, Wulf. You see me."

He kept his hand in her hair, anchoring her forehead to his so she couldn't look anywhere but him. He kept a hand on her hip, urging her faster while his own hips pumped harder. She moaned and cried out, clutching at his shoulders. Something big was happening inside of her, and she was pretty sure it had nothing to do with the orgasm that was about to happen.

If I wasn't broken before, this will shatter me.

The orgasm unfurled slowly, setting her body on fire. It started in her core and spiraled outward, causing her to lose her breath and shake uncontrollably. She let go of him and lost her balance, almost falling over. He held still and wrapped his arms around her, crushing her to him and kissing her hard.

While she was still trembling and shattering and losing herself in him, he slowly rolled them forward. She laid back and stretched out her arms, arching her back when he started driving into her fast and hard.

His hands and tongue were everywhere, making it hard to tell where she ended and he began. He was murmuring and whispering to her, things she didn't want to hear. Not when she was so upset. Then his arms were back around her, so tight she had trouble breathing, but she didn't say anything. Just wrapped her arms around him and held on for dear life while he came and came and came and came …

"No one," he was panting when she finally floated back into her body. "No one will ever be like you, Katya Tocci."

She wanted to respond, but she couldn't. She was crying too hard.

27

"I WANT TO STAY HERE."

"Then I'll stay, too."

"No, Wulfric."

"Why not?"

"Your life is in San Francisco."

"So? We'll go home eventually."

"I don't know if I'll ever go home."

"I don't care. I'll stay."

"I want you to go."

"I don't care."

"Yes, you do."

"… I don't want to leave you."

"I know. And I'm sorry, but you have to. I have to be here for my parents. I quit the bakery. I wasted enough time playing games in San Francisco – my time **and** yours. I won't do that anymore."

"The best time I ever had was when I was wasting time with you."

"Where was this silver tongue weeks ago?"

"Tocci."

"Stone."

"I don't understand."

"You're amazing. Perfection in human form. But … I don't trust you. No more games, no more confusion. I will never be able to thank you for all you've done for me, but it still doesn't change what happened in the past. I forgive you, I really do. But after everything that's happened … I don't want to keep doing this. Fighting and having sex and then wondering when the next bad thing will happen. Maybe I'm just not ready for a relationship. I have a lot of growing up to do. I'm sorry."

"So do I, apparently."

"Yes, and it feels like trying to do that together, it's just making us into worse people."

"I don't agree."

"And that's okay, but it doesn't change anything. I'm so sorry, Wulf."

"Don't be. Never be sorry."

"Still."

"I know."

"I'm sorry."

"Me, too, Tocci."

"You'll always be my teenage dream, Wulf."

"And don't you forget it."

"Never. Never, ever, never."

"I'll miss you."

"And I'll miss you. But this is good."

"It's not. Things won't ever be good again."

"Don't say that."

"I guess it's fair. You had to deal with an unrequited fantasy for years. Now it's my turn."

"Now you're just being dramatic."

"Not even a little, Tocci. Not even at all."

"Sometimes you are so beautiful, Wulf."

"Take care of yourself. And if you ever need anything, anything at all, just call me."

"Okay."

"I'm serious."

"I know you are. And I promise I will."

"But it was good, whatever it was."

"It really was."

"Katya Tocci – the best neighbor I ever had."

"Wulfric Stone – the most interesting neighbor I ever had."

28

THEY'D HAD THEIR LAST CONVERSATION TOGETHER WHILE THEY GOT dressed. Then he'd walked her to his door and he kissed her goodbye. Held onto her like he never wanted to let her go, his lips fusing to her own.

But then he stepped away. Smiled at her and pinched her chin between his thumb and forefinger, tilting her head up. He looked her over once, like he was appraising her, and for quite possibly the first time ever, she felt like she passed muster. Then he let her go and wished her well.

She walked through the party and found Vieve, gave a brief run-down on what had happened with her father. The other girl thanked her, then hurried back to her own house.

Then Katya went and found her mother, giving her a fierce hug. When she pulled away, they were both glassy eyed and fighting back tears.

Then she went up to her room and she crawled into bed. She slept for a long time. Through the rest of the party and the night. Through the morning and well into the afternoon. It was almost four by the time she went downstairs, and when her mother started talking to her, she already knew what the older woman was going to say.

"You missed it dear, Wulfric came over to say goodbye. He had to go back to work. I wanted to come get you, but he asked me not to wake you. Just said to tell you that you'd be in his thoughts."

It was awful and it hurt and she hated herself a little, but she was confident about her choice. Both Wulf and Liam had put her through the wringer. Tossed her up and down and all around, and worse, she'd let them. She didn't want to be new-Katya or old-Katya or bitter-vengeful-bitch-Katya – she just wanted to be *Katya*, plain and simple. She would have to learn how, and she couldn't do that when she was caught up in all the drama they'd created.

Seeing her mom in pain, and seeing her dad in the hospital, it had been like a wake up call. She didn't have time to figure out the learning curve of love with Wulf, and she couldn't wait around for Liam to learn what maturity was – she had a life beyond them, and it was time to focus on it. To put away childish things and start being her own kind of adult.

Even if it was really, really hard.

Her father was in the hospital for another three weeks. Normally, an amputee didn't spend quite that long, but the severity of his injuries combined with another nasty round of infections had slowed his progress.

But she could honestly say he was doing good. A lot of his eyesight had returned, which had done wonders for his mood. He still had a long way to go, a lot of hurdles to jump, but he was smiling and laughing again. He was banged up and bruised and missing a few parts, but he was still her father.

"Wow, this looks great!"

He was marveling at the sleek ramp that led up to his front door now. Katya chuckled as she pushed his chair.

"Thanks. Wulf had it done right away, after the accident," she explained.

"Sneaky man, never said a thing to me."

"He's so selfish that way, just doing things and not wanting any thanks."

They both laughed. It hurt talking about Wulf, but she thought maybe if she kept doing it, it would eventually get easier.

"I'm glad you wouldn't let anyone else come," he commented when they finally got in the door. "Being out of the hospital is bizarre. Now that I'm out here, I'm not sure I'm ready for anybody to see me."

"Why not? I think the eye patch is sexy," she teased.

"Well, of course it is. Your mother won't keep her hands to herself."

"Ew, gross, Dad."

"Hey, you have to be nice to me now – I'm damaged," he informed her.

"Nice try, dude," she snorted. "If anything, you're an improved model of yourself. Now that you've got built in wheels, we've got a whole new set of chores for you."

They both laughed again, and she almost wanted to start crying – because she was happy. Happy that they even could laugh after something so horrible. He was still her dad, still the same man she'd grown up with, still the jokester. She couldn't get over it.

"You two!" her mom groaned, coming in the door behind them and kicking it shut. "I'll show your father the changes around the house, Katya, and you go get the rest of the stuff from the car."

While she ferried all kinds of things inside, her phone started ringing. She smiled when she saw Tori's number on the screen and she quickly answered.

"Hey you, did you get home okay?" she asked. Her roommate had been coming down every weekend, helping to take care of things and keeping Katya from going insane.

"Yup yup," the other girl replied. "During the drive, I ate that entire pie you made."

"You did not."

"I so did. It was amazing."

"You're going to have a heart attack – do you have any idea how much butter was in that?" Katya laughed, dropping off the last bag. Then she went out on stoop and sat down.

"Totally worth it. I don't know how you can just give up baking cold turkey," Tori sighed.

"I'm not," Katya groaned. "I'm just taking time off. I'm still getting calls from clients in S.F., and I could find work here easily."

"Not the same."

"Close enough."

"You can't just put your whole life on hold, Katya," Tori said in a stern voice.

"Oh, okay. Sorry you're an amputee and half blind, Dad, but I gotta go have a life. Peace out!" she replied.

"Stop being a smart ass. I'm not saying leave right this minute – but you quit your job and told me to find a new roommate. You can't live with your parents for the rest of your life," Tori said.

"And I won't. I'm just gonna stay a little longer, help my dad adjust to the house. And then …"

"And then …? What? Move back here and live on the streets? Fuck that, I'm not getting a new roommate."

"Tori, you need someone to pay half the rent."

"They haven't been charging me any rent – the last check was never cashed. Liam said to stop trying."

"Figures."

"How is he?" Tori asked in a careful voice.

Liam had come down to Carmel. Just shown up. They'd had a few conversations on the phone, usually short and to the point. Not because she was still angry – she could barely remember even being mad. Removing bandages and bathing scarred and burned flesh did that to a person. She was just too busy to deal with her relationship issues with him.

So he'd taken it upon himself to just show up. It had shocked her, opening her door and finding him standing there. He had immediately apologized to her and promised that he would turn around and go home, he had just wanted to see her. See with his own eyes that she was okay.

But then she had burst out crying and he had hugged her and everything was alright. He came in and her mother cried and hugged him, too. Then she made up a guest room for him and he'd been there ever since, had become Mrs. Tocci's new best friend. He helped her around the house and ran errands and he'd been the one to drive them to and from the hospital to pick up Katya's dad.

"He's good. *We're* good," she corrected her answer.

"Good, huh. Like *good* good?" Tori questioned.

"No," Katya laughed. "Good like he sleeps down the hall and the only time we touch is when he's helping me in and out of the car. We're just friends. Probably should've always been just friends."

"I'm glad. He and I have sort of become really good friends, and I would just ... I would hate having you two mad at each other," Tori sighed.

"Nope, not mad," Katya replied. She hesitated for a second, then remembered that life was short, so she took a deep breath and decided to dive right in. "I know he's easy to fall for, Tori."

"Huh?"

"He's gorgeous, and he's funny, and god, he has that grin," Katya laughed, looking down and toying with a shoe lace. "He knows how to say all the right things to make you think you're special. Like you're the most beautiful, amazing person on the planet."

"Why are you telling me this?" Tori asked, but Katya ignored her.

"And don't get me wrong – I like him. He's a good friend, would give me the shirt off his back if I so much as shivered."

"I don't understand -"

"But I just want you to know – it's like he's programmed to say and do those things. He thinks he has to tell you what you want to hear, so you'll have to like him. Sometimes he gets out of control with it, saying things he doesn't mean and doesn't even necessarily think," she spoke in a careful voice. Tori remained silent. "His intentions aren't ever bad, but he tends to forget that being friends, or being in love, isn't about being the best or being number one."

"I don't know why you're telling me this," Tori said in a low voice. "He and I aren't like that."

"I know," Katya said, glancing over her shoulder into the house. She could hear him laughing with her mom. "But I know you like him. You have for a long time. And if you ever decide to tell him, I just want you to know all that. To be aware of the kind of person he can be sometimes."

"I don't ... I wouldn't ever ... I can't ..."

"It's okay, Tori. Really. It's okay. I'm just looking out for you. He's very blinding. Keep both eyes open."

There was an awkward silence, then Tori changed the subject. Asked about Wulf, but of course there was nothing to say. She hadn't spoken to him at all since he'd left, and she didn't feel right asking his family about him.

The entire Stone household was in somewhat of a meltdown over Mr. Stone's visit and Brie's subsequent bender. Vieve was beside herself trying to deal with her little sister *and* a distraught mother. Katya tried to help as much as she could, but what with all the help her father required, she knew it wasn't enough. Vieve needed someone to be there for her, for once. She needed her big brother, but unfortunately, he still hadn't learned that money couldn't necessarily buy everything.

Tori told some funny stories from work, then changed the subject again. Told her about how Landon Edenhoff was giving his brother a run for his money in the casual sex department. But that just lead them back to talking about Liam, a subject Tori was clearly uncomfortable with, so she came up with a reason to get off the phone and they both said goodbye.

Katya stood up and went inside. She shut the door behind her, then she leaned against it. Liam was in the kitchen, barely visible with his back to her. He was talking to her mother, moving his hands a lot and laughing. She smiled as she watched him.

There'd been a long, late night conversation with him, too. A lot of truths spoken. He admitted to being jealous of Wulf, to always feeling second best to men like him. Liam insisted he really had feelings for Katya, that he honestly cared for her. She had said that was nice but that she was swearing off men for a while.

Which was technically true, but she also just didn't believe him. Oh, she believed he cared for her. They really were friends. But he wasn't in love with her, and since she'd had a long time to think about it and go over everything that had happened between them, she was sure he never had been. He'd just convinced himself that he was – because if he was in love with her and he got her to love him, then he would beat Wulf. Prove something to himself and to Wulf and to his family and his brother and anyone else who'd ever doubted him.

It was ridiculous, but it seemed to be his approach to life in general. Everything was just a chance to prove himself. Sleep with a lot of women – proves he's a real man. Beat someone at a game – proves that he's a *better* man. It was kind of sad really, and Katya wished she could help him. But she had her own issues, ones that had nothing to do with Liam Edenhoff.

She stopped being lost in thought and she went into the kitchen. Helped her mother make dinner. Her father rolled around the kitchen, attempting to help as much as he could. He had no depth perception, which resulted in a lot of spilled items and rolled over toes. They all laughed a lot.

By seven o'clock, Mr. Tocci was done. After he took an alarming amount of pills, Katya and her mother helped him into bed. Her mom stayed with him, pulling the blankets up around him and settling in, turning on their television. She wished them goodnight and shut the door behind her.

"You're a good daughter, angel cake," Liam sighed, stretching his arms above his head as he walked into the living room.

"I try," she laughed, following him and flopping down on the couch. He sat down next to her and looked at her for a moment.

"I'm really sorry, you know," he told her. She nodded.

"I know. I believe you."

"You deserve someone a lot better than me," he said, and she nodded.

"I know that, too. Wanna watch a movie?"

Instead of answering, he reached out and grabbed her hand. Linked their fingers together.

"I hope I never do anything to hurt you ever again."

"That's not possible, Liam," she laughed. "I'm going to hurt you, you're going to hurt me. It happens. Just don't do it on purpose again, and we're all good."

"I won't. Are you sure I can't talk you into coming home? You can have Wulf's old apartment," he told her, reaching out with his free hand and brushing a lock of hair from her face.

"He's not there anymore?" she asked.

"No, he went back to his ivory tower. He wants to move Vieve in there, but I told him I wanted to wait till I'd talked to you about it."

She shook her head.

"Give it to Vieve, she and Brie can live there. It'll be good for them," Katya offered. He frowned.

"We'll see. At least move back in with Tori – she's going stir crazy without you. She tried to bake snickerdoodles all on her own and she brought them to work. I thought she was trying to poison all of us."

She started laughing again.

"God, I love that woman," she chuckled. "But no. I'm going to stay here for a while, then maybe next summer, I'll figure out my next move."

"Next summer? Long time to be away from your home and your passion," he told her.

"*This* is my home," she corrected him. "And I can bake anywhere. Don't worry about me, Liam. I'll be fine."

"But … I miss you. I miss our lunches and margaritas and all the tacos," he said softly, smiling down at her.

"I know. I miss them, too, but we'll be okay, Liam."

They stayed downstairs for a while, holding hands all through the movie. She fell asleep leaning against him and when she woke back up, she was in her own bed. She glanced around and didn't see him anywhere, which surprised her a little. Maybe he really was learning. She smiled to herself and snuggled down into her blanket.

This is good. Things will get better. Smiling will start to feel real, eventually. Just focus on you and your family, and you'll get through this.

29

ANOTHER TWO WEEKS WENT BY WITHOUT TOO MUCH NOTICE. LIAM HAD gone home the day after he'd carried her to bed, making her promise to call him all the time and visit at least once in the near future. She cried when she said goodbye, hugging him for so long that her mother eventually started pulling her loose.

Her father was adapting well to his new situation. There were bad moments, and downright awful ones – he fell out of bed in the middle of the night once, scaring about ten years off Katya's life with the way he screamed. They'd gotten him back to bed, but she and her mother had been up for the rest of the night, sitting on the couch and staring at the wall.

But mostly, he was healing. He was going to his physical therapy and he was learning how to adjust. He'd always had a positive attitude, so he applied it double time to his healing. Mr. Tocci was going to be just fine.

Her mother was also improving a lot. Nagging Katya about her love life, nagging her husband about leaving messes. She even agreed to help a friend plan a charity event, leaving the house all on her own – something she hadn't done since the accident.

Another thing that helped immensely, they now had a nurse. After her father had fallen, her mother went to have lunch with Ms. Stone during the day and apparently told her all about the incident. Within hours, a full time, live in RN had shown up. She'd been hired by a Mr. Stone, she explained, and she was given permission to do any and everything within her abilities to make life better for Mr. Tocci. Katya didn't even want to think about how much something like that cost, so she'd just smiled and shown the woman to a guest room. She knew it wasn't right, accepting that kind of help from a man she had essentially broken up with, but it still felt good. Some stress that she wouldn't have to deal with anymore.

Everything is going to be A-okay.

"Kiddo!" her dad hollered from the garage. She traipsed out there and found him at his workbench. He was frowning as he worked hard at twisting a wrench.

"What's up, Dad?" she asked, propping her hip against their rental van – a fancy one that had a lift for his wheelchair. A brand new Lexus was in the driveway, and Mr. Tocci was determined to get a prosthetic leg as soon as possible so he could get back to driving.

"I'm having a problem," he said, putting aside whatever it was he was working on.

"What's wrong? Are you hungry? Is it your pain level? What do you need?" she asked, jumping up and standing next to him. He waved her away.

"No, calm down," he urged, using the lever on his motorized wheelchair to turn himself around. "I need to get rid of something, but it's kinda big. I was wondering if you could deal with it."

"What is it?" she asked, glancing around.

"That thing over there, under the tarp."

He pointed and she followed his finger to a large lump on the other side of the van. A motorcycle shaped lump, that happened to be under a motorcycle cover.

"Your bike? You want to get rid of it?" she was confused.

"Well, I can't exactly ride it," he chuckled.

"Well, not now, but who knows what you'll be able to do with the new leg?"

"Funny thing – getting T-boned and almost dying made me a little hesitant to get back on the horse, as it were."

"Ooohhh, right," she mumbled.

"So I clearly don't need it anymore."

"I could sell it for you," she suggested. "Put it on Craigslist. Just tell me the -"

"But it was a gift!" he interrupted her. "I would feel bad about doing something awful like selling it."

"Then … give it to someone else?" she tried again.

"That's even worse, regifting a gift," he told her.

"Then I'm sorry, Dad, but I'm not sure what you want me to do with it," Katya held up her hands.

"I might have an idea," he said, rubbing thoughtfully at his chin.

"What's that?"

"We could call the bike's rightful owner, have him come pick it up."

"Dad, Wulf won't want a -"

"And he could give you a ride home on it."

Her jaw dropped.

"Dad!" she said, plunking her hands on her hips. "Okay, first of all – I keep telling everyone, I *am* home. And second of all, I am not calling Wulf. And third of all, even if we ignored all of that, I would not drive back to San Francisco on the back of a motorcycle!"

"It could do you good, sweetheart. It's very liberating."

She was flabbergasted.

"What's gotten into you!? Did you mix up your pills again?" she asked, looking him over carefully.

"Nope. I just …" he took a while to search for the right words. "I can't even begin to tell you how much I appreciate everything you've done. I always knew you were strong, Katya, but these past few weeks …"

Both of them were working hard to keep the tears at bay, she could tell.

"Daddy," she whispered, then cleared her throat. "Of course I would do anything for you. You and Mom."

"I know that, but seeing it in action – not everyone gets to experience that. And I hope they don't, at least not like this, but everyday I feel so blessed to have you as a daughter," he told her. She took deep fortifying breaths.

"Thank you. I'm very lucky to have you for a dad," she assured him. He smiled.

"Good. Keep that in mind after what I do next."

"Why?"

"Because I'm going to tell you what an idiot you're being."

That gave her a start. She glanced around, wondering if this was a prank.

"Excuse me?"

"Your mom and I love you, and sure, deep down I wish you'd stayed our little girl forever. I wish I could keep you here, warm and safe, and we could all live together forever," he said. "But that's not right. We're not children to be taken care of, and neither are you."

"I know you're not kids, I never thought -"

"I know, sweetie. But we raised you to be an independent woman, and you are at that time in your life when you should be forging your own path. You had already started down a good one – now is not the time to derail it."

"Dad, I'm not going to stop my baking career," she said. "I've even already spoken to a couple old clients, and there's a bakery downtown here that I could -"

"Horse shit."

She gasped. She wasn't sure if she'd ever heard her father curse before, it was a little shocking.

"What did you just say!?"

"You are meant for more than some bakery in Carmel, California, and you know it," he said, pointing sternly at her. "So we're not even going to discuss that."

"Okay, fine – I could go work in L.A., though. Sacramento. New York, New Orleans, lots of places. I just want to be sure you're okay, that both of you are good," she told him.

"Well then, we're good. And you aren't going to any of those places, because your heart is somewhere else."

"I swear to god, if you say I left my heart in San Francisco, I will hit you with one of those weird looking tool thingies," she warned him. He burst out laughing.

"I should have!" he guffawed. "It's true."

"Dad."

"What?"

"Just stop it," she urged him.

"Just listen to me, okay?" he asked. She sighed and nodded.

"Okay. But listening doesn't equal automatic agreement."

"You came down here to take care of me. To make sure I wasn't struggling or in constant pain," he said, and she nodded. "Well, I have Nurse Laney to take care of me, and I'm not struggling and I'm managing my pain."

"Oookkaaayy …"

"But I am witnessing my baby girl deal with both those issues."

"I'm not -"

"You are," he interrupted her. "I've talked with Wulf, and I've talked with Tori."

"You're a regular chatty cathy," she mumbled.

"Wulf is keeping his mouth shut about you – just asks that you're okay, and that's it. Won't engage in any conversation involving you."

"Good."

"Tori, however, is my new best friend."

What a scary thought.

"Oh god. Don't believe anything she says!"

"We both happen to agree that your heart is with Wulfric. Sweetie, you may be confused, and you may be hurting, but one thing I've always been proud of about you is your heart," he told her.

"My heart?" she asked, confused.

"Yes. You follow it, always. Loyally and without question. I tried to mold you into a doctor, and your mother wanted a lawyer, but even as a little girl, you followed your heart into baking. I wanted you to go to Los Angeles, and your mother wanted you to stay here, but you said no, and you followed your heart to San Francisco."

She wasn't sure where this was all leading, or what any of that had to do with Wulf.

"Kiddo, most of us are scared to follow our hearts," he told her. "Of what people think and how they'll react, but not you. When it comes to the heart, you, Katya, are fearless. You trust in it fully and you love with it wholly. I've always been so proud of you for that, and so impressed, and even a little envious."

"Wow, Dad. Thank you," she said, staring down at him with wide eyes.

"And like I said – it's quite obvious to anyone with eyeballs that your heart is with Wulf."

"Sometimes that's just not enough. We went through some rough patches. A lot of lying, a lot of fighting."

"So? Now you know what not to do," he told her.

"I'm just not ..." she didn't know how to articulate her feelings. "It's one thing to follow my heart to pursue my dreams – it's quite another to follow it over a cliff into a disastrous relationship. I don't want to give something to him if it's just going to get broken."

"That's how love goes, sweetie. You have to have faith."

"I do not -"

"Oh, hush. You're so in love with him, it's turned you stupid," he called her out. She started laughing.

"You turn mean when you talk about love."

"Well, I've had a lot of experience. Did I ever tell you how your mother and I got started?"

"Yes, you met in school – took one look at her across the track field, and it was love at first sight," she replied. She'd been told the story many times.

"That's how we met – how we actually got started, though, is quite a different story. I never wanted to tell you before because, to be honest, it's kind of embarrassing," he sighed. She raised her eyebrows. She couldn't imagine her parents doing anything embarrassing.

"What happened?"

"Because she was dating my best friend when I saw her at that track meet," he said in a simple voice. Katya gasped and pressed a hand to her chest.

"What!? You never said that! But … but … but I thought you guys went out that same night!?" she asked.

"We did. They'd only been dating a short while, I'd never met Herb's girlfriend, and she'd never met Herb's roommate. I asked her out and she said yes, that's all I cared about."

"Okay … so you guys didn't know, I guess that's not such a big deal."

"Well, it wouldn't be, if she'd stopped dating Herb to date me."

"She must have, though."

"No. You know how we went to dinner and went dancing and parked at the air field to talk," he continued.

"Yes, I remember that part."

"Well, we didn't just talk."

"I'm going to be ill, oh god."

"Oh, stop it," he rolled his eyes. "I was swept away by her! Here was this tall, gorgeous, auburn haired goddess. So funny, with these big beautiful blue eyes, and so smart, I could barely keep up with her. I told you, for me, it was love at first sight. Didn't matter if we were sinning in the back seat of an old Pontiac – I already had plans to marry her."

Katya groaned and pressed her hand against her forehead.

"So Mom cheated on her boyfriend with you the first night she met you."

"Yes. And for several weeks after."

"Seriously. Vomit. Everywhere."

"See, it may have been love at first sight for me," he continued. "But it wasn't for her. She thought we were just having fun. How do you kids say it? I was her side-chick."

Katya burst out laughing, "close enough, Dad."

"It took her a little longer to fall in love with me, and right about the time it finally happened, Herb and I found out about each other. I was so mad – that she would come between me and my friend, that she didn't care about my feelings, and that she didn't seem to love me back. After she came clean, I kicked her out of my car on the side of the street, just left her there in the middle of the night," he told her.

"Jesus, Dad. You're a stone cold badass."

"It wasn't very nice," he admitted. "But I was fairly convinced that I hated her. I cried on the way home, and then had to tell Herb, who wanted to kick me out. It was awful."

"Sounds awful," she said. "I can't believe this! Mom was some … crazy, sex-fiend coed!"

"Crazy is going a bit far."

"Oh, but sex-fiend isn't?"

"Well …"

She made a retching noise and covered her mouth.

"I wish I could unhear most of this. I can't believe it. The woman who used to measure my skirts before I left the house was a wild child in college."

"That's why she went so overboard – I think she was scared you'd make the same mistakes she made."

"Well, obviously you forgave her. What did she have to do to get back in your good graces?" Katya asked. He shrugged.

"Nothing, really."

"What!? No, I don't believe that," she shook her head.

"She apologized, of course. There were lots of tears and lots of phone calls. She showed up at my parents' country club one time, when I was playing a round with my father. I'll never forget that fight – I'm still banned from the club."

"Holy shit."

"Language, young lady!" her dad said sternly. "But no, it wasn't easy. I was so angry at her. But you know what? I really did love her. And when you love someone, forgiveness comes easier."

"But how did you know she wouldn't just hurt you again? I mean, if she was so thoughtless and selfish before … how were you so sure she'd changed?" Katya was curious.

"I couldn't be sure. I could only be sure that I loved her."

"So that's it? You were in love, so you just blindly forgave everything? I'm sorry, but that's not how it works, Dad," she said.

"I didn't say that, did I? But you act like trust is something that happens overnight. That trust should be given the first time you meet someone, and then it gets chipped away at with every mistake they make. No. Trust isn't something that's gained *OR* rebuilt over night.

"If you truly care about someone, then it takes work. Hard, tough, difficult, and sometimes just plain god awful *work*. Your mistake isn't thinking you can't forgive Wulf, because clearly, you already have. Your mistake is thinking that forgiving someone automatically takes away all the hard work that goes into the relationship. You think saying 'I'm sorry' should magically make the hurt and heartache go away. Well, it doesn't – 'I'm sorry' are just the first two words at the very beginning of a lot of conversations and a very long road of work. Welcome to love, sweetie."

Katya blinked her eyes, feeling like she'd just gotten hit in the head with a baseball bat. He'd nailed it, because she really had thought that way. Wulf had said "I'm sorry" and she'd said "I forgive you", and when feelings of relief hadn't instantly replaced feelings of hurt, she'd figured it meant those words weren't enough.

"But I just …" she mumbled. "I just don't know if I believe all that."

"Then maybe you don't care about him as much as I thought you did," her dad sighed, then his chair started rolling away from her. "But I'll tell you what – if I had behaved the way you are, and if I had held onto the hurt your mother had caused, and had refused to work through the pain and anger with her, *you* wouldn't be here, and I would've missed out on twenty-five years with the most amazing human being I've ever known."

"And what if I do all this – I talk to him and I put in the work and I go through the pain, and it all turns to shit, anyway?"

"Then at least you can say you tried. Never took you for a quitter, sweetie. I'm a little surprised, to be honest, you're usually such a fighter. Wulf clearly tried his damnedest to work something out with you – maybe he just loved you more."

"That's grossly unfair," she snapped.

"Maybe. Love is rarely fair," he sighed and started rolling up the ramp to the door. "It's messy and it's difficult and it's painful and it's a whole heap of hard work. I guess it's a good thing you found that out now."

He disappeared into the house after that, but Katya stayed in the garage. She glared at the stupid motorcycle and tried to think mean thoughts about her dad.

Of course, she wasn't able to. Instead, she thought some mean things about herself. Was he right? She felt like using his logic meant that any time a man did anything shitty, she should just be expected to forgive and forget.

But of course, that wasn't what he'd been saying at all. He'd said forgiveness and trust took work. Had she put any work into forgiving Wulf? Into actually trusting him? No, she'd been too busy playing her silly game. Too busy expecting some fairy tale romance where magic words could just erase any kind of damage and pain. She almost felt stupid now as the realization came upon her.

That wasn't how life worked. That wasn't how *anything* worked, she knew. It would be a long time before she could ever fully trust Wulf, before she would trust that they wouldn't hurt each other again. It would take a lot of work. *So much* work. Work, if she was honest, he'd tried to do. He'd been trying all along, in his own Wulfric way. He'd still be trying, if she hadn't asked him to leave. Even his final act had been to grant her wishes.

What work had she done? She'd fretted and worried and dallied about between two men. Expecting blind trust and acceptance of her actions, but not giving the same back. She'd ignored her feelings and Wulf's and she'd made everyone's life miserable in the process. All because she hadn't been willing to do a little hard work.

She was pissed off. Katya Tocci had never been afraid of hard work. She'd been a straight A student in high school, graduated at the top of her culinary class, and had relentlessly pursued her dream career, making herself one of the most sought after bakers in all of San Francisco.

Goddammit, she wasn't scared of hard work. And she wasn't afraid of Wulf, and she wasn't afraid of what the future held for them. She would roll up her sleeves and she would fight and she would yell and she would get confused and she would be misunderstood and she would let herself fall so much further in love with him, there would be no going back.

Don't ever tell me I can't do something, because then I will do it better than it's ever been done before.

As she ran through the house and dashed upstairs, she willed away the doubts that were already creeping in. Twice now, she'd walked away from him. This last time had been particularly painful and hard, and it had already been a month since then. Such a short amount of time, he would think she was a ridiculous. That she was playing with him. That she was a flip flopper who would just leave him again.

No. Stop assuming. Just talk to him. You've never ever once just told him exactly how you feel. **Do the work.**

She flew around her room, shoving a couple pairs of pants and t-shirts into a bag. As she searched for shoes, more doubts swirled through the air.

A month is also a long time. He hasn't contacted you once. Hasn't talked about you with your father. He's a very strong-headed man – he could have already shut you out. Moved on. Gotten over you. You could just be going back and ripping open old wounds and only succeed in upsetting him. He could take one look at you and wonder what the hell he'd ever been thinking.

"Stop it!"

She jerked upright and actually yelled out loud at herself.

*Just because you don't believe in yourself, **DOES NOT** mean he doesn't believe in you. Remember – you said you'd fight for him. Now is the time to prove it. **Do the work.***

She hurried down the stairs so fast, her father yelled to remind her there was no running in the house. She kept running, though, straight outside to where her mother was watering some plants and Katya hugged her from behind.

"I love you, Mom," she whispered.

"Good lord, what is this!?" her mom asked, startled.

"Nothing, just had a really good talk with Dad."

"Oh. About what?"

"About what a crazy slut you were in college."

Her mother actually let out a startled shriek and dropped the hose, sending the spray into the air. Katya jumped away and laughed as her mother got a face full of water.

"Katya Tocci!" she gasped, kicking the hose out of the way. "How dare you use that language with me!"

"It's okay, Mom. It's kinda badass, really. Two men at once! I never knew you had it in you," she teased.

Her mother glared at her for a moment longer, water dripping down her face, ruining her make up. Then she sighed and smoothed her hands over hair, putting everything back into place.

"Well, it was a long time ago," she said simply. "I was young and carefree, and quite frankly, your father and his friend were the two most attractive men on campus. What can I say? Everyone acts like that in college. It's a time for exploration."

"*Dayum*, Mom!"

"Hush. And don't ever tell anyone I said that, either," her mother snapped, pointing sternly at her daughter. Katya smiled.

"Oh, this is *all* going in the Christmas cards this year. Love you!"

Katya turned and ran back into the house, leaving her mom to sputter in front of the roses. Her dad was in the living room and wheeled up to the coffee table, fighting to open an airplane size pack of peanuts. She yanked it out of his hands and ripped it open, then handed it back.

"I love you, Dad. So much that sometimes it makes me really, really stupid," she told him.

"Completely understandable, sweetheart. Happens to me all the time," he replied.

She hesitated for a second, dancing from foot to foot while her father calmly ate peanuts.

"I'm scared," she finally said. He nodded.

"You should be. He could be shacked up with another woman by now."

"*Daddy!*"

"Of course he's not! That boy is head over heels for you. Now get out of here before you drive us all insane," he snapped, waving his hand at her, shooing her towards the door.

She hadn't asked, but she assumed her father knew she'd need some way of getting home, so she took the car keys on her way out the door. She tossed her bag into the back seat, got behind the wheel, then burned rubber as she pulled out of the driveway.

She had a two hour drive ahead of her. Two hours, by herself, stuck with her own thoughts. Not a good thing, as she now knew.

During the first hour, she almost talked herself into turning around several times. Even pulled into a rest stop once and had a full on argument with herself. Then she got back on the road and put the pedal to the medal.

The second hour was spent trying to decide what she would say. What she would do. Should she go to her old apartment, wait for him to get off work? No, that would be hours away, she would definitely psych herself out.

Okay, so show up at his office? She didn't want to create a scene. Didn't want to embarrass him or herself, at least not anymore than was necessary.

Don't want to wait, don't want to embarrass yourself. Jesus, suck it up. **GET TO WORK, TOCCI.**

About twenty minutes outside the city limits, she bit the bullet and called him. She cursed when she got his voicemail, then immediately called again. Nothing. So she took a deep breath and really fortified herself and called his office.

"The Stone Agency," his assistant's smooth voice answered the phone. "Wulfric Stone's office."

"Hi, Ayumi," Katya said nervously. "This is Katya Tocci."

"Good to hear from you, Ms. Tocci. What can I do for you?" Ayumi asked politely.

"Is Wulf available?"

"I'm sorry, he's not here."

"Oh … okay …"

"But he did give me instructions, in case you ever called," Ayumi continued. "If you need anything, I'm at your disposal, or if there's an emergency, I can go get him."

"No, no, no, no, no emergency, I'm fine," Katya said fast. "Do you know when he'll be back?"

"Oh, I'm sorry, he won't be back today. He's at a grand opening for a new business. There's a ribbon cutting, and then there's a party."

Katya's mind raced, going back over the days and weeks and months. To when they'd first ever met, in her bakery. When he'd stared at her like he hadn't recognized her.

"… I have a waiting list."
*"You have a **waiting list?**"*
"Yes. If you'd like me to make cupcakes for your party, I can have them to you in roughly three months."
"A wait list, huh."
"I'm sorry, but I'm very busy today. If you'd like to look at my portfolio, I can give you our website."
"No, no, three months is fine. We're having a party in about five months time, so if you think you can pencil me in, that would be great."

Jesus, it had been five months since that conversation. She could hardly believe it.

She never did make his cupcakes.

The universe is amazing.

"Ms. Tocci?" Ayumi asked.

"Yeah, sorry, here," Katya had forgotten she was on the phone. "Hey – could you tell me where that party is?"

30

I T TOOK KATYA A LOT LONGER TO GET TO THE ADDRESS AYUMI HAD GIVEN HER
then she'd thought it would. She wasn't sure how long the party
was lasting – was it already over? Would she be able to find him?
It would be just her luck that she'd get there, and he'd already be gone.

She parked at a meter a couple blocks away, but didn't have any
change. She decided screw it, she was on her way to figure out her
future, who cared about a parking ticket. She took off jogging down
the street.

It had been an hour since she'd spoken to Wulf's assistant. She'd
asked the other woman not to warn him that she was coming, didn't
want it getting more awkward than it already was – if he was off
guard, she could just barrel right into it all, just blurt out her feelings.

*If he's even there. It's after five – I spoke to her about an hour ago.
He wouldn't leave the party that soon, would he?*

She was so lost in her thoughts, she wasn't paying attention as
she rounded a corner. She ran smack into someone's back and almost
fell down. Someone else grabbed her arm and hauled her upright.

"I''m sorry," she said quickly. "So sorry."

"No problem," the man she'd hit said. "You okay?"

"Yeah – what's going on?" she asked, trying to look around. There was a huge crowd in front of her that was taking over the sidewalk.

"They're doing an opening ceremony for this new mall – everything is gonna be ten percent off after they open the doors," he explained. "We're all waiting for them to cut the ribbon."

"Oh my god," she breathed. "They haven't … haven't cut the ribbon yet?"

"No, but they're about to. Whoa!" he exclaimed when she pushed in front of him. "Good luck, lady!"

It was no easy task, shoving her way to the other side of the crowd. It was absolutely packed, and *huge*. She finally got to the other side and stood against a polished cement wall that came up to her eyebrows. She put her hands on top of it, then scrambled to lift herself up.

It was a gigantic fountain, water cascading over a huge shaft of onyx in the center. She carefully stood up on the edge and finally looked around.

The crowd was even bigger than she'd realized – she was barely halfway to the front of it. She sort of recognized the building, but it was in a part of town she didn't go to often, and a lot of work had been done to it. They'd maintained the historical feel, but updated everything and had added a whole parking structure on the side.

For whatever reason, she had assumed the ribbon cutting and the party would be taking place inside the building. She had also assumed it would be an office building. Ridiculous, really. Still assuming things, even after everything that had happened to her.

The ceremony was taking place outside, in front of the crowd. There were two posts with a huge red ribbon strung between them, a comically large bow in the middle. Several men and two women stood in a line behind it. Two other men were forward and off to the side, and one of them was speaking into a microphone. The other one stood stoically and silently, his hands clasped behind his back.

"Wulf," she whispered, straining her eyes to get a good look at him.

He looked the same. Tall and handsome, his face so serious and stern that he looked angry. But she knew him better now, and all she saw when she looked at him was the man who told her she was like a present. Who told her she was the best thing that had ever happened to him.

An applause broke her out of her reverie, and she watched as Wulf moved to the ribbon. A large pair of silver sheers had appeared in his hands, and while people clapped and cheered, he began sawing through the thick ribbon.

Katya frowned and started looking around for an easier way down off her perch. This wasn't right – this was Wulf's moment. She didn't like it when her relationships interfered with her career, so she shouldn't be interfering with his. She would wait around and after the crowd had gone inside and calmed down, she could seek him out. Or she could go wait at his apartment, even.

If you still have access to it. He probably took you off the list. Why should you be on it? You've changed your mind more times than a – STOP IT RIGHT NOW. NO MORE THINKING ABOUT ANYTHING UNTIL YOU TALK TO HIM, YOU RIDICULOUS, SILLY, PRESUMPTUOUS –

She had been walking along the cement edge, which had the width of a balance beam. She had noticed that at the other end, the stairs rose to meet it, and she would be able to hop down a couple inches as opposed to a couple feet. But her coordination wasn't as good as she'd thought, and one wrong move sent her careening to the right, over the crowd. She started windmilling her arms and over corrected, leaning too far to the left.

You cannot be serious. This cannot be happening again.

She shrieked when she hit the water. It was freezing cold, and there was some sort of current system in place that kept the water flowing in a circular motion. She was dragged along, coming up once to sputter for air before she was pulled back under.

Fantastic, I'm going to drown in two feet of water in front of a mini-mall. Better than I deserve, really.

She didn't drown, though. She finally calmed down enough to plant her feet. The water harmlessly flowed around her and she was able to sit upright, hacking and gasping for air. She sat there, shivering and coughing while she struggled to push her messy hair out of her face.

"What in the hell are you doing!?"

She turned her head in time to see Wulf effortlessly pull himself up onto the ledge. She groaned and twisted around, trying to get up on her knees. She was shocked when he didn't hesitate at all and just waded right into the water, ruining his expensive suit. He grabbed her arms and hauled her to her feet, standing her in front of him.

"Hi," she managed to say, her teeth starting to chatter. He glared at her, then shrugged out of his jacket and wrapped it around her shoulders.

"Thought it was a good time for a swim, Tocci?" he asked, rubbing his hands up and down her arms.

"Well, you know me and fountains."

"I do, unfortunately."

There was a second of tense silence.

"I'm sorry I ruined your ceremony," she started speaking fast. "I thought it had already happened, then I climbed up here and you hadn't cut it yet -"

"Tocci."

"- and so I tried to climb back down, but then I stumbled, and I fell, and I -"

"*Tocci.*"

"- this suction or whatever is way too strong, it dragged me down here, and I'm really, really sorry I -"

"*Katya!*" he snapped, and she finally looked up at him again.

"Yes?" she asked meekly.

"What. *THE HELL.* Are you doing here?"

She took a deep breath.

"I came to see you," she said in a small voice.

"You came to see me," he repeated.

"... yes?"

"You know where I live, you have my phone number. It had to be right now?" he asked, looking at her like she was crazy.

"Yes, it did," she nodded.

"What could possibly be so important that you felt the need to climb up here and almost break your neck and give me a goddamn heart attack!?" he demanded.

"I had to tell you something," she continued.

"It had better be really fucking good."

She took another deep breath and searched her brain for the perfect words.

"I'm scared," she blurted out, surprising herself.

"You're ... what?" he sounded confused. She decided to roll with it and let her brain go on on auto-pilot.

"I'm scared of you," she said. "I'm *terrified* of us. I'm worried that you'll get mad every time you don't understand me, and I'm frightened that I'll get confused every time I don't understand you. I'm worried this will all be too much work. I'm afraid we'll make each other miserable and horrible and broken."

They stared at each other for a long time, and if she had to guess, she'd say Wulf looked a little scared, too.

"That's what you came up here to tell me?" he checked. She chewed on her lips for a second and focused on his eyes. Those intense blue eyes that could infuriate her and terrify her and make her glad to be alive.

"But most of all," she said, barely above a whisper. "I'm scared you'll never know how much I love you."

"You ... love ... what?" he asked. She nodded.

"I think I've loved you for a really long time. And I'm scared because I've never been in love, and I'm scared because I don't know if you'll ever love me back, but … but I don't care. I told you I'd fight for you, but that wasn't really right. I'll fight for *us,* no matter how hard it gets."

There, it was out. And once again, she felt an immense sense of relief. Good or bad, ugly or not, she'd done it. She driven a lot of miles and come a long way and she had laid her heart on the table. No matter what happened now, she would always have this moment. She'd proven to herself that despite her inner voice and all her mistakes, she could make good on her promises and she could fight for him. She could rise above and be truly brave. She could be fearless.

… aaaaaand he's not responding. God, this was stupid. This was so stupid. I'm going to die if I have to stand here much longer. Literally, totally, die. Melt and swirl down the drain.

"You're scared …" he finally breathed. She managed a nod.

"*Terrified.*"

"Oh, Tocci," he sighed. "What am I going to do with you?"

"Um … you could start by drying me off with a warm towel?"

"You're horrible, you know that?" he asked, pulling her closer.

"Yes, I've become aware of it."

"I told you," he said, wrapping an arm around her waist. "Never be scared with me."

"I know," she said, staring up at him. He wiped her hair out of her face. "It's easier said than done."

"Would it help if I told you a secret?"

"Like what?"

"I think I've been in love with you since that first time we slept together."

"*You have not.*"

"I so have."

"I don't believe you."

"I kept the panties, Tocci."

"You did no-… ew, really?" she asked. He burst out laughing.

"What can I say? I'm a romantic deep down. But don't tell

anyone."

"I won't. They wouldn't believe me, anyway."

"Tocci."

"Yes?"

"Shut up now, it's time to end this with a very dramatic kiss."

They were standing in a freezing cold fountain and a huge crowd was staring at them and she was crying *so much*, but none of that mattered. He kissed her so hard she could feel it in her soul, and when everyone cheered, she thought it was her nerve endings thanking her for finally coming home.

You're very, very welcome.

"I was scared, too."

Katya snorted. She couldn't imagine Wulf being scared of anything.

"Of what?" she whispered, rolling onto her back.

"Of you," his voice was a hot breath against the side of her stomach and she resisted the urge to laugh. It was a ticklish spot.

"Of me?"

She looked down as his head moved across her body, pausing as he placed a kiss against her ribs. She could just barely make out his form against hers. They were completely under the top sheet on his bed, with only the light from a candle filtering through the Egyptian cotton.

"You laugh when you're with him. Smile. So much."

"I smile with you."

"Not enough."

"Well, you should be nicer to me," she teased, then yelped when he nipped at her collarbone.

"I knew he wasn't right for you," Wulf continued, and she groaned when his tongue circled around her earlobe. "He has a lot of growing up to do."

"He's three years older than you."

"Yet still a child. You need a man. Someone who can take care of himself and you."

"And his family, and my family …"

"I can't help it that I'm such a generous, selfless person."

"That's funny because it's actually true."

"I know. And I thought for a moment there, just for a moment … that you were going to make the wrong choice. And that scared me."

"Yeah, well …" she sighed and wrapped her arms around him before burying her face in his hair. "Me, too."

They were silent for a while. She coiled her legs around his hips, rested her feet on the backs of his thighs. His arms worked their way under her, holding her tightly while his head rested on her chest.

It was hot, being under the sheet like that, so tangled up in each other. But telling secrets and sharing souls was somehow easier to do while they were hiding away from the world. She took a deep breath and lifted her head.

"I won't stop being his friend," she said, and Wulf groaned.

"I know, we've already established that."

When they'd first gone to his apartment, there had been long talks. Confessions whispered while clothing was removed, truths told while wrapped up in each other. She'd told him about Liam's visit to Carmel, and about how she'd realized just how deep his insecurities ran.

"He needs help," she whispered.

"He does," Wulf agreed.

"He needs someone to help him realize that he's amazing just the way he is – he doesn't need to lie, or compete, or compare himself to anyone."

"And I'm sure he'll find that person some day – but not *today*."

"I worry about him," she confessed. "He's been this way for so long, he may never change."

"You'd be surprised, Tocci. People who seem to be set in stone can change in the blink of an eye. Just takes the right person to help them."

"I wanted to help him," she sighed.

"You can't anymore."

"I know ... but maybe, maybe I could help him find someone. There has to be someone out there, some girl for -"

"Just stop. You can be his friend, Katya, but you can't be his mother, or his matchmaker, or a replacement girlfriend. You have to let him figure shit out for himself. He's a grown man. Maybe screwing up with you will help him realize that, and if it didn't, then he's a lost cause."

"You're just saying that because you don't like him."

Wulf groaned and shifted around on top of her, turning his head away from the candlelight.

"That's not true," he sighed. "I don't ... Eden and I will never be friends, yes. But I don't *dis*like him. I even admire some things about him."

"Seriously?"

"Yes. He runs a good business, mainly because he's so good with his staff. He has zero fear of being disliked, because everyone who meets him adores him. Look at you, when you first met him. He's hard to resist. People gravitate towards him, he's fun, he's relaxed. He knows how to have fun, and I'm pretty sure he has no clue what stress feels like. I can't even remember the last time I didn't feel stressed. Those are all enviable qualities."

"You have enviable qualities, too," she assured him, brushing her hand over his hair.

"I know – like being secure enough in myself that I don't have to compete with everyone I meet. *Wanting* to be the best, and *knowing* you're the best, are two very different things."

"Whoa. And modest, too. Don't forget that you're modest," she teased.

"Of course I'm the best. I got the girl, after all."

"God, the ego on you."

"My ego is my most attractive feature."

"Really? I would say it's your eyes."

"You would."

"Or your shoulders."

"Shoulders?"

"Yup," she nodded, then smiled when he chuckled and she could feel it all the way through her chest. "I just wish … I don't know, Wulf. I just wish I could help him."

"Stop mothering and let him help himself. Besides, you're mine now. You need to worry about helping me."

"Wulfric Stone, I don't think you've ever needed help with anything."

"Then you're an idiot, Katya Tocci, because you have helped me so much, I'm beginning to wonder how I ever survived without you."

"Really?" she asked, looking down at him again. He pulled away and propped himself up over her, causing the sheet to finally pull free and fall away from them. She glanced around and was shocked to see the large candle next to the bed had already burned half the way down. They'd been talking for hours.

"You helped me learn that it's okay to be unsure," he told her. "You helped me learn that some things are worth fighting for. You helped me remember that smiling feels good, and laughing feels even better. You helped me become a better man, which is amazing, because before you, I was the worst. You helped me learn how to love."

Katya smiled and pressed a hand over his heart. Tried to memorize his face in that moment, with the candlelight softening his features and making his eyes glow. He looked like warmth personified, which was kind of crazy, considering she'd compared him to a stone so many times.

"No," she whispered, then she took a deep breath. "No, you

learned that all on your own, because until you, I didn't even know what love was."

"Well then, I guess that's one more thing I'm better at than you."

She burst out laughing, which was a blessing because it hid the fact that she was crying again.

"Oh god," she gasped for air, practically heaving with laughter as he fell down on top of her. "I don't know how I'm going to do this. There's barely enough room in here for your ego – how am I going to live with it?"

"You better figure it out because I'm having all your stuff delivered tomorrow," he informed her as his mouth traveled across her left breast.

"Oh sure," she snickered. "Between you and that fat head of yours, maybe they'll be room in the ... wait, are you serious?"

"How often am I not?"

"Wulf, I can't -"

"Tocci, I already paid the moving company. It's done."

"I'm not living with you."

"It's been done. Vieve is moving in with that scary roommate of yours," he informed her, and she hissed as he gave a sharp bite to the underside of her breast. "And Brie is moving into the apartment I left empty."

"Both your sisters," she was starting to pant. "Are going to be living at the Twin Estates?"

"Yes."

"And Vieve is going to take my old room?"

"Has already taken it. It's time to be quiet now, Tocci."

"No no no," she murmured, pulling at his hair so he couldn't lower his head any farther. "This is such a bad idea, Wulf. We just got back together, nothing has ever been easy between us, we always do everything wrong."

"I don't care," he breathed, his tongue sliding against her hip bone. "You have a lease with me, remember? You broke it when you tried to move to Carmel."

She gasped and glared down at him.

"You cannot be serious," she said. "My dad almost died!"

"I know. And I'm very sorry, but a lease is a legally binding contract, Tocci. You owe me at least eleven more months of habitation. My hands are tied, my lawyers are very strict about this kind of stuff," he informed her. She started laughing, but then choked on air when he bit down on her inner thigh.

"Well," she swallowed thickly. "I guess it's the right thing to do. I mean, a contract is a contract."

"Thank you. God, it's always an argument with you, and I'm always right," he groaned, his tongue smoothing away the sting of the bite.

"That's what I'm talking about. This is going to be a lot of work, Wulf. It's not all going to be sexy under-the-sheets time," she warned him.

"That's fine, because I have never been scared of a little hard work, Tocci."

She pulled hard on his hair, dragging him back up the length of her body.

"Me, neither," she whispered, kissing him deeply. He sighed when she pulled away, and she could feel him smiling against her lips. "Especially when that work creates something so beautiful."

"Beautiful," he agreed. "That's perfect."

"It really is, isn't it? I'm sorry I almost screwed it all up."

"Me, too. Now let's make it even more beautiful and see if I can make your eyes roll back again."

"I don't think that's -" she started to argue, but then his head was back between her legs and he was accomplishing his goal.

Having a good neighbor is nice, but having one that loves you and takes care of you and makes every moment feel like it's catching on fire? Well, that's just the best neighbor ever ...

EPILOGUE

KATYA NARROWED HER EYES AND GLANCED AROUND. TORI WAS STANDING AT the bar, furiously wiping at a spot. She'd been doing that for ten minutes solid – a couple more minutes, and she was going to wear off the varnish.

Liam was standing in the hallway, a stern look on his face as he spoke rapidly, his finger pointing at the person standing across from him. Landon was on the receiving end of the finger, and he was wearing the exact same expression as his twin. They both spoke in hushed tones, ensuring no one could hear them.

Brighton was sitting at the bar, her arms folded across her chest and a huge pair of sunglasses covering her face. She looked like someone had shoved a pole up her ass and she was plotting their slow death.

"Is it always this cheery in here?" Genevieve murmured, shifting around nervously at Katya's side.

"It's kinda glacial today, isn't it?" Katya commented. "I wonder how much longer Wulf will be."

"Can't be too long – Liam came out a while ago, so that must mean they're done, right?"

"You would think so."

How long can it take to sell off half a sex club!?

Liam was finally buying out Wulf's half of the business. It was something that should have happened a long time ago, really. Wulf had no real interest in the bar-slash-sex club industry, helping Liam had just been a way to make easy money. It was best to give Liam the full control he always should've had and finally leave him alone. Because frankly, it seemed like he needed some space.

After Katya had come home from Carmel, Wulf had made good on moving her into his penthouse – her stuff was delivered a day later.

It wasn't easy. The first week alone had been hell. Wulf had never had a roommate before, let alone lived with a woman. He wasn't used to having someone in his space, all the time, every day, all day. He wasn't used to another human being touching all his things and messing up his perfect arranged cabinets and moving his perfectly placed throw pillows. More than once, she'd turned around mid-sentence to find him gone. He would run away to the roof and swim away the stress.

Not that it was any easier on Katya. She'd never lived with a man, and her roommate of the past four years had been extremely laid back. She was used to having control over the kitchen and setting the thermostat as high as she wanted and not having to pick up her dirty laundry behind her – what she *wasn't* used to was dealing a cranky, taciturn, spoiled brat of a man.

But for every moment Katya got on Wulf's nerves, and for every moment she wanted to punch him in the throat, there were three more of pure joy. She'd never imagined life could be as good as it was with Wulf. That someone could love her as much as he did, adore her and spoil her.

He had strange ways, for sure, and he would never change his overbearing ways, that was obvious, but she was glad. She loved those things about him, loved that she got to see *all* sides of him. Hoped he would never change. Hoped he never stopped thinking of her as a present, because still to that day, even after three months of living together, he was the best gift she'd ever been given.

"*Angel cake!*"

She snapped out of her private thoughts and turned away from Vieve. Landon was storming towards the stairs and Liam was smiling and walking across the floor, holding his arms open. She smiled back and walked into his hug, squeezing him tightly.

Liam had been ecstatic when she'd told him she was moving home, but he hadn't been as thrilled over the news that her and Wulf were together. He also didn't appreciate the long conversation that was had about his relationship with Katya and how he had to respect the fact that Wulf and her were dating, and that to have a friendship with her, Liam couldn't play any tricks or start any shit or behave inappropriately. This wasn't a game – this was her life, and she was in love with somebody. If he was her friend, he would be respectful, and he would be happy for her.

He'd argued, at first. Tried to convince her that she was making a mistake. But when it became apparent that she'd meant what she'd said and she would walk away from the friendship if he didn't get his shit together, he'd calmed down. Promised to keep his hands to himself and his plotting to other peoples' relationships.

So far, it seemed like he was making good on his word. For the first couple weeks, he'd pulled back, which had made her sad. Despite everything that had happened, Katya really did care about Liam, a lot. She'd thought maybe he hadn't been able to handle her being with another man. Turned out, though, he'd gone on a little bit a crazy sex spree. Misbehaving on his club floor, making an arrangement with the skanky blonde from Floor Two in Katya's old building, and some sort of secret sexy affair that no one had been able to figure out.

Then, finally, he'd called her and invited her *and* Wulf to tacos. It had been awkward and stiff and weird as shit, but eventually, they'd laughed again. They made plans to go to the movies with Tori, and then to help Vieve go shopping when she decided to update her look, and even once secretly went apartment hunting for Landon.

She was a little sad because nothing had changed in the girl department, though. No solid relationships. His sneaky affair was still happening – lots of late nights locked in his office, some mysterious woman coming and going from his building. Tori was somewhat obsessed with finding out who the chick was, but he was keeping it way on the down low, for whatever reason. Katya hoped it was something good, that maybe he was finally finding love, but she had a bad feeling it was nowhere near close to that, which was too bad. Liam Edenhoff was a man definitely deserving of love.

"Hey, how did it go?" she asked, scratching her hands fast up and down his back.

"You, my dear, are looking at the sole owner of The Garden, night club and pleasure nook," he informed her. She pulled away and started clapping, then stopped.

"Wait … pleasure nook?"

"Well, what would you call it?"

"Nook is good," she laughed. "I hope you got it at a good price – I told Wulf he had to be nice to you."

"Wulf? Nice? I don't think that adjective has ever been said with his name before," Liam snorted. "You'll have to talk about it with him."

"Oh god. We talked about this. I told him not to be a jackass, he can be so -" she started to complain, but Liam started glaring over her head.

"Oh jesus," he growled.

"What?" she asked, glancing over her shoulder. He was staring at the bar.

"I'm sorry, I gotta go," he sighed, rubbing her arm affectionately. "Great seeing you – rooftop tomorrow?"

Wulf had expressly forbid Katya from having rooftop liaisons with Liam. He'd heard all the stories about what happened on roofs with Mr. Edenhoff. However, he had offered his own roof, which also had a *heated* pool, as well as lounge chairs and a covered cabana with a heater. It could be snowing, and they could still hang out up on the roof and eat tacos.

"I've already got the margaritas made," she assured him. He smiled down at her.

"Have I told you how glad I am that you stuck around?"

"Only about once a day."

"Good. Don't want you to forget it," he said, then he leaned down and kissed the top of her head before striding away.

She watched as he pointed a very angry finger in Brie's face. She smirked and said something back, which was immediately followed by Liam grabbing her arm and yanking her off the stool. Katya grimaced. Brie shouldn't have been in the club, period, since she was underage, but Liam had given up trying to keep her out, and just requested that she not come after ten o'clock, not order any drinks, and not sit at the bars. Clearly, she was having trouble understanding the rules. His anger turned on Tori, pointing between her and Brie.

Katya frowned as her ex-roommate leaned back, holding up her hands and snapping back at her boss. Lucky for Tori, she and her boss were very close friends outside of work, so she could pretty much speak to Liam however she wanted and get away with it. Good for her, too, because she eventually threw her cleaning towel in his face and stomped away from the bar.

Though she wanted nothing more than everyone around her to be in loving, fulfilling relationships, Katya was happy about Tori's single status. The girl was doing better than ever – her promotion to night shift manager had been a huge step up for her, and had come with a very hefty raise. She was proud of herself, had made a name for herself in that small space, and clearly was very happy without any kind of man in her life. In fact, she was doing better than she'd ever done with any of her past boyfriends.

…. yeeaaahhh, but it would still be fun to see the kind of guy that will finally tame her.

"Your friend is a bitch," Brie snarled as she came up alongside her sister. Katya raised an eyebrow.

"I'm sure the feeling is mutual," she replied. She'd learned over the course of her "friendship" with Brie that it was best to return her attitude with more attitude.

"Whatever. She's just pissed because Eden wouldn't fuck her if she paid him to."

"Brighton!" Vieve almost yelled. "Just because you're a miserable little girl doesn't mean you have to make everyone around you miserable."

Katya was ready to go into save-a-ho-mode, too, but Vieve's chastisement shockingly seemed to be enough. Brie's face turned red and she hesitated for a second before hurrying up the stairs.

"I'm sorry, but has she seemed … bitchier to you?" Katya asked.

"You have no idea. I went up to her apartment the other day – disgusting. She's stopped cleaning, there's food containers all over the kitchen, and a six inch layer of dust on everything. It's impossible to get her on the phone, she keeps missing our lunch dates. I'm tired of chasing after her," Vieve sighed, rubbing her hand across her forehead. Katya smiled and rubbed her back.

"Well, then … maybe you should stop chasing," she suggested. Vieve snorted.

"I can't help it, it's what I do. Speaking of which, I'm gonna go chase her down right now. We're still on for dinner?" she checked as she turned away.

"Of course. Seven o'clock. Parking is a nightmare down there, so maybe leave -"

"Early, I know. Wulfy hates when people are late," Vieve laughed. "I'll be there at six-thirty."

"See you!"

Katya watched as Vieve dashed up the stairs, chasing her sister. She was right – she was always chasing after somebody. She'd become den mother to them all. Making sure Wulf wasn't being too hard on Katya, making sure Katya wasn't overreacting to Wulf's attitude. She'd taken over cooking duties for Tori and despite being as opposite as two people could be, the two girls got along well as roommates. Vieve even checked in on the Edenhoff twins, moderating fights and even separating them when necessary, allowing Landon to crash in her and Tori's apartment occasionally.

She spent so much time taking care of everyone else, she never stopped to look after herself. Wulf had been attempting to step up, to play a more active role in his sisters' lives, but it wasn't easy. It didn't come naturally to him, being warm and inviting, and it was clear he felt awkward around them. It didn't help that Vieve automatically turned quiet and subservient around him, and Brie turned even more sullen and bratty. It would be a long road before the Stone siblings were any sort of real family unit, which was a pity because of all of them, Genevieve probably deserved it the most.

Not that there weren't other people in her life who were willing to step up and offer a shoulder to lean on. Katya knew her former neighbor Gaten Shepherd had been very interested in Vieve. They'd even gone on a couple dates. But it had never gone anywhere after that, with Vieve claiming she was too busy with work and family. After enough excuses, he'd stopped calling. It broke Katya's heart a little because she thought he'd be so good for Vieve. She needed someone to take care of her for a while.

"*Stop it.*"

She smiled at the low voice that was whispering in her ear, then leaned back as an arm wrapped around her waist. Expensive cologne enveloped her and she took a deep breath as she leaned into a strong shoulder.

"Stop what?" she asked, tilting her head back.

Wulfric wasn't looking at her, though. He was looking at the stairs, watching his sister disappear up them. Katya admired him for a moment, looked over his strong jaw and thick hair. Took in his sharp blue eyes and smooth skin. She reached up a hand and pressed it to his cheek, forcing him to look down at her.

"Worrying about everyone," he finally answered, then he leaned down and kissed her.

"How did you know -" she started to ask when he pulled away, but he grabbed her hand and pulled, forcing her to follow behind him.

"Because it's what you do, Tocci. If I didn't stop you, you'd be worse than Vieve, trying to micromanage everyone into your idea of happiness," he informed her as they headed up the stairs.

When they got to the top, they saw Vieve and Brie arguing in a corner. Katya smiled and waved. Wulf just kept heading for the exit. Outside, they nearly ran Landon over. He was standing next to the Jan the bouncer, both of them smoking. She always thought it was strange, a doctor smoking cigarettes. She scrunched up her nose and waved her hand through the air.

"Sorry, Ms. Tocci," Jan coughed as he rubbed out the butt. "I thought you'd already left."

"What, we can't smoke out here?" Landon asked, blowing a stream into the air.

"Smoke away," she offered. "It was good seeing you, Jan."

"You, too, sweetie pie. This wolf guy taking good care of you?" Jan asked, and he leveled an evil eye on Wulfric. Wulf just rolled his eyes. She laughed and wrapped herself around his arm.

"He takes the best care of me," she replied.

"Good to hear. I don't ever wanna hear different, ya got me?" he said, still staring at Wulf.

"Oh, don't worry, you won't ever be hearing anything from me," he replied.

"Your attitude ain't scoring you any points, buddy."

"Also don't care about that."

"We're leaving," Katya chuckled, shoving at Wulf's side. "Goodbye, gentlemen."

"See ya, sweetheart!"

Landon didn't say anything, just turned his back and leaned against the railing, puffing out smoke rings.

They walked out of the alley and headed down the street. It was early afternoon and they still hadn't eaten lunch. She remembered an exotic food shack somewhere nearby and looked up directions on her phone.

"Remember the burrito cart by the old bakery?" Wulf asked, shoving his hands into his pockets while they walked. She nodded and leaned against him, wrapping her arm back around his.

"Yeah. You always ate mine," she replied.

"Two times. Two times, I ate your burrito."

"Wulf, we only ate there two times."

"We should go there again," he ignored her. "Come downtown for lunch tomorrow, we'll walk over."

"Can't."

"You're right – you should go and get some and bring them to me in my office."

"No," she laughed. "I'm busy. I'm meeting with that realtor to-morrow to look at another space."

"Ah. How could I forget."

She rolled her eyes. It was a sort of sore point between them – Katya was finally biting the bullet, she was going to open her own bakery. She was going to specialize in custom orders and weddings. Wulf had been more than willing to run out and buy her the best shop he could find, but she wouldn't let him. She wanted to do it on her own. She welcomed his help and advice, but she didn't want him doing the whole thing for her.

So on her own, Katya had looked up a realtor who specialized in restaurants, kitchens, and bakeries. Wulf had checked her out, grilled the poor woman in his office, and though he insisted he could still do just as good a job, he grudgingly agreed that she would be more than capable of finding Katya a good location.

However, Wulf would not allow her to purchase something on

her own, and that he wouldn't budge on. Realty was his profession, after all, and he was very good at it. He would be there, getting her the best deal possible. Also, he was investing in her business, so he figured it was his right to be part of the final decision.

She'd been prepared to use up her savings for a down payment on a decent place, but Wulf hadn't wanted that; he had more than enough money, and he wanted to share some of it with her. So they came to an agreement – they would be business partners. On paper, with official contracts and everything. Part of the deal was that he sell out his half of Liam's business. He didn't need it and he'd be distracted enough with Katya's new venture. She wanted Liam to be free, and she wanted Wulf's laser like focus on their business. So he'd agreed, and there they were a couple weeks later, completing the sale.

"How much?" she asked after a couple moments of silence.

"How much, what?" he asked, and she glanced up at him. He had his phone in his free hand and he was scrolling through e-mails. She groaned and stood upright before stealing the device from him.

"This is my time," she reminded him as she dropped the phone into her purse. "How much did you make him pay?"

"I so love when you're halfway through a conversation before you decide to start speaking," he sighed, glaring across the street.

"Stop it, you know what I'm talking about. I told you to play nice, Wulf. If I find out you charged him one dollar more than what's fair, I will be pissed," she warned him. He finally looked at her.

"I guess you'll never know, will you," he said.

"You know I'll just ask him, and he's scared of lying to me now," she said. "He'll tell me the truth."

"Jesus, you two. What I did in life to deserve Eden, I'll never know."

"I'm sure there's a laundry list of dirty deeds that more than qualifies you for that kind of punishment. Now answer the question," she insisted, pulling him to a stop. He turned to fully look at her.

"I sold Liam my half of the business for exactly what I felt it was worth to me," he informed her. Katya folded her arms across her chest.

"Oh god. More than half a million? A million? Two million?" she groaned. She couldn't believe it. Wulf and Liam had their differences, barely tolerated each other, but it wouldn't be right if he'd gouged him. She wouldn't be okay with it, not one little bit.

"Surely you don't think I care a million dollars worth about Eden's shitty sex club?" Wulf snorted. She raised her eyebrows.

"Half a million?"

"I'm insulted. I barely ever spared it a second thought, except when it came to payments."

Her eyebrows got higher.

"Quarter million?" she guessed. That would be beyond cheap – the liquor license alone was worth that much, at least.

"Three months and you still don't know me at all," he sighed, moving to walk away. She grabbed onto his jacket and held him in place.

"Jesus, Wulf, what happened in that office down there?" she demanded. He gently pried her hands off the expensive material.

"He told me what he was willing to pay for my half. I told him he overestimated his business' worth, and that as a licensed appraiser and realtor, I calculated it to be worth ten thousand dollars, max."

Katya's jaw dropped.

"You didn't ... ten thousand dollars ..." She couldn't even believe what she'd just heard. It was like giving away his half. Her mind was beyond blown.

"Yes, but on a condition. I didn't feel he was taking good enough care of his staff."

"Uh ... huh?"

"His night shift manager wants to become office management – she needs training for that, which he isn't providing. So in lieu of paying me, he's to put that money into her education."

Holy shit. He'd basically given up his half of the club under the condition that Liam get Tori some management training.

Katya stared up at him, so in shock and awe of the amazing man in front of her. She smiled and blinked away tears.

"You're such a jerk," she sniffled.

"I can't win with you, Tocci," he grumbled, pressing his fingertips against the bridge of his nose. "Should I go back and demand a million and a half?"

"No!" she snapped, smacking him in the chest. "You shouldn't make me believe you're doing something awful when really you're being the best person there ever was!"

"Best person ever, huh," he grumbled, grabbing her wrists and reeling her into a hug.

"Yes," she replied, wrapping her arms around his torso. "That was amazing, Wulf. I can't believe you did that. You're amazing. I don't deserve you."

"No, probably not," he chuckled, and started walking forward. She kept her arms around him, hugging close to his side.

"Shut up."

They were silent for a while longer, Katya pressed against him and listening to his heart beat through his chest. When they got to the food stand, she sat at a tiny table and waited while he got them some Indian-Peruvian fusion food.

"The shit you make me eat," he grumbled, dropping the plates in front of her before taking his seat.

"You love it," she laughed.

"No, I don't," he said around a mouthful of food. Then he grabbed a napkin and wiped at his lips. "But you know what I do love?"

"What?"

"You, very much," he started, pulling something out of his breast pocket. Katya started choking on her food as a small velvet box came into view.

"Wulfric Stone," she started shaking. "If you propose to me after only three months of dating, while we're outside of a shitty food stand on the coldest day of the year, I will hate you forever."

He snorted at her and rolled his eyes.

"Please. If I proposed to you *anywhere*, you'd feel blessed and privileged and would probably pledge your undying servitude right then and there," he informed her. She sat back. "I'm not proposing, Tocci."

She sniffled and took the box from him. "Oh."

"I saw it in a store and thought of you. Just open it."

Inside the box was a little charm. A pendant, nestled into the velvet squab. She laughed and stroked a finger across the small piece of jewelry. It was a tiny cupcake, made out of platinum and with a diamond in the center of the frosting. Tucked into the lid of the box was a small piece of paper, which she pulled out and unfolded. She laughed and almost started crying all over again.

It's been over five months - you still owe me those cupcakes, Tocci.

"God, I hope you never change," she was still laughing as she snapped the box shut and dropped it and the note into her purse.

"But it's nice to know if I had proposed, I would've gotten a re-sounding *'yes'*," he commented, his voice thick with sarcasm. She chuckled and pushed her plate of food to the side.

"Hey, you gotta work for that kind of reward," she teased, moving to kneel on the table. He glanced at her once, then went back to eating.

"Where you're concerned, all I do is work," he informed her. She nodded and moved so her knees were on either side of his plate, then reached out and grabbed his tie, pulling him close to her.

"Good thing the pay off is very worth the hard work," she whispered. He nodded and watched her mouth as she leaned down to him.

"It would be, if you'd talk less and be naked more," he told her.

She burst out laughing, but it turned into a moan when he closed the distance and kissed her soundly.

Silly man, I would say yes any day. Who could resist a proposal from the most perfect neighbor anyone ever had?

THE END.

Continue for a sneak peek at Liam's story.

BLOCK PARTY

A TWIN ESTATES NOVEL

excerpt

"*OH, FUUUUUCK.*"

Liam rubbed his hands over his face, trying to wake up. He eventually managed to prop himself up and he squinted his eyes, glancing around. When he remembered where he was, he let out a deep sigh.

"*Fuck*. What the fuck is wrong with me," he grumbled.

He was in his office. His desk light and the tall lamp in the corner were still on, glaringly bright so early in the morning. At least his overhead lights weren't on, thank god. Every inch of him was sore and tired, including his eyeballs.

He fully sat upright, yawning and scratching his fingers through his hair. He hated when he slept in his office. The room was equipped for it, luckily – he had an en suite, and when he'd first bought the place, he'd spent long hours there. Being so tall and lanky, he loathed sleeping on couches, so he'd had a Murphy bed installed. Once in a while, it still came in handy.

His eyes landed on his desk, where the empty bags and containers from last night's dinner were still laying. The awkward taco dinner he'd had with Wulfric and Katya. He groaned and dropped his head.

Fuuuuuuuck. This is bad. This is so fucking bad. I have a disease, I swear to god.

"It's too early," a voice next to him mumbled.

He glanced to his right and sighed, then turned so he could fully appreciate the view.

Then again, as far as diseases go, I suppose this one isn't so bad …

A woman was sleeping on her side, her back to him. The sheets had slipped down throughout the night and were just draped over her hips, barely hiding her naked ass from sight. An ass that was absolute perfection. He also knew that hiding from view on the other side of her was a pair of equally amazing breasts that defied gravity to the point one would almost think they were fake. But after handling them multiple times, he was positive they were real. Real, and tan, and soft, and delicious, and …

"If you keep staring at me, I'll leave," she grumbled.

… aaaaaand I always forget that part. God, what a bitch.

He only knew her as Halsey – her last name. They never seemed to get around to first names. She'd shown up at his club the night before, shocking him a little. He'd only met her once before, at the Toccis' barbecue. After his fist fight with Wulfric, he'd gone to blow off steam by sulking in the Toccis' pantry and she'd already been hiding in there, sneaking a joint.

He had eyeballs, so of course right off the bat, Liam had found her attractive. Then she'd opened her mouth and he'd quickly learned that sarcasm was her middle name. They'd butted heads and had both refused to leave their little sanctuary on account of the other. They then got into a heated argument about Katya and Wulf, which had caused the tension between them to rise, which had bizarrely evolved into a sexual kind of tension, and before he knew what was happening, he had his tongue down her throat and she had her hand down his pants, and suddenly he was fucking a stranger against a sink in the home of people he'd just met.

I'm going to the nastiest parts of hell, I'm sure of it.

"Get up, I have to get out of here," he snapped back, though he made no move to leave the bed. Instead, he actually laid back down, pressing the heels of his hands into his eyes.

How did he always find himself in these situations? One moment he was looking into Katya's eyes, and he was so sure he could be perfect for her. The next, he was looking at Wulf's smug little shit eating smirk, and he was so sure he could beat the other man at something.

Then a pair of tits and ass walks into his club, and Liam's thought process goes out the window. He'd told Halsey his name in that pantry, somewhere between a blowjob and her second orgasm. Apparently, she'd remembered it and had decided to run it through the ol' Google. His sex club had come up immediately.

"*I'd never been to a sex club,*" she'd informed him. "*And I was in town, so I thought … why not come say hi.*" Then she'd scooped a cherry out of her drink with her incredibly dexterous tongue, and that's right about when his brain had started shutting down.

He hadn't intended on sleeping with her. Despite the "*fuck me*" vibes rolling off her, she still had her acid tongue firmly in place. As he gave her a tour of the club, she'd turned up her nose at the upstairs bar, criticized the décor in the private rooms downstairs, laughed at the size of the conference room, and made a face at his somewhat unkempt office.

In response, he'd told her he didn't really care what some slutty brat thought about his club or what he did for a living. She'd told him she didn't really care what some slutty club owner thought about her or her attitude. He'd told her he was seeing another woman, and she'd asked if he understood that literally seeing someone and dating them were two very different things.

"*You sad, sad man.*"

It had hit too close to home – he was sensitive about the whole Katya-Wulf subject. Even if this Halsey chick didn't know anything about it, it still pissed him off that she'd made fun of him about it.

He'd told her to leave, and she'd laughed that she was a paying customer and she would stay till she'd finished her drink. He'd warned her that he would make her leave. She'd dared him to try. He'd grabbed her arm and tried to propel her out of the room. A drink to the face and a couples shoves and swats with a handbag later, and he'd had her pressed against the door, his hand already up her very tight skirt.

He blew out a deep breath and finally let his arms drop to his sides. He could admit it, he was frustrated with the whole Katya thing, and having someone let him be a little mean, let him work out some of those frustrations ... it was nice. Clearly, Miss Halsey had her own demons, and if she wanted to work on them by fucking Liam's brains out, he supposed he couldn't really fault her.

"You *have* to get out?" she chuckled, and he listened as she rolled onto her back, the sheets rustling as she pulled them up her body. "Do you punch in and out? Have a time card? I thought you owned this business, my bad."

"I do," he said. "But that doesn't mean I like spending all day and night here."

"Hmmm, I don't know. Spending all of last night here wasn't so bad."

Don't look. **Do not look.** *You cannot keep doing this! You have someone else you care about, remember!? And you have to be at that someone's apartment tonight, you're celebrating her best friend's pro-motion.* **DO NOT LOOK.**

Liam totally looked.

Halsey was on her back, in the middle of a big stretch. She had her arms above her head, her hands pressing flat against the wall. Her spine was arching, thrusting her breasts high and into the air, her peaked nipples poking through the sheets. He licked his lips and let his eyes wander down farther, to parts that were shrouded by blanket, yet he could picture them perfectly.

"I thought I told you not to stare at me."

He cut his eyes back to her face, expecting some more of that bitchy attitude. But she seemed to be done with being bitchy for the moment. Instead, she was giving him bedroom eyes and her teeth were biting into her bottom lip and as she rolled towards him, he couldn't help but fall on top of her.

"This is so, so wrong," he breathed, then he drove his tongue into her mouth, over and over as he moved to lay on top of her.

"Then we'd better be very, very bad, and make it worth while," she panted when he moved his mouth to her breasts.

As her hand wrapped around his dick and his teeth clamped down on her nipple, he had a brief moment where he could've stopped. He knew he should've stopped, and if he'd been just a little more sure of Katya's feelings for him, he would've stopped.

But then Halsey began stroking her hand up and down, and there was simply no stopping anything at all.

Might as well enjoy this as much as I can, before I'm cast down into hell. Tomorrow. Tomorrow I'll be a better person.

Tomorrow.

The Kane Trilogy

degradation

Available Now

If you haven't met Jameson Kane yet, read below for a sneak peek …

Tatum plucked at her shirt in a nervous manner. She had tucked it into a tight pencil skirt and even put on a pair of sling back stilettos. If someone had personally requested her, she wanted to make an effort to look nice. She had blown out her hair and put curls in the ends, and toned down her make up. Even she had to admit it, she looked presentable.

For once.

Men in expensive business suits began to file into the conference room and she stood still, giving a polite smile to everyone who entered. A team of lawyers was meeting with their client. Six chairs were lined up on one side of a long table, with just a single chair on the other side.

Tate had been positioned at the back of the room, next to a sideboard filled with goodies and coffee and water. She fussed about, straightening napkins and setting up the glasses. When all six chairs were filled on the one side, she stared at their backs, wondering who the big shot was that got to stare them all down. The person who would be facing her. A door at the back of the room swung open and her breath caught in her threat.

Holy. Shit.

Jameson Kane strode into the room, only offering a curt smile to his lawyers. His eyes flashed to her for just a second, then he looked back. His smile became genuine and he tipped his head towards her, almost like a bow.

She gaped back at him, positive that her mouth was hanging open. What was he doing there!? Had he known she would be there? Had he been the one to request her? Impossible, he didn't know what temp agency she worked for – but what would be the chances? She hadn't seen him in seven years, and now twice in two days.

Tate felt like swallowing her tongue.

"Gentlemen," Jameson began, seating himself across from the lawyers. "Thanks for meeting with me today. Would anyone care for any coffee? Water? The lovely Ms. O'Shea will be helping us today." He gestured towards Tate, but no one turned around. Several people asked for coffee. Jameson asked for water, his smile still in place. It was almost a smirk. Like he knew something she didn't.

She began to grind her teeth.

She delivered everyone's drinks, then carried around a tray of snacks. No one took anything. She moved to the back of the room, refilled the water pitcher. Tidied up. Felt Jameson staring at her.

This is ridiculous. You're Tatum O'Shea. You eat boys for breakfast.

But thinking that made her remember when he had said something very similar to her, and she felt a blush creep up her cheeks.

She was pretty much ignored the whole time. They all argued back and forth about what business decisions Jameson should, or shouldn't, make. He was very keen on dismantling struggling companies and selling them off. They tried to curb his desires. His tax lawyer explained how his tax shelter in Hong Kong was doing. Another lawyer gave him a run down on property law in Switzerland. Tate tried to hide her yawns.

They took a five minute break after an hour had passed. Tate had her back to the room, rearranging some muffins on a tray, when she felt the hair on the back of her neck start to stand up. She turned around in slow motion, taking in Jameson as he walked up to her.

"Surprised?" he asked, smiling down at her.

"Very. Did you ask for me?" she questioned. He nodded.

"Yes. You ran away so quickly the other night. I wanted to get reacquainted," he explained. She laughed.

"Maybe I didn't," she responded. He shrugged.

"That doesn't really matter to me. What are you doing tonight?" he asked. She was a little caught off guard.

"Are you asking me out, Kane?" she blurted out. He threw back his head and laughed.

"Oh god, still a little girl. *No.* I don't ask people out. I was asking what you were doing tonight," Jameson replied.

She willed away the blush she felt coming on. He still had the ability to make her feel so stupid. She had been through so much since him, come so far with her esteem and her life. It wasn't fair that he could still make her feel so small. She wanted to return the favor. She cleared her throat.

"I'm working."

"Where?"

"At a bar."

"What bar?"

"A bar you don't know."

"And tomorrow night?"

"Busy."

"And the night after that?"

"*Every* night after that," Tate informed him, crossing her arms. He narrowed his eyes, but continued smiling.

"Surely you can find some time to meet up with an old friend," he said. She shook her head.

"We were never friends, Kane," she pointed out. He laughed.

"Then what is it? Are you scared of me? Scared I'll eat you alive?"

he asked. She stepped closer to him, refusing to be intimidated.

"I think *you're* the one who should be scared. You don't know me, Kane. You never did. *And you never will,*" she whispered. Jameson leaned down so his lips were almost against her ear.

"I know what you feel like from the inside. That's good enough for me," he whispered back. Tate stepped away. She felt like she couldn't breathe. He did something to her insides.

"You, and a lot of other people. You're not as big a deal as you think," she taunted. It was a complete lie, but she had to get the upper hand back. He smirked at her.

"That sounds like a challenge to me. I have to defend my honor," he warned her. She snorted.

"Whatever. Point to the challenger then, *me*. Defend away," she responded, rolling her eyes.

He didn't respond, just continued smirking down at her. The lawyers began filing back into the room and Jameson took his position on the other side of the table. She wasn't really sure what their little spar had been about, or what had come out of it. She was just going to try to get through the rest of the conference, and then she would scurry away before he could talk to her again. She didn't want anything to do with Jameson Kane, or his -,

"Ms. O'Shea," his sharp voice interrupted her thoughts. Tate lifted her head.

"Yes, sir?" she asked, making sure to keep her voice soft and polite.

"Could you bring me some water, and something to eat," he asked, not even bothering to look at her as he flipped through a contract.

She loaded up a tray with his requests and made her way around the table. No one even looked at her, they just threw legal jargon around at each other – a language she didn't know. She stood next to Jameson and leaned forward, setting his water down and then going about arranging cheese and crackers on a plate for him. She was about halfway done when she felt it.

Are those ... his fingers!?

Tate froze for a second. His touch was light as he ran his fingers up and down between her legs. She glanced down at her knees and then glanced over at him. He was still looking down, but she could see him smirking. She tried to ignore him, tried to go back to setting up his food, but his hand went higher. Daring to brush up past her knees, well underneath her skirt. He couldn't get any farther, not unless he pushed up her skirt, or sunk down in his chair. She dumped the rest of the cheese on his plate and started to scoot away. She had just gotten back to her station when she heard a thunking noise, followed by groans.

"No worries. Ms. O'Shea! So sorry, could you get this?" Jameson's voice was bored sounding.

She turned around and saw that he had knocked over his water glass. He was blotting at the liquid as it spread across the table. The lawyers were all holding their papers aloft, grumbling back and forth.

Tate groaned and grabbed a towel before striding back to the table. She glared at him the whole way, but he still refused to look at her. She started as far away from him as she could get, mopping everything up, but eventually she had to almost lean across him to reach the mess. She stood on her toes, stretching across the table top.

As she had assumed it would, his hand found its way back to her legs. Only this time he wasn't shy, and her position allowed for a lot of access. His hand shot straight up the back of her skirt, his fingertips brushing against the lace of her panties.

She swallowed a squeak and glanced around. If any of the other gentlemen lifted their heads, they would have been able to see their client with half of his arm up his assistant's skirt, plain as day. He managed to run his finger under the hem of her underwear, down the left side of her butt cheek, before she pulled away. She stomped back to the food station, throwing the towel down with such violence, she knocked over a stack of sugar cubes.

When she turned around, Jameson was finally looking at her. She plunked her fists on her hips, staring straight back. His smirk was in place – as she had expected it would be – and he held up a finger, pointing it straight up. *One*. Then he pointed at himself. One point. *Tied*. He thought they were playing a game. She hadn't wanted to play games with him, but she hated to lose at *anything*, and she never wanted to lose to a man like Jameson Kane.

An idea flitted across her mind. Tate wanted to make him as uncomfortable as he had just made her feel. She coolly raised an eyebrow and then took her time looking around the room. The lawyers all still had their backs to her – not one of them had turned around the entire time she'd been there. Blinds had been drawn over every window, no one could see in the office, but she knew the door wasn't locked. Anyone could walk into the room. She took a deep breath. It didn't matter anyway, what was the worst that could happen? She would get fired? It was a temp job, that Jameson had requested her for – he didn't even work there. Did she really care what happened?

She dragged her stare back to meet his and then ran her hands down the sides of her skirt. He raised an eyebrow as well, his eyes following her hands. When she got to the hem of the skirt, she pressed her palms flat and began to slowly, *achingly*, slide the material up her legs. Now both his eyebrows were raised. He flicked his gaze to her face, then went right back to her skirt. Higher, up past her knees. To the middle of her thighs. Higher still. If anyone turned around, they would be very surprised at what they saw. One more inch, and her skirt would be moot. Jameson's stare was practically burning holes through her.

Taking short, quick, breaths through her nose, Tate slid her hands around to her butt. She wiggled the material up higher back there, careful to keep the front low enough to hide her whole business, and was able to hook her fingers into her underwear. She didn't even think about what she was doing, couldn't take her eyes off of

Jameson, as she slid her underwear over her butt and down her hips. As the lace slid to her ankles, she pushed her skirt back into place. Then she stepped out of the panties and bent over, picking them up. When she stood upright, she let the lace dangle from her hand while she held up one finger. Point.

Winning.

Jameson nodded his head at her, obviously conceding to her victory, then returned his attention to the papers in front of him. Tate let out a breath that she hadn't even realized she was holding, and turned around, bracing her hands against the table. She leaned forward and took deep breaths. She had just started to gain some ground on slowing her heart rate, when a throat cleared.

"What is that, Ms. O'Shea?" Jameson called out from behind her. She spun around, balling up her underwear in her fist.

"Excuse me, sir?" she asked.

"That," he continued, gesturing with his pen at her. "In your hands. You have something for me. Bring it here."

Now everyone turned towards her. Tate held herself as still as possible, her hands clasped together in front of her legs, hiding the underwear between her fingers. All eyes were on her. Jameson smirked at her and leaned back in his chair. She took a shaky breath.

"I don't know what -,"

"Bring it here, Ms. O'Shea, *now*," he ordered, tapping the table top with his pen. She glared at him.

Fuck this.

She turned around and pulled one of the silver trays in front of her. She laid her panties out neatly on top, making sure the material was smooth and flat. She was very thankful that she had gone all out and worn her good, expensive, *"I'm-successful-and-career-oriented!"*, underwear. She balanced the tray on top of her fingertips and spun around, striding towards their table, a big smile on her face.

"For you, Mr. Kane," she said in a breathy voice, then dropped the tray in front of him. It clattered loudly and spun around a little before coming to a rest, the panties sliding off to one side.

As she walked away, she could hear some gasps. A couple laughs. A very familiar chuckle. When she got to the door, she pulled it open before turning back to the room. A couple of the lawyers were gawking at her, and the rest were laughing, gesturing to the display she had just put on; Jameson was looking straight at her, his smirk in place. She blew him a kiss and then stomped out the door.

ABOUT THE AUTHOR

Crazy woman living in an undisclosed location in Alaska (where the need for a creative mind is a necessity!), I have been writing since ..., forever? Yeah, that sounds about right. I have been told that I remind people of Lucille Ball - I also see shades of Jennifer Saunders, and Denis Leary. So basically, I laugh a lot, I'm clumsy a lot, and I say the F-word A LOT.

I like dogs more than I like most people, and I don't trust anyone who doesn't drink. No, I do not live in an igloo, and no, the sun does not set for six months out of the year, there's your Alaska lesson for the day. I have mermaid hair - both a curse and a blessing - and most of the time I talk so fast, even I can't understand me.

Yeah. I think that about sums me up

Printed in Great Britain
by Amazon